THE CHRONICLES OF SIN
REBELLION

MIKKI KELLS

HM
LAKE
publishing

ISBN-13: 978-0-692-24116-5
ISBN-10: 0692241167

Published by Helmor Lake Publishing

Cover and book design by Mikelynn Helmer

Printed in the USA

Readers are welcomed and encouraged to write to the author.

www.mikkikells.com
www.helmorlakepublishing.com

DEDICATION

The Chronicles of Sin is dedicated to everyone who inspired me to roar when most would whimper. For my mother, Tiffinie, who taught me to live without boundaries and to always keep chocolate in my stash. For my father, Michael, who taught me to follow my imagination with swords and other weaponry. For my grandmother, Barbara, who taught me about family, heritage, and responsibility by giving me a horse and my best friend. For my great grandmother, Afton, who took me by the hand and led me down the first steps of this long and twisting path. Thank you and I love you all for giving me the keys to unlock the doors blocking the road.

CONTENTS

1   Virtuous Sins   6

2   A Day of Wrath   117

3   Age of Greed   **261**

SINS

Luxuria – Lust

Gula – Glutton

Avaritia – Greed

Acedia – Sloth

Ira – Wrath

Invidia – Envy

Superbia – Pride

VIRTUES

Castitas - Chastity

Temperantia - Temperance

Caritas - Charity

Industria – Diligence

Patientia – Patience

Benevolentia – Kindness

Humilitas- Humility

THE CHRONICLES OF SIN
VIRTUOUS SINS

BOOK ONE

1

Atticus straightened and shrugged into his wrinkled shirt, leaving it unbuttoned. As he flushed the toilet, his stomach gave one last half-hearted heave. The complementary towel felt too soft against his mouth as he wiped it clean. In the mirror, his toned body mocked him with his shame. He was a tool, nothing more than the errand boy of *Industria* Jacqueline.

He hooked a finger under the collar of his discarded jacket and slipped into the main room. The woman's breathing was slow and even, a gentle flush still graced her cheeks. She turned toward him in sleep, a contented sigh on her lips even now, minutes before her demise. She would wake to the sharp cold blade of judgment at her back.

He swallowed and bolted to the main door, closing it behind him with a quiet snap. It didn't matter that he'd stamped and sealed her fate; if not him, then another snake in the night. At least this way, with her confession secured, he could delude himself the execution would be swift.

The corridor of the Marriage House was dimly lit in a romantic glow. Walking fast, he hurried the length of the hall toward the sleek elevator. It chimed and released a newly-wedded couple.

Atticus didn't meet either of their entranced gazes. If they felt the effects of his aura, he didn't want to know. In the elevator, he pushed the ivory dial for the first floor. He looked up as the doors whispered shut. The husband had pushed his wife against the far wall. His lips sucked at her earlobe. The wife's eyes snapped open.

The connection struck, a ribbon of desire strung between them. Except, as always, Atticus could not sense what she felt, could not participate in the twining of her desires. The wife's knees weakened and her husband shifted to support her weight. She melted, her eyes fluttered closed and her head fell back.

The connection shattered, and the hint of emotion he nearly felt returned to the grave. He stumbled backward until his back slapped against the elevator wall. The hydraulic doors hissed shut and the familiar lurch in his abdomen signaled the fifty-floor descent. He shrugged into his jacket, wincing as the tailored shirt pulled at his shoulders where the soon-to-be-dead woman's nails had raked over his skin. Emerging into the lounge, he immediately looked to the bar. The middle aged bartender, Luc frowned at him. The older man tossed his dish towel over his shoulder and flipped a tumbler onto the black top of the bar.

Bless him. Luc filled the tumbler to the top with amber-dyed synthol. The drink beckoned Atticus with all the promise of a healing kind of inebriation. In the reception room, the party was in full swing with more couples arriving to partake of their vows, no matter the licentious nature. Tonight's work proved that one of the Lesser *Industria*, who performed the ceremony, was working without a license. As long as lovers had the money for the service, she performed unlawful contracts. The Supreme *Industria* had been alerted when she gave certificate of passage an already married man to a young single member of the same sex.

The dancers pressing around him and jostling at the bar would soon be evicted after the doomed Lesser *Industria's* execution and clean-up. The Magistrate couldn't have the general populace seeing dead bodies being removed from public venues.

Atticus stepped into the pulsing crowd ruled by the skilled DJ. Immediately bodies pressed against him, the scents of men and women thick in his nostrils. With practiced ease, he slipped through the crowd like a cat through a garden hedge. The Marriage House was unusually busy tonight.

In a few moments he made it to the bar and the cold synthol whiskey beckoned. He lifted the glass and downed half of it, washing the sour taste of vomit from his mouth.

He unfolded a bill from his wallet and laid it on the counter. It was a generous tip, but as long as Luc kept the synthol flowing he didn't care, anything to take the edge off. He turned and rested his back and elbows against the bar.

"Atticus," a voice purred in his direction through the din of music and conversation.

He closed his fingers tighter around his glass, panic gripping him with sharp claws. He turned and graced the Supreme *Industria* with a bitter smile, more of a patronized grimace. The woman before him was clad in white, from her dress pants to the suede jacket about her shoulders. Her sword hung off her left hip casually. She displayed her weapons with vain pride, even in public, resting her hand on the blade's hilt. It was the same blade she'd used five years ago on him with devastating precision. He'd learned that day the City was a prison for millions principally built on truth and lies and he was trapped within it.

He tossed back more of the whiskey. The burn sharpened his mind and dispelled the slight shake of his hands.

"Jacqueline," he greeted her. "I didn't expect to see you until morning."

"My superiors wanted a report as soon as you were finished. It couldn't wait." She gave him a once over that was more thorough than it needed to be, more of an appraisal than an assessment. "I see you worked hard."

He ignored the comment. "Your woman confessed to all twenty-seven counts. She's been sliding under your nose for years it seems, bedding any man with the cash to feed her starving children." He drained his glass and set it on the bar. Luc filled the glass back to its rim with the synth as he passed.

"Did she?" A flash of excitement entered Jacqueline's sapphire eyes and she ran a long nailed finger down the handle of her sword. "I'm not in the habit of thanking lesser persons, but I appreciate your diligence in uncovering the sins of others." She sidled close, reached around him and took his drink, watching him over the rim of the glass as she sipped. Her other hand landed on his bare chest. "I wonder when I'll be sent to judge your sins."

He ignored the anger and fear shivering down his spine at her touch, anger that she dared to touch him, fear that she might require satiation from him for her own sins. Again. He took his glass out of her hand and drained the synthol. "Run along, Jacqueline," he said dismissively.

Her features twisted into a frown. "If I didn't have an execution to perform, I'd cut out your tongue."

"No you wouldn't," Atticus replied. "You wouldn't dare put me out of commission. I'm still valuable to your masters."

Jacqueline frowned. Her hand dropped from his chest and found the handle of her weapon. "Until next we meet." She turned around and snapped her fingers. Her lackeys, three Lesser *Industrias*, emerged from the shadows and fell into step after her.

"Atticus," Luc said in warning.

"It's fine," he replied and buttoned up his shirt. He needed a shower. "Give me another for the road," he said tapping the side of his empty glass. The synthol contained next to no true alcohol, but that didn't mean he wasn't going to try and get drunk. Or at least buzzed.

"You're not hunting tonight?" Luc asked as he complied and topped the whiskey off.

"I have a few prospects in mind." He let out a short laugh. Perhaps he could match the *Industria* for bodies tonight. Someone had to tip the scales and keep the Magistrate on its toes. A fight would do him some good, and Orion, the Master of Trade, kept a nice contention of guards at his penthouse out of paranoia.

"Don't get yourself sliced up again," Luc ordered. "I'm tired of drowning your friend Tobias's sorrows every time you scare the hell out of him."

"I plan on doing the slicing this time. Good night," Atticus said, and drained his drink for the last time. One thirst quenched, he now desired to quench another, and vengeance was a persistent master.

He strode into the sea of gyrating bodies and immediately someone ran into him. He reached his hands out and steadied a young woman. She was a few years younger than he, perhaps twenty two, entering the fullness of adulthood.

"Excuse me," she said, flustered, and tossed her auburn hair out of her face. Her eyes met his and she froze. The familiar connection of his aura twisting with another's jolted through him. But not her. She didn't blush or swoon from the raw temptation that comprised his aura. Her eyes narrowed and she frowned before she deliberately turned away and headed in another direction.

Did she not feel the pull of his power? He spun to watch her journey through the crowd. No woman or man was immune to his aura, or so he thought. The human body was frail and wild with emotion, prone to the influence of his Sin. Why didn't this woman react to the base temptation he offered, a temptation that so many here were dying to drown in?

She slipped through the partiers with feet that barely touched the ground, like a sparrow ready to fly at the slightest disturbance. A flash of sliver caught his eye. She carried a knife concealed at her mid-back. He wouldn't have seen it if someone hadn't brushed against her and flipped her shirt hem up in the rear. She obviously wasn't here to sign a marriage contract or to toast a happy couple. Civilians were forbidden to carry weapons.

Atticus followed her. If she pulled a knife, any chance of learning who or what she was would disappear with it. The house was being watched by several *Industria*s. For a citizen to draw a weapon in public, it could mean her death.

She moved to the back wall, out of direct light and into the shadowed recesses of the bar. He kept his power tightly wrapped around him. Even that only served to lessen his effect on most women.

"You look lost," he said.

The woman spun around, her right hand going behind her, for the weapon in the sheath at her spine. If she had any training it was minimal.

Her throat worked as she swallowed. To her credit, her wide blue eyes never strayed from his face. "This is the Central City House, isn't it?" She couldn't have been more than twenty-one, but her eyes were haunted, and he found himself caught up in them.

"Yes," he answered, bemused by the angry determination in her voice. "Do you have a husband accompanying you?"

"I'm not here for that," she spat at him and moved to turn away. He caught her arm, his power naturally reaching out.

She gave an astonished gasp and ripped her arm from his hold.

It was a struggle to keep his surprise from his face. How could she pull away so easily?

"So why are you here?"

The woman frowned and her free hand went to her hip. "I'm not looking for a date. Leave me alone."

He smiled. "I know you're not. Women searching for dates in a Marriage House don't usually bring weapons with them." She wasn't affected by him at all, which was impossible.

"How did you know?" she demanded brazenly.

"So, who is it you're here to kill? The only people here worth hunting are the *Industria* and me."

"Why do you care? I saw you with her," she spat. "You want to kill her as much as I do. Why don't you do it? You're waiting down here while she goes up to murder an innocent woman."

Heaven and Earth, this woman barely out of her girlhood wanted to knife Jacqueline. And how the hell did she know what he wanted? How dare she tread on his claim? The underworld knew Jacqueline was *his* target, and the gods help any who dared kill her before him.

Atticus pointed a finger at her. "You're way in over your head. Jacqueline will slaughter you before you even think of drawing your dagger."

She looked past him, and her full lips pressed into hard line of determination. "Out of my way," she said and stepped around him. He grabbed her arm, again and the dagger he'd been waiting for her to draw snapped up. He spun her around, imprisoning both her arms as he wrapped his around her.

"Didn't you hear what I said?" he demanded, frustrated that this woman was so determined to kill herself. He chanced to glance up and froze.

Jacqueline exited the elevator. She over looked the crowd and tucked a red-stained cloth into her jacket pocket.

Atticus swore and spun them around to face the wall. He'd meant to be long gone before Jacqueline returned from her execution. She'd made it swift this time, instead of prolonging the death, a small mercy that may have condemned him and the woman now in his arms.

"Let me go," she cried.

"Quiet," Atticus ordered her. He grabbed her forearms, and turned her to face him, intending to pry the dagger from her grasp.

Her back against the wall and with him bearing down on her, she opened her mouth and drew breath to scream. He'd seen the action enough times to recognize it for what it was.

Dropping her left hand, he wrapped his arm around her waist and unleashed the full force of his power. He heard her breath catch in her throat. Her scream died as he crushed her lips in a bruising kiss meant to silence her. She struggled, and he pressed her back against the wall pinning her between him and the bricks. Her knees weakened and she sagged against him.

You aren't immune after all, he thought, and deepened the kiss. He slipped the dagger out of her limp fingers and tucked it inside the waistband of his jeans, flicking his shirt over it. For good measure he ran his hands down her sides, searching for more concealed weaponry. Finding none, he cut off the temptation pouring out of him like a faucet.

When he broke the kiss she kept her eyes closed. Then she recovered and the flat of her palm connected with his jaw.

"How dare you?" she asked, the apples of her cheeks turning an attractive shade of pink.

"If I didn't intervene you were going to get us both killed or worse," he said, ignoring his stinging face.

How did she recover so fast? Her eyes should have been glazed over, not blazing with anger. He glanced across the club for the *Industria*. She was nowhere to be seen. That didn't mean she wasn't nearby and still a threat to this woman who wanted her dead. On any other day he might have let the woman get herself killed, but she was not just any woman. She was fascinating, but foolish.

The woman in question struggled against him, trying to remove herself from the cage of his body and the wall behind her.

"Let me go," she demanded. "And give me back my weapon."

"So you can be executed? If you want death that bad, I'd be happy to oblige. There are easier and more pleasant ways to die than under a *Industria's* blade. She has a natural sense of violence. You'd never get close enough to scratch her, let alone kill her."

Her blush deepened. Her teeth clenched, and she lashed out.

He swung his hips to the side, narrowly avoiding a blow to his unmentionables. He tightened his hold on her wrist, and she stopped her attack immediately.

"I don't make idle threats," he said, his voice dangerously quiet. "If either of us is found with a weapon, they won't kill you on the spot, I will. I'm sure you don't want to be tortured to death, or sentenced to an Undesirable's fate."

Her blue eyes hardened, and a muscle worked in her jaw.

To her credit, she didn't say anything, but nodded and allowed him to lead her through the club, behind a curtain out the back and into the night.

Who was this woman?

***

The city streets were still flooded after the downpour. Vehicles sprayed water in all directions as they passed. Darci hunched in her jacket and stomped through a puddle after the most beautiful man she'd ever seen. There weren't words to express her gratitude for the cold water soaking into her jeans. She shivered, but at least the raging heat in her veins had subsided. All it took was the memory of his lips on hers and the raw sexual power that had fallen on her like a wolf on a wounded deer and heat blossomed in her abdomen.

Worse, she could still taste the raw self-loathing behind his lips. It burned in his blood. He hated himself, hated that he made her melt like the rain was doing to her mood. She'd never sensed such a strong impression from anyone before. Rancid cherries! She'd been so close to finally sinking her dagger into the *Industria's* back, or slitting her throat, or cutting her into as she screamed.

The man was right, she didn't want to die, not yet, and for that she'd followed him. He obviously knew the *Industria* was corrupt. Through his demonic kiss, he'd taken her weapon and used her passions against her. The reasons she'd picked from his thoughts for not killing the *Industria* centered on a fear she couldn't divine. She hadn't delved that far into his thoughts. She was afraid of the thoughts a man who was walking sexual desire kept.

Who does he think he is? Darci was ready to jump him from behind, and not just to take back her weapon.

"Keep up," he said over his shoulder.

Darci glared at him again. "Where are we going?"

He didn't answer, didn't hesitate. The man continued on with a perfect, graceful stride. If swearing weren't punishable by the loss of her tongue, she'd have cussed him up one side and down the other already. Still, she'd broken several laws tonight, why not one more?

"A-asshole." There, her first vulgarity she'd spoken in the City. She tried not to flinch as though the Magistrate's gavel would hurtle down and flatten her into the sidewalk.

He stopped. When he turned there was a curious tilt to his head, and damn him, he was amused. Even the tight line of his lips couldn't hide it from her.

"I'll stay right here," she said. "Until you tell me where you are taking me." She wasn't about to let some synthol addict twist her into a knot. The strong flavor of whiskey was still on her tongue. There wasn't much distance between them and he stalked her as though she were prey that knew it was doomed. Spitting rain had dampened his hair and it fell across his eyes as he stopped with few inches spaced between them.

"My name is Atticus, not asshole," he said. "I am a *Luxurian*."

Darci drew in a quick breath. A *Luxurian?* Those were creatures she'd only heard of in stories. A *Luxurian* was a hunter of virgins who preyed on his innocent victim's lustful natures before he viciously killed them. It's a good thing she wasn't as chaste as the law said she was supposed to be, or he'd probably already have made good on his promise to kill her. Words came to her mind: non-human, black-hearted, the death by sex. She shivered.

Atticus scowled. "I won't hurt you."

"Yeah, right," she said, already backing away. He'd shocked her, but not into doing whatever he said. She never wanted to feel that out of control again. Gods, even that was a lie. Yet, his intention and thoughts were not turned toward seduction or death. Under that dark scowl, he radiated preservation. He didn't want her dead or even harmed. At the moment.

"Why should I follow you any farther?"

"We're almost to my home, and it's going to start raining again."

His lair. She stifled another tremor, and not from the cold rain drenching her. She'd recently come into the practice of not going into a stranger's home. Her sister Tara's disappearance was a harsh lesson about trust. Despite the perfection the Magistrate advertised, or laws in place, the world was not safe, peaceful, or prosperous. The man before her was more than enough tangible evidence. Men like Atticus were not supposed to exist. The Magistrate had eradicated them, hadn't they? If the stories were half-true, following a *Luxurian* would be chasing her death. She didn't intend to join her sister in final sleep so soon.

Intention never lied. Atticus didn't intent to hurt, kill, or trap her. Still, she'd known people to change their mind as quick as a coin toss.

Hadn't this entire fiasco been a gamble?

She'd alienated her parents, run away from the Grower Town, purchased a black market weapon, hunted her sister's murderer to the Marriage House, and had it all taken from her in a moment by a *Luxurian*. Until he'd intervened, she'd been so close to success. Her sister had been murdered for enjoyment. This man had taken her only weapon. She wouldn't get another one.

She could follow Atticus, or she could go home to her parents, a failure and a fugitive. It was time to throw the dice again and let fate guide her. She swallowed and nodded.

"That may be the smartest thing you've done yet tonight."

She muttered another curse, this one far more unmentionable.

He laughed, a seductive purr, and turned back down the street leaving her to follow in his wake. He led her through a maze of city streets and finally to a set of unmarked stairs hidden behind some bushes. She stopped and looked back to the night-cast street. The eroding concrete steps led to a similarly weather-worn door.

He opened it and turned to her, and his eyes narrowed at her from the bottom of the stairs.

He had to be a demon. As the embodiment of Sin he would not be easy to resist, well his aura anyway. Not only that, she did not want to venture into the darkness below. The street was well lit, and who knew what, or who, waited behind the door. He had her only weapon and as he'd said, she didn't have the skill required to win a hand-to-hand fight. Or any fight.

"If you please," Atticus said impatiently. "My home is not a threat."

Speak for yourself. With his dark gaze boring into her, she caught the cutting intensity of his purpose. Something was wrong with him, very wrong. She could almost feel the rising nausea within him as though she, herself, were becoming ill. Whatever he'd been doing at the Marriage House had affected him more than he was even allowing himself to see. Her connection to him strengthened like spider silk becoming rope tying them together. Already she'd spent too much time around him. She was picking up on the deeper things, thoughts and desires he hid, even from himself.

Darci blinked and tried to focus past the tide of heat. This was her body's reaction. Biology and nothing more. He held the door for her, forcing her into the darkness before him. She balled her hands into fists and passed into the house. Stopping a few steps into the space, she waited.

A light flicked on, revealing a Spartan, single bedroom apartment. It had a roll-out sleeping cot along one wall, a sink, a shower, and a toilet peeking behind a curtained off area. It lacked a couch, decorations and personal accoutrements she assumed a man dressed as finely as he would have. She expected it to be dripping in velvet not exuding acute depression.

"This is where you live?"

He strode past her, pulling off his jacket and throwing it into a corner. There were other clothes tossed casually aside. "Yes," he answered and studied her.

She refused to shrink under that gaze a second time.

"It was stupid of you to walk into that bar and think you'd get a free shot at Supreme *Industria* Jacqueline."

"Excuse me? I don't think this is the time for a chiding speech." He wasn't going to hurt her, but he was going to give her a tongue lashing. Who was this man?

"It is the opportune time. You obviously come from an

outlying town, a grower community perhaps. You have no combat training, no preternatural senses, and no hope of destroying a *Industria* of any rank. By law, I am required to hand you over for questioning."

"You won't."

He raised an eyebrow, an invitation for her to continue.

"If you were going to, I wouldn't have followed you. You're wrong. I can handle myself." She could watch her own back. She'd done it before, and as long as the *Industria* wasn't aware of her until the last second, it didn't matter if she survived or not. She wasn't going back home to the Grower's town where farmers turned up dead in the fields and others disappeared and were never heard from again. "Besides, the *Industria* was in the building. If you were loyal to her, you would have given me to her then."

"And if I do decide to hand you over, what information would you tell her?"

Darci didn't know what game he was playing, but she was not going to answer every single question he tossed at her. "I want her dead, that's all that matters. She committed murder and if the Magistrate can't see her corruption I will make them see it."

Atticus slid his hands into his pockets and she forced herself not to glance down, below his waist. Gods, did he have to exude such raw sexuality all the time? Couldn't he turn it off?

"How badly do you want Jacqueline dead?" he asked.

"More than you, obviously."

The small lines at the corners of his eyes tightened a moment before he smiled. "Trust me, sweetheart. No one wants her dead more than I."

Darci squinted at him, shocked at the black depths of his rage. Never before had she sensed a mind so affected by anger born of fear. Her own feelings only brushed the surface of that kind of rage.

Tara was dead, and before her death, the Supreme *Industria* had allowed things of an unspeakable nature to be done to her.

The corrupt *Industria* was one last dark spot to be scrubbed from their society's perfection and this man, believed he had a bigger claim to killing her than she did? And grasshoppers didn't eat wheat. No one had more right to take Jacqueline's life than Darci.

If Atticus did, he would have used his powers to lure the woman into a trap, long ago. But he hadn't. As much as he thought otherwise, she could handle the situation.

The tip of the handle of Darci's small dagger stuck out of the waistband of his pants. He thought she was weak, and that pissed her off.

Heart hammering in her chest, Darci lunged for the dagger. Atticus stepped backward, but not fast enough. She thrust one hand into the waistband of his jeans and wrapped her fingers around the handle of her weapon. At this range the pure anger that erupted from him as he thought she was diving toward something else, rose around her like dark water, drawing her into his depths.

She was a well-brought up young woman, not a skank ready to just dive for a man's you-know-what, no matter how beautiful or tempting he was. Reeling in shock, she raised her hand and slapped him again. Her fingers went numb like the last time.

His hand came down on her wrist and squeezed. Stubborn, she held on, a growl of frustration escaping through her lips. He probably had no idea how hard she'd worked to get the weapon. It was hers, and she was going to get it back.

His voice was laden with ice. "You will never touch me again."

Darci flinched. This was a dangerous man, and she was sticking her hand in the flames of a wildfire. His grip tightened, and so did hers.

"Don't take my things," she snapped at him and jabbed the closed fist of her left hand into the crook of his right arm. He grunted and she pulled her now free hand straight up, drawing the dagger out of his pants, but not before she'd sliced through the belt. She spun away from him, out of reach. He was the one who'd underestimated her. His problem, not hers.

Atticus took an angry step toward her and a loud rip cut through the room. Apparently she'd sliced through more than his belt. Praise be to the blade smith, the weapon was a sharp as he'd promised. Atticus's pants fell off his trim waist and he kicked them off with his shoes. It was a good thing his button down shirt hung a little loose on him and covered all his dangling unmentionables, or she'd be curious to look.

She angled the blade toward his chest. It didn't stop him. He batted the weapon aside and wrapped an arm around her waist and a hand around her wrist, bruising it further. With his body pressed against hers, it was work to remember not to relax in his grip. He wasn't even using his *Luxurian* abilities, and yet she was slowly drowning as she fought to break the surface of his aura.

The unmistakable sound of a door hissing open made them both freeze.

To her left, the wall had seamlessly hidden a secret door. In its frame a brown-haired, impossibly skinny twenty-something-year-old stared at them with wide hazel eyes. In his hands, he held a complicated array of technology. A smile split his face.

He flounced into the room with hipster-fresh flair, and gave Darci an approving once over. "Atticus, my friend, bringing work home. Bow-chick-a-wow-wow. Why'd you take a cheap dagger? There's like fifty laser-edged blades in the back."

Darci glanced at Atticus. He still wanted to throttle her, but he was distracted with trying to find an excuse to tell this new guy. Obviously he wasn't caught with his pants down very often. Or ever. She was kind of proud of the fact that she'd been the cause.

Taking advantage of his momentary hesitation, she ducked out of his grip, twisting her arm a little. His fingers had loosened and she was able to wrench free, with her dagger in hand.

"It's not a cheap dagger," she snapped at the tech addict.

"Yeah, yeah," he said and headed toward the curtained off area. "Toilet's broke in the back. If you'll excuse me." He disappeared behind the curtain with his equipment. Darci wondered why he needed the wires, c-chips or tools in the bathroom. She wasn't about to ask.

Atticus ripped the dagger out of her hands. "I'll give this back once you learn to use it."

With that, he stomped over to the pile of clothing in the corner and pulled out a wrinkled set of pants and tugged them on, making a point of pulling up the zipper.

2

Atticus led her into the front room of his residence. He slept in the front room, guarding that entrance, ready to sound the alert if Tobias needed to hide. The boy was a fugitive and he couldn't let another person be taken to the Magistrate's dungeons.

In the main room, Tobias's computers and equipment took up much of the space, leaving only a small portion of it for a few bits of furniture. He pointed to a chair.

"Sit," he ordered. She scowled at him and sat, crossing her long legs. Her wet jeans stuck to her skin, outlining every curve of those legs. He returned her frown. "Don't touch anything," he ordered.

"Didn't plan on it."

He bristled. No woman had ever stumped him so badly. One minute he thought she'd break under the strain of his power and lustily attack him, and the next second she exploded, cut him out of his pants and threatened him with her dagger. It was the fastest any woman had ever undressed him. His fist clenched around her knife. Two inches to the side and, he shuddered to think of what else she might have cut off.

He left the main room and entered the armory. It was unlocked. A chill of unease crept over him.

"Tobias," he called. "Why is the armory unlocked?"

"No idea," the techie hollered back. "You're the one packing weapons, not me."

It was unlike him to leave the door unlocked. He'd been tense to the point of being ill, not scatterbrained. His duties had been wearing on him.

Atticus tossed the woman's dagger into a box of cheap knives he collected. Bad weapons could be forged into newer, sharper, stronger blades. He turned to the wall of equipment. There were many automatic weapons, laser rifles, and a glittering array of bladed weapons. He favored the blades as ammunition was banned and near impossible to get ahold of, and laser rifles were traceable by the City's grid system and took time to warm up. Bladed weapons were stealthy, quick, and advantageous in the hands of an expert.

In the room beyond, he could hear Tobias and the woman talking. He leaned out past the door and met her gaze. She glared at him, and tapped her fingers impatiently on the arm of the chair. No, she was not affected by his aura, and probably wouldn't be unless he unleashed the full force of his power on her again. If she was, she hid it very well. Whatever hold he'd had on her at the club, she'd broken. It made him nervous and he didn't like that. He needed to get out, clear his head. The Master of Trade was still on his list for the night. Shedding blood would be a welcome distraction.

He locked the armory door before he unbuttoned his shirt. If she could get him out of his clothes period, she'd probably show up as soon as he was undressed. He replaced his shirt and pants for black carbon armor versions. He shrugged into the rib-hugging black leather harness and filled its sheaths with knives. Last, he slipped two katana blades into sheaths crossed over his spine. Grabbing his enhanced vision goggles, he moved to open the door, and hearing voices, stopped to listen.

"What did you see that made you leave your home?" Tobias asked. Even from behind the door Atticus could sense the subtle change in the atmosphere. Tobias was testing her with his *Invidia* abilities, by doing so he would draw out what hid in the deepest corner of her heart and reveal the chip on her shoulder that drove her will to survive.

"What makes you think I saw anything?" she asked in a bland voice. Atticus frowned. That wasn't normal either. Most people would be either sobbing or ranting by now and spilling their life's story. Tobias, a particularly powerful *Invidia*, was that good. When Atticus had met him, Tobias had done the same to him, and when he figured it out, he'd almost killed the boy for it. This woman sounded unaffected, or as he suspected, hid the effect very well.

"Death leaves its mark on anyone it touches. Let's just say I can sense Atticus didn't bring you here on a whim, and you didn't fight him. Usually people with knives want to kill other people."

There was a moment of silence then the door swung open, revealing a red-faced Darci. Thankfully she didn't have any more weapons on her. On the other hand, he was packing several pounds of weaponry. He stepped back out of her reach. He didn't want her using his knives to cut off his clothes again.

"Did you put Tobias up to this?" she demanded. "Don't give me that look. I know you were listening at the door. If you want to hear whatever I have to say, just ask. You don't need to use your lusty voodoo powers on me—" She stepped back and examined his clothes and weaponry. Her indignation faded. "What are you wearing?"

"Armor," he answered and slipped around her, careful to keep their bodies from touching.

She gasped. "You're going to assassinate someone."

He turned and pinned her with a cold accusing stare. "So were you."

"I have a good reason."

"So do I," Atticus said. Orion, the Master of Trade, had exported Undesirables as slaves from the city for years. His death would be a major blow to the Magistrate's operations. If he could get out and clear his head, maybe he could stop thinking about the way her lips had felt against his. He should

24

accuse her of using lusty voodoo powers against him.

Tobias stopped him. "You are not leaving Darci here with me. She's a hazard. And could you possibly be packing enough weapons?"

Atticus glanced at the woman behind him, feeling trapped. *So your name is Darci*, he thought. He liked it. The name suited her intuitive nature, but he wasn't about to tell her that. As though she were reading his thoughts, one of her eyebrows sprang up and she frowned.

"Yes," he answered Tobias's first question. "She stays."

"What? Why?" Tobias asked.

He didn't want to admit it, but he was sure she had read his thoughts earlier. He'd heard members of the Virtuous could read thoughts, but that was a rumor. If she was a Virtue, she was also a danger to them. The longer she stayed near him the more about him she would know, and he wasn't willing to risk that. He had secrets Tobias hadn't even guessed at yet.

"You are not leaving me here with him," Darci stated as though it were fact. That brushed against him the wrong way. He'd used his own power on her to get her to do what he wanted, and so had Tobias. If he left her here no doubt Tobias wouldn't be able to stifle his curiosity. Tobias had an unquenchable curiosity that had got him into trouble as often as it served his purposes. If he wanted to know more about her, he'd use his abilities until he got the information he wanted, and whatever remained of Darci when he was finished Atticus would be responsible for.

"You have to take her," Tobias said, "I have my own booty call coming tonight, and she's a distraction."

"Zeke is coming over?" Atticus asked.

Tobias nodded. "She got you out of your pants. She can handle playing watch-dog for a night run."

Atticus sighed, resigned to having this loud-mouthed and undaunted woman underfoot all night. But it was better than leaving her between Tobias the curious and his boyfriend Zeke the pick pocket.

"Fine," he said.

***

Why did he put her in armor? The black carbon fabric of Tobias's spare armor hugged her body, and she kept tugging at the seams trying to get it to sit right, which only made certain chesty parts stand out all the more. A breeze picked up and blew her hair away from her face, like dark ribbons waving across the midnight sky. He clenched his teeth. Why did he even bother to bring her home from the Marriage House? He should have dumped her on a train back to her grower's town.

"Stop it," he ordered quietly.

"Bite me," Darci snapped back. "I can't believe you think this will protect me from bullets."

He sighed and flicked the magnification on inside his goggles. "It will keep bullets from killing you." Across the street in the Master of Trade's penthouse he detected no movement. The lights were on, but he hadn't seen anyone inside. Maybe the penthouse was automated to remain lit until commanded otherwise.

"I'm going to be shot at?"

Atticus stifled a groan and flicked the magnifex off. "No. You are going to stay here." He squinted at her. "As backup."

"Backup?" she repeated.

Atticus stifled the urge to move away from her. He could practically see her gathering her anger. He'd learned fast after he lost his pants that considering expression of hers was not passive. He didn't think he'd enjoy being kicked off a twenty story building.

"I'll be back in an hour."

"Isn't backup supposed to come in guns blazing when you fail?"

He clenched a fist and reached behind him and removed a pair of handcuffs from his belt. "I never fail."

"Right," she turned away from him and he had the feeling that she could see through the lie. "Go on then. I'll be here, waiting for you to not fail."

Now it was his turn to stifle the urge to kick her off the

twenty story building. Instead, he used the handcuffs and locked one around her left wrist and the other around a pipe next to the rooftop. She jerked and opened her mouth to scream again. This time he covered her lips with his hand. It forced her to stay down and out of sight. If she didn't make any noise, someone could walk right by her and miss her.

"Keep your head down," he said and grabbed his line gun. When he felt that she wouldn't begin shrieking, he removed his hand. "If you don't make any noise, someone could walk right by and not see you."

He aimed the line gun at a point across the street, over the windows of the master suite. When he pulled the trigger it was like firing an old-world shotgun. The butt of the line gun bit into his shoulder and released a spiked rod trailing a tail of high tensile cord. The spike lodged into the far building with an audible *chink*. He pulled the line taught and secured it around a another pipe. He clipped a one handed handle that would take him down the thin line and to the master suite window.

"I can't believe you are just going to leave me here," Darci hissed at him.

"It's for your safety," he said and muttered, "and mine." He gave her one last glance before he pushed off from the edge. He really shouldn't have put her in the suit of armor.

The wind zipped past and he dropped into the air between the two buildings. He drew one of the swords across his back with his left hand and flipped it around so the end of the pommel extended past his thumb through his clenched fist. The window approached and he pulled his arm back, jabbing it forward just before he smacked into the window. Glass shattered, reflecting fractured light with a spray of crystal clear splinters. Atticus let go of the handle. He landed crouched, with two knives in his right fist.

A spray of bullets erupted toward him.

Atticus hissed as one grazed his shoulder. The armor held, but it stung like a whip had cracked over his bicep. He rolled behind the side of a large bed.

"Get the Master to safety," one of the guards shouted.

Damn it, Atticus thought. The line gun was supposed to be silenced but he'd never considered when the spike actually hit the side of the building. The impact must have tipped off Orion's security. He peeked over the bed and Orion's uniformed men were covering him and retreating.

He flung two knives, another spray of laser fire erupted and he crouched behind the bed. Two bodies dropped, one man screamed.

Atticus sheathed his sword and filled both hands with small knives. He liked these particular knives; they were sharp enough to pierce armor that laser bullets could not. He tensed and leapt twisting over the bed. Knives flew from his hands as he fell. Each blade hit its target. The four guards ushering the Master of Trade out perished before they could aim and fire at Atticus, knives lodged in their eyes.

Knives spent, Atticus came up drawing his swords. Bodies slid to the floor and silence echoed around him. He was in a lavishly decorated bedroom. Orion, Master of Trade, grabbed one of the guns from his guards.

"I'd wondered if I was next on your list," Orion said, amused. He was a lean man, his chin as pointed and his nose sharp as a hawk's. "You've been busy. Six murders in the last two weeks. Congratulations, the city is in chaos."

Atticus kept his face blank, despite the sudden unease he felt. None of the other's he'd assassinated welcomed him. Most had died in their sleep, the few who hadn't died begging for mercy. They'd had no mercy for him and so he carried their blood on his hands hoping it would wash away the blood of the innocent.

"You won't kill me tonight," Orion said with a poisonous smile.

Unlikely.

Atticus raised his weapons and moved to attack. Pain lanced through his skull and he dropped. His vision faded for a moment before the room came into focus. Someone kicked him over, her sharp heel digging into his ribs. Blood was a coppery taste in his mouth. He'd bitten his tongue. He blinked as his mask was removed by a woman.

"*Luxurian*," she said, and he recoiled at the sound of her voice, of *that* voice. "Didn't you learn from your sins the last time we met?"

"*Valerian*," Atticus spat, and blood dotted the hem of her cream-colored dress. *Valerian* Raylene was the embodiment of victory, her powers giving her an unfair advantage over any opponent. She also controlled a large number of puppet strings in the Magistrate, notably Supreme Justice Jacqueline. He grabbed the ankle of the stiletto-clad foot pressing into his chest and twisted. She fell, but not before another bolt of pain exploded in his head, blurring his vision.

He rolled over the top of her and wrenched one arm behind her back.

"Don't shoot," Raylene ordered from beneath him. "He is more valuable alive."

"And why is that?" Atticus growled. "So you can auction me off to the highest bidder? Or do you intend to keep me for your own use like you did Michael?"

"I am a wealthy benefactress," she purred from beneath him, even now trying to entice him. He tightened his hold, straining the bones in her arms. Any tighter and he'd break them. "You would never lack," she gasped.

"You manipulative bitch," he snarled and tightened his grip.

Pain split through his skull and he cried out, fighting for consciousness. He'd fought this before, he would do it again. Raylene ripped her arm from his grip just as the butt of Orion's weapon crashed into the side of his head.

When he could see, the *Valerian* stood over him again, a scowl on her deceptively kind face. "Everyone is a pawn in someone else's game, it is time you came to understand that. Vengeance and sneaking through the night, doesn't suit you."

Atticus landed with his arm underneath him. He reached for a knife at his back. The moment the pain subsided, he kicked upward, tossing Raylene onto her back. He rolled to his feet and hurled the knife in one smooth action into Orion's forehead. His eyes rolled back into his skull and the gun fell from his grip. His lifeless body crumpled to the floor.

Spinning, Atticus searched for his swords. Raylene held one loosely in her hand, a poisonous grin on her sinfully voluptuous lips. The other blade lay at her feet, unreachable.

"The room is empty," she said, kicking the other sword under the bed. "Now we can truly talk." She swung the blade in an arc as though testing it.

"How much would you give to have a few years of freedom?"

"To you?" He almost laughed. "You've taken everything from me, Raylene. The only thing I have left to give you is your grave."

Raylene's face twisted into a frown. A thrill of fear ran through him. A *Valerian* was the single most dangerous Virtue of the seven castes, and he'd learned the lesson over and over. Still, his hatred deepened. He would never do as she wished, and she would never accept that he wouldn't break, not like the others. He gritted his teeth and braced for the pain. He'd been caught and now he would pay the price for carelessness. The pain struck through him like fire, burning every fiber of his being.

He fell to his knees and wondered how long Darci would remain chained to the pipe where he'd left her before she was discovered. Would she escape?

He wouldn't. Not this time.

***

Darci pulled one more time and the handcuff slipped over her hand. "Damn him," she cursed, and shook her bleeding fist. Atticus was a master of movement. His very presence seduced the air around him, making it vibrate with power too great to be confined to his body. He'd gone unnaturally still and she hadn't noticed the warning before he turned on her like a predator, and her body had leapt with pleasure as he spun her around and chained her.

She'd underestimated him and she wouldn't do that again. Still, for such a meticulous man, he hadn't bothered to check how tight the handcuff was around her wrist.

She stood, wiping excess water off her rump. He'd left her in the rain, the jack-ass. He could forget about her waiting around for his victorious return. There had to be another way to kill the *Industria* than wait for Atticus to get his act together—

A cry split the night. Darci froze. She'd hoped never to hear that sound again. She thought her sister's cries would be the last

She spun around and searched the penthouse across the street for movement. Through the broken window, nothing stirred. What if she was wrong and he needed her to—what? Signal for back up while she was chained to the roof?

Another cry echoed up from the shattered window, and this time she saw the outline of a woman's shadow stride across the floor. She knew how he despised women. A chill pierced through her chest. Not everyone in this imperfect world would hesitate to use him. From his mind, she knew he expected to be treated like an object.

Heart pounding, Darci waited for the next cry. It didn't come. There wasn't time to race back to Tobias and get help. By then Atticus could be dead, or worse.

A phantom image of Atticus's dead body among her sister's and the many other's in the mass graves flashed before her. Yes, she knew exactly where the disobedient met their final rest, after they were too broken to be of any use to their tormentors. He must have been caught.

Darci grabbed the dangling end of the handcuffs and kicked the thin pipe until it creaked and broke with a screech. She slid the handcuffs off and looped them over the thin cord stretched between the buildings so each half hung down like handles. Taking them in her hands, she glanced down and immediately swung her eyes to the sky.

"Okay," she breathed, bending her knees. She'd never been this high in the air, ever before in her life, and now she was going to trust a pair of handcuffs to hold her weight while she went swooping in over a city street and into an apartment where there may or may not be people who would kill her. She didn't have a single weapon. What was she going to do when she blazed in with only a thimbleful of combat experience and a pair of handcuffs?

Atticus had better not be dead yet. She'd need him to help her fight. He had the experience she didn't. She adjusted her sweaty palms on the metal cuffs and pushed off the rooftop.

Darci dropped into open air and stifled a scream. The window gaped open, drawing her in with jagged teeth of glass. She glanced up at the chain hissing down the rope. It creaked, and she saw a gap widening where the links had been welded together.

"Shit," she said, a jolt of fear rocketed through her. Now she couldn't wait to be in the line of fire and possibly not falling through the air to her doom.

The second chain link creaked, and she brought her legs up as she whistled through the window. A sharp snap echoed and she dropped. Her legs buckled as she hit the plush carpet. She pitched forward, and rolled to a crouched position. One half of the handcuffs in each hand.

Atticus, hands fisted on the carpet, was on all fours. A woman in an off-white gown stood over him, her red heels stabbing the blue carpet. Several bodies were strewn about the room. All had been pierced by blades she recognized as Atticus's. A laser powered shotgun lay at her feet. She snatched it and spun to face the woman.

"What do we have here?" the woman purred. Her dark hair shone in waves, and a special kind of malice radiated from her.

Atticus's eyes rolled back into his head and he dropped. Wasn't that perfect. The super skilled vigilante was now useless. At least she had a gun.

Darci met the woman's eyes and stifled a gasp as the connection struck. She *wanted* Atticus, and was willing to torture him time and again until he willingly submitted. She lived to cause pain, and from the collage of memories circling her thoughts, she'd done a number on Atticus. This wasn't the first time he'd been at her nonexistent mercy.

Darci raised her gun and fired.

The woman cried out. Her mind turned from playful cat to enraged predator.

Darci clicked the trigger on the gun. Nothing happened. She was out of shots, and this hateful woman was gathering her strength. Darci threw the weapon in the woman's direction. She side stepped and the gun struck Atticus in the back. He groaned.

Darci braced for the power of the other woman. She threw her essence forward just as the wave of nerve-splitting torture hurtled her direction. Darci's power split through the woman's like an arrow through water. Pressure built in the room between them. Their minds flowed together, becoming a tangle of thoughts and desires. Darci reached deep into the other woman's consciousness, grabbed hold, and twisted. There was no other way, not if she was going to save herself and Atticus. The woman screamed, her long red-painted fingernails clawing her skull before she crumpled to the ground.

Darci stumbled to one knee. "I can't believe that worked," she whispered. Her hands shook.

Atticus moaned. He pushed the heavy gun off his back and tried to stand.

Darci hurried to his side to help him. He recoiled, reviling the touch of another female. He didn't recognize her. If she'd had that much pain flowing through her at once she probably wouldn't identify him either. Still, he should be able to remember someone he'd handcuffed to a pipe.

"It's me," she snapped. "Come on, before she wakes up. I don't know how long whatever I did will work."

Atticus stiffened. "Darci?" he asked and straightened. He shrugged out of her grasp. "What the hell are you doing here?"

"If I didn't know how much pain you were just in, I'd slap you for being such an ungrateful idiot." She shoved away from him and retrieved his sword.

"How did you—"

Darci held out his sword, hilt first. "Take this, I don't know what to do with it and we need to get out of here." She frowned at his scowl.

"How did you get out of the handcuffs?" he asked angrily.

"If you checked your work," she snapped, "then I would still be on that rooftop."

The woman moaned and he stared at her.

"How did *you* take out a *Valerian?*"

***

Hellfire, this woman was going to be the death of him. Atticus marched her back to the basement hideout, doing his best to smooth his shortened stride. The *Valerian* had done a number on him this time. He hadn't expected her. How was he to know she was consorting with the Master of Trade?

He swore under his breath. He should have killed Raylene when he had the chance. She'd been prone, unconscious, and he couldn't even raise his blade to slash it through her black heart.

"Are you okay?" Darci asked.

"I'm fine." He wasn't. Raylene's power didn't vanish, it wore off. He wasn't about to let Darci know that every step sent crippling waves of agony up his legs.

"Liar," she muttered. "I saved your life. What was wrong? You killed everybody else. Why didn't you kill her?"

"You didn't save my life." He wasn't about to admit to anyone that a woman had saved his life and still hadn't made a move on him. He should have known Raylene would be there, fulfilling her sinful nature by dabbling with those who had outlived their usefulness.

Darci stopped in the shadow of a pair of recycling receptacles and turned on him. "Deny it all you like, but you know I stopped that woman from ripping your heart out with her bare hands."

"Raylene wouldn't dare kill me," he growled. He wondered if Darci could see right through him, past his outer defenses and view what he hid behind the mask. There were other, lecherous reasons why Raylene would never kill him or have him killed. He was too valuable to her. The memory of iron shackles bit into his skin and pain flared in a too-familiar fashion. His stomach churned violently. Thank the gods he'd been wise enough not to eat anything.

"Why wouldn't she kill—" Darci stopped mid question. Her skin paled and she closed her eyes, swaying on the spot. "I'm going to be sick." She spun around and heaved over the side of a trash receptacle.

Atticus felt the hairs on the back of his neck rise. Darci couldn't be sensing his thoughts could she?

Her hands gripped the edge of the can so hard her arms shook. After a moment she pushed away, wiping her mouth with her sleeve and turned on him. Hellfire burned in the angry gaze she pinned him with. For any other woman he would have reacted with rage, but instead a sudden heat gripped him.

"I saw what they did to you. How can you stand by and let *them* continue to ruin so many lives? We should be out there, slaughtering them. Why don't you do something?" She reached toward him, her face flushed. Inches from his chest, her hands stopped and curled into fists. The heat in him turned to ice at her movement.

"Damn it," she cried.

At her shout, he closed the distance between them and placed his hand over her mouth. "*Quiet.* The last thing we need is the bloody Magistrate finding us."

She mumbled something sarcastic against his hand. Her lips tickled his palm, chasing the lingering soreness from Raylene's touch away. He sucked in a deep breath. How he wanted her to soothe the rest of his pains. For a moment he lost himself, wrapped in his own temptation. Darci stilled against him, her body sinking against his. Then she struggled in his grasp. Unwilling to release her yet, he tightened his hold and unleashed some of his power.

An enraged gasp escaped her and she elbowed him in the side.

"Ooff!" he grunted and let her go. Wicked bright pain flared deep into his chest from the spot where Raylene's heel had dug between his ribs.

"Stop lusting me into submission. I'm not falling for it. Keep it to yourself."

Again. She'd fought against his power and won. He hadn't been trying to seduce her, but his natural predatory reflexes kicked in. Darci should have been humming with desire. Not ready to dig out his eyes and feed them to him. It made him suspicious of her intent toward him. Why was she really here?

"Let's get back," he said. "Tobias is probably worried."

"As if," she said. "The only thing he's worried about is—" she stopped herself. "I won't say anything else. But I won't say I told you so if we get back and he's not done with...well not done."

With that infuriating sway of her hips, she headed up the alley.

Atticus hurried to catch up, his long stride quickly gaining on her. There was no way she was human, not entirely. She had to be full or at least a half-blood Virtue in order to disable the Magistrate's hell-on-heels girl. He'd been trying to kill Raylene for years and he'd never been closer than he had tonight. This small town woman had hoodwinked them both. She was a devastating variable. He needed to find out exactly who and what she was.

He caught the amused pull at the corner of his mouth and scowled.

I hate variables.

3

Darci stomped through the back door of the underground lair. Atticus followed on her heels; his power grated against her with all the feeling of silk against senses teased into raw form. After they had escaped, the exhilaration of invading Raylene's mind and stopping her attack had left Darci open to the smallest touch from his aura. Somehow she was already tuned to him, faster than she'd tuned to anyone else, even her family. It scared the fruit right out of her.

"Tobias," Atticus called into the apartment. Even now that voice seemed laced with seduction.

The unmistakable sounds of persons scrambling came from down the hall.

She turned to Atticus and lifted an eyebrow. His *Luxurian* influence must have rubbed off on his roommate. Lucky for Tobias he had a way to scratch at Atticus's infuriating itch.

He pulled his night-vision goggles off his face, revealing eyes that burned into hers with intensity. The movement had her blood simmering in her veins. In the tight hallway, they were pressed so close he'd only need to dip his head to capture her lips. She burned at the memory of the kiss from the Marriage House. He'd tasted like whiskey and temptation.

Right now, she could still taste sour in her mouth.

"I need a toothbrush," she said.

He blinked and stepped back. His brow furrowed and he glanced down the hall where Tobias and his guest were. "I have a spare." He pushed past her.

"Hold it. I don't want to walk in on them, doing whatever."

He growled and the sound had heat spreading to every party of her body. "You can follow by your decision or mine." The way he said it made her think she wouldn't like his way.

"Fine." Darci ran a hand through her long hair, frustrated.

He tensed at the movement. His eyes flicked down her body with it so did a generous portion of his power. Darci refused to reach out and touch him. He despised women who took advantage of him for his power. His chest rose and fell inches from her. It was a struggle not to touch him. The tension mounted and threatened to break over them. What would happen when it finally shattered between them frightened her. It frightened him too, and his concern shot through her as he turned and strode away from her, down the hall. With no other choice, Darci followed him. The sooner he helped her kill Jacqueline the better.

"I thought you'd be longer," Tobias said. His hands were on his hips and he was shirtless, as was the partially-dressed man lounging on the couch near him.

"I would have been back sooner," Atticus growled.

Tobias was not amused. "As if. That penthouse is a fortress and like ten stories up. You'd have to kill dozens of guards."

Darci took a good look at Tobias's boyfriend. He was also shirtless and his mind was totally trained on his lover.

"The window was faster," Atticus said, nonchalantly.

"A window?" Tobias repeated. He frowned and turned to his tablet. His fingers flew over the screen. "You'd have to scale another building and drop in at an angle and crash through double-paned laser-proof glass."

"It wasn't sword proof." Atticus shrugged, opened a closet and rummaged around inside. He came up with a small black bag. He unzipped it and removed a tiny sonic toothbrush. He set it on the table near Darci instead of handing it to her directly. She glared at him. Whatever had happened between them was making him wary of her, and that bothered her.

"So what did you do with Darci?" Tobias pushed.

"He chained me to the top of the roof."

"She went through the window with me."

Darci glared at him. If he meant to keep the fact that he'd chained her up in the rain a secret, he'd better think again. She snatched the toothbrush and turned to the kitchen at the far end of the room. She ran the water and vigorously scrubbed her mouth clean.

"I think you need to explain that," Tobias said, folding his arms. "You don't get to deviate from plans and lie to me about it."

"You chained her to the roof?" The boyfriend asked. "Seriously, Atticus. It was pouring out there."

Tobias shrugged. "He must not have chained her well if she got free. That, or there's more to her than just good looks. What do you think, Zeke?"

Darci wanted to hug Tobias and his boyfriend. Then she caught the angry frustrated twist of Atticus's thoughts and focused on brushing her teeth.

"Bad form, Atticus," Zeke said.

He growled again. "I left her on the roof and she followed."

Darci spat and rinsed her mouth. A second later, Atticus's fingers wrapped around her upper arm and he led her down a set of steps that led to a basement bedroom.

"If that's following, I'd hate to see you drag her along behind you," Tobias called after them.

Atticus didn't slam the door like she expected. He closed it softly, and she heard the click of a lock sliding into place.

Darci turned around as he flicked on the light. Whatever she wanted to say died on her tongue and became a shiver of apprehension. The congenial creature that existed in the presence of Tobias vanished here in the dungeon.

She stumbled away from him.

Atticus didn't hesitate. He came after her, all his cat-like sensuality gone, replaced by fury and death from the kind of predator who wouldn't play with his prey. The savage grace in his stride turned her apprehension into outright fear.

Darci's back slapped against the far wall, nothing but concrete, damp and cool even through the skintight armor.

He placed his hands on either side of her, caging her in again. "Why are you here?"

Darci didn't answer right away. The sudden rage of his thoughts caught her in his hold and imprisoned her there. His mind was like a gaping wound, festering and infected. He'd been through hell and had somehow risen from a life of pain, still a man who cared for the less fortunate, even as he struggled to balance his predatory nature with some semblance of a life.

"I told you," she ground out. "I'm here to kill the *Industria*, Jacqueline."

"Try again," he said. He wanted something else, but trapped in his mind, surrounded by chaos she couldn't divine what it was. She'd never felt such rage, hatred, or pain. His power slipped his control, twisting in sensual ribbons around her.

She shivered. His mind pressed against hers with growing pressure; it combined with the heat from his body to create a concoction of overwhelming sensation. If she succumbed to the temptation of his lips, of his body now, he would lash out. When she'd dropped Raylene she'd also made him wary of her. He feared Raylene. Who wouldn't fear a person with the power to make them crawl? Somehow she'd overcome *his* fear, and that terrified him even more. She was unpredictable, and for the man who knew exactly where he stood, she'd toppled his foundations and become the enemy.

Darci fisted her hands at her sides and fought to tear her gaze from his.

Atticus snarled. "Raylene has sent others like you before. Do you work for her?" His *Luxurian* abilities snapped the leash he had on them and wrapped around her, suffocating her in a grip of promised pleasure.

"No," she answered sharply. Hot desire flooded her body, mirroring the hold on her mind. "I don't work for anyone." If she could look away, the connection would break, and she'd be free from his terrible thoughts. She could see the things he would do to her to make her talk. Demons take her, but she wanted him to do those things.

No. She knew what using his powers for *that* did to him. Even now she glimpsed past images of the women he'd led to their death beds. Literally. She could not fall for his "I'm-The-Sexy-and-you-should-swoon" ploy. It would be the end of her mission to kill the *Industria*, and probably her life.

"Atticus," she said breathless. "I don't work for the Justice. I've never seen Raylene before. I don't even know what she is or how I was able to stop her." *Come on, believe me.*

His eyes narrowed. "If you can disable a *Valarian*, you would have had no problem dealing with me at the club when you wanted your knife back."

He burned through her as easily as fire rips across a wheat field. If he didn't stop with the lust she was going to erupt at him like a cat in heat.

Desperate, she fought for the freedom of her mind. Pain blossomed at the top of her head and quickly became a migraine of epic proportions. His memories stabbed at her, clawing her. She pulled, feeling as though he peeled skin from her body. There was a moment when she thought she would break under the pressure, and then she was free.

Darci snapped her eyes shut and allowed her exhausted body to sink to the ground. Unwilling to be caught by his tortured mind again while he was in this state, she covered her eyes with her hands, her cheeks wet with tears.

"How do you do it?" she asked. "How can you do what she tells you to, after everything she's done to hurt you?"

***

Atticus stiffened as Darci broke eye contact and crumbled to the floor. Her questions chilled the simmering blood in his veins, and her emotions froze him completely. She was not a weak-willed woman, otherwise she would never have been able to hold out against his influence. No woman, or man, was immune. Only Raylene, a *Valerian*, the embodiment of torture and pain, had ever been victor in the contest of pitting her will against his. Darci had beaten Victory, herself, and claimed it was an accident.

Could he believe her?

He curled his fingers into fists against the concrete wall on either side of where she'd been. He needed to know what she was. He needed to know she was not Raylene's pet sent to make him kneel in some new and horrifying way. When he'd stared Darci down, he'd felt a connection through the shield of anger. It had happened earlier, when he'd been nauseous and she'd been the one to become sick. If she wasn't working with Raylene, then tonight's trick wasn't an act. Darci had brought the woman down without even touching her.

She'd saved his life. That too made no sense. Unless it was another ploy to win his trust and then break him. Raylene knew better than anyone that he would never trust a woman. Perhaps that was why he should trust *this* one.

He pushed off the wall and bent his knees, bringing himself to Darci's level.

"Who told you about my past?" he asked, releasing her from the predatory embrace of his aura. He didn't want to. He wanted to unleash everything he was on her and force the truth from her lips. The memory of those lips was still a succulent taste in his mouth.

Darci ran shaky hands through her hair. Her eyes remained closed. "I-it's in your thoughts. The torture, the pain, the—" she shuddered, "—the bedroom games." She said the last in a whisper. "You were thinking about it, over and over again."

"You read my thoughts." So his suspicions were right.

"Yes, I did," she said, pulling her hands into fists and burying them between her knees and chest. "Not because I wanted to."

Atticus's heart pounded. No Virtue had that ability, at least none that he'd come across. He needed to see it for himself.

He reached out and cupped her cheek with his hand. She flinched at his touch. Her skin was soft.

"Open your eyes," he said.

She laughed, and pulled away. "What for? So I can see everything you regret again and get locked in it. If that happens, I don't know if I can stop myself from ripping your mind apart to get out."

He frowned and dropped his hand from her cheek. She relaxed. "You didn't see everything." His anger and fear had pulled up memories from his past. Still, if she was one of Raylene's creatures sent to ferret him out, she could have twisted his mind to her will long ago and hadn't. Most women in her position would have done that and more.

A significant portion of his suspicion dropped away. He'd never come across anyone who was that selfless.

"My sister, Tara, was marked as an Undesirable," she said. "No one knew why she disappeared. I did. I saw her from the window. The authorities were in an unmarked van. They simply took her and left. Even in a Growers Town you hear rumors about those vans. You never expect to see them." Darci opened her eyes. He recognized the raw determination in her gaze. Fueled by fury, injustice, and loss, she was willing to do anything to set things right. "Do you know what they do with Undesirables?"

He didn't. He'd been an outcast his entire life, a tool, something to do the work the Magistrate didn't do themselves. He hadn't worried much about the less fortunate, not when the City drowned in them. Unexplained disappearances were the norm here.

"They kill them eventually, but not before they use them. Most are sent to war. Those who have the aptitude to be soldiers are sent to the field. Those who don't, Undesirables, are used as target practice for soldiers."

Atticus knew which of the two Darci's sister had been. They'd tried to train him as a soldier, but he refused, even as a child, to harm the innocent. He'd watched the others torture and kill because it gave them pleasure. Darci's sister must have been one who couldn't murder on command. He wasn't innocent himself, he'd murdered his fair share of people. But he never killed simply to kill. Every one of his targets had committed all manner of acts to deserve the death he dealt them.

"I followed her mind, and found her at the compound." Darci's eyes hardened as she continued.

"The training drill was just starting. Even from a hundred yards away I felt her fear as she realized what was happening. The *Industria* was there, she gave the command to begin the attack. There were fifty of them like Tara, people who were too sweet to be expected to slaughter on command. There were twenty battle-crazed soldiers. I slipped through a fence near the back. It didn't even have electronic alarms. Anyone who was stupid enough to enter that killing field would die eventually.

"The five of them found Tara before I did. She didn't cry. I saw them through her mind, as they lunged for her. The soldiers weren't normal. The Magistrate does something to them. Whatever it is makes them stronger and gives them a desire to inflict pain. They want to hurt people. But the things they did to her—" Darci clenched her jaw, "all of it in the name of peace."

Atticus knew what those soldiers had done to her sister. He'd heard of the war crimes, the ones the Magistrate couldn't silence whispering over the broadband wavelengths from across the globe. Reports of mass murders, graves the lengths of football fields, and women used until they expired. The British Isles had fallen, and so had much of Europe under the onslaught. It wasn't unlike what happened in the city every day. Atticus was tied to this city, to the Magistrate by chains even he couldn't break. He did whatever he could to retaliate. Some days it wasn't enough. He'd ceased grieving for the doomed inhabitants of this City long ago.

"It can't go on, Atticus," she said. "You've endured nightmares, and even if you fight back, until you escape, it won't end. You don't have to believe that I'm not working for them, but I won't stand by and let you or anyone else continue to be tortured and used by a self-pleasing government."

Darci stood, her body trembling. "If you don't believe I will stop at nothing to kill the *Industria* who murdered my sister, then you have no idea what I'm capable of."

Atticus stood, and sized her up. How much of her threat was truth and how much of it was bravado? She stepped away from the wall, nose to nose with him.

"So which is it?" she demanded. "Will you trust me or kill me?"

Atticus's heart pounded. His breath caught, and a rush of heat he didn't recognize swept through his body. Could he trust her? He wanted to. She was dangerous, alluring, and full of surprises. He didn't like the combination, but she was valuable. Could he kill her? She'd saved his life. She'd been there when he needed help the most.

Darci possessed abilities that could stop a *Valerian* in the middle of an attack. Her anger and determination gave her strength. Her grief gave her purpose. She could fight, sow chaos at his side. Still, she couldn't be trusted not to turn on him, she was a woman and with her abilities he feared what she could do with them. He'd kill her if he couldn't trust his power to be greater than hers.

Giving no warning, he unleashed a surge of *Luxurian* power. Her breath hitched, and the trembling in her body worsened, a flush colored her cheeks. She opened her mouth to protest. He silenced her with his lips. He brought his hands to her waist and pulled her against him, away from the wall. She stiffened, even now trying to resist. He let more ribbons of desire weave around her. Finally, she relaxed. Her hands rose to rest against his back, her fingers curling into claws.

As she began to pull him closer, her body molding against his, he drew back.

He smiled down at her. She most definitely wasn't immune to him.

"Did you just—" she frowned and let out a furious growl,

"—you did." She jumped away from him, her back flattening against the wall, her breasts moving as she drew in angry breaths.

"I needed to double check," he said, stepping away from her and turning to the door. If he didn't leave now, he'd do something to her they both might regret.

4

"Double check!" Darci shrieked. "You didn't have to lust me into submission."

He glanced over his shoulder at her, his body half turning to give her an excellent view of his tight abs, and stunning pectorals. "I might not be able to read your thoughts, but I can read your body. You aren't immune to my abilities."

Damn him. He turned and opened the door, taking the stairs two at a time.

"You'd better run," she shouted. "You don't do that and get away with it."

His footsteps paused, and he sauntered back down, his body dressed in the skin-tight armor moving with sinful invitation. His movement alone was a calculated seduction.

"Yes, I do," he said, his eyes openly roaming her equally skin-tight clad body. What she wouldn't give for a pair of sweats and a baggy sweatshirt. "I want the *Industria* dead. So do you. If I'm going to work with you, I need to know I won't be stabbed in the back."

"Keep that up and you just might be."

His eyebrow arched, and he entered the room.

Darci's eyes widened. Now that she wasn't a threat to his personal safety, she was a threat to his ability to control himself. That could be dangerous to both of them.

"Hold it," she said, putting her hands up between herself and him. "Don't you dare point *those* kinds of thoughts my way."

"Why?" His voice tempted, urged her to let down her guard. Atticus had a messy background when it came to women and she didn't know enough about men to even think about going there with him, even if she had thought about going there more than once. If she did, it would do more harm than good to either of them.

"Because we have a working relationship. You don't like to be touched by women. I'm not, you know—" she stumbled over her tongue as his thoughts spun around her words. His *Luxurian* mind knew exactly how to hunt her. She'd revealed enough of herself to give his predatory side the advantage, and she did not have the skill to match him. This terrain was all his. "—I don't have the experience that you have, and shouldn't we make killing Jacqueline the priority?"

"You think?"

She nodded, determined not to take a step back. If she did, she knew he would be after her like a falcon after a sparrow. This game with him was infuriating. Couldn't he just have a normal conversation with her? Not that their circumstances would allow for a conversation devoid of lustiness. She would simply have to work harder not to be affected. Yeah, right.

"Stop it," she said. "I know what you're trying to do, and I'm not falling for it. I came here to kill the Justice, or be killed."

He closed the distance between them. His mind blazed with calculation, his thoughts whirling too fast for her to follow. The heady atmosphere of lust he'd created served to throw her off.

"Is that so?" he asked.

"Yes," she said.

"Good." He began to circle her. "Jacqueline is proficient with every weapon we might get our hands on. You need to practice invading minds. If you can disable her, like you did

Raylene, we might have a chance."

"*If* I can do that again," Darci said. The back of her neck prickled as he passed behind her. "I don't even know how I did it the first time."

"You can't imagine how much I want Jacqueline and Raylene dead," he murmured in her ear. When his thoughts parted and a memory rose from his depths, he caught her as her knees buckled.

Darci gasped, and closed her eyes as though to erase his memories. The electric shocks, the scalding water followed by dry ice burns. The cruelty of those two women went on for hours, each new torture a game for her. She shuddered again. His arms tightened around her. "I want vengeance."

It took two tries before she managed to respond. "I understand."

"Raylene will have Jacqueline scouring the city for us. When they find us, which will be soon, we need to be ready."

"Can you let go?" she asked. She needed to not be touching him. The combination of fear, anger, and eroticism from his aura made it hard to regain control of her own faculties. She needed to separate his rage from hers, and his carnal power from her desires before she succumbed to the dangerous mix of emotions. She struggled to get away from him.

He responded by tightening his hold. "When the Justice catches us, you will not be able to escape. Not without disabling your opponent first."

She read the open invitation in his voice. He'd frightened her, attacked her, and kissed her. That was more than enough reason to do anything to get away from him. She threw her elbow back into his side. He grunted, and his hold on her tightened again.

"In combat you don't get second chances. Try again," he growled in her ear, urging her to simply melt in his arms and let his body press into her—no! She was going to get out of this, and he was definitely going to regret it.

Darci raised her hands to rest on his forearms. When the *Valerian* had tried to attack her, Darci had split her mind and reached in, ripping and tearing as she went. If she did that to Atticus, she had no idea what she would leave behind. She wanted to disable him, not demolish him. She didn't know if she could succeed without harming him.

She gripped his forearms, pressing her nails into his flesh. Even without eye contact now, she could feel his mind. His rage was there, a boiling reservoir she didn't want to upset, but he wanted to test her abilities and fine tune them. She plunged in, the pressure of his power sliding around her with a light touch. His mind soothed and teased. She forced herself to grip him harder instead of relax in his hold. His very existence was a trap.

In his mind she found an area blocked from her. She frowned but didn't push the barrier. She didn't want to know what his deepest, darkest secrets were, especially after the small glimpse he'd given her. She steered clear and continued on.

Once she felt she had gone deep enough, she issued the command. *Release me.*

His body tensed around her. His mind clamped down on hers. His grip shifted and he grabbed both her hands in one of his. A snarl ripped from his throat as his leg swept hers out from under her. He caught her as she fell, holding both arms above her head, and straddling her waist, his knees on either side of her ribs.

Breathing hard, he hovered over her. His aura encompassed her, and she gasped, closing her eyes as his raw sexuality overwhelmed her. His rage boiled over and suddenly his lips were on hers, devouring her with his need rising around her. If she tried to break free she knew she could seriously damage him, but if she didn't, he could seriously damage her. Commanding his mind had caused some kind of defense to spring up. He was attacking her in the most primal way he knew.

She turned her head away from his, her lips throbbing from the force of his kiss.

"Stop," she gasped. "It didn't work."

Atticus froze. His mind snapped into organized thoughts

again. "What happened?" he asked, his voice rough.

Darci looked at him. He frowned at her, raw desire in his gaze.

"I tried to invade your mind," she explained, thoroughly uncomfortable being pinned underneath him.

He blinked but didn't release her. "You failed to disable me."

She struggled and ripped her hands free from his, and pushed herself onto her elbows. "Yes, and you attacked me. With your lips."

"Next time your attacker won't be me," he said.

A whistle came from the doorway.

They both jumped. Tobias stood there with his arms folded over his still-bare chest.

"No, no, don't let me stop you," he said waving a hand at them. "I've never seen Atticus in action. Darci, I must say, you have a fine way of firing him up." He gave a pointed glance to Atticus's midsection.

Darci pointedly looked elsewhere.

5

Atticus glared at Tobias. "Where's Zeke?" he asked.

"He's upstairs," Tobias answered. "Thought you might want to see the news report. You two made a double feature."

Raylene, no doubt, was scrambling to locate him. She'd want revenge for what he'd done to her. He'd had the upper hand and left her napping with the dead. She would be pissed on a new level that he'd taken victory from her, again.

It was a good thing he and Tobias had recently moved to the underground apartment. Raylene or the Justice wouldn't know yet where he lived.

"We made the news?" Darci asked, a little out of breath. She pushed on his chest and surprised him by wiggling out from underneath him. He drew in a deep breath as her movement jostled his now too-tight clothes.

Tobias only smiled. "In a grand way. You've been labeled a high risk assassin from overseas. You'll have to tell me how you managed to terrify them."

"That's a total lie," Darci said. "Why would they say we are from overseas?"

Atticus stood. "By making it sound like an enemy assassin is in the City, they can turn the entire populace into their own little watchdogs."

"That's the power of fear," Tobias added. "How did you rub them the wrong way?"

"Raylene was there," Atticus answered.

Tobias paled. "No shit. Why aren't you dead? Why am I not dead? Why didn't you say something?"

Atticus glanced sideways at Darci. She shifted her weight from one foot to the other. He could still feel her mind. His instincts wanted him to reject her presence merely because she was female and women were the enemy. Darci asked nothing of him. She was determined to fly her own flag, despite the dangers in her path. She was brave and respectful. Knowing that calmed his nerves.

"Darci had more of a hand in tonight's work than I told you. I had to make sure she wasn't a mole before we moved out."

Tobias gave Darci another thorough glance, and if Tobias had been straight, Atticus was sure he might have been oddly tempted to punch the kid for such a lingering consideration. "Right. That little scrap of barnyard fluff is a killer. Are you sure she's not selling us out to the Magistrate?" Tobias was naturally a skeptic.

"She's not," Atticus answered. "We're on a time limit," he reminded him.

"I'll get the gear," Tobias said as he turned up the stairs. "If we use the new cloaking devices, we should be safe enough until we reach the fence line." He disappeared to the floor above.

Darci's eyes widened. "It's after curfew. We won't get out of the city."

"I know," Atticus said. The light boundary that circled the city was the first of several barriers designed to eradicate escapees from reaching the wastelands. The only way in or out were the train systems. Unless you had Tobias's codes.

"Why are you so valuable to them?" she asked.

"I'm a *Luxurian*," he supplied, keeping his voice tight. "The Magistrate uses us to do the work only we can do and do easily. The last *Luxurian*, Michael, was driven insane last year."

"Atticus, this has to stop. They can't continue to use people like toilet paper, wiping their asses and discarding them."

He nodded. Emotions passed over her face. Her ability to read thoughts would make her vulnerable to the horrors he'd been prey to his entire life. He'd had Michael to guide him through the horror and make him stronger for it. The veil of perfection had only just been drawn back for her. Still, he didn't like seeing years of his pain and horror fight for supremacy in her mind.

"They have to die," she said, and pushed past him toward the stairs. "Soon, before they regroup. I think I did some serious damage to the *Valerian*. I doubt she'll recover fast."

"Then Jacqueline stands alone," Atticus said.

"Exactly." Darci jogged past him up the stairs. "And no, I didn't do the same thing to you that I did to Raylene," she said over her shoulder, answering his unspoken question.

Atticus frowned, unsettled and didn't immediately follow her up the stairs. Jacqueline would summon others like herself to help take him down. He was in serious violation of the Magistrate's law by not turning Darci in. When Michael had finally fallen and started slaughtering women at will, they brought in three *Valerians* and four *Industrias* from other city states to subdue him. Atticus would have helped his mentor, but Michael had aggressively told him to stay out of it. He would risk only one life not two to kill Raylene. Michael had failed. When they were done with him, when his mind surrendered to the *Valerian*, nothing remained of the proud and resolute man Atticus had grown to admire.

Darci had no ability to protect herself from that kind of onslaught. He might be risking her life unnecessarily. A fierce need to protect her seized him. Heat poured into his weary and strained body. His hand rose to his mouth and briefly touched lips that still burned with the kiss he'd taken from her. He'd never pursued a woman before, never wanted to.

He took the stairs two at a time. Tobias, his boyfriend's arms around him, stood next to Darci, watching the news-cast. The crystal screen flickered with images of Magistrate officials and aerial shots of the penthouse window he'd destroyed. He could see the body of a guard, his black knife buried to the hilt in the dead man's chest.

"Tobias," he said. "I think we need to give the Magistrate something to remember us by and keep them occupied."

"Finally!" Tobias crowed. "I've wanted to knock out their communications for months now, just to screw with them."

"This isn't to screw with them," Atticus said, sharper than he'd meant. "You and Zeke need time to get out of the city. As soon as they find this place they'll know about you both and you'll be dead."

Tobias sobered, but he still entered a few commands into his tablet glass, a smirk on his face. A moment later the crystal screen flickered.

"That's not supposed to happen," Tobias said quietly. He rushed over to his command center and his fingers began to fly over screens, manipulating data.

Raylene's image appeared on the crystal screen. She had a bruise spreading across one cheek.

"Atticus," she spoke. Her voice was tightly controlled, lacking the seductive quality she'd taunted him with earlier. "You will surrender immediately. For every hour you remain at large, I will spend two torturing Michael."

The recording vanished, leaving the screen blank. A moment later the news station returned.

Something in him broke. He stared at the news story. Hover cars swarmed the block of the Master of Trade's building. Bodies, zipped into black bags, flashed on the screen. Intense rage crashed through him like a glacier into arctic waters.

How dare they?

Michael had spent the last year in a cell, as the Magistrate tried to reestablish his connection to the world. He'd become the product of fear, terrified of both light and dark, cowering in the lonely corners of his mind. It would have been a mercy to kill him, but the Magistrate had ordered him kept alive. He was too valuable. Any chance, no matter how slim, that he might recover, was enough to keep his broken mind and body tethered to existence.

Atticus had also let Michael live. If there was a chance he would return, it was one worth giving him. Six months after he'd gone insane, Atticus had sneaked his way into the Magistrate's holding cells. He'd found the once proud and deadly warrior huddled on a cot.

"Gods, it's you," Michael had said as soon as Atticus opened the cell door. Sobbing, the man had stumbled into his arms, cutting himself on the blade Atticus held before him. Michael didn't notice the blood, the wound, or much of anything else. "I'm so sorry," he murmured. "Her life is worth living for. She's dead." He repeated the nonsense phrase over and over in a chant.

He should have raised the dagger. He should have struck, quick and clean. Michael deserved that much from him. It had been his own selfishness that kept him from striking the blow. Michael still dreamed of a better future, where he wouldn't have to succumb to the desires of the upper class as they terrorized the peasantry. It was a dream Atticus might still be able to give him, in some small way. He'd sheathed his weapon and left the broken man on his bed.

Within months Atticus had started to feel the strain. The work the Magistrate required of him had doubled. First it started with sudden bouts of shaking after a job. Soon he became violently ill. There was nothing to do about it. He had Tobias to look after. Hell, the boy was barely an adult, and a fugitive *Invidia*. If Atticus gave himself up, no one would be there to keep him underground and out of the line of fire.

"Atticus?" Tobias asked.

"Pack up," Atticus ordered. "It's time to leave." He avoided looking at Darci or Tobias, turned and headed toward the armory. It would take Tobias fifteen minutes at least to pack his gear and make ready.

Atticus slipped fresh blades into the sheaths on either side of his ribs. Next he crossed two old-world traditional Japanese swords across his back, and added a laser rifle to the holster along his spine. Two blasters fit snugly into holsters under each arm and on each thigh. He bent one knee to check the spring-loaded blades in each toe of his boot.

"Where will you take Tobias before you drop him off and surrender?" Darci's voice was soft but each word was a blow he couldn't dodge. He wasn't going to surrender. He would never give up to the Magistrate.

He straightened and reached for the spare utility belt on a hook. "Beyond the city. He'll activate a virus that will hack the fence grid. We'll be hundreds of miles away by tomorrow night."

"So you're going to run."

He turned at her sharp tone. "No, we are. You don't want them to find you. I don't think you'd survive longer than your sister did." He took a duffel bag off a top shelf and began stuffing it full of weaponry and ammunition.

"If we run, they win."

He hesitated. Yes, Raylene and her *Industria* lap dogs would win. But Tobias, Zeke and Darci would live another day. Michael wouldn't. Raylene would make good on her promise. His death would be slow, but at least he wouldn't spend years suffering.

"The Magistrate is everywhere. We can't run forever. Even you don't know where to go."

He turned on her. "We can try," he said. "If we don't leave, now, we fail to do anything."

Darci folded her arms across her chest. "Coward," she said. "People are dying. More than you know or think you know. You are leaving your friend to die, for the slim chance that we *might* survive."

"He's insane. Killing him would be a mercy." He zipped up the duffel and gathered the handles into one hand.

"Killing me would have been a mercy, I remember you saying."

Atticus stopped in front of her. He had said that to her, only hours ago. Now, more than her abilities made it impossible to think of killing her.

"You aren't as heartless as you think you are," she said.

Silence fell between them like a curtain. She knew his thoughts and he had no way of learning hers.

He heard a scuffle and grunt from the other room.

Darci froze, her eyes going wide.

Atticus's heart pounded in his chest. He dropped the duffel and slipped the guns on his hips out of their holsters. Now was not the time for knives.

Stay here, he told Darci with his mind. She nodded and slipped into a shadowy corner of the room. He unleashed his aura and lust twisted through the air into the hall before him. He crept down the small distance before he stole into the main room.

"Run, Atticus," Tobias shouted as his boyfriend's arm tightened around his throat. Zeke's right hand plunged a gimlet dagger into Tobias's side. He gasped, the air wheezing out of him as his eyes rolled back.

Atticus snarled. He fired and Zeke dropped, dragging Tobias with him. He'd wondered before if Zeke was a spy. Tobias had reassured him that he wasn't. It hurt to be betrayed by someone his friend had loved so fiercely.

Pain exploded between Atticus's eyes and he cried out. Raylene was here. Panic blossomed in his chest. He swept the room for the *Valerian*. She wasn't here yet. Another jolt of pain flooded his arms. The gun dropped from his trembling fingers.

He gritted his teeth and drew his sword from its sheath on his back. The specialized handle bonded with his palm print and was perfectly weighted for Atticus's arm. He wouldn't be able to aim a gun, but a sword had greater length, and he could slash and hack as much as he wanted.

He thought he'd outwitted Raylene this time. But he'd been wrong, so very wrong. He would not hesitate to kill the bitch. Not this time.

A shot rang out from the back of the lair, from where he'd left Darci.

Fear dropped into his heart and he ran back to the armory.

Jacqueline, her white clothes unstained by the fresh blood

pooling around her boots, stood over Darci's still form. Jacqueline holstered her weapon, whipping her own sword up to clash with Atticus's. Steel rang against steel, the hilts of their swords locked.

"The Masters say it's time to play," Jacqueline teased him, her shoulders shaking as she pushed against him. His control crumbled and he lashed out, punching her in the jaw. She stumbled backward. He raised his sword to attack. Raylene's power slashed at him from behind and he faltered. His lunge toward Jacqueline failed. He stumbled over the duffle he'd dropped and he pitched forward into her arms. She pressed the still cooling barrel of her weapon against his temple.

"It'll be good to have you again, at least for a few hours," she purred, tracing a finger down his chest to his belt. "Maybe this time you'll learn your place." Her knee came up, landing a blow to his groin. He lurched forward and her weapon crashed against the side of his face.

Atticus sprawled on the ground, his hands splashing into Darci's still warm blood. Stars burst in his vision. He drew his hands into fists, dragging a shaking breath into his lungs. This couldn't be it. He'd tried so hard, and to fail now nearly undid him. Darci wouldn't have given up so easily, he thought. His next breath fortified him.

Raylene's red heels clicked into view. Atticus pushed off the ground, even as a fresh wave of pain split his mind. His fingers were afire, useless to do anything but clench against Raylene's power. His sword had spun under a shelf unit, but he still had his knives. He forced himself to face the sadistic woman. Darci hadn't cowered, neither would he. Never again.

"I could kill you for tonight." Raylene's hand whipped out, slapping him. "For daring to disobey me." As her hand connected with his body, the pain lacing through him became a wave. It was meant to make him scream and beg, but today it made him angry. He stumbled and used the movement to shield his hand as it moved to his ribs.

He came up slashing. Raylene jumped back, as his knife split the dress she still wore, and several layers of skin underneath, from hip to breast. Her blood spilled forth, darkening the fabric.

Behind him, Jacqueline kicked his lower back, sending him down. The *Industria* landed several blows to the pressure points on his chest, arms, and legs, rendering his muscles incapable of movement. In seconds she had removed him of his weapons and had tied him hand and foot.

She rolled him over and stood one foot on his chest and pressed. Raylene lay on the floor screaming, sounding as pathetic as Atticus suspected she was, always the sadist, never the masochist.

Jacqueline sighed, examining the full length of him. "Atticus, I can only imagine what we are going to do to you."

6

The cell door slid back with a metallic screech, and the guards hauled Atticus inside, dropping him hard on the cold plastic floor.

"Even after those two have over-used him," the guard on his left scoffed, "he still gives off that gods-awful feeling."

"Quiet," the other snapped. "Just do your job and get home to your wife. You can take care of that itch."

"After him, I won't be able to do my job, comfortably that is."

The door screeched shut again, closeting Atticus in darkness. He coughed and spat blood. He'd bit his tongue. Below him a machine started up and the floor began to glow. He rolled over onto his back, smearing blood across the sterile healing cell and straining his dislocated ribs. The movement felt too easy to really come from him, but then again, it was hard to know if what he was feeling was real. His ribs felt real. Raylene had a fondness for stabbing him with her heels. A full healing would take hours, but he doubted Raylene's rage would go unsatisfied for even that long. She had more pairs of shoes to ruin on him.

The light around him grew brighter and heat sank into his shoulders, quickly knitting together the damaged cartilage. The energy of the cell, a unique technology not available for the common populace, warmed the rest of him. He let his eyes close against the brightness, preferring the dark, and braced for the unbearable itching that would accompany the healing. It never came.

"*What is she?*" Raylene demanded of him, his mind conjuring the voice after hours of nothing else.

"I don't know," Atticus whispered, the whirring of the healing cell tech drowning out his voice. He'd been lying. He knew Darci was beautiful, caring, unpredictable. But she was dead.

He hoped she was dead.

Once he'd been transported to the Magistrate offices downtown, Raylene had given him over to Jacqueline. The wound he'd given Raylene had taken fifteen minutes for a room like this to heal. But in that time, Jacqueline had her way with him. After that the two of them had spent hours on him, but he refused to break, refused to give them anything that they wanted, even when a vicious combination of drugs had forced him otherwise.

He took a shuddering breath. He needed Darci to be dead. If they did anything to put her though this, he had no illusions that his mind would unravel and so would his humanity. His memories of her kept him sane, tying him to his body, even as he fell closer and closer to the breaking point. They'd pushed him to that edge, and even now he teetered. The smallest breeze could topple him over.

"*Who is she?*" the demand came again, this time the voice of Jacqueline. "*Did you enjoy her?*"

"No," he whispered. "I never touched her."

"*You did. I know you did. Your aura has changed, my pet.*" He could feel the terrifying slice of her dagger again as she slowly pushed it through his skin.

He refused to cry out. He looked down at his belly and the dagger wound had closed over, but the pain was fresh. There should have been itching. Healing cells always itched unbearably as his nerves knitted back together. The fact that feeling was absent gave him pause.

Raylene wasn't done with him. He'd prayed she had finally grown tired, but he'd lied to himself again.

"You're jealous," he said, testing the cell. "Your eye twitches, giving you away."

Raylene ordered Jacqueline to dislocate two sets of ribs on his left side. He grunted at the memory, the crunch and pop still sounded as though she delivered the blow a second time.

"We could have had everything, my pet," Raylene had purred at him as she straddled him. *"If you give in now, you could be free."*

"Never," he said. "You're the Magistrate's lap dog, and could never offer me anything worth having." His thoughts turned to Darci. He would never see her again, and somehow that bothered him more than anything Raylene or Jacqueline had done to him.

The light around him began to pulse. Pain, as he'd endured for hours, speared him again. His body arched upward, writhing as he lost his ability to remain in control of the animalistic reactions of his body.

Atticus, wake up!

His eyes snapped open and the pain didn't vanish. The healing cell did. They had moved him and fastened the shackles to chains on the freezing concrete floor. Raylene straddled his hips, the tip of her dagger still pressed into his flesh. The healing room and respite from torture had been a lie. Before him was the truth.

Jacqueline stood to one side, next to a man he didn't know. He was tall skinny and bald with light blue eyes and a hawk-like nose. He frowned and moved closer. He wore the light-colored robes of an Elder. The last time Atticus had the misfortune to meet one, he'd been in deep shit.

He doubted he'd ever been in deeper shit than now.

"Stop, *Valerian* Raylene," the bald man ordered. "The structure has broken."

Raylene froze and yanked the dagger out of his abdomen. She'd been using it to channel her power into him at a higher wattage. She stepped away from him and he decided he liked this bald guy. He controlled Raylene and made her get off of him. He obviously didn't control her powers, though. The pain continued.

"What do you mean broken?" Raylene demanded.

The man closed his eyes and took a deep breath. "You test my patience," he said. "Your *Luxurian* has been shielded from my mind again."

"You are supposed to be the strongest," Raylene hissed like a snake issuing warning before it attacked, fangs out. Atticus knew that if she did the Elder would respond with fangs of his own.

"I never said there were none stronger than I," the Elder said. "It seems as though another has been found, untrained and clumsy in her work, but strong. Darci is valuable, more valuable than either the two of you. I suggest you take care."

Atticus fought for his mind, fought to locate the presence that had abolished the false memory. He wanted to crow with joy. She wasn't dead, but that didn't mean she wasn't wounded or worse.

"Her protection over him is keeping me from being able to make a decent connection."

The room he was in was large. Other fixtures were in the room, allowing Raylene more than one victim to feature in her sick and twisted games.

"Then do something about it," Raylene ordered.

The Elder stiffened, but his expression did not change. "Do you presume to order me, *Valerian?* Our mission is peace, eradication of sinful nature. I have wondered before if you have overstepped your allowances, and I wonder again."

Atticus had never seen anyone stand up to Raylene before. It made him wary. Whoever this man was, he wanted to get to Darci, and if he held power over Raylene, that was reason to fear.

Raylene bowed her head. "My apologies, High Elder," she said. "You may understand my frustration. One of my best controlled subjects has become unruly because of her."

"You have become prideful in the absence of *Temperantia*

from your city. This is one of the risks of accomplishment."
The man folded his arms by hiding each in the opposite sleeve
of his robes. "You have done exceptionally well. I will do what
I can to bring your project to heel. I warn you. I will not make
such an offer a second time."

"I understand," Raylene said. She stepped aside for the man
to have full access to Atticus.

"Bring the girl here," he said to Jacqueline.

Atticus snarled, and strained upward against the chains
binding him. Not here, not this place. The stab wound in his
abdomen ripped, and he thought his ribs might break through
his skin as well, but he didn't stop trying to break his chains.
His aura lashed out, immediately gaining the attention of every
person in the room.

"On second thought, *Industria*," The Elder said, becoming
eerily quiet as Jacqueline made eye contact with him. After a
moment, she smiled and nodded sharply before turning on her
heel and exiting.

"*Valerian*," the Elder said next. "Continue."

Raylene exchanged her dagger for a bottle of lemon juice
and a paper thin razor. "Gladly," she replied, turning on him.

Atticus felt the first flickers of real fear as his tormentor
descended on him. Raylene unleashed herself on him with
gusto as she had the first time he dared go against her wishes.
Then, years ago when she finished educating him with the
consequences of displeasing her, she'd cast him aside, into the
waiting arms of Michael. The man never said a word, he didn't
have to. He'd taken him to a small two-room apartment,
cleaned him up, and smartly slapped him upside the head.
From that moment on they'd been brothers. Learning from
each other, depending on each other, and after the work was
done, Michael had taught him to hunt the aristocracy and sow
chaos within the Magistrate.

For the next hour, Raylene educated him again. His mind
began to shut down, his thoughts became disjointed,
incoherent, more dream than reality. This time, there would be
nothing to clean up when the *Valerian* had her victory.

7

Darci paced inside her cell. She fought whoever was digging around Atticus's thoughts, enraged she wasn't by his side to tear the women who tortured him apart. They'd done this before, the two of them, she'd seen them in Atticus's memories. In the past, Raylene and Jacqueline had brutally used him for their own terrible pleasures, using drugs as aids in the torture they inflicted. It had nearly shattered him. The bindings that held him together she feared were too weak to outlast another sexual assault.

She'd woken up in a pool of her own blood, with Atticus's screams echoing in her ears. The wound through her chest had miraculously healed. But his fear wounded her deeper. Gods, what were they doing to him?

An hour ago, she'd been blocked, a wall appearing as she tried to protect Atticus. She'd fought until it had crumbled, but it wasn't enough.

She couldn't find him. Any sense she had of him had vanished. A door has been slammed, locking her in the cell. They would break him, and she had no idea what would remain when she found him, if he wasn't already shattered. He'd gone through this for years. She hoped he could hang on for a little longer that he wouldn't give up.

How could she have been so stupid as to think that Jacqueline coming through the armory door had been Tobias or Zeke? If she'd only attacked first, Atticus wouldn't be back in the hands of these monsters. Neither would she.

When did things like torture, and rape become permissible acts of government?

Footsteps echoed outside her door, followed by the chirping of an electronic lock directly outside her cell.

She rushed to the cell door, scooted along the wall, and flattened herself beside the portal. It creaked open and a tall, blonde man entered.

Darci kept her eyes wide, waiting for him to meet her gaze so she could rip his mind a new one.

As she expected, he looked straight into her eyes. Without hesitation she threw her power forward like an arrow, driving to the center of his thoughts.

She was struck by the pandemonium of his head and hesitated. She sensed his aura. It held a hint of lust, but it was muted, no, mutilated into a mix of fear and pain and longing.

Michael?

"Who's talking?" he said hoarsely. His voice held a naturally seductive tone, the voice of a *Luxurian*, but it was rough and fearful. He didn't break her gaze as he backed against the far wall. "There's a voice. In my mind. Its saying a name, I think it used to be my name. I don't know the name." He began to whimper.

Dread flooded her and she drew her presence from his, careful not to pull any of him with her. This shell of a person, this is what Raylene was turning her victims into.

"I'm sorry," Darci said, keeping her voice down. He shivered, distrusting her. She couldn't blame him, she'd done a good job of rattling the shards of his mind into a labyrinth he couldn't navigate.

"You came with him. The boy."

"With who?" she asked. His mind was so hard to traverse, and it began to affect her ability to think clearly. "Tobias?"

"*The boy*, Atticus. I saw it. You can't stay here. He can't stay

67

here, stupid boy," Michael groaned, his hand going to his mouth. He bit at already raw fingernails. He glanced at the open cell door.

"I know. How do I get him out?"

"You can't." Michael whimpered. "No one gets out." She was losing him. Whatever the *Industria* had done to him, he'd hidden as well as a broken mind could, but the barrier was as fragile as tissue paper. She'd torn into it through her rush of violence and made an already vulnerable mind into an open wound. All his painful memories, some recent, some old, all of them nightmares she'd brought to the surface.

"It wasn't me, I didn't kill her," he cried hoarsely. "I didn't kill any of them. Not my knife, only the aura. The sin."

"Shh," Darci said, moving across the cell to him. The open door beckoned her. She could make a run for it, but that meant leaving Michael to drown in his renewed anguish. She chose to help him. He flinched at her touch. "I'm not going to hurt you," she said in a soft, firm voice, the same tone she used with the children she shepherded back home.

"You said that before," he murmured. "You say that with every caress, every pleasurable kiss, but your nails rake down my back and your heels spur my sides." He began to shake. "You all say that."

Shit. She'd pushed him too far, and it had been far too easy to do. How she hated the women who had turned a strong and brilliant mind into this. Fear struck her to her core. What if they managed to succeed? What if Atticus, someone who could actually do something about the regime, became another victim of the corrupt? She might already be too late.

"Where is the boy?" she asked Michael firmly.

"They have him," he held up his hands in front of him and averted his face. "They have us both."

Time was ticking, and the longer she stayed here, the closer Atticus was to death or worse. She also wasn't willing to leave Michael behind to face the punishment of his tormentors.

"They won't have you for much longer," she reassured him and took his hand. If she were male, he would have followed her without question, but it took a few precious seconds of careful urging to get him to follow her.

She peeked her head out of the cell and glanced down either side of the brightly-lit white hall. It was clear of guards or other official personnel. Other cell doors lined the walls, their palm readers glowing every ten feet. Hers was the only open one. The hall stretched until the overhead lights became tiny specks, and there was nothing to hide behind. With her nighttime-friendly clothing, despite its blood stains, she would stick out like a red shirt in a cornfield.

She felt for Atticus. A faint flicker of something familiar directed her to the left. Senses spread, she jogged as fast and as silent as she could down the corridor, which wasn't that silent because sneaking was not one of her skills and Michael continuously muttered to himself as she attempted to haul him behind her.

The corridor ended with a door to the emergency stairwell and a vending machine set recessed into the wall. She opened the door for the stairs, and came face to face with the *Industria*, Jacqueline.

Darci didn't think as adrenaline shot through her heart. She let go of Michael and lashed out with her fist in a clumsy right swing.

Jacqueline dodged under the blow and rammed her shoulder into Darci's midsection. She gasped as she was slammed to the ground. Michael snarled unintelligibly and shrank against the wall. Darci struggled backward as Jacqueline rose up to strike at her. The *Industria* moved too fast, making it impossible for Darci to disable the woman with her thoughts alone. She needed eye contact in order to tear and shred Jacqueline apart from the inside. Darci dropped as Jacqueline aimed a kick to her chest, somersaulting backwards. Darci's shoulders smacked against the far wall.

"How did you get out of your cell?" Jacqueline snarled, advancing on Darci, her fist raised.

"I let her out," Michael said, sounding for a moment like the grown man he was and not the broken mind trapped in a predator's body. He grabbed Jacqueline's fist and punched her in the jaw. She cried out, furious, sprawling to the floor.

"Nice," Darci said in approval.

"Run," Michael roared as he took a blow to his midsection. As Jacqueline made to attack Darci, Michael grabbed the woman around her middle and bore her to the ground. Jacqueline fell and hit the shiny white tiled floor. Something snapped and the Justice cried out.

Darci scrambled to her feet. She was sure that fall had broken Jacqueline's collarbone. Now the Justice was truly angry. Darci reached for Michael and pulled him off Jacqueline.

"Come on," she said, panicking.

"She's still awake," Michael said, his body shaking. He raised his fist and punched Jacqueline once more.

"Go," Darci said, pushing him toward the stairwell.

"Don't go so fast," Jacqueline said, shaking Michael's blow off her. The punch had barely dazed her.

Darci backed away onto the landing and ran down the first flight of stairs. Michael waited for her there, squeezing himself into a corner. Whatever power that drove him to attack Jacqueline had worn out. Darci turned to face Jacqueline as she came down the stairs. The connection sparked between them and the *Industria's* dark and horrible mind opened before her.

Calm settled over Darci and she took a shoulder-width stance. She had the woman's mind. This fight was hers.

"So you'll face me?" Jacqueline asked and drew a short blade from the V of her jacket, between her breasts.

"I'll kill you," Darci promised.

Jacqueline smiled. "Very well," she said and flipped the dagger in her hand, catching it by the hilt and holding the point outward.

Darci read Jacqueline's mind and twisted as the *Industria* lunged toward her. She batted the knife away and punched Jacqueline in the jaw. Her head snapped back and she stumbled against the stair railing.

Jacqueline growled and slashed upward, forcing Darci back.

Michael caught her. Turning Darci pulled him from the wall, directing him toward the next flight of stairs. Spinning around, she caught the *Industria's* boot in her ribs.

Darci dropped, her momentum rolling her down the stairs to the next landing. She stopped at Michael's feet. Her hold on Jacqueline's mind wasn't as strong as she'd thought. Jacqueline descended toward them, the stairwell echoed with the click of her boots.

"Run, Michael," Darci ordered. To her disbelief he didn't. He offered her a hand and she took it. He helped her up and then held up clenched fists.

Jacqueline crouched, readying her attack. Darci was glad she wasn't alone; even if her partner was insane, he was still deadly, and she'd rather have insanity on her side than the madness Jacqueline employed to train her recruits.

The *Industria* leapt at them. Dodging, Darci grabbed the knife, slicing her hand on the blade. Instead of stabbing her, the blade twisted and clattered against the concrete wall. Darci attacked, using Jacqueline's momentum against her to slam her into the concrete after her blade. She grabbed Jacqueline's hair and slammed her face again into the wall. Michael scrambled for the dagger.

Struggling, Jacqueline ripped free of Darci's grip, leaving her with a fistful of hair.

"You'd better be worth the trouble of keeping you," Jacqueline said and lashed out. Somehow she'd drawn another knife and a slice appeared on Darci's shoulder. Pain spread like a fire through her arm down to her fingers. Michael had found the other knife and held it unsteadily. She was losing him.

Jacqueline attacked again and Darci dodged, feeling the knife strike her clothing. She snatched the blade from Michael's hand and thrust it upward. There was pressure and then it slid smoothly between Jacqueline's ribs.

Jacqueline sputtered before her body collapsed. Her mind sparked once, last thoughts playing across the woman's brain before it went dark. Darci had stabbed her under her breast and up into her heart.

Darci stood panting for a moment over the corpse. It was done. The *Industria* was dead, her sister avenged. Yet, instead of peace, she felt dirty. This wasn't over yet.

Darci touched Michael's arm and he looked at her with wide fearful eyes. "Come on," she said. "We have to help Atticus, he's in trouble."

Michael's shaking stopped. "Atticus? He's here?"

"Yes, and if I don't get to him right now, he's—it's not going to be good."

Michael's mind seemed to clear as her thoughts broke through the barrier of fear. He nodded, and followed her.

She flew down the stairs until she reached the right floor. By then she could hear Atticus's cries faintly through the stairwell door. She eased the door open, made sure it was clear and motioned Michael to follow her. He had shrunk back again, but he had started to trust her and took a step forward.

"The interrogation block," he whispered. "They are here with the chains, and the razors, and the—" He began to breathe hard and the trembling started again.

"No one will touch you," Darci reassured him. The things Michael said and the things he didn't say but showed in his thoughts caused rage to strike through her. She almost pitied the next person who made eye contact with her. She wanted to rip and tear and destroy, and she would do it gladly.

Michael nodded after a moment and followed her as she crept into main corridor of the interrogation block. This hall was just as white as the halls in the cellblock. She could make out the marks of blood stains in the grout between the tiles; a macabre remainder of the bodies that had been dragged out of the rooms lining the corridor.

This place was evil. She could practically smell it. It was as if the walls were imbued with the screams of the tortured, the begging cries of the doomed. She'd felt this only once before. In the old mining town her first rate school had visited. The mine itself had caught fire with over five hundred workers still inside. When she strained to listen, she could hear the screams of the dying. The walls of places where great suffering had taken place, soaked up the energy of the pain and anguish, just waiting to throw it back into the world. Here was no different.

A cry echoed through the hall.

Atticus!

A shiver of fear snaked down Darci's back. He was so close, but she had no idea who was with him, or if she'd be able to get into his tormentor's minds and wreak enough havoc to get Atticus, Michael and herself out

She crept along the wall until she reached the right door. Suddenly, it opened in front of her, shielding her from whoever was leaving. She pulled Michael down beside her and clamped a hand over his mouth, urging him to remain silent. She hoped he heard her silent command in the dark and trembling pathways of is mind. A bald man, dressed in light blue robes exited and turned down the hall heading away from Darci's position. He walked with a purposeful gait, and his posture was that of someone who was used to being looked up to. He turned the far corner and disappeared.

He must be some part of the Magistrate she didn't know about.

"Who was that?" she whispered.

"The Master," Michael answered. He refused to say more, his face white. Whoever that was, he was big trouble she guessed.

Darci turned her attention to the room beyond. A woman was talking, making cooing noises that had her blood boiling and her vision going red. Is this what they did? Torture people, and then whisper sweet promises into their ears when they were ready to break. Atticus's mind was shutting down. He was retreating to some deep place within himself. If he went too far, he might never return.

"Michael," she said, "Stay here. If I don't come out with Atticus, you run. Do you understand?"

He nodded.

Darci took a deep breath and prepared herself. She would have to be fast, and dramatic. She needed the full attention of whoever was beyond the door. She flung it open and her rage boiled over as she recognized the *Valerian,* drawing circles on Atticus's bare chest. He lay chained to the floor, his eyes closed, his chest heaving. He was drenched in blood and sweat.

Raylene looked up, shocked that she had been interrupted.

Darci didn't give a moment's hesitation. She struck with her mind, cleaving the *Valarian's* in two. The woman screamed once and Darci struck again, hooking into the woman's thoughts, ripping and tearing all that she could. It was almost too easy.

Raylene dropped forward, landing on Atticus. He groaned but otherwise did not move.

Darci rushed to his side and rolled the unconscious woman off him. The chains holding him down were thick and the locks were thumb keyed. She grabbed one of Raylene's arms and dragged the woman painstakingly to each shackle and pressed her thumb against the key pad.

"Atticus," she said gently pressing her hands on each side of his face, calling with her mind as well as her voice. "Come on, wake up."

His eyes snapped open and with inhuman speed, he rolled on top of her, both of his strong hands finding her throat. He began to squeeze and she struggled, slapping her hand against his bare thigh.

"Atticus," Michael's voice entered the room.

He blinked and his vision cleared.

"Shit." He let go of her and stood, but wavered on the spot.

Darci coughed, and stood up quickly, steadying him. "Can you walk?"

"I think so," he answered, his voice was rough, and his body showed the barest of trembling. He was going into shock.

Suddenly, Michael was on Atticus's other side, muttering something about stupid boys.

Atticus didn't react to his friends' presence and that frightened her more. By the fuzzy distance of his thoughts, she knew he wasn't in good shape. They had to get out of there fast, somewhere where she could have a minute to try and keep him together. His mind was slipping.

"I'm sorry," he said hoarsely. "I didn't mean to attack you."

"Don't worry about it. We need to get out of here."

He stiffened. "What about Raylene?" he glanced around his gaze coming to rest on Raylene's still form. "We can't leave her here."

She watched as Atticus stumbled to the tray where Raylene's tools rested, many of them coated in his blood. He grabbed the first knife, and went to his knees beside his tormentor's body.

"Kill her," he muttered to himself, his knuckles turning white around the blade's handle. Gripping the knife with both hands, he plunged it into Raylene's chest. Her body twitched once and lay still. After checking for a pulse he lurched to his feet. She felt his stomach heave once as though it were her own. Darci hurried to his side.

"Take it easy," she said, sliding his arm over her shoulder and her other around his waist. He hissed as she put pressure on his ribs, and unwound her from him.

"I can't," he said, pained.

Darci caught her breath as the tenor of his thoughts reached her. It wasn't that he couldn't. It was that he couldn't be touched by a woman. He needed to stand on his own feet, and feel the ground steady beneath them as he helped himself. He needed to know that he wasn't controlled.

"Okay," Darci said. "Let's go as fast as we can. Come on, Michael, it is time to leave."

Atticus blinked and turned to Michael. "What is he doing here?"

"He's coming with us," Darci said. "We've got to hurry."

She made sure the hall was clear before she got the men moving again.

"Which way?" she asked, Michael. He seemed to know his way around this place very well.

"We're underground," Atticus replied, turning toward the stairs where she had come from.

Michael whimpered. "Not up there."

"We can't go that way," she said thinking of the hopefully

unconscious *Nativa* she'd left two flights up. She didn't want to see the body again. "Their dungeon is back that way."

Atticus didn't say a word, but headed quickly in the same direction the strange bald man had gone. They came to a sterile white elevator. Atticus hit the button, smearing blood across the panel.

The elevator chimed and Atticus pulled her to the side. He checked the elevator before ushering she and Michael inside. He pushed the elevator button for six floors from where they were. She hoped from there it would be a straight shot to the street. Maybe they could hotwire a Maglev-car or something.

Atticus leaned his head back against the side of the elevator with a wince. Every move he made sent obvious pain shooting through his body, most notably where someone had stabbed him. In the bright light of the elevator, she got a good look at him, as he gripped the hand rail to keep himself upright. Beneath the grime and sweat, numerous small cuts and bruises lined and dotted his exposed skin. The small stab wound wept blood freely.

"Be prepared," he whispered. "When we stop, they will have the entrance guarded. We'll make a run for the doors."

She looked at him. "Can you run?" then she looked at Michael. Would he be able to keep up? The odds were against them in every way.

He opened his eyes to pin her with his gaze. "Does it matter?" He wanted them both out, but he didn't care if it killed him. Death would mean the end of all pain.

"Don't you dare give up," Darci snarled at him, catching a glimpse of all that hurt locked up inside him. It struck her to the bone, and if she didn't also have a hold of the elevator rail, her buckling knees would have driven her to the ground. He was so close to the brink of destruction. He would need careful handling if they were to get out of this alive without one or both of them going mad. He didn't want to go insane. He'd rather be dead than have a child's mind or live forever with the kind of fear he was feeling now. It was difficult for her to stomach. He was so defeated, but he still crawled on despite the odds.

The odds had been good. Neither of them were dead, and freedom, however long it lasted, was seconds away.

"I'll go first," Darci said. "If I hit them with my mind, we should have a clear path. Michael, stay close to Atticus."

The corner of Atticus's mouth gave the barest upturn. "You've been practicing."

"Sort of." She hadn't been able to use her powers when facing Jacqueline to do anything other than to predict her attack. But ripping into Raylene totally counted.

The elevator chimed again and Darci exited. There was one guard in the elevator lobby, he glanced at her and the moment her gaze connected with his, she shot a thought toward him like an arrow from a bowstring. She could practically hear the *thunk* of her mental arrow as it ripped through the man's mind and he crumpled to the floor.

"Nice work," Atticus said as he stumbled over the threshold of the elevator. She caught him by his arms and he stiffened. Darci motioned for Michael.

"Watch Atticus. He needs your help."

Michael nodded, his eyes glazed over as though he were seeing and hearing something else. "Watching the boy, the boy always needs to be watched. He's a trouble maker that one."

"Which way?" she asked Atticus, throwing her senses out. She could just pick up on the lazy thoughts of a few guards around them, down the hall to their right, some through the set of double doors in front of them. Unlucky for them, the doors didn't have glass so she couldn't be sure exactly how many people were on the other side, and how many of them were dangerous. There were a lot, and she really didn't want to go that way.

"Through the doors," Atticus directed her.

"I'd hoped you wouldn't say that."

"Why?"

"There are people out there. I don't know how many and you won't fit in anywhere with just your pants on."

Atticus paused and glanced at the guard. He also was

wearing black clothing. Quickly, Darci stripped the guard of his uniform shirt and the silly hat he wore with the Magistrate's seal stitched to the front. Atticus groaned as he shrugged into the shirt. More blood dripped from the stab wound. Lastly, she tapped the hat down on his head. Michael watched them with narrowed eyes, giving Atticus a distrustful glare now that he was dressed as a guard.

"Maybe being a guard will give us an easy way to the door," she said then paused. "You know it's weird that they haven't raised an alarm yet."

Atticus's eyes narrowed. "Yes, it is." He took a deep breath and straightened. He looked pale and ready to pass out at any second. "When we get into the main crowd, keep your head down. If you have to, there's an info desk attendant, take whoever it is out. It'll cause a big enough distraction we can get out quickly."

"Atticus, those are civilians out there."

"And they fear the Magistrate's power enough to be on their side. Everyone out there is an enemy."

His words halted her. This was a war. The Magistrate made war against the general populace of the countries they now controlled, and even against those they didn't. It was a war of fear, of swift judgment and even faster retribution. If she truly wanted to fight against the Magistrate's regime, she had to be willing make a few sacrifices.

She nodded once and opened the double doors for Atticus. He slipped through, Michael muttering conspicuously at his side. She walked close to Michael, giving him mental reassurance as they moved into the crowd. Dozens of people occupied the large lobby. Its grey interior reflected the souls of the citizens here for early morning food stamp rations or possible work visas. These people were beaten down. If they smiled, it was only a glimpse of the crumbling mask they each wore.

A woman with a crying child brushed against Michael. He panicked.

"Easy," Darci murmured, trying to soothe him. It didn't

work. The strange part of his aura she had sensed flashed out. Lust, thick and heavy, entered the room. Darci gasped. A woman near them took one look at Michael and swooned on the spot.

Guards were everywhere, posted every twenty feet or so along the walls. More guards patrolled up and down the lines of people waiting at teller booths. The guards were armed to the teeth and they were beginning to notice the sea of people who began to laugh and flirt with one another. One man passionately kissed his wife.

Atticus stumbled and Darci moved closer. "Put your hand on my shoulder for balance."

He hesitated.

"We're attracting too much attention," she hissed, taking Michael's hand in hers and pulling him toward the door.

They were steps from the doors. A guard moved toward them, a lewd smile on his face, and Darci's heart pounded. Atticus snarled at him and the man wisely tipped his hat and stepped around them. Steps later they were into the cool, pre-dawn air. The rain gave it a crisp scent, like the smell of fields after a good storm.

She glanced over her shoulder and helped Atticus down the first step. Michael jogged ahead of them into the street. No one was following them. Guards were not talking hurriedly into their radios. She didn't like it. They had just escaped from the top security holding cells of the Magistrate deep in the heart of the city and no one had blinked an eye at their escape. That couldn't last for long. Common sense told her to get Atticus off the street as soon as possible.

Somehow they made it down the steps and across the street into the city park that sparkled with dew. He had most of his weight on her now and she couldn't carry all of him. She stopped at the first set of bushes obscuring them from the street and helped him to the ground. Between the buildings the blush of morning threatened.

He groaned as his shoulders and ribs jostled.

"Why isn't anyone following us?" she asked.

"No idea," Atticus said.

A lone Magna-car hummed along street and came to a stop right near their hiding spot.

"Keep still," Darci whispered as she peered through the leaves of a bush.

To her surprise, Tobias stepped carefully out of the vehicle with his tablet in hand. He glanced at it and looked right at their location, then, confused, back to the Magistrate building. He shrugged and stepped onto the grass headed in their direction.

"Darci?" he asked from the other side of the bush.

"Tobias?" Atticus answered, in distrust. "I saw you die."

Tobias stepped around the bush and shook his head. "You saw me get shanked and left for dead. No one actually checked to see if I was actually dead, which I'm totally ticked off about. The Magistrate couldn't even have that much dignity." He gingerly lifted his shirt, revealing a lighted pulsing white patch on the left side of his ribs. "I would have died, except I woke up and my specialty med-kit was in reach. Looks like you could use a few of my nifty little patches." He noticed Michael. "Great, *another* person to look after. I thought you hated people, Atticus."

Atticus grunted something affirmative.

"The Magistrate will only take so long to figure out where you've gone after I've had my way with them." Tobias tapped a command into his tablet. "Oh, look Darci, they've discovered you are missing from your cell." He held up the glass to show a video of guards checking her cell and one shouting at the other. They ran off the screen. "It shouldn't take them too long to figure out I hacked their surveillance, and not too much longer to undo my hack job. We should go."

Darci bent down and threaded her arm behind Atticus's shoulders. "Help me get him to the car," she said.

"Right-o," Tobias said, and together they were able to get Atticus to his feet. Atticus groaned as they forced him to move. Darci couldn't believe he was still conscious.

They hurried around the bush to the sleek black car

hugging the magna rail.

"This is your car?"

"Yes," Tobias said proudly, "Now get in before he bleeds to death."

When they were inside, Darci pillowed Atticus's head in her lap. He was laid out across the backseat of the spacious Magna-car. Michael had placidly buckled himself into the front seat, and she was sure he wouldn't have even done that without her guiding thoughts. Keeping a hold on his mind and Atticus's was draining her.

"Here." Tobias handed a black bag to her from the front seat. "We'll have to move fast. When they figure out all of you got in a car, we'll have the whole city force behind us."

Darci tore into the duffel bag, quickly finding the items she needed. When the car didn't start she looked up at Tobias. He watched her in the rearview mirror. His power washed over her, filling the car and sucking information from her.

"Stop that," she said, "and get this car moving."

Obediently, Tobias pulled out into the road, but the sensation of his power in the air didn't lessen. "Who was it?" he asked.

"What?" Darci said as she wiped blood from around Atticus's stab wound.

"Your aura has changed. Who did you kill?"

"*Industria* Jacqueline."

A muscle worked in Tobias's jaw. "Hurry up and get those patches on that stab wound. I'd hate to see the man who saved me from that woman's blade follow her to the grave."

8

Atticus grunted as someone pressed against the stab wound. Dull warmth spread into his belly. He tried to sit up, but weakness kept him from doing much more than moving his arms. He didn't remember closing his eyes or getting into Tobias's car.

"Easy," Darci's comforting voice rolled over him, her gentle hands held him in place. "I have a few more bandages. Then you can rest."

He relaxed. Her hands lifted off his skin, leaving him suddenly cold, longing for her soothing touch.

"Where's the worst of it?" she asked.

"My ribs, left side. Dislocated," he answered. He lay with his head pillowed on her lap. The position felt secure. Here, they were safe for the moment, and the Magistrate couldn't be further away.

"Damn," Tobias said from the front seat. "I thought that's what she might have done with that wicked stick of hers."

"And you saw this how?" Atticus asked.

"I hacked in and duplicated their surveillance feeds so they wouldn't see you leaving."

"You should be dead."

"Tobias, just focus on driving," Darci said. She removed

another of Tobias's healing pads from the bag. She cut a strip of medical adhesive, gently secured the healing pad over Atticus's ribs, and activated it.

He caught her hand in his. She could have pulled away from him; he didn't try to imprison her as he'd done before. She shifted her fingers in his until they were intertwined, and gave a gentle squeeze.

"Thank you," he said. Now that he was out of that oppressive building, he yearned for her touch, her softness, her unwillingness to cause pain. He needed her like a child needed a safety blanket.

"I couldn't leave you there," she said.

"You could have." It would have been easy to do. She had all the time in the world to condemn him by saving herself and escaping. She'd proven the strength of her power. Given the opportunity, she probably could rip the mind out of anyone she chose. That kind of weapon in the hands of the Magistrate would give them unprecedented power over the people they controlled. They would be able to rip into the minds of their victims and their work would become easy. It would make the work that Atticus was forced to do obsolete.

"What's wrong?" she asked.

"Nothing," he answered, wincing as she placed another healing pad over his shoulder.

No. He frowned. It wasn't nothing. It was everything. They knew. Raylene was vicious and often let her sadistic lust get the better of her, but she was no fool. She would have recognized the potential of Darci's power when she was confronted with it at the Master of Trade's residence. Darci's value and possible threat to the Magistrate was a greater concern than he could ever be, especially now that Raylene was dead. Even at the cost of his own life, he had to make sure they never got their hands on her.

"Tobias," he said. "Get us out of the city. If Jacqueline and catches us—"

"Jacqueline is dead." Darci laid another bandage over some of the worst cuts along his left bicep. It stung. He could still smell the sharp tang of lemon juice.

"How?" he asked, focusing on her hands now gently exploring his skin for the worst wounds. Every feather-light touch felt as though she were lifting the memory of Raylene's torture from him. He wanted to drift with the motion of her fingers as they slid over his body, and let them erase the darkness clogging his mind.

"She was in the stairwell when Michael and I found her." Darci's hands stilled on his body. "I-I stabbed her, like you did Raylene."

"Good," Atticus said. Heaviness threaded through his body.

"Right before I found you, a bald man wearing robes came out of the room. Who was he?"

The heaviness vanished, replaced by adrenaline thundering through his veins.

"Must leave, must get out," Michael mumbled in the front seat. The heels of his hands were pressed against his eyes, and he rocked back and forth. "Go faster," he chanted. "Go north."

"There was an Elder there?" Tobias asked. He sounded as panicked as Atticus felt. "There wasn't an Elder anywhere on the feed."

Worse, Atticus couldn't remember the presence of an Elder. He would have remembered, he'd only blacked out once. But then Raylene and Jacqueline had their way with him, and the heady mixture of drugs and torture still spun through his head like a gyro.

He closed his eyes and tried to remember. He could feel fingernails grazing along his body before turning to claws and tearing his skin, but no men had featured in his torment.

"I don't remember," he whispered. But he needed to. There was something, something about warmth and light and tricks he needed to know. He sat up, his heart pounding. Wild thoughts flew from one corner of his mind to another, bashing against the walls. He knew something, but he couldn't reach it. The more he searched, the more the darkness pushed against the spider-webbed cracks.

***

"Tobias, pull over!" Darci shouted. Atticus shuddered and twitched as she reached out to touch his shoulder. His eyes fluttered closed, darting back and forth under his eyelids. His mind hadn't given under the strain. As long as she was near him, she wouldn't let him give up on sanity.

"You've got to be kidding," Tobias said, glancing back at her. "We're in the middle of a chase here. At least I think we're being chased. I hope we're not, but you never know."

"Something's wrong with Atticus."

"No shit there's something wrong with him. Did you see half of what they did to him? Add an Elder and I don't think you understand how much trouble we are in."

Atticus flinched again.

Tobias swore. "The last time he was in trouble with the Magistrate, he had fits for weeks. This is different." The car hummed at a higher pitch and they accelerated. "Last time, an Elder wasn't involved."

Darci examined Atticus, wondering what might be coming after them, or if they would escape a second time.

"He'll never tell you," he finally said. "But he's terrified of women."

Darci turned her attention to Tobias. "No, he despises women who use him."

Tobias took a deep breath and winced, one hand dropping from the steering wheel to his side. "I don't know why he likes you, but he does."

"You sure can be rude. Atticus has never been with a woman who hasn't betrayed him," Darci said. She tightened her fingers around Atticus's hand, and for a moment, she thought he squeezed hers in return. He didn't look away from the window, he didn't show any indication that he was present. That worried her. She felt shut out of his mind, like she'd dug too far again and struck an impenetrable shield.

"I've caught him screaming in his sleep more than any man should. He's also sick sometimes for no reason. He shakes when he thinks I'm not looking. The Magistrate is killing him."

"Then let's hope I can do this in a car," she said and shifted so her free hand could rest on Atticus's shoulder. The connection strengthened, but not by much.

"What are you going to do?" he asked.

"I'm going to try and fix whatever those—those *bitches* did to him."

Tobias's eyes narrowed at her in the mirror. "You've never done anything like this before, have you?"

"Don't question me, Tobias," Darci said.

"Can he wait? I need your help up front."

"What for?"

"Activating the virus, and I don't think Mike is going to be much help."

Darci hesitated. Her connection to Atticus's mind was stronger now; if she left him, would she be able to get it back?

"His aura is weak, but it's steadied out," Tobias said. "He'll be fine for a few minutes."

She let her hand slide from Atticus's, leaned over the front seat. Tobias handed her his tablet glass. Michael eyed her warily.

"Do exactly as I say," Tobias said.

Darci glanced at where they were on the road. She gasped. "You realize we are on the sky line." High rise buildings flashed past. They were twenty stories up from street level.

"Yes, and in just a moment we are going to leave the mag-lev grid entirely. Now pay attention."

In the distance, she could see the bluish line of light marking the walls of the city. Beyond that lay indeterminable darkness. Anything could be out there. The sky line curved, turning from the wall. If she trusted her sudden hunch, they wouldn't be following that curve.

She flicked a finger across the screen of the glass waking, it up.

"Okay, now listen carefully. Switch the mag-lev control to timed manual."

"Got it," Darci said. This was going to be easy, she didn't

know why Tobias was getting so worked up over it.

"Now here's the tricky part. Switch the G confab over to a 1M, follow it up with a spinning code type and key in the password 'Magistrate Sucks', with an X, so its S-U-X. That will zip us into manual mode and switch the mag into a cannon of acceleration."

"Um, say that again."

Tobias let out a growl and took the glass from her. "Take the wheel."

Darci grabbed for the wheel and the car jerked. Tobias snatched the car back into control and gave her a look that said she had seriously begun to test his patience.

"Have you ever driven?"

"Well, the field pollinator back home is worked by levers," she said defensively.

"Plagues!" Tobias said, quickly keying in a few things on his glass. "Locusts! Anything but a twenty-one-year-old who doesn't know how to drive."

"Excuse me," Darci said. "I'm twenty-two and I recently learned to hack minds like you hack computers. Don't tempt me to hack your mind and make you apologize to me every time you see me. I still haven't forgotten that you tried to make me give up my secrets earlier."

"Keep your threats to yourself. Point the wheel straight. It's going to be a bumpy ride once I punch it." He ducked under her hands and adjusted a few instruments on the dashboard to the far right.

Darci did not like the way he said that. "What do you mean bumpy?"

Tobias came up and pushed her hands off the wheel. "Get Atticus strapped into his seat and you'll find out." His tone brooked no disobedience.

Darci sat back. Atticus didn't react as she reached across him and buckled him into a series of straps that looked like a flight harness. The snap of the buckle clicking into place caused him to stiffen. His hands reached up and took hers.

His mind sharpened and his aura wrapped tight around her.

He blinked, as if finally seeing her. He frowned and the painful grip on her hands loosened. "Don't worry," he whispered, pressing one finger against her lips. "You will be safe soon. We will all be safe." He dropped his hands back to his sides, and returned his gaze to the window. His thoughts blurred. The ties of his aura dropped from around her.

"You ready?" Tobias asked.

"Y-yes," she said, trembling and strapped in. The curve of the sky rail loomed closer. Its border blinked in yellow chevron lights, warning drivers away from the edge. Other cars ahead turned on the mag-rail, but Tobias headed straight for a barrier of light.

"Ladies and gentlemen," Tobias began as he punched a button on the dash. "Please keep your arms and legs in at all times and your seats in the upright position. This is not going to be an gentle ride."

Darci screamed as a burst of sudden power threw her back in her seat. It felt as though a rocket had exploded right behind them. A deafening roar filled her ears and the car shot off the edge of the world. Ahead, the blue line of light suddenly flickered and went black.

"Yee haw!" Tobias crowed.

9

Darci stepped out of the aerial car, and walked out into the swaying waist-high grass of a meadow. The chilly evening breeze caused nearby pine trees to hiss as they moved back and forth. She'd never been so happy to be touching the earth. She never wanted to fly with Tobias behind the wheel again. At least they were stopping for the night.

"You are the most insane person here," she gasped, her heart still beating against her ribs, trying to escape. Not only had Tobias launched them off the highest sky rail on the west coast, he'd flown them six hundred nail-biting miles north, right into the middle of a never-ending mountain range. Scratch that. To a mountain range that was supposed to be radioactive enough to glow at night.

The Magistrate had been lying to their citizens. Everything Darci had learned in school as a child came back. Could she trust any of it? She'd been taught that any land north of the City was a radioactive wasteland all the way to the Scandinavian Isle. If that wasn't true, then how much of what she knew about the world beyond could she rightfully say was fact?

Nothing.

She'd been afraid to leave the City for this very reason. But she'd been tricked like the rest of the population, and because of it she and everyone else never strayed too far from home.

"It wasn't that bad of a landing," Tobias said, shutting the driver-side door. "Especially because I've never had to land an aerial vehicle before."

"We almost hit a bloody mountain."

"Well, how many people have outrun the Magistrate with a flying car?" he asked proudly.

Darci didn't give him the benefit of an answer and turned back to the car. Atticus hadn't said a word once they left the City. What if the blurred feel of his mind was simply another form of madness?

"Help Michael," she ordered as she opened the rear door.

Atticus blinked and squinted through the sun at her. She quickly undid the flight harness and took his hand. He swallowed, the muscles in his jaw working as though he were deciding whether or not to leave the safety of the vehicle.

"We're safe here," Darci reassured him, and herself. Who knew how safe they were now that they were fugitives, traitors, and murderers.

He looked around at the dense pine trees that ringed the meadow they had landed in. "As long as they hunt us, we won't be," he answered, his voice hoarse. He moved stiffly, as though Tobias's healing pads hadn't finished their work. She'd checked about an hour ago and had been happy to see his ribs looked almost normal and the stab wound had pink skin instead of a gaping hole.

A meadow lark trilled in the morning air and took flight from the edge of the trees. Another bird followed and the two flitted about one another before disappearing into the underbrush again. Atticus seemed to watch the two birds, and then he shivered, letting out a shaky breath.

"Come on," Tobias said "We're still a little ways from the place."

"Atticus?" Michael asked, stretching in the light of the sunset. "How did you know?"

A wan smile found its way to Atticus's face as he moved

closer to his friend. "You told me about this place once." He took his friend's arm and directed him after Tobias. He turned to Darci.

Suddenly, his arms went around her, and he held her. Stunned, she hesitated before she let her arms gently encircle his waist. His aura flowed over her skin, sliding along her body like a caress. Instead of his predatory possessiveness, she sensed his vulnerability and his need. He wasn't shattered, but that didn't mean parts of him weren't fractured.

A sudden snarl issued behind her. Darci turned in Atticus's arms. She tensed.

Michael crouched, his hand twisted into claws. "Get away from him," he growled. The shards of his mind gave her glimpses of deep, protective rage.

Atticus stepped in front of her. "She is not a threat," he snarled like a wolf asserting authority over another member of his pack. "Darci touched me with my permission."

Michael stepped back. His mind switched from attack to confusion. He trusted Atticus, but was confused why his friend would touch a woman. His thoughts turned inward, down some dark path, lost again from the moment. It happened so fast, Darci felt dizzy.

Atticus faced her. "We should get him where he can rest."

Tobias looked away as she turned to him. His eyes were raw around the edges. Just then she realized what he must be going through. His boyfriend had betrayed him and from what she had seen, she would have been the last person to say the two of them weren't deeply in love. As his thoughts brushed against hers, connecting with her, she sensed the depth of his guilt, his anguish. It ran as deep as his love for Zeke. She'd never even suspected his deception.

"Tobias—"

"Forget it," he said. "We're on our way to freedom. Maybe someday we can find a place where I won't get shanked by my lover with a barbed push dagger." He flashed a forced smile that didn't reach the corners of his eyes and popped the trunk of the car. He removed two bags, he handed one to Michael before slinging the other over his shoulder. "Let's go, we're exhausted and the car won't be fully charged until morning light. Might as well get some rest."

They came to a small log cabin overgrown with lichen and mosses. The tall pines must have grown around it after it had been built. By its shabby appearance, Darci figured it was close to a century in age. She had no doubt that Tobias and his clever ways had found the building even through a thick canopy of forest that shaded the place.

Tobias pushed open the door with his shoulder and they entered a very dusty but otherwise well-preserved three-room shack.

"Perfect," he said, dropping his duffel on the creaky wood floor. A puff of dust rose into the air.

Darci and Atticus entered somewhat less exuberantly than the *Invidia*. There was a main room with a couch on the right and a tiny kitchen to the left. Darci could see a bathroom down the hall and a bedroom across from that. A fireplace dominated a huge portion of the main room, and a stack of firewood next to it promised warmth.

Darci turned and gasped, confronted with a set of antlers nailed to the wall. Spiders had spun elaborate webs between the prongs. She knew people from the old world had kept parts of the animals they slaughtered, but it was one thing to know the history, and another to have it displayed on a wall.

Tobias got to work opening the duffels and setting out their supplies. He directed Michael to unrolling the two emergency beds from the duffels while he saw to the fireplace. The beds were meant to be used in the city in case of an attack or natural disaster and the citizens were forced out of their homes. But the tiny plastic squares inflated to be full-sized twin beds, complete with a pillow and blanket.

Darci moved into the kitchen. The faucet had a handle that looked more like a pump lever. She grasped the long arm of the faucet and pushed it down. There was a sickening gurgle and brackish water poured out of the spigot.

"I bet its radioactive," Darci said, pumping it again. Five or six more tries and the water changed from a dark red, to a pale yellow and finally clear.

"Doubtful," Tobias said, and keyed something into his tablet. He held it up with the sensor pointed toward the water. After a few seconds it beeped. "The Magistrate hasn't bombed this part of the world like I suspected. The water's not going to kill us, but just to be safe we'll boil if before using a purifier and testing it again. Until then—" He opened a few cupboards and removed several pots and pans. "—it will at least be good for washing." To Atticus he said, "You smell like you could use a good scrubbing."

Atticus didn't argue. He looked exhausted. Bruises shadowed his arms, ribs and across one side of his face..

Tobias unfolded a slim device specifically for boiling water and cooking food. In minutes he'd boiled enough water to fill the dusty bathtub at the end of the hall. Darci had taken a few pots of un-boiled water and rinsed the tub out.

"Let me help," Atticus said from behind her.

Darci pushed a few wayward strands of hair out of her eyes. The man was ready to start swaying on his feet. "Sit down," she said. He reached instead for the empty pot at her side, determined to do something. Darci grabbed it. "You'd better not do anything yet."

Tobias appeared in the bathroom doorway, cutting off Atticus's retreat. "You'd better the hell not do anything to reopen those wounds."

"Fine," Atticus said and leaned against the wall.

Darci's worry ratcheted up another notch. His mere acceptance of their limits on him proved how close to the edge he'd been pushed. Before last night, he would have hauled both of them out of the way, snapping as he went. Feeling the need to include him and make sure he knew she didn't think he was broken, she gave him a small pot of water to add to the bath when they filled it. His calloused hands settled over hers a moment too long before he took the pot from her. She fought the heat rising in her cheeks and turned away.

When everything was finally ready, Tobias took one look at

Atticus and said, "All right, peel them off. Let's see if they worked"

Atticus peeled off the healing pads from his ribs and abdomen. His ribs looked normal, maybe there was a little swelling. The stab wound was gone except for a small puckered line of pink skin. Even the worst of his bruises had healed under the pads. Satisfied, Tobias promptly herded Darci out of the bathroom.

"We only have the two beds and I doubt Michael is really up for snuggle time with you two in the bedroom. He's been eyeing the table in the kitchen like he might crawl under there."

"Excuse me?" Darci asked, not sure she understood what Tobias meant by "snuggle time."

The *Invidia* lowered his voice. "Atticus needs you by his side more than he's letting on. I'll keep Michael out of your way, and you keep Atticus sane while he sleeps. I don't envy him the nightmares he's going to have."

10

Atticus came awake, the scent of lemons sharp in his nose. He swallowed, stiffening on the lumpy mattress he lay on, waiting for the next bite of the knife. He clenched his hands. His fingers closed around the hilt of a weapon. Relief spread through his body, and he sagged back against the old bed. It creaked as he shifted onto his side. His ribs protested. He ignored them. He couldn't remain on his back, prone to access. The sword, Tobias had brought with them, he moved in front of his chest, hidden from immediate view. It was deadly, honed to a sharp edge. With a single flick of his wrist he could sever flesh and even bone. It was power he needed to possess.

Darci sighed in her sleep, and turned toward him. A few strands of her long hair had come loose from her braid and lay across her cheek. They fluttered as she breathed, slow and constant.

Atticus fought the urge to reach out and brush the strand of hair off her cheek. Something tugged in his chest and he held on to it. The feeling was strange, one he'd never felt. It pushed away the panic from his nightmares and seemed to promise a better tomorrow. He didn't know her thoughts, not like she knew his, but he knew the things that allowed him to trust her. She didn't hesitate when she made a decision. Even when his temptation ate at her until she trembled, waiting to touch him. She didn't have to trouble herself with saving him or Michael; nevertheless she made the effort to get them both out safe.

He admired her.

No, the emotion ran deeper than that, and it confused him. The desire to pull her close caught him and held him like no chain ever had. He reached across the short distance that separated them and stopped himself, a mere hand's-breadth away from settling on her waist. He needed—if it was okay for him to need her.

He pulled his hand back, turned and eased off the old bed, wincing with every creak and groan. Darci shifted again, and he glanced back at her. He'd never innocently slept next to a woman, enjoyed her company in bed. Again, he had to force himself away. Gripping the sword, he tiptoed out of the room and through the kitchen. Michael was sound asleep, safe under the kitchen table. Tobias snored softly on his own inflatable bed. Neither of them stirred as he crept out the door.

Outside, he walked a little ways from the cabin. Pine needles underfoot muted his steps. He took the sword from its sheath, and laid the cover against a tree trunk.

Something rustled behind him. He whirled, sword raised. A hawk, with a squirrel pinned beneath its yellow talons, regarded him with a golden gaze as though criticizing him. It rustled its tawny-banded feathers, drew itself up proudly, and stabbed its knife-sharp beak into its breakfast.

Atticus watched it tear into its prey with vicious precision. It finished, spread its dark wings and dropped off the branch into the air, soared between the trees and out of sight.

Too much time had passed since their escape. A mere handful of hours' travel was not enough distance between them and the Magistrate. The urgency to move on as the hawk had, to continue heading north to the lawless Yukon Territory, itched like the lemon juice Raylene poured into his cuts. He didn't know if it was paranoia or instinct.

He lifted the sword, holding it with a light touch, but

enough grip to make it an extension of his arm. He took a balanced stance, breathed and began. The blade whistled through the air. He stumbled and began again. The patterns were slow, each movement and placement of his feet precise. He didn't stumble this time. He gained speed, the carpet of pine needles lightly crunched underfoot. His strained body relaxed into the familiar postures.

With his sword he had power, control, and destruction. Patterns of early morning light broke over him and he flashed between the shadows and streams of sun. He began the series again. Faster, heat flowing into his limbs, the blade twisted, his body followed. Pine needles sprayed in all directions as he spun, parrying, dodging, switching the weapon to his left hand.

A dry leaf crunched behind him. He twisted. The sword tip came to rest millimeters from the hollow of Darci's throat.

Atticus froze. A bead of sweat rolled down his temple to his chin. Darci was wrapped in the fleeced blanket from the bed. Her cheeks pink, her eyes aflame with that infuriating attitude.

He dropped his sword point, slowly. His power twisted between them in the air, like the morning mist obscuring and revealing his desires. He didn't know how to do this, how to pursue her. She must think him broken or at the very least fragile, and she would be right, but not when they were together.

"If you tear one of your newly healed wounds because you wanted to play with your sword instead of rest—"

"Who said I was playing?" he asked, breathing hard from the exercise. He let a few more strands of his power loose. Tendrils of temptation spun about her and she stepped toward him.

Her eyes narrowed. She froze. "Don't even start that with me. I'm not attacking you, so you can keep your power to yourself instead of getting all defensive—" She stopped, as her mouth dropped open. "Are you seducing me?" she demanded.

Was he? He wanted to.

He moved closer to her until a hand-span separated them.

"Perhaps," he answered. He tugged at the blanket wrapped around her shoulders, and walked around her, drawing it away from her body.

"Atticus," she said, confused, holding on to the blanket and turning to face him. "I thought the last thing you'd ever want to do is seduce another woman, especially after Raylene and Jacqueline."

He'd washed the evidence of their cruelty from his body. He'd escaped their clutches, and all because of the woman before him who believed in a better world. She never faltered from her path. Despite the horrors that existed before them, she didn't yield. She split the turbulent waves around her and became the light guiding others to freedom.

By rescuing him, she'd changed the very fibers of his being. He'd been resigned to his fate as a tool, slowly breaking under the strain. Now he would be the tool to destroy them, shattering the Virtuous class with the weapon they had created.

He kept these thoughts at the forefront of his mind, wrapping them in gratitude for Darci to find. He could feel her aura close around him. Her eyebrows lifted in surprise. In response, his aura tugged against his control to be free, to wrap around the woman in front of him. He gritted his teeth and forced his power down. Even at his weakest, the last thing she would ever do was take advantage of him.

The need to feel her against him intensified into a burning ache. He tugged again on the blanket and it fell from her shoulders. She waited, watching him. He dropped his sword, and closed the distance between them.

"I'm not seducing another woman," he murmured as he settled his hands on her hips. His power tore at him to be free, his control breaking under the strain of her nearness. As he had the first time they met, he pulled her toward him, lifting her, and capturing her lips with his.

He'd taunted her from their first kiss, only because everything about her taunted him on an unbearable level. His power broke its leash and weaved around them, binding him to her. He groaned, kissing her again. He wanted her sweetness, her determination, her kindness to be his foundation.

He clenched his fists in the seams of her shirt, drawing a gasp from her lips. He could feel her mind caress his, before her hands slid up his back to catch his shoulders. She took his invitation and her tongue passed between his lips. He held her tighter, every inch of her pressed hard against him.

His hands slid under the hem of her shirt, trailing his fingers under the fabric, over her belly and up her sides. A ridge of skin between her ribs caused him to pause. This was where that bitch had shot her. A growl tore from his lips and he pulled away from her. Drawing her shirt over her head, he noticed how shallow her breaths were. He went to his knees before her, planting a kiss on the small pink scar from the laser bullet. If he could stop her from ever being hurt again, he would.

"Atticus," she breathed, and his heart responded. Warmth, true warmth from his soul kindled in his chest. Her fingers trailed through his hair. Muscles quivered and stilled at his touch. Her skin glowed golden where patches of sun fell on her. Desire to drown in her as he knew she drowned in him took over.

His hands slid down her hips and settled around her thighs, just above her knees. He pulled forward gently, her knees folding and he guided her descent, kissing her breasts, her shoulders, her neck until her hips settled over his. Why had he waited to touch her, to allow her to touch him? It was as though every second her skin pressed against his erased every moment before her. He nipped at her mouth, softly. The tension mounted and he gently deepened the kiss, savoring each dance between her mouth and his.

Her hands grabbed at his shirt, her fingers pushed up his ribs and he raised his arms as she stripped it off. She reached for the waistband of his pants. Her warmth lifted his heart. Had he ever wanted this more than he wanted it now, with her, because of her? Demanding, he lifted his hips, pressing himself against her. She moaned, and her hands gripped his shoulders with greater urgency.

His aura writhed around them and he found he could no longer wait. He rose up, laying her down before him on the discarded blanket. Her fingers had already undone his pants and in seconds they were off. Hers followed, and this close to the heart of her he hesitated. Her hips rose to meet his and suddenly all hesitation vanished. He gave her everything until the last chains of doubt broke, and he found freedom within the warmth of her arms.

11

Atticus lay panting, his blood still aflame, and Darci shuddered against his chest. He kissed the top of her head and sighed. He loved the pliant feel of her body against his and the comfort of her mind shielding his. For once in his life, all was well.

"Things aren't perfect, yet," Darci said, responding to his thoughts. Somewhere above in the light speckled pines a bird chirped.

"No," he said, "but this is as close as I've ever been."

She laughed. "You know, I got caught once with one of the farm hands behind the hay sheds. I like this much better."

"The woods?"

She turned in his arms. The pine needles tangled in her hair prickled his arms. "I like *you*, my *Luxurian* vigilante." She kissed his lips quickly. "Come on, we've got to get back. You need your rest and I'm not letting you sleep out here."

He kissed her in return. "Oh, we can. It will take a lot more than our little tumble to tire me out." He tossed ropes of seduction over her with a thought. She sighed and melted into him. He kissed her again, letting the seduction strengthen, feeling his own body respond. He could spend all day in the woods with her.

A hundred yards away, the cabin door flew open and Tobias rushed out onto the porch. Atticus pulled Darci into his arms, covering them with the blanket. Tobias hit the brakes.

"Ah!" Tobias cried, shielding his eyes. "Atticus, I never want to see you without pants again. Darci, don't get me started on you and your lewdness." Tobias turned his back on them.

"What's wrong?" Atticus asked, searching for his pants. He found them and pulled them on and handed Darci her shirt.

"We're in deep shit. They found us," he said, already returning to the cabin.

Atticus felt the world drop out from under him. He scrambled to his feet and snatched his discarded sword and scabbard, and belted it on. He didn't bother with finding his shirt, it wouldn't matter. He reached back and pulled Darci off the ground. She buttoned her pants and shrugged into a shirt.

"Come on," he said and sprinted inside, his heart beating wildly. He ran to the kitchen table and snatched his firearms from where he'd left them. How had the Magistrate found them so fast? Tobias had plotted their course through the trickiest terrain, guaranteed to lose them. He smelled a trap and his skin crawled. Zeke had access to all of Tobias's files. The rat could have fed the Magistrate the information. They never should have stopped. He should have pushed to keep going. But terror and exhaustion had dug its claws into his mind until he couldn't think. How could he be so weak? How could he put them all in danger?

The metallic whirring of an aircraft passed overhead. Atticus spun around, naked sword in one hand a fully charged laser rifle in the other.

Tobias shoved equipment into the duffel bags. Darci had coaxed a whimpering Michael out from under the table.

"Done for," Michael muttered. "You can never hide from him, not him. Never him." A chill rolled up Atticus' spine, as though the hands of Fate herself caressed him, promising the end.

"Leave it," he ordered Tobias, and shoved the other gun

into his hand. "Run!" Darci held Michael by the hand and went out the door first. "Tobias, take the rear."

They bolted into the trees, weaving between the forest underbrush. A high-pitched whistle screeched overhead, and the trees overhead parted, their branches snapping. Behind them an explosion rocked the forest. Atticus paused to glance back. A fireball arched into the sky, marking the demise of the cabin.

"We're not going to make it," Tobias said through panting breaths.

"We might still lose them," Atticus replied and ran to catch up to Michael and Darci ahead.

Before them the underbrush thinned, opening onto the meadow. A sleek, silver helicopter descended toward them.

"Get down!" Atticus ordered. Firing his rifle at the helicopter. The shots were absorbed by the black belly of the aircraft. He cursed and darted behind a tree next to Tobias.

Darci pulled Michael behind some bushes across from Atticus. Her beautiful lips were pressed into a worried line. Her focus was on the enemy descending on them.

He had to protect her.

Tobias flicked open the control panel for his weapon and shouted, "They are really determined to recapture you."

Atticus glared at Tobias. "They're not after me."

"Right. Looks like plan C is done for. And that was my favorite," Tobias replied, flicking a switch and his gun whined faintly as it powered up. "Fire this, it has more juice and their armor won't be able to absorb the blast, I hope. Don't hold the barrel. It's going to get hot." He tossed the weapon across the distance.

Atticus caught it and was surprised at the vibration radiating through it. "Whatever happens, don't let them touch Darci." He darted out from behind his tree and aimed at the helicopter. He fired and the weapon became hot in his hands before an explosion of light rocked him back a step, blinding him. A red laser blast hit the cockpit window and shattered it. A trickle of smoke leaked out the window. The echoes of shouts were heard above the sudden whine of the helicopter as it pitched forward. The rotors dragged the aircraft straight toward the far tree line. The trees whipped back and forth as though trying to uproot themselves before the helicopter chopped them into salad. Screeching, the helicopter spun, its tail snapping trees as it crashed. A gigantic pine cracked and began to list toward the meadow from midway up its trunk. It groaned and fell across the front part of the helicopter.

"No, no, no," Michael keened. His aura expanded, slapping lust against them all. Darci tried to soothe him and Atticus sensed her attention shift; less of her concentration shielded his mind and more directed at Michael.

How was he going to get her out of here?

Atticus raised the weapon and aimed at the side door. It cracked open, and he steadied the gun for a perfect shot. If it fired another blast the like first, it might give them enough time to make it to the car and take off. He closed his finger around the trigger.

A sharp pain spiked in his mind. A wall shattered around his thoughts, something cold and poisonous spilled through his brain. His body numbed and his hands dropped the laser rifle until the barrel pointed at the tree roots. Atticus gripped the weapon, trying to raise it. His body didn't respond.

"Atticus," Tobias shouted. "What are you doing?"

The helicopter's hatch slid open and a dozen heavily armed troops poured out, along with a good deal of smoke. Atticus fought to move. It felt like he was bogged down in cement.

Stop, the voice of an aged man commanded him.

A bald man wearing blue robes followed the soldiers. This was who Darci had seen leaving the torture room, the same person he didn't remember. No, that wasn't true. He did recall the Elder.

The Elder had entered his mind and promised him he would obey. Atticus had fought, but the drive of Raylene's power combined with the point of her knife lodged in his abdomen had been designed to weaken him. The same terror he'd felt in the torture room as the Elder directed his body filled him now. The man had used him like a puppet, telling him he'd become unmanageable and this was necessary. He had no way to stop this. The Elder had complete control of his body and could make him move and speak with silent command.

Bring her to me.

No! Atticus screamed, thrashing against the force pressuring his mind. He'd rather be dead than be forced to hurt her.

"Atticus?" Darci asked, her voice holding a note of fear. His stomach churned at the thought of what he was about to do.

He turned to her, terror, fear, and regret shaking him like an earthquake. She left Michael's side and closed the distance between them, innocently approaching her own doom.

12

The moment the Elder stepped from the helicopter's remains, Darci understood her part in this. He was here for her. The whisper of his malicious thoughts greeted her like a snake hissing through the grass. Michael gasped, and he turned away from the gap in the bushes from where they watched. His terror overcame the parts of him that were still rational and as a result, he collapsed. Panicked, she spread her aura to protect Atticus's mind.

"No, Atticus," she cried, and grabbed his arms. "Don't let him in."

The contact didn't spark a connection. Darci was shut off from him so completely, no matter how hard she pried, she could not reach him.

Under Darci's hands, Atticus's biceps twitched. His breaths were shallow gasps. The whisper of an aura twisted against hers like smoke. With a gasp she recoiled. Instead of Atticus, another mind had taken his place. Claws of terror stabbed into her heart.

I command you to bring her to me.

Atticus's fingers curled into fists, and then as though they were pried apart, snapped open. His hands clamped around her upper arms with bruising force. He dragged her toward the meadow.

"What the hell are you doing?" Tobias asked.

Before them, she could sense the Elder; his presence filled the meadow, and she was a bird caught in his cage. They were both trapped by the mind of the one who brought them to the Magistrate's holding cells in the first place.

Understanding slammed into her. With it came a red wave of anger.

"Don't shoot," Darci said. "If you fire, so will they. Stay out of sight."

"Like hell," he said, aiming his weapon at Atticus.

"No!" Darci cried. "Do as I say." To her relief, Tobias dropped the weapon. He stared directly into her eyes and she felt the sudden presence of his jealous power, like rough wool against her skin.

When it's time, give me the signal.

She nodded once. Atticus shoved her forward, pointing his supercharged weapon at the back of her head.

"Walk," he ground out, but his voice was strained and lacked the smooth, seduction-laced tones of a virile man. She allowed herself to be pulled forward. As she walked, she focused on the Elder, knowing who truly spoke to her.

The urge to harm the Elder, to make him bleed, clawed at her. Darci made a show of stumbling and raised her hands to the height of her shoulders. A dozen soldiers, many with scrapes and bleeding cuts, grouped around the Elder, their assault weapons trained on her and Atticus. The Elder's aura sloshed like a poison in every mind around her. He was powerful, controlling over a dozen minds in a single moment, but it spread his power thin. It left him unprotected. She controlled no one and the barrier around her thoughts was impenetrable. At least the Elder hadn't tried to break open her head yet. If he did try, he would never get in.

"Darci," he said, opening his arms to her, his light blue robes fanned like flags to either side of him. His voice greeted her warmly, and his smile was genuine. "I hoped we could meet on different terms. But it seems fate had cast another lot for us. You cut down my *Valerian* with a single thought, and for that I admire you."

Stop right there. Atticus halted her with a hand on her shoulder.

The Elder's powers, like hers, were devastating. He'd honed the edge of his thoughts to cut the ties of weaker minds. She hadn't. As a result the closer she came to his aura, the more she felt a knife slide along the edge of her consciousness. He, likewise, studied her. The wrinkles above his brows deepened like the field rows left behind a plow. This horrible man probably had never seen a field, or felt the sun on his back as he worked. She'd be surprised if he'd ever broken a sweat in his life.

"You can admire me all you want," she said. "But I'd still kill Jacqueline again if I had the chance."

His Cheshire-esque grin faltered. "This is not how I wished us to meet, my child. Jacqueline and Raylene, who would have been your sisters, did not deserve to die so horribly."

Darci kept her expression blank. Their death's had obviously struck a deep wound in the Magistrate.

"You have a strong mind," the Elder admitted.

Atticus's hand tightened on her shoulder. She resisted the urge to reach up and grab his fingers, not when he was being controlled like a robot by the tyrant before her. Even so, she needed his comfort, needed him to reassure her. She might not be strong enough to protect him after all.

"You know what I am, and you know my strength," he continued when she offered no response. He stepped forward, shortening the twenty feet between them. The edge of his aura cut deeper into hers. Her gut clenched at the uncomfortable feeling.

"I do." Darci stepped toward him, further closing the distance between them. As she did, Atticus, followed close on her heels. She took this to mean that the Elder didn't trust her. As well he shouldn't. She meant to hurt him. Knowing he feared her power gave her the advantage. This man had forced Atticus into servitude, and he did it with a smile. Determination to defeat him, here and now, infused her.

She would not see Atticus broken.

"I also understand you think your strength gives you enough reason to control the City based on your deluded definitions of peace and perfection."

The Elder smiled. Although the edges of his eyes crinkled, there was no real laughter in his expression, no true enjoyment. "It is our purpose," he said patiently. "The purpose of every Virtue is to seek perfection, and eradicate Sin."

Darci had heard those terms before, used as titles instead of concepts: Virtue and Sin.

Fear of delay, of failure drove her. She moved forward again. Atticus followed. This had to end.

"I suppose, because of my abilities, I am expected to abandon my friends?" she asked, stalling for time.

He inclined his head. "You will keep your friends, those who are not of an Undesirable status. Undesirables cannot exist in a world of Virtue." There was a note of finality to his tone.

Tobias, Darci thought, alarmed. Tobias would be counted as an Undesirable simply because of his sexual orientation. She hoped he had the smarts to stay behind his tree and keep Michael with him. She turned and looked behind herself, right into the barrel of Atticus's weapon, beyond that his eyes gazed down at her deadpan, as though the vibrant soul trapped behind them were absent.

"Is that what I would be doing?" she asked, staring into Atticus's eyes, knowing it was the Elder who looked back.

"Of course," he answered, and this time his voice came from the soldiers surrounding her, and to her dismay from Atticus's mouth too. "We are the final judgment. Our purpose is to temper the law. We are the highest power on earth."

Darci suppressed the urge to growl and clenched her teeth. She let her aura feel along the edges of the Elder's. The thin shield protecting the old man's mind was weak in places, and it didn't reach the ground. A small gap remained, where everywhere else he had wrapped himself around her tight. Her aura crawled forward, like a soldier over barbed wire.

"Only because the people fear what you might do," Darci

said.

"What we *will* do. Together *we* will achieve a perfect world," the Elder added. "I mean to have you at my side to guide the West from its days of darkness."

Darci stepped forward, again, and Atticus moved with her. This time he moved until he was inches from her back, his heat radiated through her shirt. In her peripheral vision she saw his rifle pointed toward the sky instead of at her. This close to him, their minds grated together with static friction. A charge passed between them, and her ire toward the Virtue filled her heart. "You mean, we'll be controlling people like Raylene and Jacqueline. Giving them orders about where to go, telling them who to kill."

He nodded. "It is grisly work, but you will be re-creating the world and fighting the war your parents and your grandparents have fought." She could sense he was itching to induct her into his ranks as his personal pawn.

"My sister was labeled an Undesirable. She was raped and murdered. Jacqueline, your *Industria* gave the order."

The Elder's features softened. "There is no need for anger, my child." The gentle tap of his power flashed against her aura, across her left cheek. She gasped. Her skin stung as though she'd been slapped, but the blow had felt like a feather brushing across her skin.

That pissed her off. She might have underestimated his abilities, but that didn't mean she wasn't going to hand him his saggy old ass before she was done.

"What happened to your sister is regrettable, but necessary to achieve a Virtuous city."

She clenched her fists and calmed herself. What happened to her sister drove her, but this man had no right to speak of Tara as though she were simply a memory. Even now, when she could no longer protect her she had the others to worry about. Tobias, Michael and Atticus were her responsibilities. She would not allow herself to weaken and put them at risk. The past brought her to this moment, it would not change it.

"Tell me, truthfully. How many of us are there?"

"Seven classes of Virtue and seven of Sin. Sin has nearly been eradicated through our efforts."

"And Atticus and Michael?" she asked.

"Some Sins," he began, stowing his hands in either sleeve of his robes, "can be used to infiltrate undiscovered pockets of Undesirables. Although, the measures we must take to ensure their cooperation are regrettable."

There was simply too much in this world that was regrettable.

"How long have Virtues been destroying Undesirables?" her voice, although she tried to keep it questioning, was accusatory.

"My child, you sound as though you think we are not the guiding angels who have kept human civilization alive for nearly three centuries. After the last wars, all government had collapsed. Without the Virtues, humanity would be reduced to founder in a new Dark Age. We are ready for the Final Enlightenment, and you will be on the front lines."

Darci gathered herself, pinpointing her focus. "I will be on the front lines," she promised. "Across the field from you. Now, Tobias!"

She struck, focusing her mind on piercing through his aura. It was wild but strong. Gunfire exploded behind her. Michael's twisted power of lust whipped around several soldiers. In seconds, six of the soldiers crumpled to the ground, some bleeding, and some totally zapped by lusty voodoo. The Elder cried out, his mind reacted by tightening on those who remained in his control. She felt it strike Atticus. He stumbled against her, the hilt of his sword jabbing her side.

Stop her! the Elder commanded.

Atticus straightened immediately.

Darci tensed. The only way to save herself and Atticus was to stop the Elder. She reached back with her left hand for the sword. Atticus's hand shot out and grabbed her wrist in a grip of iron. His right hand held the rifle overhead, ready to bring the stock down on her.

The blow never came.

She placed her right hand on his. "I'm right here with you," she whispered and a flare of his *Luxurian* essence broke through the Elder's failing control.

"I command you to stop her at once!"

Atticus's jaw worked. "Go," he said to her, his love for her coating his voice with emotion. His fist wrapped around the gun opened and the weapon fell, landing with a clank. His hand on her wrist loosened and Darci pulled the sword out of the sheath with a metallic rasp.

"Soldiers!" the Elder shouted. His fear sharpened the edge of his aura into a razor, cutting her defenses. The remaining soldiers raised their weapons. She sensed the mental command ordering them to fire.

She didn't hesitate and grabbed Atticus's arm. "I'm sorry," she said, and kicked his stiff legs out from under him. He fell hard, and she rolled as the first spray of laser fire whizzed overhead. "I have to do this without you."

In the distance, she heard Michael screaming Atticus's name, echoing the cry of her heart, as she came to her feet. She couldn't tell if Atticus had been shot, but she couldn't look back. To hesitate now would be the death of them all.

She struck the soldiers' minds again and a few more crumpled. The spray of fire ceased. She raised Atticus's sword. This close, she was inside the Elder's aura, and his mind slid around hers. His eyes flew wide and he stiffened. She rushed him, bringing the blade to his neck so fast the metal sang. His hold on the minds around him evaporated.

He attacked her. Darci flinched as her arms, neck and face burned as though someone had thrown boiling water on her. The blade in her hand began to inch away from the Elder. She recoiled, pushing the sword away, but her arms didn't respond. Frantic, she searched her mind but couldn't feel him. He was inside her, slowly making her pull the sword away from his throat.

She fought, throwing her mind against the Elder's. As though she'd thrown herself on the knife of his aura, he cut into her and attained unfettered access to her mind. Darci screamed and her aura collapsed.

He dove into her, tearing and ripping as he went. As he did, she could feel his essence, everything he was. He was strong, stronger than she'd expected. She pushed against him, slowing his descent to the core of her mind. Panic took hold and she sensed the end. She couldn't hold him off for long before he did to her what she'd done to Raylene. After he ripped out her mind, he would have what he wanted, another pawn to do his bidding.

Darci fought, and as she did different memories from the Elder's mind surfaced. There was attraction, women he surrounded himself with and a sharp denial. Darci grabbed for the memory, and as though she'd snatched a coal from a fire, she dropped it. The Elder was attracted, but not to females. He surrounded himself with females but there was vulnerability there.

She gasped. "You're an Undesirable," she said out loud.

The Elder froze and she took her chance. Even this deep in her mind, her body was not yet his to control. She grasped the blade tighter and came up behind him, the blade pressed against his throat.

Atticus snarled behind her, the slash of his aura shot out so fast her own knees trembled from the force of it. But his attack fell on the remaining soldiers with no effect. They were nothing but hollowed shells. Their minds had been at the mercy of a demon for too long.

Darci stabbed back at the Elder's mind and felt nothing but hatred for him. All this time, for sixty years he'd denied the very depths of his humanity. Because he had done so, he'd wrought havock and horror on the minds of those around him. Anger giving her strength, Darci broke his hold on her mind. He gasped, sweat glimmering on his forehead as she fisted a hand in his robes and pulled him close.

"This is the line," she said, pressing the blade against his throat, slicing through expensive silk of his robes and the first layers of skin over his trachea. "And there is nothing Virtuous about it."

The Elder was perspiring at an alarming rate. "You will never get a chance to save yourself from the Masters. You will be labeled a rogue—"

She applied more pressure to the blade. "I am more than a rogue. I am what you have made me, and what you should have been."

She gave him his mind, opening the doors he'd shut and released the thoughts and feelings he'd suppressed. He began to sob. Despite his sorrow, he'd still killed thousands; all because he was trying to eradicate a part of himself he wouldn't accept. In doing so, he'd become a soulless monster. She couldn't gather enough emotion to pity him.

"This is the line," Darci repeated. "I am not responsible for its creation. But I will be responsible for its destruction."

The Elder's lower lip trembled, his wrinkles deepening. "Spare me," he begged, his mind already sensing her intention.

"Who have you spared?" Darci asked. She jabbed the blade to the side across his throat as though drawing a bow across a violin's strings. Blood poured forth and darkened his cobalt-blue robes a deep purple. His blood spilled over her hands and over Atticus's blade like a waterfall.

The Elder sputtered. A gurgle issued from the gash in his neck. His body went limp and she let go of him.

Atticus approached her from behind. His heat, the anger, the lust, the desire to kill wafted off him. He laid a hand on her waist. His touch sent a volley of sensation through her, but none as fierce as his relief.

"Is it over?" he asked. His other hand slid down her shoulder, past her elbow and rested on the hilt of the sword. Gently, he pried it from her grasp and she let him.

"No," she answered. "This is only his end." The immensity of what she'd just committed to rose over her like a shadow and settled around her shoulders. And she was dedicated. The Virtuous had failed this world, even if she was born among their ranks, she would not stand with them.

He turned her and pulled her against his bare chest. "Thank you," he said, his voice quiet and his mind open to her, his love spilling forth as the Elder's blood had.

Darci took in a breath, and deep down in her something hardened. Before, she had cared, and not cared enough. It felt right to be here with him. She needed his support now as much as he had needed her. She was glad he'd kissed her in that Marriage House and decided to pursue her to the end of the earth.

Tobias marched up behind them, his aura sliding around hers, his mind calculating as he sensed them out. "You can see how unacceptable this is," he said, gesturing at them with his laser gun.

Atticus's flash of annoyance at being interrupted startled her into laughing. He kept his arms around her and turned them sideways until they were facing Tobias. He had a wary Michael by the hand and had dragged him across the field.

"There's blood all over you both. You'd better guess again before I let you back in my car."

"Your car?" Atticus asked. "I bought the damn thing, and it was not cheap."

Tobias snorted. "Hurry up," he ordered as he stomped off toward the car. "We have a long way to go before nightfall."

Darci pulled back from Atticus. Around her the bodies of soldiers lay unmoving. Without the Elder to control their empty minds, they were dying. There was nothing to be done, and it wouldn't do to remain on this killing field any longer.

"Come on," Atticus urged her.

She closed her fingers into fists and the sickening feel of blood between her knuckles frightened her. She knelt and wiped the blood from her hands on the long meadow grass. The forest around them was silent as a graveyard. Smoke billowed above the trees as the cabin continued to burn. Beyond the mountains, creeping behind them, storm clouds rose from the south.

They would come for them. The Elder had merely been the first. Many more would follow and fall at her feet. He had been right, she was powerful, and only now did she understand.

"We have to go," Atticus said, his sultry voice caressing her.

"I know." She took his outstretched hand and stood. The safety of a world she once knew was long gone and unreachable, the illusion having been shattered. She was glad to leave it behind.

In the car, Tobias started the vehicle and rested his hands on the steering wheel. "I was thinking," he said after a moment. "We're going to need more people."

"Not only people," Atticus said, kissing her cheek. "Sins, we have to match power to power."

"And Virtues," she added, turning to kiss his lips.

Michael shifted uncomfortably in the passenger seat. "Matches," he muttered, "like a game, two positives make a negative, two negatives make a positive. They match."

More people meant a greater chance of losing someone to the Magistrate's forces. She didn't want any more mass graves on either side, but the four of them, one grieving, one insane, and she was new to using her abilities as a weapon. Atticus was the only one of them with any real combat experience, and she was about to lead them all into a war she wasn't sure they could win.

None of them spoke as Tobias executed a complicated takeoff sequence. The vehicle rose slowly and steadily. Through the window Darci watched as the meadow with the bodies of the Virtuous fell away from them. Already, the wild fire had reached the edge of the meadow and drew closer to the dead. This was only the beginning of war. What would be the cost of victory? When would the cost become too great for the world to bear?

The answer came simply: No cost was too high for freedom. For the right to live and love as she wished, and to give that right to others, she would do anything.

"We'll need an army," Darci said. An army of people who would not rest, who would not stop until the oppression and fear they had lived under for so long burned like the forest below.

THE CHRONICLES OF SIN
A DAY OF WRATH

BOOK II

1

Colored streaks of laser fire cut down soldiers. Emerick watched from his perch on a cliff through the scope on his sniper rifle. He scanned the littered bodies, searching for the commander's insignia among the fallen, for her cinnamon hair, and lithe figure. She wasn't there. Fionn was not among the dead.

"Where are you?" Emerick growled, frustrated. Fionn never missed a battle. She always, always fought alongside her soldiers, giving commands as she struck down her enemies and pushed the Magistrate forces to the breaking point. He crawled closer to the cliff edge on his stomach and steadied his rifle. Fionn's rage was the fuel behind her soldiers, and her presence would guarantee the Insurgency would find the breaking point in the Magistrate lines and shatter it.

"Damn it," he muttered.

This was the most important battle of her life. If she could take these lands here and now, she would deal a wound to the Magistrate that would never cease to bleed.

Yet she was not here.

Without her abilities to give her troops the fury to push them into a ruthless battle rage they were going to lose, and lose soon. A flash of red lit up the tall spindly pines as a landmine activated. The boom echoed off the mountain face, and the concussion caused a small rockslide nearby. A fireball boiled toward the stars. The shockwave of the explosion slapped heat against Emerick's face. He cringed, the flash streaming too-bright light into his night scope.

He strained his senses, trying to catch the barest hint of her psychic scent on the wind.

An inhuman roar filled the silence left by the blast, collapsing his concentration with cold fear.

Emerick gripped his rifle harder.

"Not Hellions," he prayed in vain. "You'd better get off that field while you can," he said, hoping Fionn heeded the howls splitting the night. Nothing anyone did now could turn the tide of the battle. Every free person below would be dead before sunrise if they didn't retreat now.

A decade past, long before Emerick abandoned his post for the forbidden fruits of true freedom, the Magistrate applied a secret process to large numbers of their soldiers and created the Hellions. Horrendous things, more animal than human, with minds so twisted by carnal desire they became demons. A Hellion was capable of ripping a man's head from his shoulders.

If Fionn didn't immediately call a retreat, her people would be slaughtered without mercy. He would have given the order if he were at her side, but some other Insurgency officer was giving the orders he'd once given, just as some Magistrate commander was doing the same on the other side. He was in between, unable to call the retreat or to order the Hellions back into their cages.

The Magistrate soldiers suddenly vanished as one from the field as their tech suits engaged their invisibility functions. Hellions would kill friendly soldiers just as fast as enemies. With invisibility the Magistrate soldiers were mostly safe. Mostly.

Terrifying roars increased in volume. The first Hellion sprinted across the field and ripped one of Fionn's men apart in seconds. Dozens followed and the sounds of war became the screams of men and women being ripped limb from limb.

The aura of terror rising up from the field reached Emerick. He gritted his teeth, scanning the field through the scope. The Fionn he knew wouldn't let her men be slaughtered like this.

Screams grew louder. Insurgency soldiers fired volleys of laser fire. A few Hellions perished, but not nearly enough. Fionn's rebel soldiers retreated, sprinting away from the enemy tearing through their ranks. Instead of returning to their base lands across the lines that had separated the Magistrate from the Insurgents, they clustered close together.

"What are you doing, Fionn?" Emerick frowned. Trained in retreat tactics himself, this is not what he would have ordered. Clustering his troops into a pack with little to no shielding might as well lead the soldiers to a butcher. The Hellions closed in, snarling.

Adjusting the scope closer to his eye, he clicked the rifle into its warm-up sequence. His shots would give away his position, but he couldn't wait. Another explosion split the night into patterns of light and shadow. The mountain trembled, and more rocks tumbled past Emerick. The ring of Fionn's soldiers flared with sudden light and a barrier appeared. A Hellion sprang at the offending wall of light and with a squeal, became a steaming pile of charred flesh.

Emerick relaxed his hold on the trigger. He smiled. "That's my girl," he said. It was a good trick. A super-charged barrier, unbreakable unless you possessed the software codes to disable it. All it did for the time being was cut her wounded and exhausted soldiers off from the Hellions. If he were on the other end of the battle, he'd be hacking his way through the laser wall. It would only take a few minutes for Magistrate techs to break through.

Another explosion cut the night. Bright white blazed in his scope a second time and Emerick grimaced. He blinked and rubbed at his eyes, his night vision too slow to compensate for the blast. A quarter mile out from the small group of Yukon soldiers, another light barrier blazed into existence, and this one moved. It rushed forward, toward the first barrier.

"Fionn." Emerick stood. The sniper rifle rested useless and unneeded in his hand. "What have you done?"

The Magistrate soldiers saw the wall of light move toward them. He could sense their panic even from this vantage. The wall ripped through trees, vaporizing sections of trunk, leaving flaming timber behind. Smoke rose in its wake as it closed around the battle-field. Magistrate soldiers exploded as the wall passed over them. The putrid scent of burning bodies was thick in the air. Those who could, screamed-those who couldn't, prayed.

In seconds it was over.

He unclipped the scope from his weapon and brought it to his eye. He hadn't thought to search more than a quarter mile out. As the forest had been clear cut in seconds, he found her with ease standing at the edge of a new wasteland. A triumphant smile on her face, she stood at the front of her command still issuing orders into her comm. A great cheer rose over the valley.

There was no one now who could stand against her. Emerick hoped she was ready for the kind of attention tonight would earn her. The entire world would be looking for her now. He dropped the scope and clipped it back onto his weapon, unsure if the victory was a triumph.

A shadow moved down the mountain a few hundred yards from him. He twisted, brought the weapon up and sighted for his target, cursing himself for removing his scope. A dark-haired man, too beautiful to be called handsome, stared back at him.

Power rolled over the black mountain, a warning. A promise. The aura of desire spilling from that man—Emerick knew exactly what was coming for Fionn. The Magistrate was desperate to bring her down if they had sent one of their worst horrors to deal with her.

"*Luxurian,*" Emerick said under his breath. He'd kept a watchful eye on Fionn for over a year, always waiting for the moment when she would need him again. He thought he'd have to wait longer. She'd hate to admit it, but she needed him more than she ever had. A *Luxurian* was a Sin that could twist desire with a thought. Fionn had been bitter and angry for two years over a man, and a *Luxurian* snake would be the perfect assassin. Emerick steadied his breath and prepared for the shot—*and couldn't move his hands*. Another aura had joined the man's below twisting with dangerous accuracy, catching him between them.

"Shit," he said, and his hands dropped the weapon by someone else's command. The other enemy was probably hidden in the darkness behind the *Luxurian*, but they were also in his mind. Whoever it was, could stop him from pulling a trigger, but couldn't stop him from attacking with his own abilities.

Emerick's power, when it thundered down the mountain, stilled the air, silenced the small noises. It promised a slow, lingering end.

The *Luxurian* stepped back, his hand going to his hip. A flash of silver, and something whistled past Emerick's ear. A knife was lodged to the hilt in the tree behind him.

"I didn't miss," the *Luxurian* called.

"Leave while you still can," Emerick called back.

The *Luxurian* bowed his head once and melted into the shadows. "We will meet again," his cultured voice called from the heart of the night.

2

Fionn breathed the fumes of vaporized organics, forcing the scent of victory to imprint on her memory. She'd sacrificed hundreds for the ashen plot of land ahead. Stillness had settled over her soldiers.

"Set up a perimeter," she ordered into her comm. "Post watches and patrols. Detain Magistrate survivors."

"*Yes, sir,*" came the replies. Squadrons scattered into motion, and the frozen moment ended.

"Tech Squad," Fionn continued. "Drop the shields."

A moment later the ribbon of light miles in the distance flickered and went out. Her vision flashed with different readings. Displays of groups and their movements tracked over her irises. As the laser shields lost power, her tech connected with her first in command's. The moment the shields had gone up, she'd lost touch with over half her army.

"James," she said, heart racing. "Report."

A crackle of sound issued into her ear.

"Repeat."

More static and then, "*—alive. Send med crews—survivors.*"

Fionn turned to her assistant, a skinny teenaged corporal. "Deploy med crews, get them over there as soon as possible." The corporal saluted and sprinted toward the medical crews on standby.

"James," Fionn spoke. "Medical officers are on the way to

assess the survivors."

If there are any.

This time when James spoke, his voice was clear in her ear. *"Thank you, Commander. We await your arrival."*

Fionn signed off and strode quickly to her vehicle. A contingent of guards surrounded her as always. The squadrons were already ahead of her, she wouldn't arrive on scene first. Her personal guard silently took their places, one at each of the guns and two more in the back, before she started the vehicle and began the rattling drive across a wasteland of her own making.

The distance passed quickly and soon they were driving between piles of steaming flesh. She stopped the vehicle and exited. Men and woman, some with burns, others unharmed, smiled when they saw her. If only they knew.

She spotted her second in command and jogged in his direction. He was spattered in blood, as were most of her troops who'd made it inside the retreat zone before the barriers went up.

"We didn't lose as many as we thought we might," James said.

Fionn looked away from him, forcing the flash of temper down. "Any loss is too many."

"At least it's over," James said.

Fionn wanted to believe him. Wanted to believe what she'd seen on the field had been a victory and not another useless slaughter. "We didn't take it easily, and I doubt we'll keep it easily."

"They're desperate. Whatever they were protecting here, it's ours."

"If we can find what it is they wanted so badly. Until then, I have people to protect and lands to keep safe." Fionn stopped a passing corporal. "Get me the body count from the techs."

"Yes sir," he said before hurrying off to carry out the order.

Drawing the Magistrate into throwing all their forces at her had been risky, but it worked. If the laser fencing had done its job, only a mere handful of Magistrate soldiers could be found in a three-mile radius. For some reason, the enemy had concentrated their numbers here over these acres of land. So she'd struck where she could do the most damage. If she dealt the hardest blow possible, one they wouldn't soon forget, or recover from, hopefully she could convince them to cease antagonizing her people. Her act was brutal but meant to force the Magistrate into doing as she wanted. Altogether, her lands now spanned over two hundred miles of pitiless forest and frozen cliffs. But she'd never give it up. A five-year campaign and she had this to show for it. It was more than anyone else had.

"There are still Magistrate soldiers lurking out there," James said, keying a command into the display hovering over his left forearm. A pattern of red dots appeared on a lighted map. The dots were concentrated in the surrounding forest. A few were hidden away in the foothills of the mountains towering over them. Perhaps sixty remained of the legion who'd marched against her.

"I want them as prisoners, as many as we can get," she said. "You take a small command and round up the mountain side. I'll do the same on the forest side."

"Sir." The corporal had returned with the body count. He swallowed, his eyes downcast to the crystal tablet he held in his hands. "The count is currently listed at one hundred and seventy-three Insurgency losses."

Fionn nodded sharply, dismissing him. She knew most of those who had perished. She grew up with them, and they trusted her with their lives and the lives of their families. For a moment she allowed the grief and uncertainty wash over her. Had the price been too high?

She stared at the corporal jogging off to his other duties. Scars cut across the back of his neck and up into his close cropped hair, his badges of war. He was a man too young to have earned them.

"A high price," she finally said, unsatisfied, but still accepting the cost and the toll added to the debt she owed.

"The battle was won." James sidled up to her. "There isn't

anyone waiting to ambush us this time." His shoulder brushed against hers.

"The night isn't over," she snapped, pulling away from him. She flicked a switch on her sidearm and it hummed to life.

The smile disappeared from James's rugged face. "You're the Magistrate's prime target. Going out there is asking to be murdered or captured."

"They couldn't keep me in a cell the first time." She tipped her chin to toward the jagged mountain. "If they wanted to kill me, a sniper up there would have done it as soon as he had a shot." And he had the shot, James knew that, but whoever was up there hadn't taken it.

"If they kill you, the hope of the free people will die with you." The gaze James pinned her with was both an accusation and a challenge.

A spark of rage boiled to the surface. "I won't cower behind our walls. If I've given our people anything, it should be the will to go on despite the odds, no matter the danger." She'd kept the rage leashed during the battle. James didn't know it, but he'd pricked the inner shield, jeopardizing her self-control. He'd done it more than once lately, implying that her safety took precedence over her job.

She glared at him. A snarl caught in her throat. If she lost control because he managed dig his way closer and closer to her heart and the regrets she kept locked there, she wasn't sure he'd survive the backlash.

James paled. He didn't back down. He was a fool to think he could tame the animal she kept caged. "Then you'll have a full guard, myself included, and you won't say no. Let another officer take the mountain. You haven't slept for days. I don't want you injured on a cleanup."

Fionn forced her rage down. There was a line drawn with the blood of almost two hundred dead men in front of her. She'd given those orders. It was her responsibility to see the field secured. Every blow she could deal to that son of a bitch Tysek and his son was one step closer to settling the score. Tysek's spawn had slaughtered every reservation she had against bloodshed. His betrayal had turned her into a lord of war.

James moved closer and covered his comm. "Fionn," he said softly, "I'm not going to let you do something stupid."

Her power spilled into the air, wrapping around him. "There isn't a speck of danger out there after what we just accomplished. No one has ever killed so many Hellions at one time. We had them trapped and there was no mercy. If the Magistrate tried to attack us now, and if they succeeded in killing me, there would be nothing keeping our men from ripping them apart."

He didn't shudder, but she could tell he wanted to. He knew the stories whispered about her, and had still taken the job of first officer when she'd offered it to him six months ago. To his credit, James didn't pull back. He stood his ground and faced her.

"Understood, Commander," he said. "With your leave I will assign Thatcher's battalion to the mountain side."

"Agreed," Fionn said and checked her wrist display. "Have your men ready to depart in ten minutes."

James tipped his head and hurried to his duties. She watched his retreat understanding they would settle this matter later.

Fionn directed orderlies and helped with the evacuation of the survivors. By far, this had been the bloodiest battle she'd orchestrated against the Enlightenment. Those of her men who were wounded either had minor burns and were treated quickly, or they had missing limbs and wouldn't likely last the night. Of the five hundred soldiers she'd sent to the field, a third were dead, dying, or wounded, incapable of active duty.

With her guards trailing, she checked the pulse of a soldier who'd been moving only seconds ago. Dead. She shouldn't have checked. After so much war, she could recognize the absence of life as though it were a second sense. There was a heavy stillness, silent and persistent that identified a corpse. Wordless, she closed the soldier's unseeing eyes and stood. She looked toward the mountain, at the thin slip of moon pricking like a thorn into the night above the horizon.

"Do you hear that?" she asked her nearest guard, a man who by some weird quirk didn't feel her anger when it slipped its leash.

"Hear what?" Brax responded, following her gaze to the mountain.

Like silk sliding against skin, power rolled over her and around her. It whispered, tempted, and warned. Her anger rose. There was someone dangerous there, behind that curtain of darkness.

"What the hell is that?" one of her soldiers asked.

A moment later another power, this one infinitely more terrifying to her, lashed out. The night paused, a man's scream silenced and a whisper curled through the air. Sound ceased, the light breeze disturbing piles of ash died, and the world waited with bared teeth, promising violence.

The two powers clashed and a crackle of energy slid over the ash strewn field.

Wrath, naked and hungry, uncoiled from the depths of her soul. Her aura strained against the control. She heard the warning, the promise, as those two auras, one foreign, and one infuriatingly familiar, collided against each other. A very different battle from the one she'd just ended was underway on the cliffs above.

"*Fionn?*" James, her first officer asked over the comm. "*Did you feel that?*"

"Yes," she answered through gritted teeth. "We have some rogue *Appetence* hiding in the forest." It took everything in her to keep from answering their clash with her own challenge. She wanted to. Oh, how she wanted to cut the ties binding her powers and make the mountains tremble.

This was *her* land. How dare he return?

"Change of orders," she said to James. "I'm taking the mountain." The six men who served as her body guard for the night came to attention. "All of you, with me. We're going hunting."

"Yes, sir!" they responded as one.

Fionn jogged to the edge of the trees. James issued his orders quickly and soon a dozen men and women were in formation behind her. He matched her pace; coming abreast as they exited the waste and entered the dark, lush forest.

"Commander," he said, dropping his voice. "What are we hunting?"

"Patience," she answered, and dodged around pine with dead broken branches resembling a human spine.

If James understood her answer, he gave no response but continued alongside her.

Her wrist display showed a small band of enemy soldiers up ahead, near the pulse point of those powers. She couldn't see them from the rise. They must have known they were being tracked and ducked into a gully. They enemy would have the advantage of preparedness and be familiar with the land they'd patrolled for years. Her men were at the disadvantage.

Fionn raised her fist and her party came to a stop. The soldiers ahead stood between her and the location where those auras had clashed.

Perhaps if she was lucky and if Emerick was as much of a damned fool as she thought, the five or six soldiers over that rise were his comrades. It'd be like smashing eggs in the nest. Typical of him though, to flee the battle he knew he was losing. She tightened the rein on her temper.

Fionn motioned for her men to get closer. "James, Brax, and Smith, take the left flank. Carter, Mack, and Wells, take the right. Stay close together. If they're tracking us, their displays won't be able to tell the difference between the groups, and they will only see one person. Let's give them another surprise. The rest of us will travel up the center and put them to bed." She wanted these men alive, especially one.

"Damn," Brax said. "If we're putting them to bed, I'm not babysitting."

Fionn gave him a hard look. Brax was a bloodthirsty man, as good at cracking skulls as he tried to be at cracking his jokes. "I want them for interrogation. The rest we can ransom, or put to work." She didn't add that there was one in particular who wouldn't survive the night. "Keep the comm noise to a minimum. Move out."

The six men she'd named broke off and melted into the deathly quiet forest. Fionn motioned to those she'd kept behind and started up the incline. She moved with silent steps, laser rifle in hand, toward the target. A quick glance at her wrist display showed that the enemy was still in place.

By the time she reached the top of the rise, she moved to a crouch and sighted along the barrel of her weapon.

"*Team one,*" James's whisper came over the comm. "*We have reached destination. Over.*"

"Hold position," Fionn answered. She gazed through her scope and keyed a command into her tech-enhanced suit. Her vision sharpened and magnified. In the small gully below, not more than a brief dip before the mountain jutted into the night. Nothing stirred. She frowned. She should be able to see them by now.

"*Team two,*" Carter's rough voice spoke over the comm. "*In position. Over.*"

"*Team one, team two, are you able to confirm a target?*"

"*Negative, Commander,*" James answered.

"*Target is not in sight,*" Carter added.

Fionn frowned. They should have seen something at this distance. The hairs on the back of her neck rose. She knew when a situation was not normal, and the signs were not where they should be.

"*All advance. Put them out hard.*"

"*Roger,*" both teams replied.

Fionn took point, creeping from one dense bush, to a tree trunk. Several meters away she spotted Carter's team moving as one in a similar fashion. She couldn't yet see James. Her display began to track a movement: six individuals, one unmoving, and five who made small adjustments in position.

A rustling and scuffle sounded from the underbrush followed by a snarl that turned Fionn's blood cold.

"*Dogs,*" Carter said.

She halted, her weapon pointed toward the brush. Her team

was upwind, and the canines had scented them.

The snarl turned into a warning, directed at her. Eyes glowed from the shadow. She stopped.

"Wolves," she answered. "Scavenging. Hold your fire." She expected that the battle would have driven such cautious creatures away. But then again, battle created an endless supply of corpses for starving scavengers. Game had been scarce of late, and so it looked like cadaver had made it onto their menu.

A large, dark specimen, the pack alpha, prowled out of the bush. Its light-colored muzzle was stained dark. Its teeth were pink from blood. It snarled at her, hackles raised, fur bristling. She could tell it was underfed and desperate. The last winter had been harsh, but spring had brought more war, and with it, already dead food for the predators who had survived the blizzards.

"Don't shoot them," she ordered her soldiers. She made eye contact with the wolf and its snarl cut off. It lowered its head, not quite cowering before her, but submissive nonetheless.

She'd kept her power tightly wrapped about her, safe and under control again. Now she let a small tongue of it loose, enough to give the air a bite. The wolf jumped as though she'd struck it, and turned tail and ran. Four others whined, scampering behind it as they disappeared to the other side of the mountain.

"Why didn't you kill it?" James jogged toward her. "They'll probably start hunting the livestock."

Fionn drew her aura back. "Have we lost any livestock this winter to wolves?" she asked.

"No, but that doesn't mean—"

"They won't come near the compound," she said, with absolute certainty. "They'll hunt the Magistrate's herds."

She pushed back the bushes and revealed the mauled corpse of an enemy soldier. His sniper rifle was bent underneath his back, his eyes open, and his belly a gaping hole where his innards should have been.

"A clean shot." Brax pointed to the soldier's forehead at

the hairline, where a singed pinhole marked a laser bullet lodged in his brain.

Fionn knelt next to the body. She could feel *him*. Emerick had killed this soldier. But why? Why would he kill one of the men under his command?

"Long fall too," Carter added. He had his weapon pointed toward the cliff above them, sighting it through the scope. "No one's there now."

"Good thing he's dead," James commented. "Or we'd have lost a lot more soldiers today."

She didn't have to look at the cliff above, she could sense his absence. She could tell exactly where he'd lain, watching over the battle, after he murdered and pushed the Magistrate's sniper over the ledge.

He didn't hesitate to slaughter over five hundred of her men with his tricks and subtlety. He never hesitated to take a shot, always ready for the chance to kill an enemy. She looked back between the trees. The open ground of the destroyed field was a perfect marker. The circle of green grass in the center would have made it easy for a sharpshooter like him to kill her, or any one of her officers. Yet, he'd killed one of his own and left her, the biggest threat to the Magistrate in the Yukon Territory, alive.

Why?

3

Emerick swore. That smug bastard had the balls to taunt him out in the open and then dash off into the night. There wasn't even a psychic trail to follow. It was as though the *Luxurian* had spread wing and flown off. The notion that this possible threat had escaped him was unacceptable. He'd managed to remain hidden for two years in these mountains. If the *Luxurian* didn't have a Virtue helping him, Emerick would have neutralized him. Emerick wanted to spread his aura out farther to find the slippery man. Doing so would alert Fionn to his current position and he didn't have a death wish tonight.

The splinter of a crescent moon provided enough light that he could steal across the backside of the mountain without night vision, but not enough that he could do it fast.

The game trail he followed turned and disappeared down into the deeper shadow of the mountain. His aura brushed against someone else's. Emerick froze, scanning the mountainside for this newcomer. It wasn't the *Luxurian*, he discovered with disappointment. Whoever was hidden away with him on the mountain was not a Sin or a fellow Virtue. No, he was human. The man most likely felt only a whisper of sensation against his consciousness from Emerick's supernatural presence.

Who in the hell was up here with him? The battle ground was on the other side of the mountain.

"Captain, report," came a voice sounding like a tin whisper over the man's comm.

Hand on his gun, Emerick crouched and slipped off the trail behind a patch of ferns and a boulder. He knew that voice. That alone gave him all the more reason not to shoot the Magistrate captain until he absolutely had to. In war, information was the gold to trade with, and he never overlooked a chance to go mining.

"I've reached the coordinates, sir," the man answered. He sounded young, probably a graduate with enough experience for a small mission, but not enough for battle command. "Setting the charges now."

Emerick gripped his knife. The only reason the Magistrate would plant charges out here in the middle of the night after losing so spectacularly would be to get rid of something. Hell, he'd done it enough times to know that the clicks and beeps were the sounds of platinum grade weapons with enough bang to destroy half the mountainside.

"Charges are active. I repeat, detonation in t-minus ten minutes."

Shit. There wasn't nearly enough time to get off the mountain before it came tumbling down. The soldier must have an air lift or something. Emerick unsheathed his knife and crept out from behind the ferns. He'd have to wait until the soldier left and then deactivate the charges before they blew. Or he would take out the captain and steal his ride. The man would be focused on his task, thinking he was alone, that his displays would alert him to anyone in the vicinity.

How wrong he was.

The soldier wore a standard stealth suit and was plugged into his tech like a leech on a vein. No wonder the Magistrate just had their asses handed to them by a bunch of farmers turned soldier. Especially if *this* was their special ops agent.

"Tell me, Captain," responded the commanding officer on the other end. *"Do you have family?"*

Now that he was closer, Emerick could clearly hear the timbre and lilt of *that* voice, and he began to sweat. His father was personally commanding this operation. Which told him how terribly important thus cover up was.

Hell, yes, Emerick was going to intervene.

The captain froze. "I'm sorry, sir. I don't think this is the most appropriate time to discuss personals."

"Answer the question, captain."

Emerick waited, rethinking his plan. He'd heard those words from his father's lips before. He knew exactly what they meant. Somewhere above in a stealth aircraft or on the next mountain over, a sniper was waiting, finger on the trigger. The deed was done, and this mission would take the captain to the grave. Whatever his father wanted hidden would stay hidden.

All the more reason to interrupt.

Emerick waited for the moment. If he moved closer now, he'd be in the sniper's scope and an instant target.

"I have a wife," the captain answered, hesitant. He must sense, must know that something about his mission traveled down unfamiliar and treacherous paths.

Don't answer, Emerick silently told the man.

"What is her name?"

Emerick could see the captain sweating under his helmet. "Gemma."

"I will send her my regards," Emerick's father answered dispassionately. *"You did well."*

A bolt of light zipped through the air. The soldier crumpled. Dead.

Emerick waited a moment. The shot was taken, but the sniper would wait to confirm his kill if he was worth anything. In the emptiness beyond the corpse, the faint glow of the charges shone against wet rock. A nervous tick appeared in his right leg, he had short minutes to take care of the explosives.

Unwilling to wait longer, Emerick sprinted toward the light, leaping over the corpse. He immediately went to his knees, drawing his knife, and started with the first of six charges. Using the tip of the blade, he pried off the casing and revealed the complicated control on the inside.

"Shit," he muttered. If there was any subject he failed in, it was explosives. He worked, waiting for the bite of a bullet to end him, or the white-hot heat of a wrong move to set the detonation off early. The first charge went dark and the shadow crept in. Emerick didn't stop and moved on to the next. The minutes shortened and a cool calm poured over him. Another went dark, and another. Ninety seconds until detonation and the final platinum grade weapon powered down.

Emerick sighed and sat back on his heels, wiping the sweat from his palms on his pants. He stood, intending to leave with his new cache of explosives and a set of intelligence to leak to the Insurgency. His boot bumped the captain's body. Waste not, want not.

He searched the soldier quickly, taking his unused belt knife, sheath, a few rations, and slipped it all into the bag that had carried the charges. He would have taken the man's other weapons, but they were heavy and would weigh him down. He'd need speed to reach Fionn's compound in time to warn her about this and the *Luxurian*.

By now his father would have noticed the total absence of a blast spearing into the sky. This hidden corner of the mountain, made by the point of two cliffs meeting together, obscured him from immediate sight. Without the faint glow of the charges, the darkness around him had thickened. It provided high contrast with the dark blue sky above, as though the difference were between deepest night and dawn's first light. A shiver of unease fell over him and he spun on his heel so his back did not face that darkness. He felt the urgent need to leave.

Whatever was deep in the shadow cast by the cliff above had been the target. This was as far as the soldier had ventured into that unfathomable depression. Emerick sensed it would be unwise to travel farther in. What was here, his father wanted hidden, and because of that he couldn't leave it unguarded. Not for long at least. He'd send Fionn's men its coordinates or return himself with the light of day at his back—

The ragged click and rasp of chain links across stone

echoed from the shadow.

Emerick kicked his sniper rifle up. He *knew* the thing trapped back there would not be harmed by something so mundane as a bullet. He reconsidered leaving with the charges. Maybe he should have let them go off.

Beyond the shadow, a hiss issued like a snake's warning and Emerick backed away, carefully stepping over the body of the soldier.

The whirr of an aerial vehicle broke the night like the swarm of a hive. Glad for a reason to turn tail and run, Emerick sprinted back up the trail. A spotlight split the night like a spike, illuminating the dead soldier. The light stopped sharply a few feet from the body, failing to pierce the darkness beyond. With the bright light, he couldn't identify the aircraft as the Magistrate's but he doubted it was the Insurgency's.

A low whistle cut the air. A bright orange explosion engulfed the Magistrate scout. Its camouflage melted away to reveal its silver color and the white eagle of the Enlightenment painted on the side. The whirr of its engines turned into a scream as the scout plummeted. Another missile screeched through the air, finishing its chances of survival. The missiles had come from another aerial vehicle still hidden behind the veil of night. The downed craft slammed on top of the dead soldier and flames spurted upward.

Emerick waited for the flames to break that deep shadow. But they didn't. Instead the fire turned away, arcing back toward the destruction.

No wonder his father wanted that black place hidden under a landslide. It was impenetrable and repelled fire. What a weapon that would be? If his father could harness the darkness, the Magistrate would have a new and frightening tool to terrify the free people of the earth into submission.

He needed to reach Fionn before the *Luxurian* and before his father found another way to cover his tracks.

10

"What the hell is this?" James asked the corporal who'd brought the report.

"I don't know. The pilot didn't know either." The corporal kept a stiff upper lip, which with a man like James, all six feet, broad shoulders and his chop-a-tree-in-half-with-one-swing reputation gave the young man a certain credit. Fionn sat back in her chair watching the exchange, knowing she had a few moments' rest before the corporal's report made it to her desk. Since when had warfare become mostly about paperwork and less about mission? Lately there'd been more paper cuts to worry about than bullet wounds in her life. Now that Emerick was on the loose and nearby, she was itchy to be out of command and on the hunt.

"Send another pilot up and have him report."

The corporal saluted her then James before he scurried off. Fionn gritted her teeth as she stared at the screen and figures in front of her. Lists of the dead, lists of those expected to die, and those who'd survived to die another day. Then there were the lists of Magistrate numbers. For every dead of hers, an average of six enemy soldiers had been killed, and only because of the little trick she'd devised. She should be happy; her people were safe, for now. But this victory felt hollow. Someday the Magistrate would be back, and they'd have a trick of their own.

"One of our aerial patrols found a Magistrate scout on the east side of the mountain and brought it down. He stayed in the area. A half-hour later another Magistrate scout was sent to the same position. Forty-five minutes later, another. All three were shot down. The pilot looked for a reason why they would be there and he found this." James swiped the report onto the crystal screen in front of her.

A map and a set of images appeared with times listed next to them. James pointed to a particular image, lit up in the light of the flames of a recently downed craft. From the overhead angle, it was impossible to fake. The flames, instead of pushing back that dark spot, had bent *away* from it, back toward the heart of the blaze.

Her intuition bleeped a warning. "Double the patrol there. Let's get the rest of this settled, then we'll schedule a survey team. Right now we need as many men as we can spare out there holding the line. Tysek won't let us rest for long."

Brax, who'd been quiet since their return to the compound, snorted. "Spare any more and we'll end up sending the sheep and chickens to hold the line."

"Tysek's advance is pushing against the center. Not many but enough to tire our troops," James said, dropping heavily into his place across the table.

Fionn stood. If she stopped, if she let herself relax, she'd lose the hard-won hold over the Yukon. She'd lose that line, and they couldn't afford it. The future of every free person under her protection depended on it. And winter was only a few months off.

"Let them push our forces," she said. "And we will push back as we always have. This is our land now, and they'll have to slaughter every last one of us to take it from us." But she was worried, and she hoped one of them wouldn't call her bluff.

"I wasn't saying we should consider a partial retreat. We need more recruits," James replied. His tone scratched at her, picking at her temper.

"What recruits?" Brax asked. "From where? All we've got

left is the chickens and the children chasing them."

"Brax is right," Fionn said, keeping her temper buckled down. "There aren't any more. We need something to give us an edge and finalize the Magistrate's respect for our presence. Something that will further convince them that this is lost ground and they will never regain it."

"'Scuse me, miss," inquired a voice from the door, startling them all.

Brax surged out of his chair, the rough-hewn furniture clattering against the concrete wall as he drew his sword.

Fionn spun. Not many caught them, any of them, unawares.

A skinny lad, perhaps no more than sixteen, cowered against the door frame, a tablet in his hand.

"Stand down," Fionn said quietly to her men. None of them had heard the door open, but it was late and after the massive explosions of her trip mines to bring up the fencing, temporary hearing loss was a bane for them all. "What do you need, boy?" she asked.

"One of the officers asked me to bring this to you," he said, holding out a crystal tablet. The boy glanced down at her fist with wide innocent eyes.

A knife was in her hand. She sighed and sheathed the blade. Brax lowered his weapon, muttering something about motherless brats sneaking through the bricks, and kicked his chair upright. She reached for the tablet and keyed it to life.

It was a ransom note. One of her officers on the west end had been captured. She frowned. He was a minor officer; why would the Magistrate send her a ransom note so soon after the battle? She'd pay the ransom of course. She'd funded her army with the limitless supply of gold she'd found right under her feet, but the timing made no sense. This sort of wartime pleasantry would come later, a week or so from now.

A sharp movement caught her attention. She shifted her right foot back and missed the blade aimed at her chest. It swiped down, cutting through her leggings at the hip. Pain bit into her side, and she dropped the glass tablet. It shattered with a tinkling of crystal shards. The messenger boy had a sharp grin of triumph on his thin, underfed face that now seemed rat-like.

James shouted, but she didn't hear.

The rage deep in her lashed out. Like thorny vines, her aura cut into the would-be-assassin as sharp as any blade. Small pricks of blood appeared on his arms, but he never lost the smile. Even as she squeezed and sliced the life out of him, he didn't stop smiling. Her anger boiled over, the walls and ceiling shook with the force of it. Red ran like tears down the boy's arms, dripping off his fingers into a pool at his feet. In minutes, boy's eyes rolled into the back of his head, and he dropped.

The threat gone, Fionn cut off the flood of power. She stumbled backward against the rough-hewn table. Her hand went to her side and came away wet. The knife blade had been paper thin and wickedly sharp. Still, the sensation of a torrid rage in her veins didn't fade as she regained control; instead, it got worse. Nausea gripped her suddenly, and a sharp pain pierced into her abdomen.

"Poison," she muttered, fighting to make her thick tongue work.

"Bastard," Brax growled, making sure the assassin was dead. He kicked the poisoned blade against the wall and checked the hall beyond for more assassins. "Should have known better." His face was white.

"Sound the alarm," James ordered. He reached for her arm.

Fionn flinched away from him. "Don't touch me," she growled.

"We need to get you to medical," James answered, and disobeying her order, reached for her again.

The raw anger seething and writhing against the surface of her skin lashed around his wrist. James's blood dripped loud against the war room floor. Fionn stumbled farther away, fighting to stop her from striking her second in command. Oh, but how she wanted to let her power crawl up his arms and over the rest of him in punishment for daring to disobey a direct order. A wave of weakness splashed through her.

James stepped away and out of the reach of her aura. "We'll follow you," he said to her. "Brax, cut down anyone who tries to stop us on the way to medical."

A siren blared somewhere. James would have sounded the alarm, of course. It would confirm she'd been wounded. Her people would panic, but they would be ready for an attack in under five minutes.

Fionn repressed the urge to snarl at James. Despite his good intentions, she was ready to continue the slaughter. She clutched at the wound in her side and stumbled to the door. Brax slipped past her, careful not to make contact with her and took point, his sword in his right hand, his hunting knife in his left. Anyone who dared face Brax would be in for a surprise. James guarded her rear. With uneven steps, and a hand on the wall to keep upright, she made the journey and left a trail of blood in her wake.

A squad of soldiers charged around the corner. Fionn growled. Her tenuous hold on her power loosened and her aura filled the corridor. Their squad leader caught sight of her and blanched. The team of soldiers stopped, their eyes going wide.

"Get back," Brax said.

The soldiers didn't move.

"Did you hear what I said?" Brax raised his sword. "Unless you want to die, you'll turn tail and run."

The squad leader nodded and ordered his troop back the direction they had come.

Word would spread faster than snowdrifts in a blizzard about her condition. The last time she lost control, she'd escaped the dungeons of Admiral Tysek and only his soldiers had witnessed the destructive rage she'd unleashed on those who hadn't run from her. She refused to lose control here. Her people didn't need to know why the Magistrate called her the Blood Commander.

Red lights began blinking overhead. The alarms went off again, summoning the reserves to man the underground turrets and patrol the first six levels. The light blue of medical lay at the end of the hall. Spots appeared in her vision and she let out the breath she'd been holding. Her legs gave out and she tripped, going down on one knee.

James's hands were instantly pulling her up. Her wrath cut into him, but he held onto her, his blood soaking her shirt.

Brax hollered down the hall. Nurses with dark half-moons of exhaustion under their eyes, appeared rushing a gurney toward her.

"Don't let them touch me," she growled.

"They can't help you otherwise," James said.

Fionn ignored the gurney, ignored the shocked faces of the medical staff and their questions, instead continuing to the medical ward. Her rage had abated, but the smallest upset would break her painstakingly constructed mental barriers. Her control was as fragile as an egg shell.

"Let go of me," she ordered James once she had reached a hospital bed behind a lockable door. She gripped the baseboard of the bed, refusing to lie down. To lie down would be to give in. Torture hadn't broken her. A thousand soldiers couldn't kill her. Neither would this.

The med staff flitted about her like hummingbirds, their forms blurring, instruments glittering in their hands. They muttered things about conditional poisoning, and rattled off her vitals.

"Commander," the head of medical addressed her. Her voice was soothing and without threat. "You have to keep your rage under control. This type of poison is synthetic. It reacts to your abilities."

"You've seen this before?" Fionn ground out. Her body felt as though it were both on fire and freezing. She wanted to lash out again, the need slammed against her instincts like a hammer on a nail.

"Yes," the woman said shortly, scanning her again with her instruments. "You have to fight against using your power. The poison works to trigger it, using it as fuel to kill you faster. If you give in you could be dead in seconds."

Fionn heard the warning. She trusted Doctor Blanc. The woman had escaped her lowly position as a physician from the Magistrate city almost five years ago. The day she'd arrived in Fionn's camp she stood up to her without breaking a sweat, telling her she was the most experienced doctor in the north and there wasn't anyone else Fionn should have on her team training her healers. If she said she knew something, then she did and Fionn didn't ask questions.

Fionn nodded. "I'll try. Keep your staff out of this room. I'm likely to kill one of them if they touch me."

"I need to administer to you," Doctor Blanc said stubbornly. "You'll bleed out before you overcome the poison."

Fionn shuddered, forcing down rising rage. "Just you," she managed to say. "Get everyone else out."

The head of medical turned and exited Fionn's vision. Her fists tightened on the bed rail. Giving in was not an option.

James stood a few feet away. Blood still dripped from his wounded hands. Brax stood guard at the door, appearing menacing with his sword glittering under the bright lights of the ward.

"Get out, James," she said.

"You need me here."

"Not in this room," she snapped, a portion of her rage breaking loose from its chain. She winced as nausea rolled over her. "You're the Commander. Protect the people. You must hold the line, or so help me, when I've beaten this, I'm coming after you."

"Fionn," he said grimly. "The line will hold. You're going to be fine." He was pale, almost sickly grey in complexion. She'd only seen women who'd just lost sons to war, turn that color.

That pissed her off.

"Chicken shit," she said, her voice sounding raspy and distant. Her hands and feet were cold now. Something on the display panel peeped out a shrill warning. "Get out of here before I kill you."

He stared at her. He believed her. She would kill him. If he didn't, after seeing what she'd done to that brat who'd attacked her, then he was a fool and he deserved the death waiting for him. There was fear in his eyes too, and stubbornness. His instincts would tell him to fear her, but his gods-damned stubbornness kept him from giving in.

Doctor Blanc swept back into the room. "Do as the Commander orders, sir, before I make you leave."

James gave Fionn one last lingering glance then he wisely exited. Nurses waited just outside the door and immediately began to see to the wounds her aura had given him.

"I'm going to give you a few meds," the doctor said as she approached Fionn.

Fionn gritted her teeth and nodded. The doctor began fussing with load of syringes from her pocket and pricked her shoulder, the back of her hand gripping the bed rail, and another needle stabbed her just above the wound on her hip.

"I need to get these clothes off to see how bad the damage is."

"Do whatever you need to do," Fionn said and began the battle against herself to save everyone around her. She thought of the men and women who gave their hearts, and souls to protect their freedom, their children, and their families. She thought of her officers who mercilessly gave everything to hold the line. She thought of her first officer.

"Can you lie down?"

Fionn closed her eyes forcing back the rising tidal wave of wrath and nausea. The poison was in her now, burning through her, freezing her, pushing her powers to the surface and breaking the chains keeping them at bay.

"That would be unwise," Fionn said.

James.

In another life, she could have loved him. Even if he was a stubborn hard-headed brute.

She never would. That place in her soul for another had already been filled, and ripped out. Death was racing toward her, toward everyone around her. It was only a matter of time before the poison won and she unleashed the rage in her. It would kill every last person within her strike radius. Emerick would have given that information to Admiral Tysek. The stab of betrayal cut like a fresh wound.

She'd already loved. She'd already lived.

5

Emerick gauged the horizon. It was early, almost four in the morning, and the sun was rising. They gained fifteen minutes of sun a day until the solstice, when there would be a day without night, and then they would lose that much sun until the night without a day. By now the *Luxurian* could have made it on foot back to his father's barracks or to Fionn's underground compound. He was still ten minutes from the compound's first fence. Emerick didn't care if the *Luxurian* went back to his father, but he wasn't about to take the chance that he'd slipped past Fionn's defenses. With the power of seduction and desire, it would be too easy to infiltrate the hearts and minds of the men, and especially the women, guarding the entrances. Emerick didn't have another way to cross the ten miles to her the compound except on foot.

Birds woke, chattering at him as he traveled under the spindly northern pines. The trees formed stark contrast in the night. Their boughs seemed to reach down toward him, like claws. Somewhere in the distance the hair raising call of a loon split the air. The sound seemed ominous, as though that darkness he'd left in the cleft of the mountain cliffs followed him, the rasp of chain upon stone and the sense of watchful hunger reached for him. There was a relief in heading into the heart of enemy territory, carrying charges, assorted weapons, and risking Fionn's wrath. The intelligent thing to do would be to leave his weapons behind, and to approach the woman unarmed and without threat. But he couldn't, because the threat of a snake in her den was worth more than his self-preservation. He'd rather risk her wrath than risk her death.

Emerick shifted the bag on his shoulder, moving a little faster.

A creek sang over and between lichen-spotted rocks, creating a natural bridge. Emerick stepped onto the first rock and hesitated. A lark trilling nearby cut off mid-song, leaving a fractured echo of melody on the wind. Graveyard quiet pervaded the forest, tension rode the air. The rock beneath him trembled.

Emerick leapt across the rest of the water. The grassy bank vibrated with energy. It wasn't an earthquake, no, that would be accompanied by a whip-crack of sound as the earth split and shifted. *This* was different; the sensation of the earth trembling was psychic, not physical.

Anger, hot and blistering as desert heat rolled over him, turning his blood cold.

"Fionn."

Emerick dropped the extra weight of the bag of explosives and ran. He was still several miles from reaching the borders of the compound. If her power had an effect on him from this distance, the amount of energy she'd let loose was enough to drain her. Draining her would leave her open to another attack.

He stumbled and slid down the steep side of a hill. Rolling, he hooked an arm around the slim trunk of a silver aspen and used it to bring him back to his feet. Her pain washed over him with the rage. He leapt over a log, sprinting through the tall grass of a meadow and into the trees again. The wave of her rage grew stronger, rose higher until he choked on her aura. The last time he'd felt this, he'd been shackled to a wall, miles away and unable to help her.

He'd been locked in his father's private compound. Those hours spent feeling the lash of her anger, her fear, her desperation had finished any ties he'd had with his father, the Magistrate, or any mission of peace. Hundreds of innocents had died under her hand, and he was to blame for it and for the Magistrate's Enlightenment. He wouldn't fail to be at her side this time.

Another, fainter slash of her power cracked through him.

She was fighting for her life. What other reason would she have to react so violently?

He stumbled over an exposed riverbank and crashed through the glacial mountain water.

He stopped at the edge of the clearing and engaged his cloaking shield. Her people would be on high alert, and he couldn't help her if he was sniped before he even entered the compound. He spread his aura out, sensing for the *Luxurian*. Only another *Appetence* would have the ability to block that much power and survive. Any other human would be struck down the moment that anger focused upon them.

Suddenly, Fionn's power cut off. Panic gripped him and he reached for the top of the electric fence ringing the pastures and pulled himself over. Electricity zinged up his arms and rattled his teeth. Nothing short of death would stop him now.

Gods, he couldn't be too late.

The hangar to the underground landing bay gaped open, swallowing a section of lush green field. Emerick sprinted toward it, drawing a weapon.

He threw his aura deep beneath the earth and snarled.

The *Luxurian* was here, and he'd brought company. Another *Luxurian*, and another Sin, someone with very little power who shouldn't be there were present. Four possible assassins. If she was dead, they would soon follow her to the grave.

The world darkened as his aura thickened in the air, becoming a destructive force. He formed his power close about him like armor. At the edge of the hangar he stared down, reflecting all the fury Fionn had unleashed.

Rifle in hand, he stepped off the edge of the hangar bay and dropped below. He landed crouched on the dorsal side of a great transport vehicle being winched to ground level for take-off. His camouflage flickered and died, the program using the last of the battery power he carried with him. A few steps to the nose of the plane and he leapt down onto a first level gangway. The guard posted there kicked his weapon up against his shoulder and pointed it at him.

Emerick struck with his aura. The guard's movements slowed. Slapping the soldier's weapon aside, he slashed at the man's carotid artery with the side of his palm. The soldier's eyes rolled back and he dropped. Emerick caught the man before he fell over the edge and down the ten levels to the hangar bay floor. He dragged the man back from to lean against the door leading to the honeycombed labyrinth of the compound.

A red alert light flashed in each corridor as Emerick jogged toward the medical wing. She was still alive. He could feel her there, like a thorn in his mind, ever-present, worrying deeper into him, her power jolting through the earth in intervals.

A young man, armed and uniformed, jogged toward him.

"Soldier," he said, using the tone of a superior, "What happened?"

"I don't know. Word is, the Commander's been assassinated." By the squeak of his voice the soldier hadn't outgrown his youth.

"She's alive," Emerick breathed. "What else have you heard?"

"The assassin had a knife, it was poisoned."

Emerick swallowed, his grip on the knife at his belt made the leather handle squeak. "Thank you," he said curtly to the soldier. "Back to you duties."

"Yes, sir!" he answered, saluted and did as he was told.

Emerick liked the boy, but he was stupid, answering a complete stranger's questions and calling him "sir" as though he were an officer and not some ragged man dressed in a faded patched uniform. The news and the soldier's lack of diligence stirred his ire. A *Luxurian* wouldn't have had to seduce his way past any security point with weapons smuggled under his coat, or even in his hand as Emerick had.

Unable to stop it, Emerick's power rolled on silent threat,

breaking over on the enemy's presence, as though shouting a challenge from the roof of the world. The *Luxurian's* aura, answered and slid over Emerick's like a caress, as though beckoning him to his very own velvet lined grave. Emerick answered back with a quick jab, promising that it didn't matter where the *Luxurian* hid, or for how long, Emerick would find him, and have his revenge.

A weak flicker of something rough and violent brushed against the sensitive tendrils of his power, and he continued his course. He had to see her first. She had to live. He'd waited this long to see her again, and he would not lose her now, not at the pinnacle of her campaign when she was so important to more than just him.

A security guard and his companion stepped forward to bar him from the medical ward. Emerick didn't give them time to speak before he threw his power around both men cutting off their desires to intercede and block his entrance. The men blinked at him placidly and did nothing as he swept past and inside.

Harried nurses and doctors scurried back and forth between rooms. Like a hive following an attack on the queen, the personnel here swarmed over their domain with efficiency borne of practice. Five years of battles with wounded to care for had prepared them well. The wounded were being treated on nearly every surface from the floor to counters. The dead were covered in sheets and laid out in what was normally a lobby area.

Fionn had been moved to the back of the ward. No one noticed him immediately, despite his being fully armed. He was surprised he made it halfway.

"Corporal, who is that man?"

Rather than get a shot in the back, Emerick stopped and turned. Fionn's new first officer James held his ravaged hands over a basin as a nurse sewed the deep cuts across his palms closed. The cadet on James's left, drew his sidearm and pointed at Emerick's chest.

"Identify yourself," James demanded.

"She's dying," Emerick answered.

James jerked toward him, a curved suturing needle half-way through the meat of his palm and trailing string. "Who are you?" The officer's features darkened. Emerick could tell he'd slipped over the edge from being a reasonable man to being one with murderous intentions. He was also obviously very protective over the commander.

"If you don't let me help her, the poison will cause her to lose control and every person on this level will die shredded, just like your hands." Emerick glanced pointedly at James.

James's eyes narrowed. "Impossible, Fionn doesn't have that kind of power."

Emerick wanted to laugh at the man's incompetence. *This* was his replacement? Instead he cast patience over the corporal with the weapon still trained on his back, deciding to deal with the most immediate threat. The cadet lowered his weapon a placid expression on his features.

James didn't stop him. Something like resignation passed in front of his eyes.

"You're a fool. I've seen her lose control, all it took was a few moments and she'd skinned a man." He turned on his heel, leaving James to trail in his wake. "You have no idea how powerful she *might* be."

Her nearness grated against Emerick's control, a sensation that sent fear scattering through him. He'd lost control already. If James had refused to let him pass he would have killed the man without hesitation. He wouldn't let one man tip the balance into the Magistrate's favor, she had to live.

He stopped outside the closed door hiding her from view. The familiar guard with his blade drawn didn't move toward him.

"I thought you were dead, Emerick," the guard growled at him. He raised his sword, light gleaming off its diamond sharp edge.

Emerick stared at the man built like a boulder with legs and arms like tree trunks. Under different circumstances they would have shook hands and slapped each other on the back.

But times had changed. "Brax, took you long enough to crawl your way to the top." He stripped his rifle from his shoulder and the knife from his belt and handed them to the man who'd saved his life once before. At one point the two of them had been friends.

James stepped between them. "You know this man?" he demanded of Brax.

Brax was about to reply when the door to Fionn's room opened and a terrified doctor ran out. Emerick caught the woman in his arms and steadied her.

James rushed to her side. "Doctor Blanc, what's wrong?"

The woman turned to James with red rimmed eyes. In her hands she clutched a crystal tablet with vitals and other medical babble flashing across its applications.

"The synthetic poison is shutting down her systems. The more she uses, the faster it kills her." Only then did Emerick see the long lines of blood dripping from underneath the woman's lab coat.

"Get her help, she's bleeding." Emerick moved the doctor aside and into the hands of a waiting nurse and turned back to enter that room.

Brax's hand on his arm stopped him. "You won't survive if you go in there."

"Beware the fury of a patient man," Emerick replied. He opened the door and closed it behind him.

Fionn snarled at the sound of the door's click. Her power struck out at him. The front of his neck stung painfully. Her back was to him.

"Get out before I kill you," she snarled. She gripped the bed rail as though she hung on for life. The slap of her power in the air made him shiver, not with fear, but with familiar longing. He thought he could stand against this, but gods, he'd die to feel her, all of her consume him again.

"No, Fi," he answered. "I'm staying."

She whipped around. Strands of her red-brown hair had escaped the tight braid she kept and framed her face like wings of fury. Recognition lit in her eyes and her features blazed with emotion.

The destructive slash of her rage caught him across his chest. Hot blood dripped from the shallow cut over his pectorals and dampened his shirt. She groaned, one hand clutching her belly. Her power cut off. The screen next to the unused bed blinked red warning signs.

Emerick rushed to her side, gathering the full force of his power and filled the room with it. She flinched at his hand as he brushed against the tight shield of her aura.

"You betrayed me." Her hands tightened on the bed rail before she pushed off and rounded on him. Sharp razors cut into his arms, his thighs. His power did nothing to shield against the raw energy and emotion she forced upon him.

"You killed them." Her power grabbed onto him and began to tear. *"There were children there, you promised to keep them safe!"*

He stumbled forward and slid his hands over her arms. Behind her the monitors had begun to squeal Fionn's imminent death. Like a whip, her essence raked over his back, shredding his shirt and searing his skin. Once upon a time he would have asked again for that lash. Maybe later, maybe in another   life.

"Stop," he ground out, pulling her against him.

"Not until you're dead." Her breath cut small slices along his neck.

"You can kill me later. You have to live first."

Emerick's power swirled like lazy eddies of mist in the air around them. At his command, the energies coalesced and descended around them.

An enraged scream ripped from her throat and her power surged against his. The two met and clashed, fractured and shattered. Lines like claw-marks appeared on the floor and the walls, but met the fortification of Emerick's power and stopped. He pressed close, cocooning patience around her, forcing stillness into her.

Her body stiffened, rejecting the absolute calm his power demanded. Lines of sweet pain coursed through him and he held her tighter. Her rage demanded his submission. How he'd denied her this long caused a different kind of ache in his chest. Like a wolf to his mate, he wanted to give her everything, even his life if she demanded it, but he wouldn't allow hers to end before his.

Fionn's breaths became long shuddering pants and her body weakened further. Her aura wavered and dropped. Quickly Emerick wrapped his power tight around her, shielding her. He pressed a hand to her throat, feeling the strong beat of her heart, and let out a shuddering breath of relief. The monitors against the wall were in the green.

It was over, for the moment. He'd suppressed her power enough to force the synthetic poison into regression. A few hours on a blood filtering system would completely eradicate the toxin and when she woke, she'd be as enraged as she'd ever been. He'd deal with the two *Luxurians* and the other intruders in the compound and be well on his way by the time she thought to have him brought to her.

Emerick gathered her limp form in his arms and laid her gently on the bed. Only now he looked down and saw the wound just above her hipbone wrapped in gauze. He smiled. She still wore her lucky underwear for battle, a delicate pink brief with vertical cream colored stripes, totally at odds with her personality. Her blood had ruined them. She'd be angry about that too. It made him smile. Unfolding the sheet and blanket from the bottom of the bed, he tucked the covers around her.

Gods, how he wanted to stay here with her. He brushed strands of her hair back away from her lips. Unable to resist, he bent and kissed the round apple of her cheek. His lips were bleeding and left a stain of his bottom lip on her white skin.

"Emry," she whispered in sleep, her sigh one of longing.

He turned to find her first officer watching him from the doorway. Emerick straightened, feeling the numerous slices in his skin, the damp stickiness of his clothes. Now that one threat was put to bed, another waited in the doorway. If he had the use of his hands Emerick was sure James would have shot him.

"Get out," he said. Emerick read the possessiveness in the man's voice, and his own anger, fueled by vestiges of Fionn's power still coloring his aura, urged him to kick James's ass down the hall. He suppressed the urge, unwilling to disturb Fionn's healing rest for even a second.

Emerick hesitated. Leaving her to hunt down her would-be assassins meant leaving her open to attack again. Yet, as much as her people loved her, anyone who dared attack her now would be stupid to do so. He tore himself from her bedside and exited the room, making sure to close the door behind him.

"She'll be fine," he said to the doctor who was being bandaged by a nurse. "The toxin is still in her, but it won't rouse her power."

"How did you do it?" the woman asked.

Emerick took a deep breath, feeling the gash on his chest pull and sting. "Like calls to like," he answered. "I am her opposite, if I use enough of my power over hers they neutralize." He made a point of meeting James's eye. "That won't change."

"*Patientia*," the doctor breathed. "Thank you," she said and called over a team of nurses before disappearing through Fionn's door.

"You're bleeding everywhere," Brax pointed out. "She sunk her claws in deep."

"I know you now," James said. "You're the bastard who allowed an entire contingent of this army to be captured by the Magistrate as they escorted refugees to the compound. Every last one of those brave men and women died. Entire families were slaughtered."

"Allowed it?" Emerick repeated. "I spent two months under the hand of a lesser *Industria*. I didn't allow anything. I tried my damnedest to save those people. And I failed. I won't again." Emerick ripped his useless torn and bloodied shirt off his back and tossed it in a receptacle. "There are four intruders in the Compound. Two on the upper east levels and another two camped out in the mess hall. Fionn is here in the middle.

Do your job and protect her. I'll do mine, and slaughter the sons of bitches my father sent to assassinate her." Emerick had spent all his power, all his ability to remain patient and reasonable. There wasn't enough tolerance in him to keep him from decking the first officer for much longer.

"Your *father*?" James asked, his face turning a shade of purple. "You're the spawn of that murdering psychopath."

"Who were you the spawn of?" Emerick shot back. There was only so much patience in him.

Brax laid one of his massive hands on James's shoulder. "I'll watch him. If he tries anything, I'll kill him. If he says there are intruders here, he's right."

While Emerick doubted Brax would kill him, the possibility of those gigantic hands around his throat slowly squeezing him to death was very much a reality. Brax might not be a *Appetence*, but that didn't mean he wasn't one of the most dangerous Insurgents.

James nodded sharply. To Emerick he said, "If you use your power against the people here, I will personally skin you alive and roast you slowly over a pit of coals."

Emerick believed him. The man cared deeply for Fionn, something that rankled with him but also assured him of her safety. A man in love was foolish, as he well knew, but a man in James's position could become dangerously overprotective.

"I wouldn't touch any of Fionn's people," Emerick said in a low voice. "Because I know what she'd do to me if I did. Nothing you can threaten me with is worse."

He turned and opened a cupboard he knew held extra uniforms and found a neatly pressed and folded green t-shirt and pulled it over his head. Next he pulled on a jacket that would hide the blood stains from the several shallow cuts Fionn had given him.

"Ready, Brax?" he asked, holding his hand out for his rifle. James laid the rifle aside and instead gave him his own belt knife.

Brax checked his sidearm. "You know she's going to kill you the moment she wakes."

"I'm planning on it," Emerick replied.

6

Emerick didn't like leaving Fionn in the sliced-up hands of her first officer. The man exuded the kind of threat only another man interested in the same woman could sense. They were rivals, and unlike Emerick, James hadn't ripped her heart out. James was a good man, but he'd failed to protect her. Emerick wouldn't mind if Fionn killed James instead of him when she woke. Still James had managed to fall down the same dark hole he had.

What a glorious descent.

He hoped the man landed on spikes when he reached the bottom.

"She likes him too much to kill him," Brax said.

Gods, he'd been muttering out loud again. Too much time spent with rocks, trees, and streams for company instead of actual people.

Brax ignored his growl of frustration and continued jogging after him down a side corridor.

"How did you know there are other intruders?" Brax asked.

"You felt Fionn's power."

Brax shook his head. "Not like you did."

"It feels like a whip with razor blades. Every *Appetence* has a unique signature in their aura that another *Appetence* can track. I can sense them even when they aren't using their powers."

"That's a good trick. Can you sense your father?"

Emerick stopped and turned. "Like attracts like," he answered. How else did he explain how he knew his father was alive, and father was currently locked behind the walls of his military complex, bristling with soldiers armed to the pits? "In the same way, your uninvited guests can sense me coming, if they're paying attention."

"Right." Brax replied. "So guns blazing like the sting op from two and half years ago."

"Not exactly. I want information first. If we can capture them without killing them we should. Besides, they could have friends without powers. I can't sense powerless enemies," Emerick said.

"What kind of Sin are we after?"

"Two *Luxurians,* an *Invidia,* and the fourth must be weak. I can't get a read on him to even tell if he's a Sin. We're going after the two most dangerous. The others are somewhere else in the upper levels. They'll be caught in the lock down."

"You know," Brax said. "If a *Luxurian,* let alone two, had managed to get in, wouldn't this place be a lonely man's wet dream?"

Emerick laughed. He liked Brax. "Normally." The absence of lust thickening the air did worry him. He'd studied the successful training techniques of cities who managed *Luxurians* for years. It was strange that the Sin hadn't acted other than to observe the field of battle and break in.

When they met above the battlefield the *Luxurian's* message had been clear, whatever the *Luxurian* wanted, he didn't want Emerick's interference. Which was exactly why he was going to interfere. The *Luxurian* was a city creature, and the diabolical ways in which his kind were used, made them unsuitable for work in war games. It was exactly the unpredictable move he expected from his father.

Brax tightened his lips into a hard line as he considered. "He could start up at any minute. I'm not attracted to you and don't want some sick Sin changing that. Let's get this done, fast."

Emerick let his aura roam, sensing out the rest of the underground town. Far to the left and down near the mess hall, he found that sensual pressure.

"He's a strong bastard," Emerick said. This wasn't going to be easy. He knew Fionn's ways and mannerisms and had felt the unbearable lash of her power before, but he didn't have any handle on a full-fledged *Luxurian's* abilities. "My father would have had the most powerful Sin he could find sent in. There's only one I know of and he's still in the cities."

He prayed it wasn't *him*.

Brax patted the side of his laser rifle. "Lead the way, Master Virtue."

"You have a talent for sarcasm." Emerick slipped through a narrow corridor, a short cut to the lift, the fastest way to get to the mess hall.

Before they reached it, the lift opened and a pair of kids scurried out. They stopped in front of Emerick and Brax, their eyes going wide. Emerick glanced at Brax with raised eyebrows.

"What are children doing this close to the surface during a lockdown?" he asked through gritted teeth. Didn't anyone follow the protocols he'd developed?

Brax frowned at the children. "Sandy, Jacob," he chided. "What'll I tell your mother when she hears your running upward during a full lockdown?"

"Pssh," said the older of the two. She was tall and just beginning to fill out as a woman. "It's just a lockdown. It's not like there's anything to worry about. This place is impenetrable. You said so yourself."

"Maybe I was wrong. It was a kid that just tried to kill the commander."

The younger boy, about twelve, with a shaggy mop of hair in desperate need of a wash, puffed out his chest. "We'd never do anything like that."

"I didn't say you'd do it. I said others your age from the Magistrate are doing it." He turned them toward the nearest stairwell. "I need the lift. You get down those stairs and back to your mother."

Sandy stuck out her bottom lip. "What about you?"

"I'll be home for supper."

That satisfied them both and they scampered off down the gang way, their well-worn shoes slapping against the metal. Emerick slipped into the lift and Brax followed him.

"Yours?" Emerick asked.

"Might as well be. Their father died a year past. My sister's had her hands full trying to keep it together." Brax punched the control and entered in his coded password to take them down the ten levels to the kitchens and dining halls. Emerick noticed the lift now extended to twenty-six levels below the surface. That, at least, was good. He'd told Fionn the best way to get at the rich deposits of oil and gold beneath the Yukon was to dig and dig deep like a weed so the Magistrate would never be able to uproot her.

"I didn't know you had a sister," Emerick said.

Brax shrugged. "Before Fionn was captured and you left, the two of you only had eyes for each other and the grand empire you were building. You should hear what the people said about you. To this day, no matter what Fionn says, most don't think you were responsible for what happened."

Emerick forced down the flash of resentment, and the sense of failure. "Do they even know what happened?" She'd said it was his fault. That if he hadn't wormed his way into her life and changed everything, those doomed men, women, and children would have been safe. That five hundred lives wouldn't have been lost.

"What happened?" Brax asked.

Emerick leaned back, hearing the overused gears of the lift grind. "I was sent here three years ago as a spy. My final orders, I knew going in, would be to murder her."

Brax's features darkened. "You were going to do it."

"I was. But then, she showed me a different way to live, and I realized I'd been living a under the whips of my masters for so long I'd become confused about what freedom actually was. I disobeyed my orders and became a traitor." Emerick stared at Brax, envious that the man had spent the last two years guarding her while he'd been cast out because of his father's actions. "For people who've been at war non-stop, the Insurgents are the happiest I've ever met. I fell for the freedoms, the people, and I fell for Fionn. I'll kill my father for the assassination he ordered on her life today, and I'll make it slow because of what he did to her five years ago."

"I'm happy to hear that," Brax said and readied the sword at his side. "No one really knows what happened that day. Most people think you're dead. Your stunt with Fionn will resurrect you. All that matters is who you are now. When the nights were longest and cold, you got the Insurgency off its ass and sent us running into the future. Without you we wouldn't be the threat we are to the Magistrate regime today."

"No," Emerick said. "Without Fionn, all of this is impossible."

The lift ground to a halt, bouncing them with a light jolt.

Emerick considered the words that had passed between them. He'd still give these rebel people who were free and happy everything he could. He would give their leader even more, his life if she wanted it.

Brax slapped him on the shoulder. "The people still need you. I don't think we're any closer to securing these lands then we were when you left. She needs you."

"I'll try and remember that when Fionn has me on the rack," Emerick said.

"Hell," Brax answered. "I'll be handing her the tools, if she decides to use them. I want that woman on my good side. But the Insurgency needs both of you, now more than ever."

The lift doors opened inviting in the delectable smell of crisped bacon and scrambled eggs that were being served for the early morning breakfast. The punch of *Luxurian* power overrode the demands of Emerick's rumbling belly.

"Careful," Emerick growled. "He's powerful."

Brax held him back with a hand against his chest. "What is he capable of exactly?"

163

Emerick gave Brax a once over. "If you try to kiss me because of his power over lust, I will kill you myself."

"Good," Brax said and rolled his shoulders. "I've got my own woman to think of and I'd rather die by your hand than hers."

Emerick snorted and stepped out of the lift. He glanced around for anything out of the ordinary, soldiers in mismatched uniforms or the shiny pieces of Magistrate tech. He could sense the *Luxurian*, but not a power-absent soldier hiding under the guise of one of Fionn's men. It was possible the man he hunted was back up in case Fionn didn't die. Brax followed, his laser rifle in one hand, the barrel pointed down, his other resting on the sword at his belt as though he could use both at the same time.

"There could be more soldiers here than just the *Luxurian*."

Brax swore. "Fine, I'll follow your lead."

Falsely relaxed, they entered the main portion of the mess, a large room decorated with Insurgency banners and symbols.

Emerick kept his own hand at his belt, flexing his fingers and resisting the urge to toss the hunting knife Brax gave him the moment he saw the *Luxurian*. He spotted the Sin immediately. The man hadn't shaved in a few days, and still the shadow of stubble did nothing to hide or roughen his entirely too handsome face. The thick pelt of a wolf had been turned into a coat, serving again to turn the *Luxurian* into a striking figure, instead of a rough-spun refugee. The coat was a perfect place to hide all sorts of weaponry, and as Emerick knew well, the man could strike a target in the dark with a flick of his wrist and a slim knife.

Emerick stopped. Here where darkness could not hide the man's identity, He recognized him. By the look of surprise on his opponent's face, the shock was mutual. Emerick never worked with *Luxurians*. They were unruly, difficult to control, which is why they were usually kept as underlings of a *Industria* within city walls.

"Change of plans," Emerick said quietly. "Let's get breakfast and have a nice chat before we take him out."

"A chat?" Brax repeated, sounding unconvinced. Emerick didn't have to see him to know the man was shaking his head.

"Have a little patience," Emerick said, and strode through the crowded mess hall. The absent din of the place, which normally rolled at the level of a roar, gave the mess an eerie overtone. Men and women ate in determined silence. More than one person wiped at eyes wet with tears. Friends and loved ones had died the night before, and there were still more battles to come.

A woman with dark circles under her eyes stood from her table and hurried over. She gripped Brax's arm.

"Brax," she whispered. "We've heard terrible things. Is it true?"

"Fionn's fine, Agnes," Brax replied with a lowered voice. He glanced at Emerick. "That man saved her life."

The woman's shoulders lifted and tears gathered in her eyes. She placed a small hand on Emerick's bicep. "Thank you," she said and then returned to her table.

Emerick didn't have a moment to respond. Out of the corner of his eye he watched the *Luxurian* shift in his seat. The man's raised eyebrows now shadowed his eyes with dangerous meaning.

Atticus! The name sliced through his mind and with it he was thrown back to the terrifying nightmare that had been the Military Preparation Academy. *Appetence* were sent to the Academy to gauge their potential as soldiers. Emerick had passed with flying colors; Atticus had failed and been sent on to the City. They'd been fourteen last they'd met, and here they were again, on opposite sides of the battle. Only this time the tides had reversed.

"Change of plans," Emerick said.

"You ever going to just stick with a plan?" Brax asked.

Emerick ignored his companion's frustration. "If he pulls a knife shoot him."

"Got it. Which one?"

"The pretty one sitting with the skinny kid."

Emerick moved along the hall, toward the kitchen.

Atticus's *Invidia* accomplice didn't give any indication he'd noticed anything amiss as he sat hunched in his seat, tapping away on his crystal tablet. The kid looked more like a tech than someone with powers that could open a heart faster than any blade. He couldn't have been older than nineteen.

"Damn," Brax said. "How the hell did they get past the check points? That kid is stuffed full of tech gear and the other is packing a fuckton of cutlery."

Emerick didn't reply. He continued to the serving line, swiped a tray of food and a set of utensils. Brax followed his lead; instead of one tray he took two.

"You need more than one?"

"This," he gestured to his brawny body, "doesn't keep itself going, and if we're eating, might as well make it count."

"Morning," Emerick said brightly to the *Invidia*, startling him as he set his tray on the wooden table with a loud *snap*. He pulled out the chair and dropped into it, using the motion to loosen his blade at his belt. Brax did the same across from him, keeping one hand on the stock of his rifle. The fold of Atticus's coat was open and Emerick spied a glittering row of knives.

Good, they were both packing. This time it would be an even fight, if that's what it came to. In school it had always come to a fight. One thing he remembered about Atticus was his unwillingness to back down, his resolve to win and dominate any contest. As children, Emerick possessed the advantage of being a Virtue among others of his kind, and the training of a lifetime of combat. Here, as adults, it might be an even match.

Emerick didn't let that thought distract him, choosing instead to unroll his fork and knife from the rough-spun napkin. He left the napkin on the table close to Atticus and forcefully stabbed a strip of sausage with his fork. The sound of metal on metal reverberated through the mess, turning heads in their direction, ensuring that if something happened between them, there was an audience and enough combat-trained professionals to kill the *Luxurian* if he decided to fight.

"I said we would meet again," Emerick said.

Atticus's eyes narrowed at him in recognition. "Emerick."

Women would swoon over the sensual lilt in his voice, but then it was a tendency of the *Luxurian* breed to be walking sexual temptations. As it was, all the women in the mess were sneaking him quick glances. Atticus had indeed grown up and become a lethal creature. Well, so had Emerick.

"Atticus." He bit into the sausage. "You're supposed to be in the city. Or dead."

Brax was happily shoveling food into his mouth, but he watched the exchange with the intensity of a hawk. The *Invidia* had ceased his attention to his tech gadgetry and leaned back in his chair. It was unnerving that he also seemed unperturbed by the company he found himself in. Either the young man was damn cocky or stupid.

"The city hasn't learned its lesson if they sent you to collect me." The threat in Atticus's voice was palpable.

"No," Emerick replied. "I'm not doing the Magistrate's dirty work. They have other Sins for that. How did you escape?"

"The same way you did from the Academy every other seventh day."

"That bad?" Emerick asked. It was a rush, escaping the high-walled confines of the Academy on Sundays to dally with friends in the local circuit. Until he got caught. Then it became trickier every time he tried to sneak out.

The *Invidia* leaned back in his chair, folding his arms across his chest. "Atticus, first you find a girlfriend in the middle of nowhere, and now you've got a bromance going on. I give up."

Emerick bristled. "Excuse me?"

Brax pushed one tray aside and started on the second. "I like him." Brax pointed his fork, a sausage speared on the end of it, at the *Invidia.*

"Tobias," Atticus addressed his companion in a warning tone, "Zip it."

"The last time I saw you, I wasn't sure you would survive," Emerick said.

There. The barbed sensuality of Atticus's anger slapped against Emerick's aura.

Atticus's aura thickened with the promise of violence. "And you were given extra marks for trying to kill me."

Brax set down his fork, and Tobias leaned forward.

Emerick took a deep breath and forced his fingers to release his knife under the table. "We all have regrets." The mess stilled for a moment, his own power slipping his hold, before the sound of knives against plates and conversation began again. Atticus had a hundred reasons to hate him, a thousand more to hate the Magistrate.

"I never thought you'd join a militia, Magistrate or otherwise." Emerick took another bite of sausage.

Atticus's temper flashed again in the edges of his aura. "I haven't," he answered.

Tobias snorted. "Darci would say otherwise—"

"*Tobias,*" Atticus growled, and the air thrummed with power.

Emerick swallowed his mouthful of pork links and swigged the bitter gritty coffee. The coffee hadn't changed since he'd last had it. Brax mirrored his movements as Atticus and Tobias glared each other down. The young man wouldn't be any trouble; his aura was faint. Atticus, on the other hand, was still armed to the teeth. Even if Atticus hadn't been behind the assassination attempt, danger cloaked him. It didn't matter if he was a refugee, he was still a threat to the Insurgency.

It was possible that Atticus had signed on with mercenaries. Whoever this Darci was might be his commanding officer. There were plenty of mercenaries who chomped at the bit trying to pry through the cracks in Fionn's infrastructure to get even a handful of the rich gold and platinum deposits she had both hands on. Most of them failed in the attempt. So how did Atticus gain access to the compound?

"Hey," Tobias said to his companion. "I have work to do. Your girlfriend wants a hand with some adjustments on the injectable for Mike. I'm here babysitting you instead of doing my work."

Both Emerick and Brax straightened in their seats at the seemingly offhand comment. Emerick dropped his fork with a clatter.

"Mike" was the code used for the type of micro-robotic poison designed to turn a Sin or Virtue's power against them. Micro Injectable Kill Envenom. M.I.K.E. for short.

He drew his blade, drawing the remainder of his power with it. He'd been too hasty in thinking Atticus might be here for peaceful reasons. Fionn had been poisoned and he wasn't about to let some kid get past his defenses and endanger her a second time. His abilities conquered all noise in the room, stopping the sound waves so fast even the air seemed to freeze a moment. The rasp of his short hunting against the air echoed as loud as a platinum-grade explosion.

Atticus stood in a serpent-like movement. He reached inside his coat and withdrew three blades held between his long fingers. The other diners stared. Some had their hands clasped over their ears. A few reached slowly for their side arms. With Emerick's power in the air it was impossible for them to move at any great speed.

"I should have killed you that day," Emerick growled. His voice like a shout broke the shroud of power in the air.

"You should have," Atticus replied. "Tobias, get out of here." Atticus's aura flashed out, not at Emerick, but to the direction of the others he'd sensed, no doubt sending a signal to them. Atticus then raised his hand, fractured light reflecting off his knives.

Emerick shifted his grip on his own weapon and Atticus's hand released. Light splashed off the blades for a fraction of a second until Emerick threw all his power forward. Two of the knives ceased their travel toward him and hung for a moment suspended in mid-air before clattering to the floor. The third bit into Emerick's left bicep, embedding itself like a porcupine quill into the muscle.

Bloody knives are barbed!

Emerick cursed, raising his weapon to block the fourth knife, batting it from the air. He reached up and wrenched the blade from his bicep, flexing his fingers against the pain.

Atticus's hand whipped out. More knives flew from his fingers.

Emerick blocked them again, ducking under the few he couldn't stop. Keeping Fionn from killing herself and forcing the micro-robotic poison into dormancy had taken most of his energy. He needed to end this quickly if he was to win.

He leapt forward, slashing with one knife, a twelve-inch blade with a serrated edge. *Did Brax really have to take his rifle?* Emerick caught the four blades clutched in Atticus's fist on the serrated edge and blocked the punch to his gut. Atticus's power lashed around him, breaking the spell their dual powers had cast over the mess hall

Screams erupted. A woman swooned as backlash from Atticus's power struck her.

Emerick dropped, brought up his leg and landed a blow to Atticus's ribs. Atticus grunted and stumbled away, crashing into a table. Trays of food scattered across the floor.

"Don't hit him in the ribs," Tobias shouted. "Do you have any idea how hard it is to get those to heal correctly?"

Emerick scowled at the boy standing on the sidelines of the fight next to Brax. Damn his hide, Brax was smiling.

"What the hell?" he asked the man, ducking yet more cutlery as it hurtled through the air toward him. He lunged forward again as Brax smiled at him and pulled Tobias farther out of the way. The bastard wasn't going to intervene. Not that he needed the help.

Atticus darted toward him. Emerick dropped, kicking Atticus's legs out from under him. He landed hard enough that Emerick heard the air whoosh out of his lungs. Emerick leapt on top of him and lunged for the six-inch throwing knives still gripped in Atticus's right hand.

"Uh, Atticus?" Tobias asked. He held up his crystal screen, the pinhole camera mounted on its backside filming the battle.

"What!" Atticus ground out. His left hand came up, trying to grip Emerick by the throat. Emerick blocked and retaliated by punching Atticus's pretty face, splitting his lip. It felt good to get the drop on someone who could actually fight back against his powers. He was tired of sneaking through shadows, silencing the sounds all around and stabbing his opponents in the back or throwing them off cliffs.

"Darci's telling me to tell you to stop fighting. Oh, and smile." A flash of light appeared from the back of the crystal screen, blinding both of them.

"Tobias!" Atticus snarled.

"Making memories of freedom. Darci is going to love this. Atticus, the great lusty extraordinaire grappling with another guy."

Brax laughed.

Emerick punched Atticus in the ribs again. Atticus stiffened, his movements becoming less fluid. Emerick took the shot and grabbed at the knives in Atticus's fist. He slammed the back of his hand against the ground again, and again. Finally, the knives went skittering in all directions.

Atticus punched him in the side. Emerick responded with another blow to the man's jaw. "Working for women, Atticus? I always thought you'd end up on the bottom."

Atticus yelled, landing a wild punch to Emerick's jaw. He felt his teeth cut into his cheek and stars appeared in the vision of his right eye. Emerick blinked and realized he'd rolled backward off Atticus. His left arm hit the ground and pain radiated from his elbow to his fingertips, followed an instant later by the tingle of a numbed arm. He'd landed square on his funny bone. Head spinning and senses ablaze as Atticus's power closed around him, Emerick stumbled to his feet and right into the barrel of Brax's laser rifle.

"Shit, Brax," Emerick said as pain lanced across his forehead. "Point that elsewhere." He spun to face Atticus as another blade whipped through the air. He threw up his power again and the knife halted, dropping with a metal clang against the floor.

"Drop the knives," Brax ordered with a smile, pointing his rifle at Atticus.

Emerick turned to see Atticus advancing on him with yet

another set of knives gripped in each fist.

"Where the hell are you keeping all of those?" Emerick asked. Atticus lunged for him again, a promise of death in his eyes.

"I said drop them!" Brax shouted, the smile now gone from his face.

Atticus flicked a glance at him. A rope of pure Sin whipped out from Atticus like a viper striking its prey. Emerick felt the blood drain from his face. Brax's weapon never wavered.

"Cut the crap, *Luxurian*," he barked. "Or I'll shoot you here and now. Your powers can't touch me."

Emerick gave Brax a once over. He wasn't immune, was he? Atticus must have had the same hesitation as his power wavered. Emerick lunged just as Atticus struck with his venom. His aura crashing through the air. Instead of striking Brax, the full force of the psychic blow struck Emerick. He gasped as a true sense of Atticus's abilities ripped through his aura as though it didn't exist. Emerick was trained to use his powers with efficiency. Atticus used the pure force to accomplish what he wanted. Emerick lunged, bearing the *Luxurian* to the ground. He rolled with the movement and brought his arm around Atticus's throat and grabbed his wrist with the opposite hand.

"Game over," Emerick said, applying just enough pressure onto the carotid artery to make Atticus's vision waver but wouldn't make him pass out.

A dozen soldiers and officers had their side arms trained on them. Emerick released Atticus and backed away. A sense of satisfaction spread through him.

Atticus glared at Emerick. The bastard still looked ready to beat him senseless, death by laser fire be dammed. Emerick caught the flicker of another knife in Atticus's hand. He braced himself to defend again. Hadn't he won yet?

"Atticus," Tobias's voice was the only sound in the room. The other patrons had cleared out. "Darci says to stop it now."

"Who the hell is Darci?" Emerick panted. Damn, but fighting like this was a good workout. It definitely served to take the edge off his frayed temper.

"What was the 'or else?'" Atticus asked Tobias.

Tobias glanced up from his tablet, furrows appearing between his eyebrows. "Or else?"

"There's always an 'or else'," Atticus didn't lower his weapons, and his power threaded through the air, coiling around the onlookers, whose fingers itched to pull triggers.

Tobias cocked his head to the side as though he were listening to something far away. "She says you'll never get the chance to do the unmentionable thing that you did last Tuesday ever again."

Atticus growled. A muscle spasmed in his jaw a moment before he dropped the knife, got to his feet and raised his hands. He stepped close until his nose was inches from Emerick's. "We're not finished. I owe you for six months spent in rehabilitation and a lifetime of work under the twisted hands of your government."

"If your assassin had succeeded, you'd be dead," Emerick promised.

"Assassin?" Tobias repeated. "We're not here to assassinate anyone. We're here to join the cause. You know. Rebellion, add our skills to the team. Go freedom, right?"

Brax, thankfully, intervened, pushing Emerick away from the *Luxurian*. "Arrest those two," he ordered four of the closest soldiers. "The rest of you escort them to isolation."

"If I get stabbed for this," Tobias said as soldiers converged on him, "I am never forgiving you. Being your wingman sucks when you're out picking up men."

A soldier frisked Atticus and ripped off a specially designed bandolier from under his coat. There were slots for over a dozen knives. Most of them were still full.

"There are more in my boots," Atticus added. The soldier removed another three knives from each of his calf-high boots. "And the soles." He bent down and took out a knife from the toes of each boot and handed them over.

Emerick exchanged a surprised glance with Brax. How many knives was he packing? He didn't trust the man's sudden acquiescence. Whoever this Darci was had a lot of sway over him.

"You break that tablet and you'll be breaking six years of work from a genius," Tobias warned as another soldier frisked him and stripped him of several pieces of complicated gadgetry. Tobias turned to Atticus. "If we get tortured by a *Industria*, I'm not making more bandages to heal your sorry ass."

Atticus wiped a dribble of blood from the corner of his mouth. "Relax. They don't have a *Industria* here. It'll be the old fashioned way if they decide to interrogate you." He allowed two soldiers to cuff his hands behind his back. "Emerick," he said as the soldier's marched him away. "Who from the Magistrate would try and assassinate someone under your protection?"

"An idiot," Emerick replied.

"You know I'm not," Atticus added before he and his companion were led into the lift.

Emerick picked up one of the knives Atticus had carried. Paper thin, perfectly balanced and incredibly sharp. It was a weapon designed for stealth, skill, and speed. An interesting choice. He'd underestimated Atticus. He would not do it again, but he had to concede the man was right. Atticus wasn't that stupid.

Emerick knew what the City Magistrate did to keep their Sins compliant with their wishes. Atticus would have been given every cause to hate them. There was absolutely no reason why he would attack Fionn. Hell, Tobias had even said they were here to 'join the cause.' He figured the loud-mouthed *Invidia* had told the truth.

Shit. Now he was back to square one. Someone trying to kill Fionn and the one and only true suspect was his father, locked behind his armies, his gates, and his overprotected military office.

Emerick took a deep breath, and the skin over his ribs stung. He lifted his borrowed shirt and revealed three deep cuts across his left side. Had he even seen Atticus swipe at him there?

Brax moved next to him. "He moves a lot faster than you do."

Emerick sensed this was only the first of many contests to come before the end.

The end of what? Nothing good. It was as though Atticus's presence here, during the battle, and now in Fionn's compound, signaled the beginning of a new phase in the war. What was it his companion, Tobias, had said? To join the rebellion, add their skills to the cause.

"He didn't do it," Emerick said to Brax, who'd come to stand next to him. "If Atticus thinks something is worth protecting, he'll fight to the death to keep it safe. He wouldn't come here without a damned good reason. He was trained by the Magistrate to kill by seduction. If he wanted Fionn dead, she would be and she would have walked into the trap without a second thought. We're not in the clear yet."

Brax went back to his tray of uneaten food and used one of the throwing knives he'd picked up to spear the last sausage. "Don't let it get to you. The place is on lockdown, Fionn is healing and alive. Only thing left to do is to wait for new orders. You're under arrest too, by the way," Brax said around his mouthful of sausage.

"Locking me up won't stop someone else from trying to finish what the assassin couldn't," Emerick snapped. He wasn't in the mood for Brax's games or his smart-ass comments.

"No, it won't." Brax finished off the rest of the sausage and wiped the blade clean on his pants leg. "But it will keep *you*, technically a traitor, under lock and key."

Emerick narrowed his eyes at the soldier.

"Besides, you're bleeding all over the place." He waved a hand and the remainder of the soldiers approached. "After the stunt you pulled in medical earlier, I figure the only way to keep you from killing yourself is to lock you up and send a nurse down to stitch you back together."

"You are not going to do that until I find the bastard that tried to kill her."

Brax swore. "I want you at one hundred percent when this breaks open. James doesn't like you and neither does Fionn. When Admiral Tysek pulls his head out of his ass and attacks, I want you and any man willing to fight ready." He took the cuffs from the soldier hands and snapped them around Emerick's wrists himself.

"Admiral Tysek isn't a fool, Braxton," Emerick said as he allowed soldiers to take him by the arms. "He'll attack the moment he thinks he has the advantage. Right now he does."

"We'll know when he starts to mobilize on the front," Brax said. "Fionn will need you at her side before the end. I'm going to make sure you don't do something stupid. Take him away," he ordered.

"This is something stupid," Emerick shouted over his shoulder. No point in fighting. Not when the third soldier had a rifle aimed at his chest as they marched him away, toward the same lift that had disappeared with Atticus moments ago.

7

The soft glow of daylight lamps against Fionn's skin made her to want to sigh into blissful relaxation. She hadn't slept so hard or so well in years. She took a deep breath, trying to savor the limp heaviness threading through her body.

"Easy," a soft voice said, breaking the tranquility like rain on a sunny day. "Doctor Blanc said to take it slow."

Fionn opened her eyes and blinked against the gentle glow from the display panels. Her medical history listed across a large crystal screen in complicated notes. A few words stood out, Nano-poison, filter time: eight hours. A list of anti-toxins and their doses. She turned her head, her unbraided hair rasping against the rough pillow beneath her.

"James," she acknowledged the man at her side. Was that her thin and weak voice? She cast her thoughts back. So much rage. Had she been out of control? A flicker of sharpness, of danger—of fear, sparked within her.

"Commander," he responded. "Time is fifteen forty. Enemy forces have been silent since the attack."

She let out a short laugh, more and more of that luxury feeling abandoning her to be replaced with the burden of duty. "No they haven't. Admiral Tysek wouldn't let something like nearly killing me give him a few minutes rest. He's been up to something. Find out what it is." She tried to sit up, and her vision spotted with black dots. After a few breaths the moment passed.

A whirring caught her attention. Two red tubes were attached to a machine, their ends in either of her arms. She recognized it as a filtering machine. The nano-poison must not be completely out of her system yet. That explained the lightheadedness.

"There hasn't been any news," James replied. He had a hand out as though he were going to help her. She saw the thick gauze wrapped around his palms.

"What happened to your hands?" she asked.

He pulled his hand back, his clear blue eyes meeting hers without fear. "You didn't want anyone to touch you, but you wouldn't have made it to medical without the help."

"I—my aura." She took a deep breath and the flickering spark of anger rose again, lending her strength. A few more of the events leading to her internment at the hospital gained clarity. Most distinct, she remembered ordering James to keep his hands off her.

"Dammit, James! I know the limits of my abilities. I know what I can do to someone when those abilities suddenly have no limits. It's a miracle I didn't reduce you to a bucket of guts and glory."

"My apologies, sir," he said testily. "But you hold this army and these people together. I don't. I wasn't about to let you die out of fear of your supernatural capabilities."

"Was anyone else hurt?" she asked. After that first bite of the knife, she knew she'd killed the boy who delivered the poison. Everything after still remained mired in a scarlet haze of blood lust and unquenchable rage. She could have left them all untouched, or she could have left mass slaughter in her wake.

James hesitated. He stood from the chair by her bed and faced away from her.

"Today of all days," she said, too quiet. "Do not try my patience."

Patience. The thought shot through the red fog like a blaze of brilliant light. *His* voice, *his* touch. Gods, she'd tried to kill *him*, and failed. *Again.*

She felt the rage, hot, wild, and hungry. A shiver snaked into her core, fully replacing the tranquility she awoke to with the sweetest and most dangerous anger, absent from her for as long as he. Her soul began to stir after a long winter of hibernation.

James rounded on her.

"I had no idea last night we were hunting the man who'd made it possible for half your army to perish, would be the same man who would save your life."

"*He's still here?*" A series of chemical responses, panic, fear, apprehension, the ever-present rage, sharp as glass, raced through her veins only to be filtered out by the machine. The last time she'd allowed him close, she was captured, tortured, and then half her army and who knew how many refugees were torn to pieces.

James took a breath. "He's in the brig with a *Luxurian* and an *Invidia* he ferreted out after—" James gestured at her. "I can't tell you how much I hate to say it, but if he hadn't breached our security, you'd be dead."

"Three powerful hostiles, an assassination attempt, and yet no alarms were raised. I want our security checked and then double checked. Over a thousand free souls and just one *Appetence* with the wrong intentions could jeopardize that freedom. If you don't already know how dangerous some of them can be without trying—" she glanced at his hands "—then you have sorely underestimated our enemy." *And your commander.*

James moved as though to place his hands on the back of the chair next to the bed, but thought better of it. "I understand. Other than those three, there haven't been any other break-ins. The front has been quiet."

Quiet? So soon after a battle? They hadn't won the war yet. And who was giving the orders? Brax? Carter? Hopefully Carter, Brax was too cavalier, but at the moment any one of them would be better than James who seemed to have lost his nerve. She'd have to figure out how to keep him off the front lines until his brain reconnected.

"Who's working Command?"

"Carter has point. He's reporting no movement."

Doubtful, they had just taken a huge swath of land from the Magistrate. "Think, James. What about the front, the flanks, anything?" she asked. "What about that report we received, the concentration of craft over the east mountain slope?"

James frowned. "The front reports no attacks, or activity. Same on the flanks. The extra patrols I ordered on the east side of the mountain haven't reported anything unusual. It's quiet."

"And that doesn't worry you? Tysek has had—" she checked her history chart "—six hours to recuperate and you've just given him that."

She'd bet her entire command Tysek was up to something. Just because they weren't receiving reports about it, didn't mean that sneaky bastard hadn't already subverted her defenses. He'd ordered her death, and sent a child to do it. He knew her well. She wouldn't have suspected an innocent. He would have counted on her death but what about his son? Would he have factored Emerick's sudden appearance or had he ordered Emerick here? Was this another ploy to win her over? Tysek had once offered her a position in his command. She'd told him to take it to hell. The bastard reacted by ordering the torture to continue. A man that cold would never think twice about killing her, but she wasn't dead. Tysek must have sent Emerick here to confuse her. Whatever he had done to her saved her life. Why save her now instead of finishing the job?

She wasn't about to fall into the hole Emerick's betrayal had left in her.

She closed her eyes and filtered through what she could remember of his saving her. A door slowly closing, her awareness aroused. She couldn't have stopped the rage breaking loose to kill him. The nano-poison was designed to increase the use of her power, as the little parasites used her unique energy to kill her faster, destroying cells, tissues, and finally entire organs. Lashing out at him had done nothing to release the pressure building inside her. Yet his power had frozen hers like a creeping frost, battling against the wildfire and overcoming it. She'd demanded his death, and he'd fought against that demand and forced her to submit to life.

A less than steady breath escaped her. She pushed herself into a straighter position. The needles in her arms connecting her to the machine pulled painfully. A feeling of imprisonment captured her and long-dead panic returned with a vengeance. She couldn't be here chained to a hospital bed. Her place was at her command, now more than ever.

"Get the doctor," she ordered, focusing on remaining calm. He gave her a considering glance, and she returned it with a glare of her own. She wasn't recovered, but staying out of the line of fire was not an option. Her enemies had to know, without a doubt, that they could not stop her.

James straightened and exited with a salute that was lacking in its normal energy. Minutes lengthened, and the whirring of the machine became like a metronome ticking away time with every change in its cycle. James wouldn't normally take this long. She glanced around her room, reading her medical chart more thoroughly. The room had taken a beating; scars of her power had left jagged burn marks that stopped at the points where Emerick's power had intervened. Even now, she could feel the echoing clash of her power with his. She forced muscles that wanted to clench to relax.

The door opened. James and Brax entered, along with the head of medical.

"You shouldn't be sitting up," the doctor chided. "Not with this machine hooked up. Break one connection and you could have all your blood pumped onto the floor in a few minutes."

"I'm fine, Doctor Blanc," Fionn responded.

The woman shook her head. "I can't believe you survived. The toxin was self-replicating until Emerick barged his way in here and shut it down." She pressed something against the crook of her elbow and sudden nausea gripped Fionn.

"If I see you back here again anytime soon," Doctor Blanc

threatened, "I'm going to chain you to this bed."

"I don't plan on being back."

"That's code for keep the bed open and your scanner handy," Brax said, giving the doctor a playful wink.

Doctor Blanc didn't laugh as she continued her work. In moments the blood cycling through the machine drained back into Fionn's body, and the tubes were removed.

"When do you want to see him?" Brax asked.

"When I'm damn good and ready." She didn't have to ask who he meant. Of all her officers and personnel, only Brax would be brazen enough to confront her with Emerick, her once-upon-a-time lover. She threw back the covers.

James sucked in a breath and turned about-face.

"Commander," Brax said with approval. "Who knew *that* body was under your fatigues?"

Fionn swore at him but didn't bother covering up. She'd been dressed in a short tank that ended at her ribs and a pair of clean white panties which served to show off the several scars that crisscrossed her torso, legs and calves.

"Doctor Blanc, some pants please," she requested.

"Yes, sir," the woman said and slipped out of the small room.

Brax flashed Fionn a smile. "No wonder you have that man tied up in knots."

She swore at him again. "Quit ogling me and get over here." She swung her legs over the side of the bed and more spots appeared in her vision. After a few deep breaths, the spots vanished. She grabbed Brax's huge forearm to steady herself as she stood.

"Commander!" Doctor Blanc cried from the doorway. "You sit your ass back down and take this in steps. Don't you dare rush through all the work we put into keeping you alive."

Fionn straightened. Her body felt weak and stiff as though she'd taken a beating. A beating she could handle, and the stiffness only served to tell her she was still alive. There was work to do, people whose protection she had to secure.

"Give your attention to one of my men who's in worse

shape than I." Fionn said. With Brax's support she made her way to the doctor and took the pair of pants and slipped them on.

"Fionn—" James started, turning back around.

"Don't even think about trying to order me into a sick-bed," Fionn threatened him. A tongue of temper colored her aura. "We're in the middle of a war that could turn against us at any moment. I grew up under the whips of Magistrate law. I won't let a failed assassination attempt keep me from our mission."

She dropped Brax's arm as her aura condensed with her frustration. Using him as a support would only give him slices along his arms at this point. She hadn't meant to reveal details of her dark past or her fears of the future. Letting slip those details would also expose that her drive to challenge the Magistrate might not be entirely fueled by the decisions of a sane person. Maybe they weren't, but she'd managed to keep thousands of refugees safe, had rebuilt the lives they had lost, and maybe had given them chances at new ones. That couldn't count for nothing.

"I need those reports," she said as she moved past James toward the door. The stab wound strained, but a slight limp and the promise of another scar were small badges for having escaped death again. "Have them sent to my quarters."

"Yes, sir," he answered quietly.

Fionn opened the door and stepped into the crowded hospital ward. The whole medical bay silenced at her emergence. Those who could came to attention and saluted. Nurses paused in their work. A woman cradling a solider much too young to have lost his life met Fionn's gaze with one of grief.

Fionn straightened her shoulders and despite the stiffness all over her body or the pain in her hip, strode to the woman. She knelt and laid a hand on the woman's arm.

"What was his name?" she asked.

The mother's chin lifted with the resolution of someone who knew too many pains. "Geoff," she answered.

"Geoff made it possible for thousands to live in freedom. We are in his debt, and in yours." Fionn squeezed the woman's arm and stood. In silence she strode out of the medical ward. The walk was long to the lift that would take her to the fifth level and her living quarters, but she accomplished it with straight shoulders and a head held high. Brax followed closely, along with two other guards. Word of her survival would spread from medical and reach the deepest levels within minutes. In an hour the entire compound would know she lived and walked again. From there it was only a matter of time before Tysek's spies told him of her survival. She expected that soon after he'd hear about the execution of his son, and she hoped he trembled in his shiny black boots when the news reached him.

She pressed her thumb to the key pad on her door and it opened on silent hydraulics. Her bed was perfectly pressed and made up in the corner. The, large desk and work area were studded with crystal screens showing maps, strategy, and lists of active duty soldiers. An ever scrolling list of the dead blinked a message that it had been updated.

Brax pushed past her and quickly checked the small kitchen and bathroom area to the right.

She counted another thirteen reported dead since the last count had been posted. She even recognized a few names. Geoff's was there. He had been eighteen, her age when she started this campaign.

"All clear," Brax reported, his voice soft.

"Thank you," she said and walked toward the bathroom and her closet of military clothes, uniforms, camouflage gear, and special equipment. With her weapons in their appropriate holsters, she shrugged into her uniform jacket. Her rank was embroidered in black over her right breast with the Insurgency's emblem, a wolf ringed by the Latin phrase: *In potestatem noctis sicut lupus.*

A soft chime signaled the door. Brax opened it and she heard him greet James.

"She's in there," Brax said.

A moment later James appeared behind her in the mirror. In the reflection she noticed permanent lines starting to appear between his eyebrows.

"You look like shit," she said, wiping her face with a rough towel and turning to him.

He held out a crystal screen to her, despite his fairly useless hands. "It's been a rough day in the Insurgency."

She took it and leaned back against the sink. The first report was a set of images of the same wreckage from early this morning. The wreckage no longer blazed with fire and the mountainside was brightly lit. Her eyes were drawn to the darkness behind the debris. By the angle of light, she should have been able to see everything against the cliff face. Instead, she saw, if possible, an even larger spot of black. The previous images had shown flames arcing in a crescent *away* from that darkness.

"What is that?" She pointed at the shadow's deepest part.

James's frown deepened, and he moved closer to see the image. "No one reported it."

"Send a survey team. Whatever is there, I bet Tysek is after it. If we've shot down two carriers over it, then it's a high interest position."

The next reports were normal. Lists of dead, wounded, and active duty soldiers. The numbers were better than she'd projected. The final report was a squadron who'd heard wolf howls during the day from the direction of the Magistrate's retreat lines.

"Did you look at this one?" she asked, reading the notes. "'Wolf howls. No concern.'"

"The wolves have been hunting closer and closer to inhabited areas over the last winter."

Fionn didn't like the shadow of doubt growing in her mind. "What else sounds like a wolf howl?"

James didn't answer right away. "Hellions."

"Exactly. We've never been able to successfully get a drone shot from over Tysek's complex. He might not have unleashed his entire Hellion force last night like we hoped. Add a few more men to that watch."

"What about techs?" James asked. "If they are Hellions, sending more troops will only invite a slaughter. With techs they could erect another barrier."

"Don't send any senior officers. We can't afford for any of them to fall into Tysek's dungeon."

"I agree. I'll send two in addition to the six already there," James's shoulders straightened more. He seemed relieved that her earlier displeasure had abated. It had, but his desire to protect her or look after her best interests instead of the people's irked her. The people's protection was their first duty.

"Fionn—" he started.

"James," she kept her voice down so the guards wouldn't hear. "Please, don't. When I needed you, you were there. I don't know if I can be that for you." *Or for anyone.* Not after what she would have to do.

What she'd taken for friendliness from him ran deeper than she gave him credit for. He wanted to be closer to her. Perhaps he even wanted a relationship. There might be a chance, but then there was Emerick. His presence changed everything.

"I know," he said, but he didn't drop the issue. "You're the best of us. You shouldn't have to be alone."

Fionn moved to walk past him. She hesitated, giving him the chance if he wanted to stop her. He didn't take the chance, or didn't see it. Another would have. Instead he looked down and let her pass. His nearness broke the space of her aura, an aura charged with enough energy to make him flinch.

"When the time comes," he said, stopping her with his voice before she entered the other room, "I will still be here."

Then he nodded sharply and saluted. "I'll see to the patrols and get the techs on their way." He hesitated. "You'll be visiting the brig?"

"I promised him he'd be dead if he ever returned."

"You don't need to do this."

Fionn's ire grew and she couldn't keep her voice from shaking with the intensity of the power coursing through her. "We agreed, James. I perform executions, no one else. You have your orders, I have mine."

8

Emerick straightened in his shackles. Something had woken him. He groaned. He'd been resting with his bare back against the six-inch-thick plastic, and his skin had become stuck to it. Sitting up so fast felt like he'd ripped the stitches the nurse had painstakingly sewn into his back.

A quick glance around the plexiglass cell, its walls several inches thick, told him nothing had changed. He was still locked in the underbelly of the compound with his new companions for comfort. The rattle of the chains echoed loud in the enclosed cell, just like every other noise.

"Get excited," Tobias said, from across the cell where the boy was likewise chained to the wall. "You are the jumpiest person I've ever met. Weird for a guy whose supposed to be the epitome of all things patient, *Patientia*."

"Tobias," Atticus said with his eyes still closed. "Shut up."

The *Invidia* glared at his companion. "Is that what you do when you get arrested? Sleep?"

"Not usually," Atticus answered.

"Been arrested often?" Emerick asked. He twisted carefully, trying to see if he had ripped his stitches. When the nurse arrived, she'd had a bitch of a time trying to get the bleeding stopped. Emerick hadn't realized how badly his clash with Fionn had wounded him. Fifteen sutures across his chest, a few more on his back and legs, another several from Atticus's blades to his ribs. Hours later he still felt like he'd been put in a meat grinder.

Atticus opened his eyes and stared at Emerick. "Not arrested, punished. Turns out I don't like authority figures."

"Make sure you don't tell Commander Fionn that," Emerick replied. "How did you get out?"

"The city or its dungeons?" Atticus's stare was unnerving.

"Both."

"I met a woman," he answered.

Tobias let out a snort, not looking up from his examination of the shackles around his wrists. "I wouldn't call Darci just a woman. She had you from the moment you met. I could read it in your aura."

Atticus continued, "She wanted revenge. The Magistrate had culled her sister and used her as training practice for their soldiers. Not just any soldier, a special breed."

Hellions. They were monstrous, infused with some kind of tech or chemical that turned a normal man into a savage cannibal. What the Magistrate had created were so inhuman they were given the name Hellion. Undesirables, those members of a city or community deemed to be irrelevant or sinful in nature were sometimes given to the Hellions as fodder. Emerick had never been to a training of that sort, but he'd heard the stories and spoken to the officers who'd watched. It was madness, in raw animal form.

"I saved her life, and she's been saving mine ever since."

"So we should expect her soon," Emerick said.

Tobias threw the chain attached to his manacle down. "Primitive, yet effective contraptions," he pouted.

"I thought you'd follow your father's fast track to leadership," Atticus said.

"I met a woman," Emerick answered. "I was sent to kill her, and I couldn't do it."

"I heard." Atticus smiled. "So things didn't work out between you and Eliza?"

Emerick looked away. The day Atticus had been expelled and sent to the city for focus training, he and Emerick had fought. It had been over Eliza, a *Carita*, who'd tricked both of them into pursuing her by playing on their adolescence and naïveté. After the resulting fight, any innocence they'd had was shattered.

"No," Emerick answered. "No, Eliza was marked as Undesirable the next year, for conduct unbecoming a Virtue."

"The Magistrate is slaughtering more and more people. The citizens don't believe in the Enlightenment. Any hint of rebellion is being crushed and it's happening by the hundreds," Atticus said. "Those who can are escaping the cities." Atticus didn't have to say what was happening to those who didn't escape. Emerick knew about the mass graves filled with millions of dead that dotted the post-American countryside.

Emerick stood, attempting to stretch his legs and shake off the horror he felt. "Rebel cells are popping up in all the rural areas. If there's anything sustainable, colonies are sure to be found. There's enough gold and oil here to keep us going for centuries."

Atticus nodded. "There are a lot of rumors about Fionn circulating in the cities. We chose to come here specifically because she fights back. She doesn't hide from tyranny. She's hidden this place very well. We searched all winter to find it."

Tobias snorted. "Who searched? I hope you know how hard it was to find the exact coordinates. This far north the sun doesn't shine for almost a month straight. Using efficiency solar panels so sporadically pretty much fries them. We got stuck living in an igloo. Burning everything we could find just to stay warm."

"Most refugees searching for the compound don't make it more than a week after the first snowfall." Emerick said, genuinely impressed they'd survived.

A prick of something pinched the edge of his aura. It was faint, but steadier now. His mouth went dry and his hands curled into fists.

"The commander is on her way," Atticus said. He stood and stretched his hands overhead. "And she's pissed off, on an epic level."

"I know," Emerick said. "She promised she'd kill me if ever she saw me again."

"And still you came to save her life?" Tobias asked.

The sensation of Fionn closing in made him feel like a fox sniffed out by a wolf. Her ire trailed like the tips of fingernails across his aura, even from this distance. He closed his eyes and waited. She was in the lift now, hurtling toward him.

Minutes later, the cell door creaked open. The jailors unshackled him. One held a laser rifle aimed at his chest.

"This way," the one with the keys said.

"Keys!" Tobias exclaimed. "Yes, that's it. So old fashioned in these modern days but quite effective."

"Quiet," Atticus ordered. To Emerick he said, "See you on the other side."

Emerick didn't bother replying.

He was led to a dark cell, concrete on all sides instead of light and glass. His wrists were attached to different chains, tying him to the center of the isolated interrogation room. The jailors left. The one with the rifle backed out, keeping his weapon trained on Emerick's chest until a thick concrete door slid into place turning the cell into a tomb.

Would she kill him? Would she hesitate?

He felt her emerge from the lift, her aura immediately raked over his with enough rage to make him shiver. He let his aura flow beyond the walls of the cell, acknowledging her. The cell door opened again with a metallic grinding. She strode around the door with a limping step, but her shoulders were straight. The skin-tight pants accentuated her curves and his chest tightened at the sight.

He met her blank gaze, but saw the swirling heat of emotion behind her eyes.

Her power struck him. Pain sparked along his entire left side. She followed, stepping inside the cell with the purposeful stride of command. His gut clenched.

How long would it take her to finish him?

The door rolled shut after her, leaving them alone.

Where were her guards? He was dangerous. Hadn't he

proved that already? She should be accompanied by at least one. Especially if they thought mere chains would hold him.

"You came back," she said and stepped into the light. Gods, he wanted to rip the jacket from her shoulders and let her tightly secured hair down and run his fingers through it.

Another slash of energy cut against his legs. It was a blow meant to send him to his knees, but he fought to remain standing. "You were dying."

"You came here to kill me," she accused. "Again."

So his father had told her that much. "I was sent to kill you two years ago, but I couldn't. I came back to save your life, and slaughter the son of a bitch who tried to kill you."

Her anger and rage filled the room. Bands of power constricted his chest and it became difficult to breathe. Her rage intensified, raking with the sharpness of her emotion not quite cutting into him, but close, oh so close. The familiar desire for more rose in him.

His breath came out in a stutter, not a release, but not begging for it yet.

"Why?" she demanded.

She ripped holes in the shield of his aura as though he'd cloaked himself in gauze. He pushed back, fighting to extend the moment, forcing the walls between them to shatter.

"You know why," he panted.

"Liar," she snarled, and he felt lines of suture on his back rip open. He cringed, gritting his teeth against the indulgent sounds wanting to slip past his lips. "My scouts saw you walk out Tysek's main gate unharmed."

"My father's *Industria* doesn't have to leave a mark in order to torture his prisoners. I don't know why he released me." His vision blurred as her power whipped over him. A moment exists when the body begins to absorb the pain, and it becomes something else, something sweeter, like being stung by a bee in order to get the golden honey. Emerick felt himself sliding into that moment. His heart thundered in his chest and his pulse thrummed deep in his core.

When he could see again, she had moved closer, but still

out of his reach.

"You betrayed me. You betrayed the people. Do you know how many refugees were torn to pieces because of you?"

Emerick's own anger broke the sweet trance he'd been sliding into. "I defied every order my father ever gave me to protect you. I'd kill him a thousand times over because of what he's done to our people."

"They are not your people," she hissed. "If you really wanted him dead, he would be." Her power cascaded over him like a shower of sparks and he cried out. He threw his power against hers in reaction and the two opposing forces twined together.

"So would you," he replied. He'd waited, letting her have the free shot at him. She hadn't taken it. He strained against the shackles, as he had once before, in his father's dungeon, when he couldn't break free to save her. Patience coursed down his arms into the chain links, freezing the molecules as her anger snapped over him again. The links shattered, and the pieces plinked sharply against the floor.

He lunged for her, locking his fingers around her upper arms and pulling her against him. Tiny slices and cuts appeared along his hands and arms as she struggled against him.

"I gave you the chance to kill me," he growled into her ear, as he pulled her hair free of its tie and buried his hand in it. He crushed his lips against hers and their power clashed, twined and broke the last barriers remaining between them. It was like trying to force oil and water to become one, and succeeding.

Her teeth dug into his lip, drawing blood from the cut she'd made earlier. He broke free, gasping, and smiled.

"You waited two years." She twisted, dropping out of his arms, and straightened a few feet away, her fists raised in front of her.

Now they were getting somewhere. "I would have waited longer, but you were dying."

Her eyes narrowed and she attacked. Her rage swept his knees out from under him. Her kick, aimed at his chest, laid him out flat.

"You're an idiot," she said, standing over him.

"Then kill me," he invited. "If you can."

A scream ripped from her throat and she straddled him, the flat palm of her hand finding his cheek. Her power burned through his bones, urging him to give in to that sweetness ripping him apart.

He wanted to.

Instead, he wrapped a leg around her back and, using his elbow, twisted and brought her beneath him. She struggled, but his hips grinding against hers pinned her. She gasped.

"Keep doing that," he snarled softly into her ear, "and I won't hold back." He nipped her earlobe. Her shudder had heat traveling downward in a single rush. Her hand flashed out and grabbed the back of his neck, warmth searing where she touched. She rose up to meet his lips with hers.

She kissed him with all the hunger and desire he'd held in check, unleashing whatever he'd held back. Gods, how could he have stayed away from her, from this bliss? Two years seemed like an eternity. With each undulation, each scratch from her nails, he plummeted toward another set of shackles, these of her making.

"*More*," he demanded as he had years ago. His hands ripped the stiff-pressed jacket from her shoulders; the three black buttons popped and clattered against the floor. He could feel the warm trickle of blood down his spine from reopened wounds and didn't care. He'd let her flay him alive as long as she didn't stop.

"No," she said. "Emry, stop."

He shuddered, unwilling to claw his way back from her, to separate his aura from hers. He wasn't sure if he could. She demanded, and already he'd taken enough. He wasn't dead, and there would be other times to break the bonds of her command.

His hands fisted against the concrete, and he dragged a ragged breath into his lungs. He buried his head against her bare shoulder, breathing her in. He kissed the spot where her neck curved to meet her shoulder, then her jaw, her lips, and her forehead.

"Gods, Fi," he whispered. "I'll do whatever you desire. Next time don't ask me to stop. Because I won't." He drew back, hovering on all fours above her, aching from the distance.

"I came here to kill you." There was pain her eyes, not the pain that scarred over with pink skin, but the kind that wept unending, from wounds to the soul.

"Then do it," he said, knowing now that she wouldn't.

The sound of dripping liquid caused her to flinch. She glanced at the noise and gasped. "You're bleeding."

"I know," he answered. Moments ago she was angry enough to rip him apart with her mind, and now she was worried about a little blood?

She pushed against his chest and he let her up, helping her to her feet. His legs were still shaking, and he was glad for the thick fatigues he wore that helped to hide other tell-tale signs of her effect on him. She turned him around and pushed him against the wall. The cold concrete made him realize he'd lost his shirt. How did that happen?

Blood ran freely between his shoulder blades, each drop traced down his spine. Now that her aura had released him, he realized there were far too many burning lines across his back. Maybe he had taken them too far.

"How did this happen?" she asked. Her fingers probed the places on his back and ribs that had been stitched together.

"You, the *Luxurian.*" He hissed as she touched a particularly tender spot. "Don't go picking a fight with Atticus. He's wicked fast and his knives are sharp."

"What the hell is wrong with you?" she shouted, her voice reverberating too loud in the cell.

"Yeah, it was stupid to try and save you when I wasn't sure if my power would shut off the M.I.K.E.—" he hissed as she pressed something against his back.

"How bad were you bleeding before they stitched you up?"

"Dammit that stings, and not in a good way."

"*Emerick,*" she warned him, pressing harder against the

wound.

"I don't know," he turned to look at her. She had wadded up the jacket he'd ripped off her and was using it to stanch the bleeding. While leaning on him, she used her fingers to key-up her wrist display. "I wasn't paying attention. I was trying to keep you safe and the compound secure."

"Like hell you were." The display blinked to life. "Brax," she bit out.

"*Commander?*" Brax answered.

"Get me a nurse."

"*Damn, Commander, what did you do to him this time?*" Brax's voice issued over the comm.

"Just do it, and open the bloody cell door." Emerick noticed she kept her temper in check, despite her frustration.

"Thank you," he said after a moment of silence.

"For what?" she snapped and the end of her anger sizzled up his spine.

He sucked in a breath. "If you don't stop, I'm going to—"

"Do what?" James's voice cut through the charged cell air like lightning through a storm.

"James," Fionn said, and the undertone of her voice changed, sharpening into disappointment. Emerick would have smirked at her first officer in triumph, but as she turned the rough fabric of the jacket shifted, grinding into him like sandpaper. He flinched.

"You're needed in command." James presented the report to Fionn with all the stiffness of a brick wall.

Emerick sensed the moment between them ending, that he would be locked up again until she was ready to face him once more. He couldn't let that happen. She'd work herself into another, perhaps more determined rage and then beat on him until he *did* die from the wounds. This was war, and even if she did kill him there were other more important things she needed to know. His father wanted whatever was hidden on that mountain side, and if he or his overlords desired it bad enough, Fionn's devoted army or her anger would not be enough to protect the Insurgency from what might be coming.

A cold sweat broke over him. His father had planned the perfect distraction. Any harm to Fionn would directly wound her army. It meant the victory she'd won last night might have startled Tysek, but he hadn't used the formidable forces at his disposal to retaliate, just a child with a poisoned knife. His father was mustering his strength for something else.

"Fi, we need to talk."

"It can wait." She pressed the jacket over his wounds and her power licked at him again, eliciting a groan from him. If she wasn't leaning on him so hard, he might have slid down the wall.

Brax entered, escorting a team of medical personnel, he stopped. "Holy shit, Commander."

"Get a transfusion running," the orderly directed his assistants as they rushed over. "What happened?" he asked.

"You ever pissed off a woman?" Emerick asked. "The Magistrate isn't—"

Fionn pushed the jacket harder against his back. "You're about to do it again," she murmured.

"Bring it," Emerick challenged.

"Don't tempt me," she snarled, before handing the duties of sewing his skin back together to the medical staff. "Keep him under until I return. I'm not done with him yet."

"Yes, sir," said the orderly.

Emerick spun around, knocking the sedative out of the orderly's hand. "Like hell."

"Restrain him," Fionn ordered.

The soldiers accompanying the medical staff tackled him to a floor that was as cold and terrible as their commander's voice. Emerick could have fought, but he hesitated, watching the woman who would be his savior or executioner depending on her mood. She changed, her features remained the same, but the sizzle of her power drew away from his and she disentangled herself. As the distance grew between the touch of their auras, she became frigid and closed off.

Her laying into him minutes ago had been the release of rage and emotion she couldn't reveal to her people. He caught the concern on James's face, the quick flick of his eyes up and down her body, searching for injuries. Even with only his merely human senses he could feel the raw power she'd unleashed, and its sudden disappearance. She took the report from James's hands, scrolling through a set of images. Her jaw clenched, a muscle twitched the more she focused.

Emerick didn't resist as the guards pinned his arms and legs. The medical staff descended on him like white crows upon a body, needles pinched between their fingers.

"When were these taken?" Fionn asked.

"Fifteen minutes ago," James responded.

Fionn was already gone, her wild hair, the snap of her wrath. The shadow he'd seen on the mountain pressed close in his mind. He needed to tell her before whatever his father prepared for the Insurgency was unleashed. The first prick of a needle brought a cold numbness to the burning skin on his back. It was nothing compared to the cold fear gathering around his heart.

9

"How many dead?" Fionn asked as she paced in front of the long wall of crystal screens in the command room. She tapped on a section of the screen, keying the magnification, and searched in vain for any of her uniforms among the tree line. But there were none, as she knew deep in the pit of her belly that there would not be. Not with Hellions out there.

She resumed pacing, seeing only bits and pieces through the aerial view of dense tree cover, failing to find the bodies of her men. The enemy she saw were blurs, swarming under the dark canopy with restless movement.

"Another seventy or so," one of her officers answered. His tone grated on her. These weren't just numbers. These were people with loved ones left behind.

"We are in a state of emergency, gentlemen. We cannot afford lose seventy soldiers to oversight. Why weren't we alerted?"

Brax stood. "We were. We didn't react."

James frowned. "The wolf howls."

Fionn wanted to growl, strike, lash out, *something*. Admiral Tysek had orchestrated this perfectly. *That bastard.* He'd crushed the resolve of her men by trying to kill her and now he'd shattered the lines those men had worked to create. She thought her trick with the wall had eradicated his Hellion hordes, or a large percentage of them. On the screen were double, maybe triple what her men had faced the night before. It was hard to get an exact count with the tree cover. That many bodies would pile up at her walls as they died running into them and the Hellions would scale the corpses of their fellows to get in to the compound.

The sudden, very real possibility that the compound would be overrun by Magistrate forces weighed heavy on her. They could be infested by a breed of soldier that didn't have morals, and who possessed a thirst for violence she'd never encountered, except in herself. Yet, Tysek's monsters waited at the tree line. They'd broken her first line of defense and done nothing else. Beyond that line, Tysek's tech scramblers made it impossible to predict how big a force he sent against them. She wanted desperately to believe that the mass of Hellions was a farce. This had to be a scare tactic.

Could she be wrong? What if Tysek had developed some new weapon, as she had? She couldn't see the great and fearful Tysek sending a mass of confusion her way, not a man that controlled and strict. He simply didn't have that many monsters at his disposal.

Or did he?

"Order a flyover," she commanded.

The order was quickly given and one of her airmen reported that he was en route to the coordinates.

"They must be waiting for an invitation," Brax said. "I don't think they're simply hiding in the foliage. We can see them just fine on the perimeter."

"*Approaching target,*" the flyover pilot said over the comm from the cockpit of his single passenger stealth craft, a costly machine. "*No, sign of—wait—there. Transmitting footage, over.*"

The screen flickered and video from the craft appeared across the wall.

Fionn stared at the three dimensional projection of the valley she'd left barren in the wake of the last battle. Parts of it still smoldered small streams of smoke trailed upward. At the edge of the tree line, between the thin pines as they crowded each other, she spotted them. Some foamed at the mouth.

Others were drenched in blood, the simmering rage on their faces unmistakable: Hellions.

"Shit," she whispered under her breath. There were more than she'd thought. It wasn't a farce, and the scare tactic was working.

Still, the niggling pinch of doubt lodged in her mind. Tysek had purpose in every movement. There was a reason he had drawn her surveillance here.

A distraction?

She pulled her personal crystal tablet toward her across the table and opened the report she'd been given before the child had stabbed her. The image of the craft wreckage bothered her, the flames again catching her eye as they curved away from that indeterminable inky blackness pushed against the cliff-face.

Fionn leaned over James in his seat and pushed the comm. James moved fast and keyed the comm off.

"If Tysek is listening," he said, "If his techs got past the encryption he'd recognize your voice. I'll give the commands. Let him think you're still out of commission."

James was right. It would be to their benefit for Tysek to believe that she was still a dying invalid. She nodded sharply.

"Order the pilot to the site of the wreckage from these photos."

James reached over and turned on the comm. "Pilot," he said and read off the coordinates.

"*Roger, base. Adjusting flight. Over.*" The video redirected as the stealth craft swung over the forest. More Hellions lurked in the trees closer to the mountain face. Some had even climbed them and hung in the branches, bouncing and shaking them like monkeys in a rainforest. Most of them paced like lions in cages, with heavy steps that exuded the power and menace. She'd seen a Hellion rip a man in half without so much as a blink of hesitation. The man had still been alive, screaming until he bled out. Such creations were despicable. If she could, if she knew how, she'd eradicate every last one of them.

The footage angled up and began to circle around the

crown of the mountain. A thick layer of snow ended several hundred feet above the area of concentration, lines of ice ran down creek beds cutting across the cliffs and rises.

"Sit down, Commander," James said softly.

She glanced at him repressing the urge to let loose an animalistic snarl. Did she look like she was dying on her feet? She'd survived worse than a mere poisoning. Hell, today with all its surprises didn't even rank in her top five worst days ever. Close, but not quite.

The day isn't over, she reminded herself.

"If I sit down, I'm going to split this table in half," she said to him. The others in the room stilled at her comment, work ceased for a tense moment.

"My apologies, Commander," James said.

On the screen the smoking wreckage of more than one scout craft lay like sacrifices before the darkness. The ink-black shadow hadn't lessened, even with full sun beating in its direction.

"There," Fionn breathed. "Halt and continue hover over the wreckage."

James keyed the comm and repeated her orders.

Brax, left hand gripping his sword pommel, came to stand next to her, and examined the images. "If that's a shadow, I'll jump naked into the lake next December."

"I'll take that bet," James said.

Fionn stepped closer to the screen. Her officers might make a game out of this, a tactic to release the valve on their rising stress levels, but she was in no mood for games. The pressure focused her, kept her on task, and restored her energy.

The video feed rotated as the craft circled the spot of darkness.

"Move in closer," she said, a dark suspicion forming in her mind.

James repeated the command.

"*I'm experiencing vibrational inconsistencies. Over.*" The whine of the craft's engine was now audible through the comm link.

James looked to her. She held her up her hand in a fist: Hold position.

"Maintain hover, Captain," James said.

"*Roger.*"

Fionn studied the darkness. It appeared solid, but after a brief scrutiny she spotted variations. The darkness churned, like mist. Its surface was simply that, a surface hiding what was underneath. The mist, the slight movements were made from something within that paced incessantly and disturbed the shadow keeping it.

"Looks like you're jumping in the lake," Fionn said.

"Did you see that?" Brax asked.

"Gods," Carter whispered from the back of the room.

Fionn pointed her thumb in the air and motioned upward.

James bent over the comm. "Gain altitude and maintain safe distance, Captain."

"*Thank you, sir. Over.*" The relief in the pilot's voice broke the tension in the room. A great breath released from the men around her. The room again seemed alive with the hearts of the strong as though the aircraft's distance could eradicate their fear. For a moment, these great men of this Dark Age had been quelled by something immense. Something that hid under the beds of children, which none of them possessed an explanation for.

Fionn froze an image of the shadow.

This is what they were fighting over. Something about that darkness seethed and crawled under her skin. Now that she knew it was there, she realized she'd always known. The granite mountain had drawn her here. Why else would she have dug into the bedrock, developing new technology to survive underground surrounded by earthen walls carved from the permafrost with technology even the Magistrate hadn't mastered?

She needed to go to that place, stand before that darkness herself. She felt fear, as though within that yawning black she would find her doom or her victory. She had to know which.

"Oh, no you don't."

Three swords and five laser guns ripped from sheaths and holsters, aimed at the doorway. A woman, perhaps a few years younger than Fionn, stood in an open door that had only seconds ago been shut. In the silence, they should have heard her enter.

"Identify yourself," James ordered the woman, his sidearm steady in his hand. Fionn noticed he'd set the laser weapon to maximum output. It would kill the woman instantly if he fired.

"My name is Darci." Her clear, summer-sky eyes fell on him and he shivered. "I'm not here to hurt you. But I am here to keep you from getting yourself killed." At last, her gaze came to rest on Fionn.

An aura, clear as crystal and as faceted as a gem brushed against hers. Her rage rose in response.

I swear that I will not harm you or your men. Darci did not open her mouth, but her voice projected clearly into Fionn's thoughts.

"What are you?"

Darci smiled. "Well, for starters, I'm a refugee, I came accompanied by the two men in your dungeon and a third who was tortured into insanity by the Magistrate city overlords. We escaped last year." Her lips closed and her aura, strange and knowing, touched Fionn's again. *I am a rarity among our kind.*

"*Temperantia*," Fionn said. She sized the woman up. Her build was slight, but Fionn sensed an energy and capability under the standard issue coat, sweater and pants given to new refugees. The woman was not what she expected of the rarest Virtue that could be bred. She was dangerous, and Fionn would do some damage if she tried to attack her, but at what cost? What would such a precious Virtue want with her?

"I killed the *Temperantia* that had my sister raped and murdered, tortured one of my companions into madness, and tried to do the same to my boyfriend, who is currently being held in your dungeon. But you have tried to do none of those and your mind and the minds of your soldiers are pure."

Fionn's anger abated. Somewhat.

Brax sheathed his sword and put his hands on his hips. "I

guess we know who the 'or else' is." He looked over his shoulder at Fionn. "And you thought you had it bad trying to fend off Emerick. Imagine if he could read your thoughts."

Fionn's rage came spiraling back to the surface.

"Holy shit!" Carter exclaimed, his hands flew over the controls in front of him.

Everyone in the room spun to the screens, except James. He kept his weapon trained on Darci.

"*Mayday, mayday!*" came the panicked voice of the pilot still circulating around that point of the mountain.

The screens flashed, like lightning through darkness. Fionn's rage dialed down to anger, then to astonishment as she watched. The display in the corner showed the pilot's altitude at over ten thousand feet and climbing, yet on the camera, the darkness *moved.* It reached toward the stealth craft in jagged black lines, faster than her pilot could gain altitude. One of the video feeds cracked and a ragged beeping issued from the comm.

Fionn cut her anger completely. The clawing darkness froze in motion and slowly retreated back toward the mountainside.

"*Captain Stewart requesting immediate instructions. Over.*"

James flicked on the comm. "Return to base, Captain. Repeat, return to base for debriefing."

"*Thank you, sir.*"

What in the seven hells was that?

Good question, Darci's mind responded.

James turned to her. "Your call, Commander." His face was pale.

Fionn moved to the screen and keyed up the replay. Goosebumps appeared on her arms as the slow circular trajectory of the stealth craft's camera caught the distinct eruption of that shadow. First it seemed to undulate, the definite line of shadow sloshing like water in a bathtub against the mountain side. Then fingers of black jutted out, faster and faster, reaching for the stealth craft. The video jerked as the first line of dark touched the craft, and the landscape spun in a wild rotation. As if someone had turned off a switch, the dark froze and melted back into its heart.

It hurt to swallow. Her throat was suddenly dry. It couldn't be coincidence that the shadow had lurched for her pilot the moment she let the rein loose on her anger. She'd felt the answering shudder of rage storm through the earth around her. Her power had controlled that shadow's movements, given it strength. How long had this been happening? Had she been so ignorant?

"That shadow is in the heart of Tysek's operational radius. We need to find out exactly what it is."

"Commander," Darci spoke. Nearly everyone in the room jumped at the sound of her voice, all of them having forgotten her arrival in the wake of this alarming revelation regarding their newly acquired lands. "I need a moment of your time after what we just saw. There's something you should know."

Fionn straightened her shoulders and regarded the woman. Darci appeared just in time to witness the unexplainable occurrence. But there was no one else in her command who had the powers to understand what they were dealing with.

"You have five minutes." The pilot should be back by then, and there were still the Hellions to consider. "James, sound the alert and prepare the ranks. I want as many squadrons as we have, prepared for battle within the hour."

A quick check proved the Hellions hadn't broken the line and crossed into land Fionn now claimed. That didn't mean they wouldn't.

10

Emerick winced as the last stitch was completed, drawing a line of flayed skin closed. Fionn's power had whipped against his body with devastating force. Gods, he hadn't even realized how much damage she had done until the medical unit began their torturous sewing.

The pain wasn't anything like the glorious heat and energy of the kind Fionn could inflict when she lost control. The dip and tug of the needle and suture were emotionless, and he'd rather feel the hot hard death of the Commander's fury than this.

"He's all yours." The doctor moved away, and the guard approached, black boots tromping toward him.

They'd snapped manacles back on his wrists, replacing those he'd broken. Even though Fionn had spared his life, he wasn't free yet. He suspected it would take a month of fending off her rage before she even began to trust him again. It was going to be a good month, although the thought of continually having to endure his skin being sewn back together lessened the rise of his excitement.

A shudder passed through the earth. Power slammed into him. His skin prickled like it had been splattered with grease from frying bacon. The charge of pure rage heated his body until it was replaced by a cold fear.

Rage shot through the earth, but he did not recognize Fionn's power.

This was something else entirely. It felt dark, and he sensed true bitterness in its pulsing vibration. Fionn might be angry with him, but her anger was hot, full of passion.

What was going on up there? Dungeons, shackles, and Fionn's wrath be damned, this was a war he would not let her fight without him at her side.

"Get up," the guard ordered him.

Emerick cringed. This was going to hurt, again, and not in a good way.

He groaned, giving the guard a show of trying to push himself upward with his hands bound in front of him.

As expected, the guard bent down, his leather boots squeaking, his rough hand wrapping around Emerick's bicep. Emerick allowed the doomed man to take most of his weight and rose up to his knees. The line of quick-heal sutures tugged a warning, which he didn't heed. He stumbled and led with his right arm down, throwing the guard off balance. As the man tilted forward, Emerick twisted, slamming his left fist into the man's jaw, directing his power with the blow, and the guard dropped.

Emerick straightened and hissed. "Son of a bitch!" He'd probably ripped two or three of the stitches out. At least the nursing team had taken the initiative to lay down a swath of adhesive medical tape over the splits in his back and across his chest.

He pushed the guard over and searched him for the keys. With a jangle of old world tech against the shackles and a quick twist he was free. Sort of. This many levels below the surface, it wasn't the chains that kept prisoners locked up. He ran to the cell's open door, disappointed again in the lack of security. He would have had the door shut until the guard on the inside was ready to escort the prisoner out. These were simple concepts that had been drilled into him from Academy days. Fionn needed his help and expertise. And whether she wanted it or not, she was going to get it.

Voices echoed from where he'd first been imprisoned. It wasn't hard to imagine Atticus and Tobias arguing. Atticus was powerful. He'd be handy in the fight ahead. The lift entrance was tempting, Fionn was in danger. But, he knew his father, and he wasn't about to leave any weapons locked up while enemy forces overran the compound.

He turned and headed toward Atticus's cell.

"Finally!" Tobias shouted, his voice muffled by the walls of their dungeon. Emerick slipped around the corner and slammed into a wall of raw Luxurian power. The other absent guard lay slumped at Tobias's feet. The young man's shackles dropped from his wrists. He thrust his fist into the air, something metal shined between his fingers. "*This* is a key. I told you I'd get us out."

"What the hell is this?" Emerick demanded. Atticus had seduced the guard, and by the rapid swelling of the man's eye, had knocked him out.

"We're under attack," Atticus said as Tobias un-shackled him.

"No shit. You didn't have to hurt the man. Gods, Atticus, you're as bad as ever."

Atticus shrugged, but the air of danger in his aura increased. "We don't have time to wait for them to let us out. By then it'll be too late."

Tobias practically skipped out of the cell's open door.

"You felt that too?" Emerick asked, turning to head back toward the lift.

"We did." Atticus grabbed his arm. "Listen, I've spent enough time in the city to sense where power comes from. When that rage came through here, it came from the earth and it originated from miles away."

Emerick nodded. "I know. Let's go warn the commander, before she does something else stupid."

"Like kill you for real?" Tobias asked, eyeing him. "Because she took her claws to you."

"Yeah."

"Darci says they're heading toward the hangar bay," Atticus said.

Emerick glanced at the ceiling. "I know." At the moment, Fionn was a churning mess of anger heading toward the south end of the compound and the hangars, some twenty floors above. Until he knew what his father's diabolical scheme was, she wasn't leaving the Compound. Even if he had to tie her to a chair and take the beating for it.

11

Soldiers marched in hurried steps to their garrisons. Expectation hung in the air like cut glass. One wrong move and you'd be the next to bleed. Fionn knew she'd caused it. Word had spread like wild fire, and rumors had begun to circulate, whispers that the poison had changed her. Her unnaturally fast recovery time, added to the way she'd destroyed the assassin and then her failed execution of Emerick aroused suspicion and, for some, fear.

Emerick. She could feel him, sense his location in the dungeon—no, he was in a lift, and headed her way. How the hell had he escaped the isolation cell? His aura was twined with hers still, and the feel of it served to make her temper more explosive. He was the one who had the balls to demand more from her. She'd give him more.

A shiver of anticipation coiled into her belly and the warmth grew. She took a deep breath as though that would cool the coals of desire he'd ignited. The flare of warmth was making her increasingly uncomfortable. Hell be dammed, if she was blushing—

"You are," Darci whispered at her side.

Fionn growled, and her officers stiffened further. Tensions were high as it was. Her officers stood behind her overseeing the preparations being made to receive and quarantine the stealth craft. She had no doubts about their trust and loyalty, but she was suddenly having some of her own. What awaited them from above?

The blare of a warning siren sent the deck crews scattering as the bay doors were winched open with a grinding and groaning of well used mechanics. Daylight cut inside the darkness with the alacrity of a blade.

"So that's how you get that paint job," Brax said quietly near her.

The underbelly of the craft had been slashed with jagged stripes cut into the camouflage of its hull, some flickering blue, some green, some sparking flares of yellow from damaged circuitry. She stiffened and sensed Emerick's response even at this distance. He was still a hundred or more yards away. From what she was sensing of him, he'd come barreling through the lift doors like a bear out of its den. She couldn't be the one seen to intervene.

Fionn glanced first at James, changed her mind, and turned to the least likely of her men to kill on sight. "Brax, Emerick escaped his cell. Meet him at the lift."

James snapped to attention like a bloodhound on a scent. She could practically see his hackles rise and the physical effort it took to keep from baring his teeth.

"Did he now?" Brax's eyes crinkled with amusement. He slid his sword from its sheath. "After what I saw in that cell, I'm impressed your ex can still move."

"Emerick is back?" asked another officer. "*Alive?*"

"So there was a relationship," another of her officers whispered from behind her. It took effort to keep her temper locked down. After unleashing so much of it on Emerick and after the events of the morning, she was surprised there was still any energy left in her. But there was. Enough to lay waste to all her men with a single thought, and the closer Emerick got to her, the more unstable she became.

"He was never my anything," Fionn lied under her breath before she gave Brax his orders. "Go meet him, and if he tries anything, knife him."

"Tries anything with me, or with you?" Brax asked.

She snarled at him, lashing out. As usual her power flowed around him. Not touching him. He smiled, saluted and jogged toward the lift.

"Why didn't you kill him?" James asked. His question was smothered with jealousy. James was a determined leader, an idol of the people, and on his own way to the same legendary status Emerick once had. And she'd been stupid not to see that she let James replace Emerick's presence. What could she say to the man who she could never be anything but a leader and superior to, but who'd given her his full allegiance?

"Who says I still won't?"

Smoke began to trick out of the stealth craft's portside engine. Fionn keyed the comm on her wrist display.

"All hands prepare for hazardous landing procedures. Repeat, situation is dangerous."

Fionn's clothing moved in the breeze stirred by the craft's complicated system of hover jets. As it lowered to the secure deck, the other decks closing behind it as it entered the underbelly of the compound, she could see the full extent of the damage the shadow had done to it. It was a wonder the craft was still airborne.

A shrill whine screeched from its engines. The hum of the engines cut off was replaced by the sudden captivated breath of the hangar crews.

The craft fell. It listed to the right as it sped toward the ground with illusory force, seeming almost lazy and slow like some great beast lumbering toward its final resting place. The impact shook the entire floor, knocking a whole crew of craft engineers off their feet.

Shouts rang out. A giant plume of smoke erupted from the right wing of the dying craft.

"Put it out!" cried a lieutenant. A large truck with a tank of fire retardant sped from the sidelines toward flames. "Before it hits the fuselage!"

Fionn tensed, ready to leap into the fray. She could see the pilot thrown against his controls through the cockpit. The man was her first witness to whatever the Magistrate was hiding.

She needed him alive.

"No," Darci's hand grabbed her arm before she could act. "Don't." The *Temperantia* appeared frightened, her eyes wide to a degree that revealed a soul-deep terror.

"Darci!" a man shouted from behind them.

Fionn turned to see two people she recognized as the prisoners from Brax's report. Emerick was there too. She glared at him.

The one named Atticus immediately wrapped Darci in his arms, bent and kissed her thoroughly on the mouth. The bite of lust rose from the two of them. Darci pushed against him, her chest heaving.

"We are *working*, Atticus."

"Like hell," the *Luxurian* replied. "I know that half these overworked officers were staring at *my* lady."

Darci's eyes narrowed. "Mark your territory later," she turned to Fionn. "Half the time I don't know if I want to have his babies or kick his ass."

Atticus nodded, frowning as he examined the situation.

"Brax," Fionn snapped. "Please explain to me how half our prisoners have escaped the brig."

"Hell if I know, sir," Brax said. "Besides, from my observations, none of them would dare harm any loyal to the Insurgency."

A cavernous pop like a pellet gun shot into a round barrel silenced the chaotic order of the bay.

"Who's that?" Emerick asked, pointing at the cockpit.

Fionn cut off her anger and stared. The pilot was banging a bloody fist against the glass keeping him inside his craft, smearing red in front of where he shouted something at them.

"Clear the deck," she called. "Open the hatch." Her entourage of officers and prisoners followed her as she jogged the several hundred meters separating her from the craft.

"Fionn, wait!" Emerick's shortened stride revealed how injured he was. That irritated her. He should be recovering, not chasing after her. Gods, she should have just killed him. The thought had her chest contracting uncomfortably. She hadn't forgiven him for the deaths of her people or what she'd endured under the orders of his father. Having him in her compound was screwing with her self-control. Even now she wanted to force him to the floor and finish what they started earlier.

A primal scream filled the closed hangar and instant fear and anxiety swallowed the constitutions of all present.

"By the light of day," Brax whispered drawing his sword again.

A terrible knowledge clicked into place in Fionn's mind even as what had once been one of her few pilots leapt from his craft. His fingers were curled into claws, and foam dribbled down the side of his mouth. His blood-shot eyes locked onto the closest deck hand, and he let loose a roar.

Fionn jerked out of Emerick's grip on her arm and engaged the enemy. Her first kick sent the rabid man rolling.

People were shouting, but she couldn't hear them past the pounding of her heart thundering in her ears. The shadow had risen from its cliff-faced corner as her anger and rage had roared from the depths of her soul with startling ease. The contact with that darkness had damaged the stealth craft, and forever changed the man inside.

"Hellion!" James cried drawing his side arm. That name was like a signal for hell to break loose. Men scattered toward exits. Those who were armed drew their weapons and took aim.

The monstrous man rose up, blood now streaming from a cut on his forehead. He didn't hesitate and launched himself at her. Fionn gathered her power and met the creature head-on. The Hellion's skin split, revealing red, bulging muscle beneath the dermis. His clawed hands swiped at her, his teeth snapped. She lashed out again, and the creature screamed like a wounded boar.

It moved faster than she'd expected it to, and its blood slicked hands wrapped around her throat. She let loose her power, hearing the screech of metal as her rage scored the decking. Warm blood splashed against her arms as she vainly punched at the Hellion's sides.

"It's her power," Emerick's voice issued clearly through the rush in her ears.

The sweet calm of his aura fell over her and the Hellion like a tranquil ocean wave, persistent in its peacefulness. Her first instinct was to deny his power. This was her fight and she would not fail.

The Hellion's hands tightened and a choking sound issued from her throat. Spots appeared in her vision.

Emerick's persistent power thickened around her like sand that had suddenly become hard, fooling her with its soft appearance. To deny his peace was to succumb to the rage monster's hands ever tightening around her throat and die. She would not die, so she gave in.

Her body went limp and her power vanished from the air, her aura returning to hover just above her skin. The zap of close range laser fire echoed from a distance and the hand around her throat dropped away. She fell to her knees gasping over the unmoving body of the pilot. His open eyes stared at her in accusation. Cuts split every inch of his exposed skin.

You did this, his eyes that even as she stared, glazed over in repose, *this death is your fault.*

She pushed away.

Gods, was she to blame for all of them? Every time she'd unleashed more rage upon the Hellion, he'd become stronger, more monstrous, his lust for destruction feeding directly from her as though she'd been the adrenaline in his veins.

Cool, firm hands were lifting her. Emerick.

She pulled and stumbled away from him, her injured hip straining at the awkward movement. She would not admit that he had saved her life again.

"That's the second time today," he said.

She gritted her teeth. The desire she'd experienced when he'd pinned her to her dungeon floor wasn't something she should have felt. Even now she was tempted by him, and she didn't want that. Or did she? Instead of answering her own stupid questions, she turned toward the craft. Parts of it still issued small streams of smoke from its cracked and broken hull.

"Quarantine that craft," she ordered. "I want every inch of it analyzed. Put the body on ice until our medical staff can perform a necropsy."

"Commander," the skinny kid, Tobias, said. He held up a scanner. "I'm reading widespread fiber fraying, and all artificial intelligence systems are shot. All I can see from the memory banks are rolls of repeated codes that don't make a lick of sense. Whatever infected your pilot got a good bit of the virus in with the hardware and the software of this baby."

Her lead tech officer looked up from his own readings. "He's right, Commander."

Brax wiped the blood-stained blade on his black fatigues. Fionn noticed the multiple wounds pooling blood from the dead pilot's side. Brax had stabbed the man through almost every major organ. Her power had given the Hellion energy, it had fed off her rage. "As superstitious as this sounds, I believe that shadow was capable of causing every bit of this."

Emerick's power flashed out and the hangar silenced. "What shadow?"

Darci, who was still secreted behind Atticus, pushed him aside. "You've seen it," she said. "You've been there."

Emerick's face hardened and his aura became a shield. "Stay out of my head," he warned the woman. Atticus snarled at Emerick, the dangerous heat of desire pressurizing the air.

Fionn stepped toe to toe with Emerick. "You've seen a shadow before, something impenetrable by light?"

Emerick's aura rushed against hers, prickling her skin with the force of winter wind. "It's not a shadow," he said, "My father wanted to bring the mountain down over it. I disarmed the charges, and your flyover found it. My father has too much to answer for if he's been using you to create these. I think it's long past time he and I had a talk."

"What were you doing there?" Fionn demanded.

"Worried about my safety?" Emerick countered.

"What did you find?" Fionn asked, aware that her entire

command scrutinized her. They all saw what her anger had caused. It couldn't have merely been coincidence that triggered the shadow to react every time she unleashed her power.

Emerick glanced at the other officers. "I didn't see anything. Like you said, it's impenetrable. But more significant is what I heard. There's something imprisoned there and the Magistrate will do anything to keep it hidden. They don't want you to find it."

"He's lying," James said. "Why would Emerick just stumble across this?"

Darci snarled, and her power coiled about them all. "Emerick's mind is devoted to keep this place safe and protected. Our single greatest threat is whatever his father has kept hidden. It must be destroyed or removed from Magistrate control."

Atticus stepped between James and Darci, moving like a snake coiled to strike. The anger from the two of them was a palpable wave of heat to Fionn, and suddenly the bond between them was clear. Darci, a Virtue, gave Atticus direction, driving him like a stake into the heart of the conflict, and in turn Atticus gave her every protection, his movements promising destruction to anything that threatened her and her desires.

Fragments of that relationship Fionn could see reflected in the conflict between herself and Emerick. They had the same interests; he never would have driven so hard to bolster the Compound's defenses, or develop ways to live in this treacherous place in the world, catching refugees like butterflies in a net to keep the machine of his invention moving. All she had done, even after she thought he'd betrayed them, was to continue his suggestions and plans, and work to push the threat of the Magistrate back from their borders and protect their people.

He, a Virtue, gave the direction, and she, a Sin, provided the protection.

This discovery terrified her. She'd been haunted by Admiral Tysek's words for years. She couldn't just give up on what she'd known for so long.

He betrayed you, and gave me your position. Without my son, you'd still be safe behind your lines little girl.

However, Atticus was right. Whatever threat they faced was perhaps fueled by the shadow on the mountain. Its discovery had resulted in the death of a good pilot, but it had revealed how the Magistrate was creating Hellions.

"Brax, assemble a team." Fionn ordered. "James, give Emerick your comm."

James unclipped his comm from his wrist and with a glare at Emerick tossed it to him.

Emerick caught the comm and snapped it on. His face hardened as though the prospect of talking to the man who'd kill thousands of innocents was one step closer to ripping the man's guts out. "You'll want to record this."

Fionn nodded to the techs, automatically including the new kid. They immediately began to work their expertise. Tobias was the first to give a thumbs-up go ahead.

Emerick keyed up the display. While they waited for the connection, his gaze met hers, searching. A flicker of that energy before that had shattered the bond slipped over her aura, like the once reassuring touch of his hands massaging her shoulders from long ago.

Something changed in that moment.

She needed him. Without him, she would never have found the drive to accomplish the impossible and save the lives of thousands from the Magistrate's Undesirable label. If it weren't for the permanent fusion of his aura with hers, and the sting of betrayal, she would have succumbed long ago to the Magistrate's enlightenment.

The comm beeped softly in the silence and Emerick's aura thickened, his jaw clenched, and he keyed the command to activate the link.

12

The sensation of waiting was like a blistering wind. Fionn's steady stare did nothing to help him focus. He opened a link.

"Come in eagle outpost, do you copy?" Emerick's voice echoed in the deathly silent hangar. All eyes were on him. James gripped his sidearm with more force than was necessary. Brax noticed too and placed a hand on the man's shoulder.

"Relax," he whispered. "You'll get the chance to kick his ass later."

"Quiet," Fionn snapped.

"This is eagle outpost. Requesting identification. Over."

"This is lieutenant commander Emerick Tysek of the first rank, requesting direct link to Admiral Tysek."

There was silence, for several moments. The minutes lengthened. He didn't dare look at Fionn or anyone else. The heat wave of her temper as he'd spouted his old ranking was a touch of a sore note. After all he'd technically reached a rank higher than hers, even if she was the commanding officer of her territory. The title was proof of his wildly successful, yet short, career as a Magistrate soldier. He'd surprised everyone on both sides of the war when he took the lesser position of first officer.

A crackling came over the line. The static signaled another person listened in on the conversation from the other side.

Emerick struck first, taking the high ground. "Father," he

said.

"Son," his father's age-roughened voice spilled over the connection. "I trust you have an acceptable reason why you are transmitting from within our enemy's territory.

"I don't. What's your reason for hiding your shadow on the mountain?"

His father's breath hissed over the connection. "You were there," Tysek said.

Emerick heard the rare emotion in his father's voice and pressed his advantage. "I disarmed the charges after you sent your lieutenant to his rest. What's on that mountain? I won't ask again."

Even across the miles separating them and the lines, Emerick felt the slap of his father's power, and his own aura's flaring response.

"I gave you one chance to save yourself, Emerick. Returning from exile has signed your death warrant."

Emerick fisted his hands.

"You signed it the day you sent me to murder Fionn. You should have known better than anyone, I wouldn't be able to destroy my opposite. The Magistrate is losing ground. You should turn back and leave the Yukon in darkness. Your Enlightenment has no place here."

"The Yukon was never intended to be saved." Tysek paused. When he continued his words were hard and sharp, "The darkness here is a cancer. Surrender now. I will spare the children."

Emerick thought of Brax's niece and nephew. His father wasn't kind enough to spare children, and there weren't enough children to make it worth Tysek's effort.

"No, you won't," Emerick bit out. "You'll slaughter anything that lives like you always have. Surrender is not an option."

"This final stunt has forced my hand. We would have conceded some loss of ground. The Seven have decreed the Yukon is to be stripped and quarantined."

If ice could be formed by sudden, deep fear, Emerick's

body would have been coated in it. He swallowed, tried to speak, and gulped again.

"Then this truly is the end," he said, his voice steady. "No terms."

"You will not surrender," Tysek said. "Sin cannot be suffered to exist and must be brought into the clear burning light. The worst of those sins, immortal in nature and damned in tormented sentence, will forever remain in the darkness. The knowledge of true Sin shall remain chained with them." The words Tysek quoted were the teachings all academy graduates memorized. The words held new meaning.

Was his father trying to tell him what was hidden on that mountain?

Emerick clenched his fingers. "I told you once if you destroy what I hold dear, you'd live to regret it. The Final Order has forced *my* hand, Father. I will send the Seven your head before I come for them."

"It has already begun, my son." His father's voice held no shred of guilt, only the cold hard emotionless patience of a man who ran his life as his overseers commanded. "I'm sorry I could not save you from this darkness."

Emerick's hands shook as Fionn's aura twined with his own again.

"No you're not. Not yet." He removed the comm from his wrist, the link going dead and the tech automatically dying without contact with a pulse point. He weighed the piece of tech in his palm before he spun and hurled it against the closest wall. It shattered.

"Emerick," Fionn said. "What is the final determination?"

He turned. "Exactly what it sounds like. Tysek is going to unleash everything he has against us."

"Us?" she asked, her heat washing over him, wrapping around him, giving him what little comfort it could provide.

"Yes, I said us," he answered. He stepped toward her and propriety be damned, he grabbed her by the shoulders. Her well-trained officers whipped up their weapons. "You'd better scramble the troops and lock this place down. If the Magistrate thinks the people here are truly lost to them, they won't try to save anyone." He ran his hands down her arms. "It *will* be a slaughter."

Fionn pulled away, her anger growing.

"All this because of that shadow?" Darci asked.

Emerick turned to her. "No, it's whatever casts the shadow. Whatever we stumbled across, the Seven Generals fear enough to kill every living soul in the compound."

Fionn paced back and forth. With each step Emerick could see her mentally ticking off her possible choices, backing into the corner the Magistrate had trapped them in. When there was no place left to turn, no choice but the worst, that deep and abiding rage would break its bonds and crash over his father's forces as she'd unleashed herself on him, and he'd be at her side. The resulting destruction would be a massacre.

Warmth dripped like honey into his midsection. Gods, he'd go to war for her and mete out any destruction she willed from him. He would not see these people, he would not see her, bent under the lash of the Magistrate and slaughtered like cattle.

"By the Seven Generals, you mean the seven most powerful virtues of each class, right?" Tobias asked, not looking up from his tablet.

Emerick turned to him. "Yes. With their power, it's rumored they have attained true immortality."

"Cool, just like the legends."

"What legends?" Atticus asked.

"Oh, well supposedly there are seven great sins and seven great virtues unleashed upon the earth by Pandora. It's debatable that the Magistrate's Seven Generals are the legendary virtues," Tobias said. "Based on my readings of the singularity, um, the shadow, it's not very well protected. I'd bet he's collected a few *Ira's* and locked them away there."

"So it's a prison," James said.

"Pretty much," Tobias answered. "I'm bouncing an old satellite feed down at the mountain and every time Fionn, you know, does her thing, the singularity responds. It's like dark particle physics with a little quantum science factored in."

"Tobias," Atticus said in warning.

"Oh, right," Tobias said with as much attitude as he could muster. "You only speak lust. Let me offer a simpler explanation. Dark matter particles are like magnets. Like attracts like. You get two dark matter particle users, like you and Michael running around, pretty soon you sync up. When you let a little power loose, his aura will respond. If you let a lot loose, it'll be like sticking him with a bunch of needles. His aura will react as though you were attacking him, sending out just as much if not more dark matter particles around him, thereby expanding his aura."

"Huh," Brax said, sounding impressed. "I think the kid's onto something there."

Fionn took a deep breath and closed her eyes. "My power is manipulating whatever the Magistrate has locked under that shadow?"

"Essentially? Yes," Tobias said. "Sort of. It's a huge dark particle source. It could be manipulating you."

Emerick frowned. If it weren't for his own power rooting him to the ground, he would have begun to pace too. He disliked feeling so much chaos. It was everywhere, bearing down on them from every direction, and his meager abilities as a *Patientia* were nothing compared to those that they were up against.

Tobias finally looked up from his crystal tablet, a stunned expression plastered across his features. "I'm not so sure it's a coincidence that you founded the Insurgency here, just miles away from what could be the actual source of *Ira*. I mean, if the legend is true, and the original *Ira* still exists, this could be it."

"If the Magistrate has control of the source of wrath, that explains the Hellions," Darci said.

"Hold on." Brax held up his hand. "They're using *Ira* to turn innocent people into monsters?"

James stepped in, close to Fionn's other side. "What can we do about *Ira*? Right now there are hundreds of Hellions massing on the borders. We'll have to deal with those first. We must concentrate on securing the Compound."

Emerick narrowed his eyes. James had moved inappropriately close to Fionn, closer than a first officer needed to be.

"The Magistrate is giving the Final Order," Emerick said. "Unless we defeat them from every direction and every angle here and now, the Seven will erase us completely." He took a deep breath, feeling the walls close tighter, and hating the only crack he could see to save them. "If the *Ira* is the only motivation they have to claim this frozen waste, we—"

"What's this we?" James interrupted. "You're a traitor who got a lucky break. I swear, you won't get another one."

"Forgive me, *first officer*," Emerick spat. How he'd love to rip into him and teach this upstart a lesson. "Every person in this Compound will either live or die today. The best chance we have is to split the forces. Defend and attack." Anyone could see the utter puppy love James had developed for Fionn, and that just plain pissed Emerick off. He doubted the man would last five minutes alone with the full force of Fionn's passion flaying the skin off his bones.

"Stand down," Fionn snapped with enough ire to startle both of them. "If the Hellions attack, and we assume Tysek still has some cannon power after yesterday, it's only a matter of time before they break our defenses. The laser fence can be decrypted as fast as we keep encrypting it. Soon they'll have us. Emerick's right. We need to catch them at their heart, and kick them in the balls."

"I like her style," Tobias said. "Like attracts like remember? Your best bet is to reach the other *Ira,* and tap into the power source. If you can zap Admiral Tysek's forces like you did Emerick, and you know, turn them into shredded-cheese versions of themselves, Tysek won't stand a chance. If he's smart, then he knows that, and he'll have all his best little soldiers there. So be prepared for a fight."

"Can't we destroy the *Ira*?" Brax asked, checking his weapon.

"No," Tobias answered. "The amount of energy that would require is monumental. Seriously, when I said 'sun,' I mean like the actual sun. Okay, well not that bad, but it would take more—" he gestured wildly "—everything to accomplish the task. I highly suggest not trying it. It's better to try and manipulate the energy, if you can."

"How?" Emerick asked.

"Not you, you're a Virtue, it'd probably kill you if you tried to use it. Fionn has to do it. She's an *Ira*. Besides we already know she's been manipulating the energy. Get her close enough and I promise you'll see something cool."

"Sounds like a plan," Atticus said. "I'm ready for another fight. The last one didn't count." He flashed Emerick a smile.

"Don't worry about your encryption," Tobias said, a dangerous glint in his eye. "I'll make sure the enemy can't set foot within a mile of the compound. None of the Admiral's techs have my skill or modification ability. Plus, they're all idiots if they haven't already figured out how to crawl through the obvious cracks in your defense system. No offense."

Fionn nodded sharply, her mouth set into the grim line signaling that she'd come to a decision, and she'd deal with the consequences as they came. "James, you have command. Set Tobias up with a control system. I want every system we have up and running at max until this is over. I will lead the away team. All special ops units with me in fifteen. Make it clear, it's either us or them. We didn't sacrifice so much to lose it all. Emerick, get your friends suited up. You're not supposed to be here anyway. Dismissed." Her commands cracked over them all with the intensity of a whip's lash.

"Sir, yes sir!" The shout rang out as her officers saluted and a flurry of activity broke out.

Emerick saluted and turned to the *Appetence* who'd been given to his command under Fionn. Tobias jogged off after James, leaving Emerick, Atticus, and Darci.

"Where do we suit up?" Darci asked, turning her deep, soul-piercing gaze on him.

"Do you have any weapons training?" Emerick asked. The

woman was in her early twenties and too thin to really be of any use against a Hellion. Her abilities as a *Temperantia* would have to be more than enough to—

"If you keep insulting me with your thoughts, I'll be forced to defend myself," Darci said. "And you won't like me as an opponent. I can see what you're going to do even before you know it."

The way she said it had Emerick reassessing his earlier evaluation. He coughed. "Right. This way."

There would be no going back after this. He'd been serious. He would murder his father if the man attacked. If Tysek did attack, he'd accompany his troops in his command craft, like a Roman war general in his chariot. The last time Emerick had faced his father, he'd summarily had his ass handed to him. Emerick was strong, but his father had always been stronger and had taken every opportunity to make sure Emerick knew it. It filled him with a certain kind of trepidation and a deep boiling frustration. The man had done everything to tear him down and was doing it all again.

Somewhere a siren began to blare. Lights installed on every level flashed as the alert sounded. Grim acceptance dropped into his chest like a stone and made it hard to breathe. The attack was beginning. The end was near, for one of them or the other.

"He gave the final order," Emerick said, as he and the other *Appetence* followed Fionn to the lift.

"So did I." Fionn pressed the button that would take them up. Overhead, the hangar doors were opening, and a few craft were already taking off. These men and women knew how to do their jobs, and they had the drive and determination to protect their home, the last place on the continent they could be free.

Admiral Tysek had no idea the fury with which these hardened people would dig deep, root in, and fight until they were free from his oppression.

13

The thump of the cannons as they took off vibrated the air all around. Below, Hellions swarmed like a hornet's nest toward the Compound's hills and bunkers, tearing into anything they could get their claws on. With each cannon shot, ten or fifteen of the monsters were removed from action, but for every enemy destroyed, there were two to take its place.

"Where the hell did they all come from?" Atticus shouted over the rotating blades of the helicopter.

Emerick looked up from the clear gaze of his sniper's scope. "My father's no idiot. He would have prepared for this day. Isolation coffins aren't new tech, and you'd be surprised how much space he has under his feet."

"You never said anything about this," Fionn shouted at him.

Emerick glanced at her. "Three years ago those storage facilities had just been built. No one knew what they were for."

A bright blue shield flickered like an old world bug-zapper every time one of the Hellions got close enough to the compound to try and jump the wall. Every now and again, whole sections of the line flickered as though they would go out, and then the coding kicked in and the line blazed brighter than ever. Without Tobias, they would have been down under the attack of Tysek's techs in the first ten minutes.

Emerick moved past Darci and Michael, and stopped at

Fionn's side. The warning flickers of caution spat at him like sparks from a fire as he neared. He answered with enough of his own power to make her hesitate.

He keyed his comm off, and spoke next to her ear, the silk of her hair stinging his neck in the high wind. "You keep flaring up at me, and I *will* take you for another round."

The sudden bite of her aura twining with his was like a hot breeze. "We're here to work," she replied.

He flicked his comm back on. Atticus nodded at him.

"Keep it to yourself," his friend shouted. "I'm having enough trouble concentrating as it is."

Emerick gripped the stock of his rifle, resisting the urge to kick Atticus's *Luxurian* ass out of the craft. It was tempting, but they needed his help.

"*Approaching target*," the pilot informed them.

Emerick, Darci's voice echoed in his mind.

Startled, he turned to her. His gaze locked with hers and her voice became loud.

Tobias told me, that if Fionn can't channel the Ira's power, if she loses control only an equal and opposite power will stop her. Be ready.

Suddenly she was gone from his mind. He nodded, letting her know that he understood. He could stop Fionn's powers if he needed to. But what could he be ready for? He barely knew what they were approaching, a faceless imprisoned wretch locked in darkness? Or the destruction of the largest and last group of free people on the continent?

"Shields!" Brax shouted, diving away from the open hatch. "The bastards are cloaked."

An explosion rocked the craft.

Fionn's rage took flight. She let go of her handle, swung her rifle on its strap behind her back, and grabbed a long-barreled blaster from the rack behind the cockpit.

"Get out of the way," she ordered Atticus who was firing useless laser bullets toward camouflaged and shielded enemies.

She knelt next to the door and fired. Light blasted from the end of the long range blaster. Moments later, in what appeared to be empty air space, a craft flickered into existence. Smoke billowed from its engines. Fionn fired again, finishing them. As the craft spiraled toward the steep mountainside, her rage abated.

"Wolf two," she addressed the other craft who was supposed to be offering air support. "Keep your eyes on the airspace. They shoot us out of the air and we're finished."

Unlike Tysek's craft, the Insurgency would most likely be spotted even with camouflage engaged. They had decided to make this as fast as possible. Their speed would blur the camo, and although they wouldn't be immediately spotted, they definitely wouldn't pass unnoticed.

"Twenty seconds to the drop zone."

Emerick could sense the darkness like a mouse smelling a snake. He adjusted his weapons: two side arms, and a few knives were all he had to protect Fionn, help wrangle the source of wrath into submission, and defeat his father. He didn't like the odds of his succeeding.

"Say your prayers," Brax said.

Darci frowned. "There are Hellions down there, on the mountain."

"How many?" Atticus asked.

She closed her eyes. "Their thoughts are like one single mind. I-I can't tell them apart."

Emerick went to the open door of the craft. He could see nothing on the ground as they whooshed over tall spires of trees. The wreckage site and the waiting shadow were clear of enemies. "I don't see them."

"They're there." The weight of Darci's tone caused absolutely no doubt in Emerick's mind that they were.

Fionn joined him, glanced out, then stepped back. "That bastard. He's dressed a squad of Hellions in camouflaged armor."

"Shit," Brax said, checking his handgun and shoving it back into its holster. "We are not prepared for this."

Fionn's rage grated against his skin like rough stone. "Camo up," she ordered. "Unless we run right into them, we should be able to sneak by."

"*Fifteen seconds*," the pilot said. They were speeding past the mountain-side, banking right and losing altitude.

Suddenly the cockpit exploded. Smoke filled their compartment. The craft jolted forward throwing them all to the floor. Emerick's rifle slid across the floor. One look told Emerick the pilots were dead and they were next.

"Wolf One down," Brax shouted into his comm.

"Evacuate," Fionn cried, choking on the smoke. Her jacket was caught on one of the instruments she'd been thrown into as they were struck.

They careened toward the mountain, nose first.

Brax didn't waste any time and jumped out of the open door. Darci screamed as Atticus grabbed her and followed Brax, launching them into the sky as their camo suits flickered on and they vanished from sight.

Emerick grabbed his sniper rifle as it slid past him and slung it over his arm. He ran to Fionn and ripped the sleeve of her jacket off. He didn't hesitate and tossed her out the side of the craft, diving after her.

The craft hit the ground a second before they did and cartwheeled into the cliff slide. Rocks and dirt sprayed in every direction. The howl of a Hellion followed the screech of the wreckage.

Emerick rolled to a stop and got to his hands and knees. His skin had split along the lines of stitches in his back. Too late to worry about it now. He scrambled upward, gasping as the air had been knocked out of him. He looked up and saw Fionn picking herself up a short distance away. Only her left arm was still covered in a shimmer of invisibility. The rest of her suit had been too damaged to carry a circuit. He looked at his own, and realized he was just as exposed. The others were nowhere to be found.

"Fi," he shouted. "You're humped." He raced toward her and yanked her to her feet.

The *pit-pit* of laser fire rained down around them. A sharp whistle gave Emerick a moment of de-ja-vu as the battle broke out over them and an explosion rocked across the sky.

Another missile screeched through the air and found its target. An enemy craft flickered into view over them, spinning wildly into the ravine far below on their left side where the ground sloped steeply down.

"We're on the ground and kicking," he reported into his comm.

"Cover the Commander," came James's voice in his ear. "Fire at will upon all enemy aircraft."

"Hellions ahead," Brax said. Emerick turned and could just see his outline ahead of them.

"All camo off," Emerick ordered. "The more of us there are, the greater chance we get Fionn to the *Ira*."

"This day just gets better and better," Brax answered, his camo flickering off a few yards up the slope.

A screeching and howling erupted around them as one by one they were spotted by the still cloaked Hellions. Emerick grabbed Fionn and pulled her behind a boulder. Atticus and Darci were right behind them. Darci was bleeding from a small cut above her eye, but otherwise the others were in good shape.

"Did you know these suits can slow a free fall?" Darci asked.

"Next time, warn me," Atticus growled, palming his knives.

Emerick pulled a grenade out of his cargo vest. He ripped out the old-fashioned pin with his teeth and lobbed it over the boulder. "You weren't frightened of a little fall, were you," he asked.

Atticus grunted.

The explosion caused the mountain to shudder around them. A rain of pine needles showered them. Screeches erupted as the boom subsided.

"The way is clear," Darci said. "They are still here, but disoriented. Something's confusing them."

"Let's go piss off the Magistrate," Brax said. He raised his rifle, a crazy smile on his face.

Fionn's power lashed in the air around her and an answering tremor whispered beneath Emerick's feet. "We'll need to clear a path to get to the wall. Tysek has lined them all up nicely." The Hellions between them and their destination set to howling again.

Emerick slapped her back, throwing his own energy around her. "Not yet," he said. "Wait till we get closer or you'll just give the Hellions more rage to kill us with."

Fionn brought her weapon up. She didn't argue, but her power didn't lessen either. "Move out!" she ordered. She turned and leapt over the top of the boulder, the piercing blast of her laser fire erupting in a controlled burst as she began the attack. Emerick followed close on her heels. His grenade had shattered the tech of many of the Hellions' camo and parts of their bodies appeared: a leg, a head, half a chest. Emerick fired at those he could see, shattering more of the tech and dropping Hellions.

A flash of metal and three more dropped with knives lodged in their eyes. Atticus kept pace with him, his knives in each hand. Emerick raised his rifle, providing more cover fire as they sprinted toward the mass of smoldering wreckage that marked the shadowed area of the cliff face. He picked off two Hellions, but where those fell, more took their place.

"Where is that air support?" Emerick shouted into his comm, and squeezed off a few more rounds.

A strange pressure wrapped in the air. The closest Hellions stopped, and turned about-face before attacking their fellows.

"Darci!" Atticus cried. He dropped his knives and caught her as she stumbled.

"I'm fine," she said, shaking her head. "That will hold them off."

A whine of air craft signaled their air support. A rocket whizzed overhead and trees exploded into splinters. Emerick turned and followed Darci and Atticus around the still smoldering pile of wreckage.

"*You are clear, Commander,*" James said.

Fionn whirled to face Darci. "Do you sense anything?"

"Rage," Darci said, her face white. "Anger, hatred. Are you sure this is what we need to do?"

"What the hell?" Fionn asked as they came around the wreckage and face to face with the wall of black.

Emerick hadn't noticed it in the dark, but the color had been leached out of the grasses and rocks nearby. A shiver trailed down his back. Emerick grabbed Fionn just as she moved to step toward the shadow.

"Keep your distance," he said, unsure of how they were actually going to access the *Ira's* powers. He hadn't felt the *Ira* before, but now the sense of pure wrath was overwhelming. There was only one *Ira* that he could sense. It meant Tobias's legends were correct. This was the source of wrath.

"Who thought this was a good idea again?" Brax asked.

No Virtue is welcome within the realm of Sin. A hiss of chain, the clink of links dragging over stone, and rasping breath issued from the shadow. *Begone from this place or die!*

The shadow receded, and then a harsh grating laugh rose from within its depths

"Can we hurry up?" Brax shouted as he let loose a spray of laser fire. "I don't plan on being someone else's dinner." He lobbed a grenade over the wreckage. A loud pop and a shower of gravel followed.

I have waited for you, Fionn, great of many. The darkness stirred and Emerick caught a flash of light, and a haze of red before the shadow obscured the *Ira* again from view.

He pushed Fionn back and threw out his hands. A jagged arm of shadow struck against the sudden shield he'd created around him and Fionn.

The *Ira* screeched, the sound like a thousand birds shrieking. A slice of pain struck over his entire body. He cried out and dropped to one knee. The shield of his aura faltered.

You presume to stop me? Ignorant child. The voice wasn't something he heard; it was like Darci inside his mind, but different, rancid, and putrefied by years of imprisonment. It wafted from the shadows like the ashes of hell itself. A rumble gathered beneath his feet. More jagged lines raked out from the shadow.

"Fionn," he said. She shook herself as though waking from

a dream. Fear, true fear, struck him deep. Something was wrong. Fionn was sharp in the field of battle, but the lazy, almost casual look she gave him was not the woman he knew, the woman he'd give his life for. They should have turned back; they should have waited for an opening, a weakness in Tysek's defenses. Not this.

"Commander!" Brax yelled. "We're surrounded."

Fionn blinked and raised her weapon. She moved differently. Slower. Behind her the air shimmered.

"Get down," Emerick pushed her behind him, firing over her shoulder. A Hellion, foam coating its lips, crashed to the ground, dead.

"Heavy inbound—position compromised—" James's voice came over the comm in broken fragments.

"Shit," Emerick said. He turned to find Fionn reaching toward the shadow as though mesmerized. To his horror, the shadow seemed to reach back, a jagged line of black rising from its depths. He grabbed Fionn and dragged her away.

An inhuman cry issued from the shadow accompanied by the ominous crack of chains.

Howls rose all around.

"Put me down," Fionn growled, and the sharp bite of her power whipped against his forearm.

Emerick released her, keeping his weapon aimed at the air around them looking for any sign of escape from the camouflaged Hellions no doubt closing in on them. He fired two shots at random from hip level. The shots struck several feet away and two Hellions dropped, holes in their chests. The air shimmered around them as though a shudder had passed through them. "Gods," he said, checking his wrist display. They were ringed in a steady line of enemies.

"James," Fionn snapped into her comm, seeming to wake up from her trance, "Where is my air support?"

There was a crackle of indistinguishable sound from the comm followed by a complete silence. The Hellions breathed like animals, deep and heavy. The line they held remained steady as though awaiting a command to attack. Emerick reached for another explosive from his belt.

"Looks like we're all alone," Atticus said as he backed toward them, an arm held out protectively in front of Darci. "Any idea of how to tap into that power source would be a good one."

"They don't have any thoughts," Darci said. "The Hellions, they're like drones."

"Brax," Fionn said with eerie calm. "Try and establish contact with the Compound. The rest of you, create a perimeter. Don't shoot. Anything might set them off."

"Keep a rein on your powers," Darci added. "If the *Ira* created them, and Tobias is right, any of our powers might cause like to attract like."

"All signals are being jammed, Commander," Brax said as he keyed commands into his wrist display. "We're cut off."

Emerick glanced at Darci.

"We're too far from the Compound for me to reach Tobias," Darci said, answering him before he posed the question.

Fionn turned and examined the looming shadow they were trapped in front of.

"Don't get near that," Emerick said. "Disturbing the *Ira* could get us killed."

"Maybe for a Virtue," Fionn countered. "I'm here to use its power and I plan to. Do you feel that?"

"If it's fear," Brax said, "Then yeah, I feel it." He cast aside his laser weapon and drew the broadsword at his side. "If we're going to die—" Brax spun the sword with enough force to make the air sing, "—Let's make those bastards work for the right to have the last dance."

In the distance an explosion thumped like a heartbeat over the mountain. It was as though the battle were following them here. Emerick glanced at his wrist. The feed of information was broken, the hologram images flickering like fireflies. What little information he could glean told him a massive Hellion horde that had been headed to the Compound when they set out was now stampeding in their direction.

"Like attracts like," Emerick muttered.

Fionn paced back and forth. Her aura clashed with his at every pass. Emerick grabbed her arm, the fury inside her aura clawed at his fingers to let go. He didn't.

"You have to channel the *Ira* and you have to do it now."

A grating cackle, something akin to a laugh, cruel in nature and chilling to the bone, issued from that darkness.

"The daughter of my soul has finally sought me out. After so many centuries, I shall again walk the earth. Our darkness will balance the light and we will triumph." The voice was rough, sickening to hear.

Emerick spun to face the shadow. The mountain trembled under their feet, and a low growl rose around them from the Hellions. He gathered his power, bolstering his aura, ready to throw everything he had between them and the *Ira* if she attacked.

"Stand down," Fionn ordered him. He sucked in a breath at the intensity of her energy. The power locked in the shadow answered, the dark churning like mist. The sharp whip of Fionn's aura wrapped around his wrist, drawing blood and breaking his grip. She pulled away. "I'll be fine. Hold the line."

The shadow's movements became more animated. Claws of darkness reached out drawing Fionn in even as she stepped toward them. Panic gripped him with sensation more painful than those Fionn could conjure. He'd lost her once.

"Like hell," Emerick said. He jumped after her, grabbing her hand. The black closed around them, the howls of monstrous men disappeared. All that remained was the rasp of chains and crushing weight of *Ira* stripping him to the core as he stepped over the threshold of light into darkness.

14

The tickling sensation of dry, brittle leaves scraping gently across Fionn's skin caused her to shiver. Power, greater and deeper than hers, surrounded her. This was *wrath*, wrapping dangerous tendrils of death around her, ready to catch its prey in the trap of its thorns. She'd never once been the prey, always the predator. With *Ira* she was determined it would be no different. Emerick's hand tightened on hers until her fingers were pinched between his.

"Welcome."

Fionn jerked as though exiting a trance and waking in a different place. The darkness parted and revealed the source of the voice that echoed from every direction.

Ira, the embodiment of the power coursing through Fionn's veins, stood before her. She appeared younger than she sounded, just a little older than Fionn was. Bright chains shone at the woman's wrists, ankles and neck. The grimy tunic she wore was cinched at the middle by a rotting leather belt. The woman's skin gleamed white, her naked toes pale against the black. Her fiery red hair hung well past her waist. Despite her ragged surroundings, her lips were turned in a pleasant smile. But it was her eyes, blazing with hatred, her irises a deep glowing red, which caused Fionn to hesitate instead of attack. She could feel *Ira*'s gaze on her, through her, and in her like someone had peeled back the layers of her flesh and laid open her soul.

"Free me, Fionn." *Ira's* voice grated the demand, struggling to speak.

Fionn saw the shackles again, the silver-white chains, blindingly bright. Power radiated from *Ira's* bonds. The Sin had been imprisoned, and the manner of that imprisonment had her wondering, was the Magistrate behind her captivity?

"Why?" Emerick asked next to her. His power flared, crackling as the two opposing energies were forced to tangle.

Fionn tensed, her fingers closing tighter around his. She didn't dare look away from *Ira's* gaze. She'd had her dealings with predators. To look away was to show weakness and invite death.

Ira laughed and in her voice Fionn heard the wet snap of unused tendons and crack of old bone like a promise. The sound turned into a shriek as Emerick's power split *Ira's* aura.

"*Patientia*," *Ira* spat. "You are a fool to follow Fionn, greatest of many before her into my domain. I promised to kill you for your use of me, and now you come to me in such a weakened and pathetic state. Have you lost all your precious dignity at last?"

Fionn stepped forward, striking with her own wrath. "His life belongs to me." The shadows churned like ink in water. An answering echo of power erupted from beneath their feet.

Ira stiffened as Fionn's warning struck her. The red of her eyes brightened. "Life must exist in perfect equilibrium. For nearly a thousand years I have been locked here, the first of seven shadows, the first of seven demons, the first of seven to be imprisoned. The first to be betrayed by the lies of love." The ground shook, vibrating with the molten wrath coursing from *Ira*. "*Patientia* must be vanquished. I will have vengeance!" She screamed the last and Fionn heard a distant, echoing roar that sounded like the pained cry of a man and the eerie song of a wolf. The shadows closed in tighter.

Emerick cried out and his power pushed against the aura crushing him.

"Stop!" Fionn demanded, her anger exploding from her like

a freight train. *Ira* stumbled backward, her hair flying about her face as she slammed against the cliff face.

"Why?" *Ira* snarled in return, lunging against her chains. "So you can fall again for the betrayer, the bastard of lies? I have watched you, Fionn. I called you when your mother was murdered, when your father abandoned you to the Magistrate. I called to you when all hope was lost. I carried your soul through the sweet nights and the painful days until your empire was on its feet. When he—" *Ira* pointed at Emerick "—locked you in chains, I gave you the strength to break free."

Fionn glanced between them. *Ira* thought Emerick was one of the Seven.

"Emerick never locked me up. Admiral Tysek did. "

Ira hissed, and her attack ceased. Her red gaze rested again on Emerick, suddenly with a mix of interest followed by unmistakable revulsion. "The son of *Patience*."

Fionn tightened her fingers on Emerick's. Something wet coated their hands. She didn't have to look to know it was his blood.

"You want Tysek dead," Fionn said seeing her chance. "So do I."

Ira smiled, a wicked grin. "Free me, and I swear it will be done. Together we shall cover the world in darkness as the Virtuous have paved the way. There can be no light without the dark."

"I'm here to save the thousands of innocents under my protection," Fionn said. "I will not release mass slaughter upon a world that doesn't deserve it."

"Doesn't deserve it?" Howls rose all around, and the swirling darkness seethed like snakes, coiling tighter around them. The edges of *Ira*'s aura became jagged and sharp like spikes. "The world has succumbed to imprisonment. Only destruction will beget freedom."

Emerick stepped forward. His aura was weak, the slightest blow might crumble his defenses. "Is my father's death all you want?" he asked.

"The balance!" *Ira* screeched, and the thorns in her aura

stabbed at them. Emerick flinched and he stumbled against Fionn. "The balance must be restored or even your people will perish. This world will die and everything with it. The Seven of the Light have forgotten."

"If we promise to correct the balance, will you give her the power to defeat my father?" Emerick ground out.

"You, son of *Patience*, would risk your life for the balance?" Ira asked.

Emerick snarled, his power parting the darkness. "I have already given it." His hand tightened on Fionn's.

Ira began to pace back and forth, the length of untarnished chain scraping behind her like the train of a gown. Finally she stopped and pinned Emerick with a shriveling glare. "Do not disappoint me mortal, or I shall take back the gift of my immortal rage."

Heat rushed all around and the shadows fell upon them. Fionn gasped as her aura was infused with the pure unadulterated rage of true wrath. The power laced with hers, distinctly different than her own but submitting with eagerness to her will.

Ira shrank back into the farthest corner of her shadows, until the light of her eyes and her bindings were all that remained.

"Go forth and destroy," *Ira* commanded.

15

Fionn turned, blinking in the sudden shine of the mid-afternoon sun as it descended toward the horizon. The Hellion Horde was now visible, and they formed a ring around her team like wolves. They snarled, crouched in animalistic preparation for the slaughter, seething together like a mass of single minded creatures.

He used me to create them. Ira's voice came from the shadow behind them.

Fionn could see now the balance *Ira* spoke of. The Virtues had taken the world for themselves, locking Sin away in the darkness.

Emerick shivered next to her before his hand slipped from hers. "Promise me we will never do that again."

"Seven hells," Brax said. "Where have you been?" He was spattered in gore, and streams of red dripped from his sword. Bodies of Hellions lay around him and the others.

Darci turned to them, not a speck of blood on her, but the bodies strewn about her testified to her destructive power. "Their minds might be empty, but they still think in order to attack."

"What happened?" Fionn asked.

Atticus jerked a knife out of the chest of a Hellion, keeping an eye on the steady line of snarling brutes. "They attacked the moment you stepped into the shadow." He held out his arm to look at the backside of his bicep. "They have a hell of a bite, and they're totally immune to my powers."

"Imagine that," Emerick replied. "Mindless monsters unable to feel anything other than rage not succumbing to your lusty wiles."

The whizz of a high speed projectile sounded. Twenty meters away, the cliff-face towering over them exploded. Fionn was thrown to the ground along with the rest of her team. Bits of rubble pecked at her back and legs. Immediately her ears began to ring, and with the strike her instincts lashed out. Her power crashed against the stealth craft hovering overhead. Spider-webbed cracks appeared across its underbelly and all at once its stealth tech failed. The craft wobbled in the sky.

A slash of *Patientia* power in return caused her throat to constrict.

"Tysek's on that craft," Atticus shouted. He pulled Darci to her feet and sent his own bolt of power against the craft. It wobbled some more in the air.

"Bring it down," Fionn shouted. Her weapon was a few feet away, a giant boulder crushing the stock. All she had left was the handgun at her side, a belt knife, two grenades, and her supernatural abilities. More than enough to bring Tysek to an end and secure the Yukon territory.

She needn't have ordered the craft brought down. It landed and Admiral Tysek, dressed in a white suit and accompanied by a guard of fully armed soldiers, exited and marched toward them. His power fell over the Hellions and they stilled, their inhuman snarling dying down. Patience curled around Fionn's aura like water breaking around an immovable object. Out the corner of her eye Atticus stiffened.

Come to your doom, my love. Ira's voice crooned. Fionn shuddered once, and then what power *Ira*, Goddess of Wrath had possessed passed into her.

Emerick brought his weapon to his shoulder aiming, in the direction of his father. "Stop!"

Tysek continued to stride forward. The Hellions parted like water. Even though wrath gave the monsters strength, it was patience which focused and controlled them. They were his father's puppets.

The admiral's guards had their weapons on Fionn. At this range, her armor wasn't enough to stop the laser bullets. Tysek himself didn't appear armed, but then a man who could freeze the bullets in the air didn't need one.

"I'm surprised, Lieutenant Commander." Tysek strolled forward with the air of someone who was in control, in their element and unconcerned with the enemy presented before him. "You have executed your orders perfectly."

Fionn bristled and the new power allotted to her reacted like a whip, cracking from beneath their feet as though the mountain itself were breaking. She'd let Emerick live. He'd saved her life. Yet the feelings of betrayal Emerick sensed were still too close to her heart. With those simple words, Tysek had managed to bring all her simmering hurt to the surface.

16

Fionn's rage slammed against him. Emerick threw up his hands in front of him as her blow sent him to one knee. A moment later her power let up, and he felt it thunder through the earth toward his father.

"No," Emerick shouted. "Your orders mean nothing." He stood and rode the next wave of Fionn's power and followed behind her like a hammer driving the sharp blade of *Ira* deeper into his father's shield. The air cracked and split with the pressure, static electricity sparking between them.

Tysek stepped backward. His father recovered and the air hummed as Tysek's power rose again.

"You will obey," he said with total conviction. "Or die."

Emerick tried to block, but his father's power was the source of his own and it passed through his aura.

Fionn cried out and fell to the ground. She scrambled to her feet, blood dripping down her face. Rage blossomed in her eyes. Another crack issued from the ground.

Emerick tried to follow her power with his own as he had the first time. He might as well have flicked his finger against a pane of glass for all it did to harm Tysek. Exhausted from a day of stretching his less than divine powers to their limits, he had precious little energy to work with. His father had laid the last straw against his back, and he would not allow Tysek to break him further by killing Fionn, or worse, turn her against him a second time. He'd rather shatter his powers than let her think for a moment that he would ever betray her and endanger the people she loved.

"I follow no orders given by the Magistrate, *Father*."

Tysek's expression was impassive. Without warning, his power collided with Emerick's, ripping at him with all the force of a hurricane. Pain struck Emerick deep, as though he were being cleaved in two.

"I'm stronger than you, Emerick," Tysek said. "I will simply absorb your attacks. Still, you have carried out your orders, whether you knew them or not. You have given me the Insurgency's commander, and you managed to drain *Ira*'s power."

Emerick shouldn't have been surprised. The Magistrate was master of manipulation. They'd managed to bring entire continents under their control with nothing more than suggestion. Now Emerick knew why they had been unchallenged. They had locked any threatening powers who could keep their greediness in check in chains where they were useless.

"You thought your little rebellion against my authority would succeed?" Tysek asked, moving closer until the thick power of his aura wrapped around Emerick, with an ocean of deep silence. "From all my offspring I could have chosen as my heir, I chose you. Centuries of children I've abandoned and at last when I decide to culture one, I find I have picked the worst of the lot. Your mother, after all, was a street whore living in squalor. Still, her Sinful powers were formidable, but the whelp she birthed is nothing. In half a millennium I have never been so thoroughly disappointed."

So his father was as old as *Ira*. *Ira* had called him her mate. Yet Emerick knew she wasn't his mother. He'd seen his genetic code and read his own file of the woman he'd been born from. She was long dead, her sins eradicated after she'd done her duty and bore him.

His father's power let up, and Fionn attacked. She slashed with *Ira* and the mountain trembled. The blow stopped a foot from Tysek and dissipated.

Emerick clenched his fists, trying to steady his breathing. His father could stop his powers, even take them away, but this time his father had been focused on Fionn and hadn't finished the job. A corporal's error. Emerick filled his lungs, a shudder passing through him. Energy coursed anew through his veins. *Ira* had willed her power into Fionn and unknowingly, his father, God of Patience had done the same.

"Don't delude yourself, Father," he said, feeling steadier. He stepped around Fionn. He was only a few strides from the man, the closest they'd been in years. "You did abandon me. You've just been lucky we haven't met before now."

He met Fionn's gaze, *Ira's* light in her eyes, and nodded.

Fionn unleashed every ounce of her power. The ground beneath their feet bucked and shook. Emerick let *Patientia* loose, and the dust particles in the air froze.

Tysek threw up his hands, absorbing the strike. Sweat beaded on his forehead, gathering in the lines of his permanent frown. "I warn you Emerick," Tysek said, "you cannot control the Hellions. Your power is weak."

Emerick closed the gap between he and his father. "We have *Ira's* power. I don't want to control them, I want to destroy them," Emerick replied, strangely calm. He brought his right fist up, throwing his weight behind it and forcing it into Fionn's power, using it as a weapon. He felt the skin of his knuckles split on his father's jaw.

The Admiral's head snapped to the side and he stumbled. *Ira's* power raced up Emerick's arm, slicing the skin. Neither he nor his father was immune to wrath, and Emerick was counting on it.

His father spat into the dust, blood spattering on bits of rubble. Tysek's frown had disappeared, and his eyes were wide. "The final determination has been ordered, son. Attacking me won't save yourself, or your slut of an Undesirable lover."

"I'm not worried about my life." Emerick gestured again to

Fionn. She smiled, let loose her power and he struck again. Tysek's mouth curved into a grin as his fist came toward him. The admiral moved and surged upward, striking for Emerick's kidney. Emerick dodged, expecting the move, and landed a blow to his father's exposed back. *Ira* blanketed them both and jagged slices appeared in his father's uniform. Tysek twisted in a blur, catching him in the jaw with his boot. Emerick stumbled backward over a piece of wreckage and fell. A few more stitches popped in his back.

How the hell did his father move so fast?

"I'm centuries older than you, Emerick." Tysek's face fell back into its permanent frown.

"And that makes you somehow wiser?" Emerick asked. He watched for the bunching of muscles. Now that he had a gauge of how fast the man could move, the game had changed.

"I am the God of Patience. For the good of the world, I locked my mate away. Don't you dare think I wouldn't sacrifice my son for the same good."

Emerick knew his father, like so many other *Appetence* had bred for the sake continuing the line of power. At one time, Emerick had expected he would do the same. Whatever love Tysek may have felt died long before his conception and had been replaced by indoctrination and the drive toward a clear and perfect future. Like a flawless gem, Tysek couldn't see the past the brilliance and find the feathered cracks revealing its weaknesses in the stone's heart.

But for that one moment when Tysek spoke of his mate, of *Ira*, there was a flare of emotion, deep and just as vibrant as his obsession with perfection. *Ira* wasn't Emerick's mother, his mother had been mortal. His father had never loved the woman who'd carried him, but he was still obsessed with the Goddess of Wrath, just as she was obsessed with him.

"You love her still, and yet you let her rot in chains." Emerick surged forward, his power seeping through the growing cracks in his father's aura, and hooked into the teeming well of *Patientia*.

Tysek snarled, and he dropped his aura as Emerick hoped

he would. The horde of Hellions echoed his father's animalistic cry as he attacked. Emerick fell back, holding on to the cracks in his father's aura, and pried them apart.

Fionn cut past him. The rocky ground around Emerick and his father exploded in an eruption of fine dust particles. Emerick opened himself to that power, succumbing to it. Instead of tearing him to pieces, Fionn's energy slid past him and stabbed through the crack in Tysek's aura.

Tysek winced and stumbled. His power faltered. Whatever had been holding the Hellions back failed, and the cannibalistic monstrous remains of once good men leapt forward. Emerick heard the familiar crunch of Brax's sword as it struck bone. Darci cried out as Hellions descended on her.

"No!" Atticus screamed from behind them.

Tysek, blood welling from thousands of cuts in his skin, turned toward Fionn away from Emerick. He drew his sidearm, a small silver weapon with maybe enough charge for one killing shot.

Fionn reached for her own weapon strapped to her back. Emerick could see by her face she knew she wouldn't draw in time.

Emerick had waited long enough for his chance. There wouldn't be another.

He slid the blade from his sheath and plunged it into his father's back. The blade was sharp and glided smoothly between ribs and cartilage, striking a lung. Tysek's power cut off, his grip on the palm-sized weapon failed and it clattered to the ground.

Fionn turned on the vast horde and Emerick shivered as she unleashed everything she was upon the wave of death rolling toward them. The first few ranks were ripped to shreds. Atticus grabbed a discarded rifle and fired, expertly ending the closest. The horde turned and ran.

Tysek fell to his knees and Emerick caught him, easing him down to the ground.

His father's face was contorted in pain. Blood trickled out of the corner of his mouth, and the short rasping breaths of a man drowning in the end of his own doing were loud, even with the sounds of battle continuing in the distance.

"It is done," Tysek found the breath to speak.

Emerick nodded. He expected to feel nothing, he expected to feel everything, but he did not expect the crystal clear calm that settled over him. There was no going back after this. His future and the futures of thousands, perhaps hundreds of thousands were changed by this one act of patricide. It was right, and it was wrong, but it had to be done.

A great keening echoed from behind him. He discerned *Ira's* wail as a mere dying vibration trembling through the mountainside.

"Yes," Emerick said, finding his voice. "It is done."

"I was immortal," Tysek said. He coughed and a red bubble formed on his lips. "Mortality will find you as it has found me, my son. The light will eradicate the shadows."

His father's eyes rolled back, and a few more wet, raspy breaths were all that passed between his lips. The final stillness of death descended.

"Without light, there wouldn't be shadow," Emerick said to his father's corpse. Gently he closed the man's unseeing eyes, stood and silently returned to Fionn's side. The Hellions had fled and he'd promised to destroy them.

17

The room slowly emptied of Fionn's officers and errand boys, for the night. All of them were exhausted from keeping thousands of people fed and rested. The week had been spent cleaning up the messy leavings of the great battle. Fionn had left Emerick behind, instead taking James and Brax, her two favored guards, to "take a walk, and get some food." This had been the longest damned walk Emerick had ever waited through. He knew she was avoiding him. They still had unfinished business, and the furtive glances they gave each other in passing were merely an acknowledgement, not a settlement.

Emerick sat hunched over the plans for extended security measures across the southern front, his aura closed tight over him like a shield, keeping off the flickers of power from the other *Appetence* in the room. Tobias had his corner of crystal screens with the other techs. Atticus and Darci had taken residence across from each other at the long table. Darci was scrolling through some kind of report, no doubt something to do with her new duties as refugee organizer. Atticus had his head resting on folded arms, sleeping. No one had questioned his presence as her bodyguard, as he rarely left her side. Michael, their insane companion, was under Darci's careful watch.

Fionn's power stuttered out, breaking his musings. He stifled a growl.

It had been a week, gods be damned, a week of waiting with the flick of her temper around every corner, in every frustrated snap of her power. He'd waited for that moment alone. He could feel her pacing like a caged predator up on the observatory decks. With *Ira*'s power strengthening her aura, he could sense, even at this distance the seething nature of her thoughts.

"Hell's bells!" Darci cried out.

Atticus woke and leapt to his feet, the reflective flash of a knife in his hand. "What is it?"

The whole room had jumped, except Tobias who had plugged his headset into his tech and most likely couldn't hear them over his music.

Darci stood, her hands braced on her console, and glared at Emerick. "I have had it with your mopey, miserable thoughts. Get out." She pointed to the door.

"Excuse me?" Emerick asked.

"Atticus," Darci snapped. The man in question stiffened, meeting her eyes. Emerick didn't hear what went on between them, but it was obvious they were having a private conversation.

A slow smile spread over Atticus's face. He sheathed his dagger, turned to Emerick and tipped his head toward the door. "Let's go."

Emerick didn't need any encouragement. He'd seen Darci drop a soldier with nothing more than a glance. He had work to do and didn't want to spend the day snoozing on the floor.

As soon as the command room door shut, Atticus leaned against the wall with a fluid grace that had Emerick suddenly thinking, *predator*. "Emerick—"

"Shut it," Emerick said. "I don't need help from you with this."

A dagger zipped through the air, inches from Emerick's nose, and embedded in the wall with a resounding thud.

"You do, and you'll keep your mouth shut," Atticus said,

his voice going dark. "I was a sex slave for the Magistrate for six years."

Emerick had guessed some of what Atticus had suffered at the hands of his father's government. So he shut up and folded his arms across his chest, waiting for whatever advice his friend had to impart.

Atticus uncoiled. The languid way he closed the distance between them startled Emerick enough that he moved backward, his shoulders hitting the wall. *Luxurian* power wrapped around him like silk.

"I can read desire." Atticus reached past him, and a ribbon of *Luxurian* power brushed against his aura. The man was pissed, and not for the first time since they'd become tenuous friends, Emerick worried if he would stab him. "You want her, and your unsatisfied need to tangle with her is affecting my tangling with Darci. If I see you before morning, and you haven't figured this out with Fionn—" Atticus jerked back, ripping the dagger from the wall "—then I *will* put you out of your misery."

The door they'd just left hissed open.

"Whoa! Sorry guys, I didn't realize you were here."

Atticus smiled and pushed off the wall. "Tobias, excellent timing as usual."

Tobias smiled. "If I didn't know how straight our *Patientia* friend is, I'd be jealous." He slipped past Atticus and headed down the hall.

Atticus gestured down the hall toward the lift that went to the upper levels. "Until dawn."

Emerick glared at Atticus and marched down the hall.

By the time he reached the lift, he could sense Fionn's agitation growing. No doubt she'd felt the quick strike of Atticus's power. Emerick still did, and it pissed him off. It was a good thing Doctor Blanc had removed his stitches this morning, just in time to give him new ones.

Brax stepped out of the shadows when he neared the observation deck hatch. "Ready for round two?" he asked with a wry smile.

"She doesn't need a bodyguard. You should get some sleep. No one would be stupid enough to touch her now."

Brax glanced at the closed hatch. "Who said I was here to guard her?"

A possessive fury gripped Emerick. "Where's James?"

"Where do you think?"

Emerick cut off a snarl. "You should go."

Brax let out a breath. "I had a bet with Tobias you'd be here sooner."

Emerick ignored the comment and keyed the code for the hatch. The scent of wood smoke was still thick in the northern air. Because of the permafrost, and the number of bodies, they wouldn't have been able to bury them fast enough before decay bred sickness. With the pyres they were able to send the spirits of the dead into the afterlife, if there was such a place, the day after the battle.

Fionn paced the length of the observation deck. The sky outside the thin slotted windows was red with the late night sun. This time of year the sun didn't quite set. It lingered on the horizon. In few minutes it would begin to rise high in the sky.

Fionn had stood with him three days before as he'd watched his father's body become ash on the wind. He'd needed to see it himself. To believe that what he'd done had truly happened. The flames of a hundred fires had erased the Magistrate's shadow from the Yukon. They'd stood alone, silently sharing the end of the struggle, with the blood of their enemies still dried in the cracks of their hands.

In the days following, she'd retreated into herself. So had he, but enough was enough.

"Fionn, stop," James said, breaking Emerick's reverie. The officer grabbed her arm as she strode past where he stood near the wall.

Fionn turned on James, and Emerick sensed the quick jab of her powers. The other man winced.

Emerick stepped over the threshold of the blast doors. James caught his eye and stiffened, moving away from Fionn.

"I don't believe you were ordered here," James said.

For the last week, James had hovered around Fionn like a fly, irritating the hell out of him. Besides, the man had flinched under her power. He'd been right that he'd never be able to survive the full force of Fionn's ire like Emerick could.

"I don't believe I need your permission to approach my commander," Emerick answered, the bite of his aura in the air.

"You should leave, Emerick." Fionn's eyes reflected some of the red glow she'd inherited from *Ira's* power

"No," Emerick said. The last week had been filled with enough "Yes, sirs" for a lifetime. To James he said, "If you don't leave now, I won't be held responsible for your injuries."

"Is that a threat?" James asked. His hand drifted toward his sidearm.

"It's a promise," Emerick said. He let enough of his power free to cut out the hum of the compound's noise and force James to comprehend how dangerous the situation was for a mere human. The only sound was the whisper of his and Fionn's power sliding against one another like static electricity. James made the right choice. He swallowed once, and nodded at Fionn before escaping through the hatch, closing it behind him.

The metal clang of the door locking shuddered through the room. Far off a howl rose across the expanse of fields. Fionn turned to the open window.

"Hellions?" Emerick asked. They'd spent the night he killed his father hunting every last one of them down. If there were more, they would need to finish them. He'd never forget the eerie hair-raising sound of monsters who had once been men.

"No. Those are the wolves," she replied, fondness for the beasts thick in her tone. She'd always loved the wolves. "What do you want, Emerick?" She sounded tired, but her aura curled around his, the barbs of her power scraping along his skin. As before, heat followed where her power trailed over his body. A thin line of red appeared down his right arm as though she had dragged her nail from the sensitive skin of his elbow to his wrist. He sucked in a breath, and forgot about men and wolves.

"More," he whispered. The sensation of her nails trailed over his chest. He stepped closer. She turned and faced him, standing her ground, red flaring in her gaze. He rested his hands on her waist, her sharp power snapping against his exposed arms, but she held back.

He bit back a growl.

"Two years thinking I betrayed you and that's all you've got to throw at me?" He taunted. She was keeping her wild power in check, probably thinking that the warning she'd given him would fend him off. Like hell. He tightened his fingers and pulled her hips against his.

"Get your hands off me," she said, dangerously quiet. "You might not have betrayed me, but that doesn't mean I've forgiven you for it." Her energy whipped across his back. The dark t-shirt he wore shredded, and the cool night air brushed against his skin. Her hands moved to his arms, clutching his biceps as though she had claws.

"I'm not letting you run from me."

She pushed against him, trying to move him. "I am *not* running from you."

"Then stop running," he said. "We both know what we've spent the last week dancing around. If you think James will be able to handle the waves of power—"

She froze and her power raked down his arms like claws. "James has nothing to do with this."

Emerick shuddered.

"I warned you, Fi," he growled. "You had your chance to be rid of me and I've lost my patience waiting." He locked one arm around her waist, holding her against him, relishing the feel of her warm body against his. With his other hand he reached up and gently tugged the tie in her hair, freeing the severe bun she'd twisted her shoulder-length tresses into. Gentle still, he twined his fingers in her auburn locks, and tilted her head back, bringing her wrath to the surface by compromising her stance. He had her, and her instincts would cause her to fight back, stand with him toe-to-toe in challenge.

He accepted.

"Keep it up—" he urged, pausing to nip with his teeth at her exposed throat, "—and the wolves won't be the only ones howling."

Her power surged around him and their auras weaved together, cracking like lightning. Her nails dug deeper into the skin of his shoulders, pulling him toward her. He fisted his hand tighter in her hair and dragged her lips to his. He heard a ripping sound and suddenly he was shirtless.

He broke off the kiss. "I'm going to run out of shirts," he chided, not minding in the least bit. He didn't give her a chance to respond and ripped open her uniform jacket, the buttons clattering on the metal flooring. He pushed up her shirt.

"More." She returned the demand, her nails digging into his back.

Where skin touched skin, a sizzle of current clashed between them as polar opposites were forced together. Her shirt fell to the ground and he picked her up, his hands gripping her firm buttocks. Her legs wrapped around his middle as she devoured his mouth, and he pushed her against the closest wall.

"If you stop Emry—" she gasped, the fingers of her left hand pushing under the waistband of his pants. Her power flared, rippling over them both. "—I will lock you up again. I might even kill you."

He smiled into her hair, nibbling on her earlobe as her movements sent heat spreading from his core. With her new powers it would be easy to rip him to shreds. Like now, he'd gladly accept the night when she finally ended him. But he wasn't about to make it easy for her.

"You can try."

***

Fionn's hand shook against Emerick's chest as she gasped for air. The cold breeze trailing through the lookout openings was welcome against her too-warm skin. She felt flushed all over. She ran her hands over his chest, his shoulders, feeling the scars she'd made and the new raised welts, evidence of their lovemaking.

"At least I'm not bleeding," he said from where he still hovered on all fours over her. The heat pouring off their bodies was enough to keep out the chill, but not for long.

"I'm not as angry at you now as I was," she said, helpless to keep from smiling. Unlike before, she'd been unable to score his flesh. Not for the first time, she wondered if in killing his father, some of his immortal power had been transferred to him. It was the only reason she hadn't ripped him apart, not that she hadn't tried.

He lowered and kissed her again. There was a pale light in his eyes; it hadn't been there before. "So does this mean you'll stop avoiding me?" he asked.

"As long as you follow orders."

He kissed her neck, her collarbone. "Never." He spoke, lips moving against her skin. Heat followed his touch and lingered.

She wrapped her leg around his hip and surged upward, flipping him onto his back. "You are my subordinate," she reminded him, her nails gripping his shoulders.

He turned his head to the side and kissed her left wrist. "Only when we're working."

Her comm, discarded along with the jumbled pile of their clothing crackled to life. "*Commander?*" Carter's voice asked.

Emerick stopped and she closed her eyes, reaching for the infernal device. His hand found hers, stopping the motion. "Let the officers handle it, Fi. I think you've earned a night off. Several in fact."

"Emry," she protested. Still, she was seduced by the promise of neglecting her duties for a few hours at least.

The comm crackled again. "*We've been contacted by a rebel faction. They are requesting assistance. Tobias shows the signal originates from the outer edge of the new territory to the east.*"

Fionn frowned. "There isn't another rebel faction east of here."

"One of the scout craft reported seeing Magistrate activity to the southeast yesterday." Emerick reminded her. He reached for the comm over her body. "We'll be right there," he replied.

There was a pause. "*Understood, uh- sir.*"

"I'd hoped the Magistrate would give us a break," Emerick said as he began searching for his clothes amid the strewn mess of discarded shirts and pants. "You didn't rip off my pants, did you?" he asked.

Fionn handed him his pair of mostly undamaged fatigues and reached for her own. "We aren't the only ones out here trying to survive, we just happen to be the most successful."

Emerick's aura withdrew from hers as he retreated into himself. They'd not talked about the death of his father, or that Emerick had wielded the blade. He'd killed one of the Seven, and she possessed the pure power of *Ira*. The Goddess of Wrath had faded, and only a small shadow remained where she'd been locked away. They hadn't spoken of that either. Fionn knew *Ira* was gone, now preserved inside her. There wasn't anything to talk about.

"If the Magistrate can't break us, they'll break any possible allies we might have," he said.

"Then we'd better get a move on, Lieutenant Commander." Fionn yanked her pants on and threw her shirt over her head followed by her now useless uniform jacket.

Emerick paused buttoning his own pants. "Did you just promote me?"

"I believe I did."

"I accept." He pulled her in for a quick kiss and when he stepped back there was mischief in his eyes. "Shall we return...General?"

She arched her eyebrow and took her boots from his hand. "Watch it," she said, aiming a slash of power at his thigh. The fabric of his pants split.

He shook his head and followed her through the hatch.

Command was a hive of activity when they reached it. All available officers had convened. More than one stifled yawns and rubbed sleep from their eyes. Silence fell as she filled the doorway. All eyes landed on her, and then Emerick behind her. A few of her men smiled in approval. She saw Atticus dip his head in acknowledgement, his stare on the man following her. It was a good bet he'd *arranged* Emerick into confronting her. She'd have to remember to thank the man. Not only was he a lethal soldier, but a helpful ally.

"James," she said. "Report."

James glared at Emerick, who was still shirtless. "They're on the comm," he said.

"I've been receiving interference signals from the Magistrate," Tobias said. "The order for the attack originated from a little place I used to call home. Magistrate central."

"The people asking for help aren't lying," Darci said, opening her eyes. "They *are* refugees. Without *Patientia* blocking my powers, I can sense maybe five hundred or more people from their location."

Fionn clasped her hands behind her back and glanced at Emerick. He winked and went to his console. She moved to the front of her Command. Her people straightened in preparation for another battle. Her trust was reflected in the attention they gave to her.

"All hands to stations. I want all available ground troops to the carriers. Brax, lead the advance guard and provide air support. We'll be fifteen minutes behind you. James, you have the command. Atticus, Darci, Tobias—" she allowed her gaze to wander down Emerick's chest, "—Lieutenant Commander, let's go meet our neighbors." Her commands were punctuated with "yes, Sirs" and the scramble to action.

It was time to fulfill her promises to *Ira* and return the balance to a world broken with fear.

Energy and anticipation filled the room. These people knew their enemy, and they knew how to fight, how to win; and they had the patience to wait to strike and the rage to bring the Magistrate to its knees.

THE CHRONICLES OF SIN
AGE OF GREED

BOOK III

1

Above the humming of the generators and the pit-pat of constant rain, a woman's scream cut the morning mist. Cadence tightened his small fingers around the plastic-wrapped book. If he looked back he would be tempted to unleash the power inside him, stop the screams and the man who caused them. Turning back would mean being sick for weeks afterward, it would mean being punished for challenging the King. He growled in defiance, low enough that his voice twisted with the generator's noise and became nothing. If they found his secrets, if they followed him and found... He shivered.

The militia would lower the drawbridge and the accompanying force field in a few moments. He would have seconds to make his escape. The floodlights swept the courtyard again, illuminating the centuries-old cobbles. This fortress had been a stronghold of a barbarian chieftain, before time transformed it into a ruin. But Angus, the new King and Cadence's stepfather, had built upon the old foundations. His metal fortress, more a box than a castle, was the only surviving rebel outpost on the isle. The rest of the land, surrounded by turbulent seas and the ever watchful Magistrate, was a radioactive dead zone. Because of the waste land, an echo of a centuries-past war, not even the Magistrate was willing to cross and force their surrender. It was why this small city had evaded its eye. They were free from the pressed and perfect tyranny of the Virtuous. Cadence gritted his teeth. Even freedom, he knew, had a price. His mother paid for it more and more. Time would tell how long that freedom would keep her, or any of them, alive.

The roving spotlight passed Cadence's hiding spot, leaving him in darkness. He darted forward until he reached the small drain on the other side of the yard. The drain ran under the wall and was too small for an adult, but not for him. He grabbed the grate covering it and strained against its weight to open it. It should have been bolted down, but someone had left the tools unguarded and he'd stolen the bolt cutters. The grate screeched open, metal against the stones.

"Did you hear that?" one of guardsmen asked. The scuff of boots stopped nearby. Cadence froze.

"It's nothin'," the other guard said. "Just your ears fooling you."

"They're not fooling anyone."

Another shout fell through the courtyard. With it came the echo of a power burst. Cadence shivered as the familiar energy tingled across his skin, the power of *Invidia*, envy.

"The King is at it again," the first guard said, his voice a little younger, less rough than his partner's. "Makes me wonder what his wife said to him this time."

"Quiet!" his older companion hissed. "There have been enough hangin's this month as it is. I don't want to be up there swingin' in the wind next."

Cadence pushed sodden hair out of his face. The guards hurried away, no doubt both unnerved by the prospect of being caught gossiping about the King. They should be. Cadence had seen his stepfather do worse than hang a man for even a sideways glance. The truth of the matter was, Angus struggled to support the fortress and its inhabitants. The growing stress of trying to keep a hungry population fed had led to an unpredictable temper. It led to obsession and unbridled greed, both things Cadence knew too well.

Rain blurred his vision as he slid into the drain, legs first.

Immediately his clothes were soaked as his body blocked the drainage of water from the yard. Cold water into his boots. He closed the grate, keeping a grip on it with his right hand, his left holding the book, as he hung half suspended toward the drain's black hole.

Some day he would be too big to fit through the drain tunnel and he'd get stuck. He hoped today wasn't that day.

He let go.

His backside slammed against the drain as it sloped under the wall. A second later he shot out into open air. He had enough time to suck in a gulp of breath before he hit the water. Clawing upward, he gasped when his head finally broke the surface. The drawbridge was fully lowered, covering his escape. The book floated in its thick plastic wrapping nearby. He grabbed for it, and clutched it under his arm. Hampered by the book he swam toward the opposite bank like a frog. The far bank was muddy when he reached it. Still, he scrambled through the sludge caked on the side of the moat. Following his usual path, he reached upward for the ledge... and found nothing.

Fear stabbed him. It was pitch black. Had he swum in the wrong direction, back towards the castle?

"No," a familiar voice said. A hand somewhat larger than his own grabbed his, and he was suddenly jerked upward, landing with a splash in the crescent of a pipe. "You went the right direction, as always."

"What are you doing here?" Cadence demanded. He struggled to speak over the shivers wracking his body. The moat was cold. "What if they catch you?"

Green flashed from the other boy's eyes, a few feet above him. "They couldn't catch me with a nuclear weapon; they won't catch me here. Besides, I thought I'd save you the trouble of traveling to me. It's cold this morning." His friend said it as though it was too cold for him to be out in the turbulent weather. Cadence had seen worse. This year's winter had stretched far into spring, threatening to broach summer. At least they'd had spring, wet and dismal as it was.

Cadence stood and looked back toward the castle. He shrank into the darkness of the tunnel. From here he couldn't see the light of the room where his mother and stepfather were.

"Angus came home without any new food," Cadence told the other boy. He didn't have to say that his mother was taking the anger that would otherwise be meted out on some other unfortunate soul. "He'll force me to use again tomorrow."

"Today, Cadence." The other boy came to stand next to him. He rested his hand on Cadence's shoulder. There was warmth in that hand and it flowed into him, stopping the chattering of his teeth from his plunge in the moat. "It's morning, remember?"

As if on cue, a swallow trilled nearby, probably hunting the bugs that flitted back and forth across the moat's surface.

"You promised you'd stay away. He kills all citizens without registration."

The rain tapped slower against the water's surface.

The other boy's hand tightened on his shoulder. "I have something for you."

Cadence turned away from the castle. "Another book?" he asked, knowing what it was.

The other boy's eyes flashed green, and in the brief light they cast Cadence could see the crinkle of a smile at the corners of his friend's lashes. "Good guess. How many books is that this month?"

"A few," Cadence answered.

"You read faster than I do." Cadence could tell he was pleased. "No, I didn't bring any books this time. I brought something else. You need your strength." The older boy placed both his hands on Cadence's shoulders. The familiar feel of the other boy's aura pulled at him sharply. Hot energy rushed into him. The power infused Cadence with warmth, strength, and a renewed vigor. It was over much too quickly. His friend stumbled against the side of the pipe, weakened.

Cadence's friend had done this before, shared his power with him, but never so much. It filled his aura. He felt as if he'd had too much to eat. Nausea overrode the ecstasy flowing through him and he ran to the edge of the tunnel. He gagged. Perhaps if he'd had warning he wouldn't feel so sick. There was simply too much power. It strained at his skin, pushing his aura out unbearably.

"Easy," the older boy said, coming close, but not touching him again. "Breathe. It'll settle. *Avaritia* doesn't like to be forced. It does what it will. I wouldn't have given you this much if you weren't going to need it."

Somehow the boy, the other *Avaritia*, always knew when Angus lost his temper. Each time he had failed to provide for the city. And Cadence would be forced to cast his aura to appease the King's need to survive.

The first time Angus had forced him, Cadence was sick for days afterward. The other *Avaritia* came in through the window, scaling the castle walls using nothing but his fingers and toes. He'd reassured Cadence that this sickness would pass. He'd given him a small drop of power, enough to help him recover before he slipped out the window and disappeared. The next morning Cadence had felt stronger than ever. After that, every time he'd been forced to cast his aura, his friend had brought him books, and a drop of power to help ease the sickness.

"Why so much?" Cadence asked. The power had started to settle, mixing with his own. He could do anything, go anywhere, and no one could stop him.

"I said take it easy, boy." His companion's voice echoed with sudden age, a ragged old man's voice. Not the voice of the adolescent he appeared to be. Cadence wasn't fooled. He knew his friend was ages old. That was the problem with insatiability: those who held dominion over greed could always sense the truth behind a greedy heart. "This much power could go to your head. I've warned you before. You are dangerous. If you do not use in moderation, you'll tear yourself apart."

Cadence considered the words. "Is that why you gave me Beowulf last time?" Beowulf had been blinded by his greed for power and wealth. It had led to his downfall.

His friend was silent. He'd moved to the opening of the pipe, the lightening sky giving him a subtle silhouette. "It has a few good lessons, if you care to learn them. It took you a long time to read it."

"It's a big book. And it's very boring."

The other boy turned, and now Cadence could see the smile on his profile. "Tell me, what did you learn?"

Cadence had already formulated his answer beforehand, knowing his nameless friend and mentor would ask. "I learned men are inherently greedy."

"You knew that before."

Cadence had expected that response and had his reply ready too. "Yes, I did. Beowulf confirmed that men have always been greedy and will never change."

Somewhere close by someone screamed. Cadence jumped. Another woman. Another child missing. The woman's sobbing drew closer. The drawbridge was nearby. She'd be heading for that. Cadence moved to the mouth of the pipe and stood next to the taller boy.

"My daughter," the woman cried. "She's gone!"

One of the guardsmen replied, trying to calm her, but it did nothing to stop Cadence's racing heart, or the fury in his veins.

After today, hers wouldn't be the only screams to be heard in the morning. More children would disappear. They had been disappearing for weeks. Everything had a price, something Angus hadn't learned yet.

Cadence suddenly felt like Grendel, the wretched creature who'd terrorized Beowulf's people. He was even hiding under the drawbridge, like a legendary monster waiting to snatch its prey as it crossed his threshold.

"I feel like Grendel," he admitted, breaking the silence between them.

The other boy turned to him, a curious intensity darkening his features. "No, you are not Grendel. Don't even think it."

The woman was crying again. She would wake the castle, and the town. Her daughter was missing. Cadence knew where the girl would be. She'd be with the other children, the others who were lost, sold to pay for what Angus couldn't scavenge, grow, or raise. Cadence's powers couldn't satisfy the greed, only fuel the desire for more.

Angus had vowed to find the children and bring them back. They would never find them. They'd been taken far away, in the white air craft that landed on the beach when no one was watching. Cadence wondered when they would come for him, when they would place the blame where it belonged and look under the bridge to kill the beast destroying them bit by bit.

"How am I not Grendel?" Cadence asked. "Someday what Angus's greed demands will create a monster he cannot control. He forces me to do what he wants. He doesn't know what that is doing. I am the monster he's making. The damage won't stop until someone finds a Beowulf to stop me. You know it's true."

The distant cries of the woman quieted. The rain had stopped and the swallows were out in force now. Their darting, arrow-shaped bodies whistled in the morning.

"Beowulf still had to contend with the dragon," his friend said, his green eyes lighting the darkness. "Angus needs allies in his fight against the Virtuous. No amount of greed will help him in that. What band of warriors might come to join his ranks, I wonder."

Cadence didn't have an answer. An answer didn't seem necessary. He stared at his nameless friend, wondering who he thought would play the part of the dragon.

2

"It's a treaty," said Fionn, once upon a time rebel commander and now admiral of the Insurgency. She paced in front of her comm screens, the council members from the other compounds watching from the displays. One screen showed the brief request that had arrived from a small rebel block located in, of all places, Scotland earlier in the morning. They were all that was left of the country.

Michael sat in the furthest and darkest corner, where he wouldn't disturb the proceedings. Hours of endless arguments and decisions weren't his business, but he'd been "asked" to attend. Fionn never asked for anything, her requests were orders no insurgent would disobey. He'd have been happy in his bunk, left alone. This cramped underground command room, the many tempers and people it contained, made him jumpy. They wouldn't hurt him—he knew this—but it didn't stop his skin from itching.

"That's not worded like any treaty I've ever read," said Lieutenant Braxton, Fionn's right hand man.

Emerick, her general and soon to be husband, pushed off from the wall and held out a hand, stopping Fionn's incessant pacing. Michael understood the kind of attraction that existed between Fionn and Emerick. He'd felt it himself once, before his mind had been shattered.

"Fionn, stop," Emerick said from his place. "This isn't a

treaty. It's another ploy to get us to show weakness."

"What if it isn't?" Fionn replied. "What if there are starving people on that nuclear island?"

The bite of Fionn's wrath caused Michael to flinch. No one else panicked when her power, so similar, at first, to an Industria's, brushed against their auras. Fionn's aura was cutting. The many stresses of running the entire Yukon, her increased powers and responsibilities fending off the constant attacks from the Magistrate, had worn down her control. Lately, the entire compound was on edge. They weren't hiding anymore. They were fighting and gaining ground. Accomplishing these insurmountable tasks had been wearing on the entire underground compound. Michael tried to settle into his chair, hoping his bored expression would keep him from being noticed. He didn't need to be here, so why was he?

"We can't help everyone," Emerick said quietly.

"Then what is all this for?" Fionn retorted.

Her anger grated against Michael's still fragile mind. He'd been tortured into insanity by the Magistrate, and used as a slave for years before that, like every other Sin who fell into their grip.

"Easy," Darci, the healer and *Temperantia* who'd pulled him from the depths of insanity, said gently. Her powers were over the mind and the heart. Without her constant monitoring of his mental faculties, he wouldn't be whole enough to be of much use. Since she'd rescued him, very little of his mind had been his and his alone. She reached for his hand now, but he shifted, bracing himself for the intrusive touch of her calming thoughts. Atticus, his onetime apprentice, reached between them and took his wife's hand.

Atticus nodded at Michael. As a fellow *Luxurian*, he could sense his desires better than anyone else. A *Luxurian* was a master of desire. Any kind. As such, he and Atticus possessed dangerous and seductive abilities, and they knew each other's aura as well as they knew their own.

Atticus knew he didn't need Darci's power reaching into his thoughts and rearranging them again like a puzzle with pieces that didn't quite fit together. She said his mind was still fragile and Michael agreed. His thoughts still felt feather-like, waiting to be blown off a cliff to twist and grasp at empty space again. But he couldn't depend on her power to keep him on the ground. The time had long since passed for him to be himself without Darci's assistance.

Emerick's *Patientia* power flowed into the air, negating Fionn's simmering anger. The room visibly relaxed. Another thing about Sinful and Virtuous power: where opposites collided, they canceled each other out, as long as their powers were equal. Emerick was Fionn's opposite, and they clashed like the sea on a rocky shore. There was beauty and pain in watching them together, so perfect, so made for one another.

Michael took a deep breath and crossed his arms over his chest. He'd hoped the empty pain in his heart would heal, but time had instead deepened the wound. He shouldn't be here. His tenuous hold on his own power was a danger. Fionn never ordered anything without a reason. By the direction of the current conversation, he liked her reasons for having him here less and less. The command room, with its press of volatile auras, was no place for him.

Admiral Fionn took a deep breath. "I apologize. The Scottish people are an ocean away. We don't have the forces to send over and help them secure their borders from the Magistrate on their word alone."

"Most likely," said one of the other council members on one of the many screens, "they are already compromised by Magistrate influence."

"Most likely?" James, Fionn's first officer, added. "Of course they have infiltrated them."

"Tobias," Fionn said. Tobias had been with Michael, Atticus and Darci when they escaped the Magistrate's capital city and fled to the Yukon. He was a genius, better at crafting technology than the Magistrate. If the Magistrate had been more willing to employ him than condemn him for his personal choices, they would have probably quashed the Insurgency by now.His valuable inventions were a driving force behind their efforts. He also possessed the power of *Invidia*, also known as envy, yet he never used it. "Send the council members those images you were able to pull from the satellites."

Tobias flashed a thumbs-up and went to work, his fingers flying over his controls. "Sure thing, Boss."

After a moment the council members' eyes widened and muttering broke out as each conversed with their own people off screen.

"*This* is London?" the bulky man from the UNF asked. His people had dug out an existence behind the great Niagara Falls, hence the unimaginative name Under Niagra Falls. He had nearly six hundred people in his stronghold, an impressive number of refugees.

"This *was* London," Fionn corrected.

The picture flashed up onto Michael's personal screen on the table in front of him. The city had been razed to the ground. Parts were still on fire. Most of it was rubble, with a few stubborn walls remaining. The Magistrate had bombed it recently. He'd seen a picture of the once proud city; it had gleamed with a thousand years of mismatched architecture. Last month there had been rumors of rebel settlements there. Now, these new images proved any such rebellion had been crushed. The Magistrate was no longer willing to turn a blind eye to any uprising.

"This happened yesterday," Fionn said. "Our potential allies are requesting aid as the Magistrate has started their hunting here"—she gestured to the south end of the isle— "and are working their way north."

"That place is a nuclear waste land. How could anyone survive?" another council member asked.

"How do *any* of us survive the Magistrate?" Fionn replied. She turned from the screens to her people. Her red-tinged gaze landed on Michael. "We need someone to ascertain whether or not we should lend our assistance."

Michael glared back at her, challenging her to call him out, give him a reason for his presence in this meeting. She tipped her head to the screen, the red glow of her eyes, a mark of her immortal power as the strongest *Ira* walking the planet, grew brighter for a moment. Her powers made her a goddess in her own right, as her husband's made him a god. Still, Michael didn't feel the need to cower under that gaze, as so many others did. He knew how mortal they truly were.

Out of courtesy he looked at the satellite image of a large fortress, surrounded by a river. It was obviously a militarized compound. The banner of the dragon flew from its ramparts, gold on a green field.

Michael narrowed his eyes at Fionn.

So that's why he was here. Someone needed to take the trip and she'd chosen him for the job. He began to question her intelligence. She'd better have a damned good reason to send him away from the compound.

"If the Magistrate is bombing rebel outposts," the man from the UNF said, "this won't be a diplomatic exploration. It'll be a rescue. Assuming they are not allied already with the Magistrate."

Fionn placed her hands on her hips. "I believe the best course of action is to send a small team to investigate and make contact with King Angus, their leader. In a few days a small team can research what they are really up to. That will give us enough time to plan our engagement with the Magistrate and assemble our forces for a joint strike."

"Do you have someone in mind for this mission?" the UNF leader asked.

"No," Fionn said. "I'd like volunteers."

Michael took a steadying breath and settled back in his chair, hoping he didn't look apprehensive, excited, or terrified. Everything he felt and more. She had ordered him here specifically for this. He wanted to volunteer. He was tired of Darci's worried touches, always checking the structure of his mind. And Atticus, well, he needed his distance from him for a while. Besides, his powers would only be a bonus to whoever else joined him on the mission. A *Luxurian* could sense desire, and desire wasn't simply sexual in nature. Atticus's power was formidable enough, but Michael had always been stronger. Just as he could now sense Fionn's desire that he volunteer, he would be able to sense the desires of this King Angus. He would know almost instantly if the man was trustworthy.

Next to him Atticus stirred. "What's wrong?" he asked, so quiet his voice was only a low rumble.

Before he could answer, Brax stood. "I volunteer, Sir," he said.

"Sit down," James barked. "We need you here in case the Magistrate attacks."

Brax rolled his eyes. "You've got a powerhouse of Sins here. The last direct Magistrate attack at our doors was over six months ago. I barely bloodied my sword. This place is making me stir crazy. No offense, Fionn, but I have to get out."

"I accept," Fionn said after a moment.

"How small a team were you thinking?" Brax asked.

"Two," Fionn answered.

Michael tensed, his heart pounding. He stood, before another could take the spot. "I volunteer."

Fionn glanced at him, and the corner of her mouth turned upward. "I accept. Council dismissed. Lieutenant Brax, Lieutenant Knight, you will depart within the hour," she said, calling Michael by his last name.

Michael waited until the room was empty before he left, feeling the weight of his decision. Atticus gave him a long look before he followed his wife toward the door.

By the time he reached the modest room assigned to him, he was shaking. This mission came out of the blue. Why would Fionn assign him to infiltrate possible enemy territory? He couldn't even walk through these underground corridors without feeling trapped in a dungeon again. There were no chains, but the instinctive fear of closed spaces remained. Over the last few months, he'd somehow managed to keep it together. If he went on this mission, he knew he was risking his sanity. If he lost it again, he would never regain it.

But not going meant staying. It meant looks of pity on every face, and special treatment for his presumed inability to cope. There wasn't a corporal, gunnery sergeant, or bilge rat who didn't know he had been tortured into insanity and how it had been done. He couldn't continue confronting that day after day.

His bed was rumpled, yesterday's uniform tangled in the sheets. His standard issue duffel was large enough to hold the few items he would need, with ample room for more gear he wouldn't. He was packed in under five minutes.

A knock sounded on his door. A brush of consciousness scraped against the outer wall of his aura.

Michael stiffened and closed his thoughts.

"Come in, Darci," he said.

She opened the door and her aura immediately flowed over him, checking for weaknesses, pieces of his mind that were out of place. It was a ritual between them every time she greeted him. Satisfied that he was fine, she withdrew from him and shut the door softly.

"Are you going to be able to handle this?" she asked.

"I'll be fine," he said, turning to zip up the bag. He wasn't an animal to be appraised at every opportunity. Whatever it was she searched for in his aura, she never found it.

"This might be too much. You don't have to—"

Michael spun to face her, letting the refined edge of his aura lash out. "I'm going," he said, closing the matter. He grabbed his bag and approached her.

Her eyes widened. She shrank away from him and the door, toward the back of his bunk. She wasn't as powerful as Fionn or Emerick, or even Michael. If she hadn't moved, he wasn't sure if he'd have struck at her again, and this time caused damage. He wrenched the door open and came face to face with Atticus. The boy he'd once mentored had grown into a formidable warrior, and for the first time they were suddenly on opposite sides of the game board. Atticus was a protective man, and technically Michael had just threatened his mate.

"You aren't leaving like this," Atticus said, with more threat in his velvet voice than had ever been directed at Michael before.

Michael ground his teeth together. This constant race of emotions between them was making him unstable. He'd never fully recover if he stayed.

"Get out of my way," he ordered. He was taller than Atticus, and if he wanted to he could have pushed him aside. He refrained, knowing that to do so was to push away the bond between them. He did care for Atticus, but the man was no longer a boy. He was capable of taking care of himself. He didn't need Michael's guidance, hadn't needed it for years.

Darci slipped from the room, placing a hand on her husband's arm. "Make it quick before Fionn or Emerick come looking." Then she left.

"Listen up," Atticus said, shoving Michael back into his room with enough force to bruise, and slamming the door. "I don't know what the hell you've been going through the last few weeks, but I wouldn't have suggested a mission outside the territory to Fionn if I didn't think you could handle it."

"You're behind this?"

Atticus's eyes narrowed. "I'm not going to have to rescue you, am I?"

"I am not an invalid," Michael retorted from between clenched teeth.

"Prove it," Atticus said.

A knife appeared in Atticus's hand. With a flick of his wrist, he sent it whistling toward him. Michael side-stepped, stretched out his hand. His fingers caught the flat tip of the knife. He whipped his hand back and the blade sailed past Atticus and embedded to the hilt in his door.

Atticus smiled. The tension in the air drained with all the sluggishness of a clogged pipe. "Good. Fighting always did bring out the worst in you."

Michael straightened. The simple exchange had shifted something inside him. He felt steadier, more himself than he had for months.

"You've never seen me fight," Michael said. This time when he approached, Atticus opened the door for him.

"Of course I have," Atticus said. "I've never seen you do

that though."

"You've never seen me fight," Michael repeated. They walked side by side toward the hangar. Atticus remained relaxed. Michael was not.

"You never did tell me exactly what happened," Atticus said quietly.

Michael's gut clenched. It had taken three Virtues, and twenty heavily armed soldiers to bring him down while he gave her time to escape. She'd been wounded from the first shot, when the Industria found them out. A tryst between a Sin and a Virtue was forbidden. Such a relationship between a Sin like him and a prized Virtue like her was the worst kind of trespass. He should have known they would be discovered eventually. His dearest wish was to relive those moments, do something differently... Fight harder, escape the city. He prayed she had. Eleven years later he still didn't know if she'd survived. Even if she hadn't, the Magistrate would never forget the carnage he'd wrought that night.

They'd had to shatter his mind in the effort to subdue him.

"I'm not going to tell you," Michael said. "It's better not to know. I'd rather forget."

Atticus's aura withdrew from his and they were once again on separate sides of a vast field. Atticus still trusted him. He hadn't attacked him, as his instincts must have urged him to, when he unleashed his temper on Darci. Michael sensed he'd done something to sadden Atticus. But he wasn't ready to trust anyone with this part of his heart. There wasn't anything Michael could do about that. Some things Atticus would never know about him.

"Protect her," he said when they reached the hangar. They both knew who he meant.

"I will," Atticus said. They embraced, Atticus slapping him hard on the back. Then Atticus returned to his duties and Michael entered the busy hangar deck.

"What was that?" Fionn demanded the moment he stepped through the door. "You know the rules about fighting."

"It was nothing, Admiral," Michael called over the sounds of machines and engines. He joined her and Brax at the bottom of a boarding ramp next to a small aircraft. He could tell the vehicle was equipped with the tech they might need for the trip and then some. It was one of Tobias's projects, fit to fly better than a falcon.

Fionn's aura thickened, her formidable power filling the air.

"That better be the last *nothing* between you and anyone else here."

"For a while, at least," Tobias called from inside the craft's open hatch. "It'll be nice to have only one *Luxurian*'s aura to deal with around here."

"What do you mean?" Michael asked. He genuinely enjoyed Tobias's company, the streetwise genius Atticus had saved from being culled as an Undesirable, but the boy was irritatingly vague and intrusively curious most days. It was one thing to be intelligent and quite another to lord it over the entire compound. Michael wasn't even sure the kid knew he was doing it.

"You two have been clashing on the aural level for weeks," Tobias said. "Me and everyone else are ready to press skin to skin at the drop of a hat." He nodded to Fionn. "No offense, Admiral, but the way you and Emerick go at it could cause an earthquake. And there's enough desire to go around the moon twice in this place."

Fionn blinked, the tech having successfully shocked her into silence.

"Don't worry," Brax said. He slapped Michael's shoulder. "I'm taking him away. He can spice up the Magistrate's soldiers and spread the love over the nuclear waste lands."

"Bastard," Michael said under his breath, moving out from under Brax's hand.

Brax smiled. "See? I said this would be fun."

"Zip it, Brax," Fionn said, giving Tobias a look that said they would talk later. "We have new information. The Magistrate's forces are moving faster than we anticipated. You'll most likely be surrounded when you get there."

"I thought this was a diplomatic mission," Michael said.

"It still is, but if we're going to be diplomatic there have to be people to make treaties with. You may need to keep the Magistrate at bay. We won't have the manpower to send anyone to assist you until the away team returns from the UNF. You'll have to function as a two man army. Guerilla tactics. Gods know you have the power and strength for it. Good luck, gentlemen." She nodded to Tobias and saluted them. They returned her salute and she left the hangar.

Tobias keyed up the display on his crystal screen. An image of a man flashed up onto the tablet. "This is our new friend, Angus, from across the pond. He claims to be the leader of the little town you'll be visiting. These are the scans from my ancient satellites. He's not doing the best job. His resources are low. There's very little farming being done, and the crops are poorly managed. Beyond that, this tiny city is pretty well defended, but they've seen better days. If the Insurgency didn't keep the Magistrate so busy, they would have been blown off their island months ago just for living without a license."

"This Angus looks like he'd deep six a puppy," Brax observed. "Why are we trying to play nice with him?"

"Judgmental much?" Tobias asked.

Michael didn't comment. He studied the image of the man, his deceptively friendly eyes and the way his nose had a slight bend. The man was as hard-boiled as they came, but his shirt was a little too clean for the state of his city.

"Yeah, keep that in mind when you speak to him," Tobias said. "He's a slick talker that one, so don't trust him. But, you know, don't kill him. We're supposed to be allies. Moving on."

Angus's image dropped away and was replaced by one that punched Michael in the gut and recreated the hole where his heart should have been.

"Harley," he whispered. Her name hadn't passed his lips in over ten years. The sound of it had him reeling. All the pieces of his mind rattled, threatening to break apart.

"Yeah," Tobias said. "How did…?"

Michael felt the brush of the *Invidia*'s aura. Tobias would know in an instant exactly why she had such an effect on him. Michael glared at him, daring him to say a word.

Tobias blanched and coughed. "Um—yeah, so Harley is Angus's right hand lady. I don't know what she's there for, but Angus keeps her close. Try not to go too crazy, Michael. People change. Oh, and I added some extra supplies I thought you might need. It's a long flight, so take the time and please read the manual on your way over."

Michael took a steadying breath. Fionn would have to break his mind again, and tear him limb from limb to keep him from this mission now. This Angus was a dead man if he'd so much as placed a hand on Harley.

"Michael," Brax's voice held a warning. "Is this going to be too much?"

He tore his eyes from Harley's face, from the eyes he knew so well and suddenly not at all. His aura snapped about him with a vitality he hadn't known he possessed since before that fateful night.

Brax took a step back when Michael glanced at him.

"When do we leave?" he asked.

3

Angus hesitated when the knock came at their bedroom door, and Harley sighed. She pressed her cheek into the carpet.

"It wasn't me," she said softly, her voice less audible than the whisper of rain on the windows.

"Shut it," Angus hissed in the brogue she'd once found charming. "If I catch you using your powers again, I'll make good on my promise. The wastes are an unfriendly place. If it weren't for your valuable son, I'd have done it long ago. I can't afford to keep Virtues under this roof, not when there's famine. If I find you're to blame for the shortages, I may not be able to keep the people from tearing you apart." His heavily booted feet crossed the floor and the metal door slammed behind him.

Harley struggled to her knees, stifling a groan. He'd known exactly where to place the blows. The bruises were beginning to show. He wasn't hiding his actions from anyone. Last month, she'd overheard him say the fields were rotting; they wouldn't have enough seed grain to plant next year. They wouldn't even have enough to feed the populace through this year. He blamed her. He blamed everyone but his own poor management. And now the Magistrate was breathing down their necks, getting closer each day. She'd come here years ago as a refugee. She wasn't the only outsider, but she was the only notorious person wanted by the Magistrate. Angus had many reasons to suspect her, even though none were the right reason.

She stumbled to her feet, steadying herself with a hand against a polished bookshelf. Once she'd run to Angus with her bleeding heart, now she crawled out of his sight. If she could, she would leave. But there was nowhere to go, no place but the waste, and that was certain death. She closed the bathroom door. She'd been so stupid to think she'd ever been in love with him, that he could love her in return.

The mirror revealed that Harley's eyes were puffy again with unshed tears. She refused to let any of them fall. Her face had once been the most beautiful in the Magistrate city. Now, she saw the wife of a man. A world-beaten woman who was nothing more than a placeholder, until someone more convenient could replace her.

Angus was a wildly powerful Sin, but he had no heirs. He had tried to father a child of his own by her. He needed an heir of his own blood. Cadence wouldn't satisfy the townspeople's demand that Angus's son be a son of his, not just hers. She'd agreed to try. She'd miscarried twice, and together they had grieved over the loss. Yet his relentless drive meant that her sole duty was to present him with a child; and with each passing month, when there was no sign of a pregnancy, his anger grew. He had begun to resent that he needed her, a Virtue, to produce an heir. Any offspring between Angus and herself was guaranteed to be powerful, able to rule over this land.

Power begets power. If Angus had chosen another Sin as the bearer of his children, the two negative energies would result in a child with the abilities of a Virtue. Angus despised anything to do with the Magistrate, as did most of his citizens. It was why his people weren't allowed to marry Sin to Sin, only Sin to powerless human.

After her escape from the Magistrate, Angus had found her crashed upon his shores. He looked upon her face, and whatever he'd seen had convinced him to take her to his castle. A few weeks later she discovered she was pregnant with a dead man's child. She'd done the only reasonable thing she could and agreed to marry King Angus of Ardtornish.

His delight when she gave birth to an *Avaritia* had terrified her. For the sake of her son, she'd enslaved them both.

Harley splashed water so cold it was almost painful against her face. The icy water ran in rivulets down the line of her neck, to the hollow where her clavicles met and still further between her breasts. The water traced invisible lines that had been branded upon her senses by the hands of a man long since dead. Now, years later, she couldn't forget him. His ghost haunted her, marked her, and chained her to his memory. She shivered and grabbed for the towel. Even after she'd endured so much, the mere memory of him could still raise sensations all over her body.

If he had lived, if she'd done something to save him, perhaps he would be here now. She wouldn't find terror waiting in her bedroom, but tender protection. Their affair had been illicit; her overlords in the Magistrate would have had her executed on the spot when they discovered her treason. But times had changed. The Magistrate's light was encompassing the globe. She knew from overhearing Angus's conversations that he suspected the Magistrate had infiltrated the castle.

He was right. And he was a liar. He'd been the one to invite the Magistrate spies in. If she revealed his secrets, he'd execute her. She was caught between two deaths, clawing for life.

She would never go back to them and she couldn't stay here and let Angus use her son. They had to escape. Somehow.

A pounding sounded at the bathroom door. Harley froze.

"Y-yes?" she asked tremulously.

"Another child went missing during the night. Stefan's informed me Cadence is missing, again. I will search for the village girl. Find him. He hasn't left the castle."

"All right," Harley answered, injecting false meekness into her reply.

"We're to have guests this afternoon. Make yourself presentable." Angus's heavy steps paced away from the door.

Guests? She didn't believe in coincidences. Angus's

contacts in the Magistrate couldn't be coming here, could they?

Harley's hands shook as she readied herself. Angus would be away searching for the lost child. Possibly for hours. And they had guests. They didn't receive guests. They found refugees and inducted, or rather forced, them into the ranks of Angus's tyrannical rule, convincing the new peasantry class to do as he commanded and call him 'King' in exchange for protection. His greatest argument and biggest lie were that any refugee would be safe from all things Magistrate. That promise was also why Harley's *Castitas* powers of chastity and moral purity were so offensive to him. They shouldn't have been, she was a failure in both regards. He despised her power, but without her he would have no possibility of a child and there would be no one to control her son, Cadence. Without Cadence, the castle and those its armed force protected would have been starved into submission by the Magistrate years ago.

She cracked open the bathroom door, checking the room beyond for occupants. It was empty. Below the window, in the courtyard, horses had been saddled, various forms of stolen gadgetry attached to the beasts and to the men astride them. Angus mounted his great black steed, a laser rifle twice the length of his arm held in his right hand, the reins in his left. His shouted orders were muffled by the glass. He didn't look back at her as he spurred his horse, leading the search party out of the courtyard and across the drawbridge.

Only when the yard was empty did Harley leave the room. She hurried to Cadence's room down the hall. There were bolts attached to an electronic locking mechanism on the outside of the door to keep him in, as he'd been found wandering farther and farther into the ruins of the wasted city.

"Cadence?" she asked, opening his door. She checked under his bed, in the closet, and found nothing. The room was empty, save for the stacks of books by his tidy bed and the small bundle of dirty clothes at its foot.

A maid met her at the door. "He's nowhere to be found, Milady," the other woman said, worry in her voice.

"You checked all the usual places?" Harley asked

desperately. The clock on her son's bedside informed her it was only minutes past dawn.

The maid nodded.

"Get me the cook," she ordered. "He must have eaten before he snuck off."

The maid twisted the hem of her shirt. "I checked with cook first, Your Highness. He hasn't seen him."

Harley pushed past the woman and flew down the stairs as fast as her sore body could carry her. He couldn't have been taken. Angus wouldn't dare sell him to the Magistrate too.

"Cadence!" she shouted, her voice echoing off the cold stones of the castle halls. Her heart squeezed in her chest, making it difficult to draw breath in her panic.

It would be easy to find Cadence if she were allowed the use of her powers. But she shuddered to think what Angus would do if she did. It hurt to breathe, it hurt to move, it hurt to think after he'd punished her on mere suspicion. If she used her powers and found Cadence, Angus would sense the flow of her power in the castle stones. Old stones seemed to soak up power, so much so that one could sense the passing of a Virtue with the lightest brush of fingertips across them, reading the memory.

They had time yet. Angus wouldn't be back until well after sunrise and he'd mentioned his guests would be there late in the afternoon. Cadence was always discovering new ways to sneak out. He always returned. Always.

"We have some time," she whispered to herself.

"I'm sorry, Milady," the maid said, confused.

"Nothing," Harley said, a little too sharply. "Search the castle again. Find him. Check the storerooms. He can't have gone far."

4

The control panel blinked in lazy, continuous readouts. Nothing had changed in the last four hours of flight time. The ceaseless whine of the engines in the confined space dug under Michael's tolerance. They were still an hour out from their destination, the endless gray seas cresting beneath them in tiny white dots of foaming waters.

"Who is she?" Brax asked from the pilot's seat. He keyed a few commands and auto-pilot resumed. He swiveled his seat to face him.

Michael forced himself to exhale slowly. What could he tell him? What should he reveal to Brax about the woman who'd changed his life? She'd inspired him to escape, to rebel. For her he had challenged his masters and the cost had broken him. She made him volatile, and Brax's inquiry loosened the rein on his temper.

He fixed his gaze on Brax and the man stiffened.

A tense moment of silence passed. Michael wasn't sure which of them would strike first. He'd issued the challenge and Brax wasn't the sort to take the invitation unless it was worth it. Danger scented the air. Brax dropped his gaze. Michael hadn't been sure he would, for a moment.

"Don't tell me then," Brax said, turning back to his controls as though they weren't about to come to blows. "Atticus said you can handle this, and that's what I'll expect."

"I'm here to do the job," Michael said. "Nothing more." His words did nothing to convince either of them that he didn't have a personal interest in the mission.

Brax was silent. The engine noise filling the craft became a roar.

"While we're being stoic and unreasonably secretive, let's prepare for approach. Scan the next fifty miles out for enemy craft or ships and begin looking for a safe place to land near our new friends."

Michael understood why they didn't want to land at the castle. They were here to see whether Angus was an enemy or not. It would be stupid to simply hand over their escape vehicle. They would land somewhere else, shrouded from view, and keep the camouflage on until they were ready to return to the Insurgency.

Michael keyed up a display and began running scans ten, twenty-five, and fifty miles out. Red dots began to appear on the map's jagged coast line. About every three miles an enemy watch was posted. By the ring of Magistrate soldiers placed throughout the thirty miles of countryside he'd scanned, their potential allies were surrounded.

"If we land inside the green zone," he said to Brax, "we'll be surrounded by enemies. If the Magistrate advances, we will be overrun before sundown."

"I'm not turning around now because a few soldiers are tromping around with their chests puffed out," Brax said.

"I wouldn't let you," Michael said.

"Aha!" Brax crowed. "So it is about the girl."

Michael didn't respond. Let Brax think what he wanted. Harley was his responsibility. There wasn't anyone else Michael trusted with her life but himself.

Brax gave him a sidelong glance. "I don't like the look of how many Magistrate battalions are down there waiting for us. We should find out what the Magistrate's plan of attack is."

"How do you propose we do that?" Michael asked. "We meet Angus in forty-five minutes. We'll already be late, and Fionn will be pissed if we don't meet her deadline." He didn't like the options. It was obvious by the clusters where the Magistrate's main column of soldiers and supply was located. The Magistrate was well equipped to keep intruders and spies, like them, out.

Brax gave him a hard look. "Imagine how thrilled the Insurgency will be when we can give them the entire attack plan. Defeating the Magistrate here will be a cakewalk. They can't be that heavily reinforced for a tiny fortress like this. We don't have Tobias to hack in for us. We'll have to infiltrate."

Michael forced his hands to release their grip on his controls. He was making the screen flicker. He swallowed and pulled his aura close about him in a shield. The tighter it became, the more it supported him and kept his hands steady as he gripped the armrests.

"You mean to let one of us be captured," he said carefully.

Brax winced. "No, but one of us will need to explore their camps. And I'm better suited for it than you. They'll have an Industria with them for sure, just by the size of that force. There isn't anything an Industria can do to me."

Michael shuddered. "You're wrong," he said with absolute conviction. "They don't use only their powers to interrogate. Don't think for a moment that I'll come and rescue you when they have you begging for mercy."

"Do you fear them that much?"

"No," he said. "I fear myself. I've been insane for years because of what they did to me. I had enough of myself left to control my powers, the last time. If they take that away, there'll be nothing to keep me from becoming their deadliest weapon."

"I doubt they'd use you to lust us all into submission."

Michael focused on the gray clouds, making his voice as bland as the color. As with the clouds, it was impossible to hide the turbulence caused by the storm of emotions inside him. A deadly mix of fear, rage, and untapped desire. "Wouldn't they? They tried it on an entire city, and it worked."

Brax tapped a finger against the dash. "We can't be late for our meeting with Angus. If we are, he'll be liable to do something stupid, like attack, or join the Magistrate's side to prevent his people from perishing."

"Then what do you suggest?" Michael asked. He tried to pretend he wasn't relieved. But he was. He couldn't be trapped behind Magistrate lines.

Jacqueline is dead. It didn't matter how many times he reminded himself, he still bore the scars from her misuse of him.

"I'll infiltrate the Magistrate," Brax said. "You make friends with Angus. I will join you by morning."

Michael arched an eyebrow. "And if you don't?"

"Don't come looking for me. Assume I'm dead. I can take care of myself better than you, right now. Make sure you report in by eighteen-hundred hours, or Fionn might send the team after us early. I don't know about you, but I've had my ass saved by Tobias too many times in the last year. If he gets the chance to throw it in my face again, I'll never get my dignity back."

Assume I'm dead. The words triggered a switch in Michael, and his grip on the hand rests of his chair increased until his knuckles cracked. He'd told Atticus the same thing once. Atticus hadn't listened to him, and the young man had rescued him. Could he let the same fate happen to Brax, without the hope of a rescue?

"You'd better come back," he informed Brax, his tone mild, hiding the threat and determination he was promising. "Or I'll drag you out by your balls."

Brax laughed and punched a few controls. "Initializing landing sequence," he spoke into his comm, recording their procedures and logging their progress.

In minutes the gray mist of clouds parted, revealing a rolling green plain that dipped in deep folds close to a rocky shoreline. A sparse and patchy forest greeted them with the promise of many clear places to land.

"Welcome to Scotland," Brax said.

Michael felt the tug of familiarity. His heart raced, and blood pulsed hard and fast in his veins. "I know this place." It was a place of kinship, of bawdy song, of deep history.

"Like hell," Brax said. "No Magistrate slave has ever been let out of their cage this far until now."

Michael tore his eyes from the landscape and turned his attention to the control panels. He knew, without understanding how, that this place had once been his home. But that was impossible. He'd always been the Magistrate's plaything. Brax knew and so did he. Didn't he? There were things he couldn't remember. Maybe this wasn't the first time he'd been here. Much of his life, before he'd been forced to join the Magistrate, he couldn't remember.

An indicator on the control panel began to blink. "Radiation levels are high." A topography map showed pulsing red in the low spots between the trees. In those places the grass was a sickly yellow and the trees were stunted in growth. "Most of those low spots aren't safe to land in."

Brax cursed. "Of course they aren't. Let's find someplace closer to the castle." He directed the craft further north, toward the peninsula of land on which the castle perched, a ring of murky water surrounding it.

As they landed, the heavens opened, spilling a deluge of gray rain that plinked against the craft's hull. Michael gritted his teeth. The castle's curtain wall could be seen in the distance, surrounded by a dark ring of water. The city sprawling before it was small and in a disastrous state. Whole buildings had collapsed and most were in disrepair. At least the defenses ringing the decrepit city appeared sturdy; at least there were defenses.

Michael pushed his aura out toward the city in the north and the Magistrate in the south, sensing for other Sins and Virtues. It hurt to extend his aura, like a muscle he was forcing beyond its traumatized capacity. At the compound, he didn't dare unfurl his power. Two *Luxurian*s in residence, both stretching their auras to fullness, would have devastating consequences. The human heart could only withstand so much of a single sensation before giving out, and he dared not risk Fionn's armies or her wrath.

His aura extended past the craft and into the air, meeting the tree tops and sweeping down their trunks.

"Michael?" Brax asked.

He flinched and his aura snapped back against his skin like a rubber band, stinging. He opened his eyes, wiping away a bead of sweat.

"I was scanning the proximity."

Brax's shoulders tensed, his mouth set in a hard disapproving line. "Just keep your hands to yourself," he said, sounding more than a little shaken. "And remember not to look at Angus that way. We want to make friends, not corpses."

Michael didn't reply, but closed his eyes and pushed his aura out again. The surrounding countryside was free of—. A wave of pure energy slammed into his aura. It was foreign, familiar, angry, and protective, warning him away. For the second time in as many minutes his aura snapped back, this time with a kick, as though it had been thrown at him.

He came back to himself with a snarl.

"Someone's out there." It was not Harley who had defended against his aura. Harley was a Virtue. This was a Sin, and one of great power. He was startled enough that he couldn't tell exactly what power.

"There's a whole city of rebels here," Brax replied. The reverse thrusters kicked in and the craft landed with a gentle jolt. The engines powered down with a shrill whine. "Don't get paranoid. Besides, if they attack you, we'll know for sure they aren't friendlies." He had the audacity to smile.

"Bastard," Michael growled. His hackles were still raised, and until he knew whose territory he found himself in, he'd be on alert for the threat.

"Always was, always will be," Brax said, unclipping himself from his flight harness. "The craft's camouflaged. Unless someone walks face first into it, it'll stay hidden. Let's get a move on. Make sure you take a nice change of clothes. We want to impress these people. Then again a man like you or Atticus could make rags look like riches."

"Being camouflaged now doesn't eliminate the possibility that someone saw or heard our landing," Michael said.

Brax glared at him. "You know I thought this might be a fun trip. But you have to respond with cold practical statements and not even a smile." He slapped his shoulder. "We're on vacation. Live a little."

They checked the gear each of them would be taking. For Brax, tactical weapons, armor, and gadgets specially designed for infiltrating Magistrate perimeters. A comm, a dress uniform, armor, an extra semi-automatic pistol, and a laser weapon with extra battery cells went into the small bag Michael carried. He slipped a knife into his boot, and another handgun remained heavy in his palm, the safety off.

"Ready?" Brax asked, reaching for the release lever to open the hatch.

Michael didn't answer, just shifted his grip on the handgun.

"REBEL CRAFT," came a loud announcement from outside their vehicle. "YOU ARE SURROUNDED."

They both froze.

Michael felt the cracks in his mind widen with strain. They had come for him. They would take him back. Fragments of nightmares stabbed into him. *Heels spurring him on, drawing blood. The clink and bite of chains around his limbs. Endless torment, breaking upon him in waves of pain. The cutting presence of the Industria. Her lips whispering promises of blood and death in his ears. Only death never came.*

Brax swore. "Aren't you supposed to innately sense the Magistrate?"

"Fuck you," Michael replied, matching Brax's anger. He tentatively stretched out his aura, searching for any hint of a Industria, waiting for the stabbing crush of pain to rip into him again. He felt nothing. He gripped his weapon harder, steadying his hands.

Brax was frantically checking the read-out. "They're not showing up on any scanner we have with us." He drew the sword strapped to his back.

"Unless they have a tech with them."

"One better than Tobias?" Brax asked. "No such creature exists."

"OPEN YOUR CRAFT DOOR AND EXIT WITH YOUR HANDS ABOVE YOUR HEAD. ANY ATTEMPT TO FLEE WILL BE SEEN AS MILITANT ACTION AND YOU WILL BE SHOT DOWN. SURRENDER IS YOUR ONLY OPTION."

Brax paced in front of the hatch, a span of two small strides. His brawny bulk made the craft bounce and shudder on its landing gear. The space really was too small for a man as broad-shouldered as Brax to move around in. "We're two miles from the castle's outermost defenses. Which gives us enough space to set up our own little operation. Looks like the Magistrate had the same idea. How the hell are we supposed to get out of this?"

Michael grabbed the belt of explosives. "Get out of the way," he ordered.

Brax froze. "We're not going out there without a foolproof plan."

Michael pointed his sidearm at Brax's chest. His hand was steady, but his heart pulsed blood through his veins so fast he heard a buzzing in his ears. "I'm not going back."

"No one's asking you to." Brax's voice was calm, steady, placating him. "Atticus said you might not be totally stable. I mean, are you ready to—"

Michael cut him off by hitting the control that unlocked the exit door. The hatch hissed open to the side on its hydraulics. The rain swept in on a fierce gust of wind, curling around Michael as he pulled the old-fashioned pin from the grenade. He lobbed the egg-sized explosive toward the small force of five men. Their leader, his wrist at his mouth as he sputtered a report into his comm, froze as the grenade bounced to a stop at his feet. He frowned at the device before realization made his eyes widen.

"Grenade!"

The team of Magistrate soldiers went down. Brax grabbed Michael and pulled him inside the craft as the heat-wave from the explosion blasted through the hatch. Bits of debris clattered against the metal flooring.

"Gods," Brax said. "If you ever pull that shit again, I'll put you on ice until I can cart your sorry ass back to Fionn for demotion."

Michael shoved the man aside. He wasn't afraid of losing his rank. He was afraid of chains and pain. He strode through the hatch, his fingers gripping his weapon. Bodies and parts were strewn about the forest clearing. The gore was quickly being washed into the earth by the pouring rain.

One of the Magistrate soldiers, his white uniform now red and black, moaned. Michael didn't raise his weapon, but struck with his aura. The man shuddered, writhed, and groaned. Pink foam bubbled between his lips. He gave one last twitch then lay still. Blood seeped from the man's nose, ears, and unblinking eyes.

"What the hell was that?" Brax asked behind him. "You didn't even touch the man."

Michael felt bile in the back of his throat. He forced it down, breathed, and focused on the feel of rain dripping in cold rivulets down his neck, under the collar of his uniform. The open air above him, the forest surrounding him. No walls, no chains. He stared, pitiless, at the Magistrate soldier. By the pattern of bars on his comm he'd achieved a high ranking position, a captain or lieutenant. Michael couldn't tell accurately as part of the man's comm and hand were missing.

"He desired to live," Michael heard himself say. "Not as much as I wanted him to die."

"You're a scary son of a bitch," Brax said, sheathing his sword. "Even I felt that much energy."

Michael took a deep breath, feeling freedom again, feeling whole. There were cracks, places where the light could still burn the darkness in which he shrouded his mind, but he'd passed the first test. He could stare down the enemy and know they could not touch him unless he willed it. He hadn't lost his edge, but it did need honing.

"There's a powerful Sin between us and the castle. I will

stop there before meeting Angus." Michael blinked rain water out of his eyes.

"How powerful?" Brax asked.

They both knew the Magistrate had been collecting gifted people to do their bidding in the war. Or neutralizing Sins and Virtues if they refused to convert. Emerick's father had been one of the seven Magistrate Generals, the God of Patience. He'd been stationed in the Yukon, guarding the imprisoned Goddess of Wrath. *Ira* gave Fionn her power, and together she and Emerick were able to defeat his father. Since then, the Insurgency was on the watch. The Magistrate had locked the most powerful Sins away, thinking that doing so would bring the world into harmony. Removing the dark only shifted the balance in favor of the light and sowed chaos. To restore the balance, the remaining six gods and goddesses of Sin needed to be located and released.

"This Sin is not that powerful," Michael said. He'd never forget the feel of *Ira* unleashed. It had shaken the entire mountain, ripped through the earth with ease. This was a lesser Sin.

"You sure?" Brax asked. "Having one of the six here would explain a damn lot."

Michael wasn't sure. If the Sin was cloaking its aura, it might be possible. That much power was hard to hide. He thought of *Ira* and how the Magistrate had kept her hidden for nearly a century.

Brax began stripping one of the Magistrate soldiers of his bloodied uniform. "You'd better go or you'll be late. Fionn will be pissed, and I'm not taking the blame."

"Watch your back," Michael said as he stepped around a body toward the north edge of the trees.

"You watch yours," Brax called after him, and they went their separate ways.

This forest did not compare to the richly living forest growing on Fionn's lands. The trees here were obviously sick and too thin for their height. The underbrush grew with all the lethargy of a poisoned existence, as though the nutrients had been leached from their half-dead leaves. It was late summer. The leaves should be large, instead of so small. After listening to his surroundings, he realized the sounds of insects or the flap and twitter of birds were curiously absent.

Something was in the process of sucking the life out of the land.

Michael had studied the potential uses of each Sin, their positive properties and negative. Only one type could take life, and it was impossible for any but the incredibly strong to take this much life and leave rampant famine in its wake. It made him angry. This land was starving, and what little nourishment it possessed was stolen from it. Like a thief stealing the food from a child. As if the Magistrate's radiation poisoning wasn't deadly enough. In months, this beautiful land would be nothing but a muddy waste. It was one thing for the Magistrate to destroy humanity, quite another for it to destroy the earth.

Michael pushed his aura out again.

There! He jerked to the right, raising his sidearm with unusually steady hands. The Sin was clumsy, not hiding his presence, perhaps cocky in the knowledge that he was the most powerful here.

Michael weaved through the trees. A few yards from the edge of the forest he spotted movement and froze, sighting along the barrel of his weapon. The hair on his arms rose. It didn't come from the drizzle of rain still leaking between the leaves.

He spied a small form sitting atop a large boulder, sheltered by the branches of a lone tree. He strode out of the forest into a clearing, his weapon aimed between the shoulder blades of a boy. He wasn't yet a teenager; young, perhaps eight or nine years old.

He frowned. A boy? What in the seven hells was a child doing out here in a militarized zone? Where was his mother? He lowered his weapon a fraction of an inch.

"Excuse me," he said, command suffusing his voice.

The child stiffened and glanced over his thin shoulder, most of his face hidden in shadow. His wild eyes flashed at him with inner green light. Michael felt the rush of another aura clumsily brushing against his. The child's eyes widened. He snapped the book he'd been reading closed and leapt from the rock.

"*Avaritia!*" Michael called out, breaking into a run after the boy. The child was quick, but so was he. He caught him easily by the back of his mud-soaked shirt a few feet from the edge of the forest. The boy shouted something unintelligible and twisted out of his grip, the thick, leather bound book with crumbling edges clutched against his chest. He leapt away from Michael and dropped through the ground.

Michael hurried to the spot where he'd disappeared. A small pipe—no doubt a leaving from some past sewage system—marked a hole in the ground. The slapping of shoes against water echoed from below.

A strong *Avaritia* could easily have sucked the life out of the forest. By the green light in the boy's eyes, Michael had just found a very strong Sin possessed with the power of greed. Even more intriguing, he now sensed two *Avaritia* auras. This boy wasn't the God of Greed, but the god was nearby.

Fionn would want to know about him as soon as possible. While the orders were to assess King Angus's reliability as an ally, the entire Insurgency was on the lookout for the other six gods of Sin. They might fight against the Magistrate, but there would be no winning until they had restored the balance.

5

Angus stared at the mangled remains of one of his men kissed by the incoming tide waters, the sea foam turning pink. The man was only identifiable by the knot work of tattoos on what was left of the corpse's bicep, and where an iron band— the man's comm—still encircled his pulverized wrist. The rest of him was reduced to bits of cracked bone and pulped flesh, strung together by what tendons and ligaments remained whole. The other fifteen men were nowhere to be seen. Only the gentle tap of rain in a puddle created by a large boot print catalogued the incident.

Angus repressed a shiver. He knew what had done this. For the sake of his people he'd made a deal with the devil, assuring their survival. A few deaths were no more than they would face if starvation found them come winter. He'd made assurances they wouldn't starve. The price was still very, very high.

"And the children?" he asked of the man at his side, Demark, a stalwart companion in these desolate times. It surprised him how easily he could evoke a caring and strained demeanor, even though he knew the children were in good hands, Virtuous hands. All of them showed promise with their powers. The Magistrate had quickly agreed to trade the children for supplies; at least, that's what they had said. He hoped he hadn't damned the children only to damn them all.

"No sign, Sire." Demark shifted his stance. His boots

squelched in the mud. The man hadn't met his eyes since they rode to the beach, following the "trail" the child had left behind.

Angus straightened and surveyed his men, taking note of their green and frightened faces. "Their mothers are getting restless," Angus said "Continue the search" Several of the men nodded and made to do as he ordered. He took the reins of his horse from Demark.

"Sire," Demark urged, "let us return to the castle, before whatever took Hamish returns for the rest of us."

Angus turned and scrutinized Demark's face. "Whatever did this is no threat to us. We're in more danger from the Magistrate than whatever took the children." That, at least, was the truth. He mounted the strong steed, a black horse of steady nature and sleek hide, settling into the saddle.

"The tide will see to the remains," he said.

Demark's lips drew tight over his teeth. But the man was wise not to say anything.

"We're expecting guests," Angus said. He didn't wait for the remainder of his patrol guard to return to their horses before he turned and spurred his own back toward his warm hall. The ride over the moors was cool, in defiance of summer's heat. He had fields to tend, and seed to manage. His time was wasted searching the marsh for men he already knew were dead and children who were given to better places than this. He had to try to improve his city. He wouldn't dishonor his ancestors further. He slowed his horse when he and his men reached the main thoroughfare into his realm.

"Make way for the King!" Demark shouted at his side, having caught up to him.

The midday crowd rushed to the sides of the cobbled street. Women clutched children to their sides. The road cleared and Angus urged his horse through the gates of his castle's walls. A hundred years ago the fortress was a crumbling ruin. The weeds growing between the stones were more valuable. His father before him had begun to rebuild it and Angus had finished the work. Now the façade was strong. The walls were reinforced with metal shielding and defenses worthy of the era. The people were protected and the Magistrate was kept out.

The sleepy courtyard sprang to action as he and the six men with him and their horses clattered in.

Angus leapt from his horse before the stable boy had a chance to catch the reins. He stripped off his gloves as he strode through the heavy, armored doors.

"Fetch my wife," he ordered Demark, who followed on his heels. "And the boy."

"Yes, Sire," the man's tone was less than savory.

Angus stopped in the wide entryway and turned to him. They stared at one another for a moment before Demark lowered his gaze.

"I'll be in my rooms."

Angus caught his reflection in the crystal screens he'd stolen, as he sat behind his desk. The lines of the kingly tattoo on his temple flexed as his jaw clenched. He touched the screen and it blinked to life with unread notices. One stated there were six dead calves.

He swore and pounded a fist against the desk. Six! They couldn't afford to lose half a dozen head of beef stock.

He didn't look up from the next set of reports when he heard the timid steps of his wife approach through the door.

"You sent for me," Harley said, her western accent revealing her nervousness.

Angus looked up then and frowned. There was something about her features, some emotion there that irritated him. He stretched out his senses, and she flinched when his aura touched her. He could barely sense her powers. Good.

"Where's your son?" he asked.

Harley appeared shocked, though he'd told her of his plans, of the people's terrible need to eat. "He's exhausted, Angus. You can't make him use again so soon."

"I didn't call you here to listen to you whine. We have a guest coming. Make yourself presentable."

Harley's attention pricked, and she turned her head to the

side and blinked in that infuriating way that used to be so coy and alluring. "Who?"

"You'll meet him tonight."

The door opened and Demark strode in, towing the young and very dirty Cadence behind him.

"I found him in the store room, Sire."

Cadence jerked out of Demark's grip. "Let go of me." The boy had dark hair unlike his mother's, and his eyes were a piercing shade of green. In his hands he carried one of his many useless books. This one had the word "Charlemagne" written on its hardbound cover.

"Store room?" Angus asked, taking in Cadence's dirty and soaked clothes. "If I hear you've been in the moat—"

"Like hell," Cadence snapped.

Angus caught the defiance in the boy's eyes. Cadence knew he was growing stronger as he matured. Soon he would reach puberty and there would be no stopping him. Angus hoped he'd have the boy's acquiescing compliance before Cadence's powers eclipsed his own. His people needed Cadence to want to do his bidding; he just needed to convince the boy.

"You'll keep a civil tongue in your mouth," he growled. Angus waved a hand at Demark, dismissing his second.

Demark bowed, glanced at Harley and Cadence, then slipped out the door, closing it on squeaky hinges.

"You wouldn't recognize civility if it stood before you," Cadence said, unusually articulate for a child his age.

"Cadence," Angus said with forced patience, "we had six calves perish this morning. I need to you try again. And this time, no deaths."

"It's too soon," Harley said, breaking her frightened silence. Her power slipped into the air, flickering like the forked tongue of a snake, and just as unwanted as the sound of her voice.

Angus glared at her. "You dare, in my presence?"

Her face whitened and she swallowed. "No, I-I..." she glanced between him and Cadence. "I apologize. I didn't mean to cause offense."

He remained unconvinced. She knew the terms of his

keeping her in wealth instead of poverty, at his side instead of in the streets with the grime.

"Cadence, do as you're told."

The boy's fingers tapped against the cover of the book. "You already found the gold."

Angus smiled. The boy was unusually attuned to any form of wealth and its comings and goings. "It's not the gold I need more of. We have guests. If we are to survive the Magistrate's fire we must impress these foreigners so they will give us soldiers. We need their defense." He may have bought the Magistrate, but he had no intention of being a slave to them, and the Insurgency was the last cog to secure in his plan. His stepson would make sure the plan was in perfect motion.

Cadence's nostrils flared. "My power cannot give you soldiers, Angus."

Angus nodded. "Aye, that's true. But it can make these men believe they need to send us aid."

"You want me to lie?" Cadence clarified, as though the idea was the very opposite of what he wanted.

The boy's belligerence, following so closely on the heels of his mother's use of her Virtuous power, had worn his patience. "You'll do it. *Today*, boy."

The child's chin lifted. A fraction of an inch, but it was a fraction of defiance.

Angus surged out of his chair and grabbed Cadence by the front of his stained shirt. "Do not test me."

Cadence winced, his book slapping against the floor as he dropped it to pry at Angus's fist. Angus's power was stronger than the boy's. Still, Cadence fought him, defying him. Angus couldn't have that. Tossing Cadence aside, he turned on Harley.

She shrank from him. "Please, Angus."

Angus ignored her. "Now, Cadence," he ordered, and advanced on his wife.

"Stop it," Cadence shouted before he reached her, pressed against the shelves. "I'll do it!"

Angus cut off the stream of his power and faced Cadence.

The boy's eyes were greener than he remembered.

"You don't know what you are asking for, *King*," Cadence said, spitting his title as though it were an acrid poison. He glanced once more at his mother's silent tears then back at Angus. The wave of *Avaritia* power flooded the room, coursed through the castle halls and stretched over the town. Dust disappeared from the shelves, tarnish was stripped from the metal fixtures and a sense of wholesome abundance replaced the fear and apprehension.

"More," Angus demanded.

Cadence began to shake, but his defiant gaze never left Angus's. The sensation of wealth, fulfillment, and the easing of the ache in Angus's own belly was priceless.

Finally, Cadence's power flickered out, once, twice. His eyes rolled up into his skull and he collapsed atop his forgotten book. The power cut off, and with it the morning seemed brighter and the rain pouring outside crystalline in its brilliance, despite the overcast sky. By the time the emissary arrived, the entire town would appear beautiful and lively.

6

The broken, pitted and crumbling single lane road that began at the forest's northern edge crunched under Michael's boots. A shout echoed a few seconds after he stepped from under the tree's sparsely leafed boughs. There were three trenches between him and the outermost city wall. Sections of laser fencing, razor wire and even medieval barriers, constructed of sharpened tree trunks angled toward him, stood between him and his destination.

"Drop your weapons!" someone from one of the nearby turrets shouted down at him.

Michael slipped his side-arm back into the holster at his hip and held his arms away from his sides. "I am here as an emissary from Admiral Fionn of the Insurgency," he called back.

There were a few moments of silence, then the massive gate creaked open and a troop of six men marched toward him, fully armed. Their patchwork armor was stained and dirty, but no weaker than their faces, set with seriousness. Michael noticed that cheekbones and chins stood out too much under their scratched helmets. Their eyes were little more than sunken spots of glittering willpower. They had their weapons trained on him, and Michael didn't doubt that if he so much as flinched they'd fire.

His heart pounded and his skin became hyper sensitive as

his senses shifted into overdrive. The formation, the march, the weapons, and the soldier's fortitude were not things he'd been prepared for.

How many times had he been guarded in such a formation? Never unbound, always dragged and forced.

He straightened his shoulders, forcing the waves of paralyzing fear back into the shadowed cracks of his mind. He thought of why he was here. He was here to find Harley. He was walking into this of his own will, no shackles he hadn't already chosen freely.

The shaking stopped, and the ground steadied beneath his feet.

"You're late." The man checked the comm strapped to his wrist. Like everything else in his possession, the comm was scratched and dented from wear. "Should have been here over an hour ago. Lucky for you, so was the King."

"The Magistrate is almost at your doorstep," Michael said. "I ran into some trouble."

"That's as may be. I can't have you entering the keep armed. Hand over your weapons," the captain of the little troop ordered.

Michael bit back a snarl, but handed over the sidearm and the rifle at his back, and his bag containing the rest of his gear. It would be searched, but they wouldn't find anything out of the ordinary.

"And the others." The man still held out his hand.

"I'm a Sin," Michael said, with forced congeniality. "The other weapons you can't take from me."

The captain narrowed his eyes. "Are you now? I'm under orders to detain any Virtue that tries to pass my gate. The last Virtue to cross the gate the King ordered hanged. I had the pleasure of watching him kick. I'd love another show. I think we'd better check and make sure you're a Sin." He grinned showing his crooked and rotting teeth.

Michael didn't flinch at the words. He'd wished for death many times before and never been granted his rest. No one here was powerful enough to stop him. When he let his aura loose, it was a small fraction of his strength.

The man's eyes widened, then he smiled. "This way then."

He turned on his heel, giving Michael his back. His men swarmed around Michael, as though he were being led to slaughter. When the troop moved, he noticed the sloppy formation, the out of synch stepping. Fionn would never have stood for such shoddy work. Against a perfectly drilled Magistrate army, these men would be cut down in minutes on a field. Behind their walls, they at least stood some chance of survival.

They passed through three check points, the guard around him gaining more men at each entry point. Michael began to wonder how quickly Angus would spring his trap if he was playing Fionn's trust. He was led under a high arch with a set of spiked iron doors ready to snap shut on him.

Angus's city reeked. The stench of human and animal waste was a thick undertone to the clean scent following the rain. It was almost as strong as the lingering despair oozing from between the chipped cobbles. The sewer system must not be functional, because the streets were not clogged with refuse. The few rickety modular buildings that stood were in good repair, several older buildings were nothing more than crumbling brick mounds with spaces which windows once filled.

The city seemed caught between the old world and the new, not sure to which it belonged. Likewise, the people reflected the indecision of their town. Many were skinny. Few appeared well fed. Some wore simple tunics, and others modern uniforms. No single piece of clothing he saw was new. All were patched and frayed. Michael, even wearing the rough-spun uniform of the Insurgency, was better dressed than any he'd yet to see, and the few people he saw stared. The place remained a victim of the war ravaging it. It was a wonder the Magistrate hadn't already overrun the city or reduced it to a pile of ash strewn rubble.

Women and children stopped and stared as he was marched past. Many turned tail and scurried back to their dwellings, some pulling horses or goats behind them. One boy held a chicken and was crying, "Mamma!" while the hen squawked her displeasure. The men and boys were in uniform, armed and manning the walls, or playing at soldier guarding the mishmash of streets. If Angus wanted to outlast the Magistrate's superior numbers, technology, and powers, it was clear he'd need allies. He might be able to engineer a siege for maybe a few days; more likely a few hours. Angus's resistance would only test the Magistrate's hand; and, lately, the six remaining generals were fond of calling the Final Order.

The Final Order was a scorched earth command. It meant the Magistrate no longer wanted these rebel small holders to fill their ranks and convert to their Enlightenment. They'd given the people fully to the darkness, and the only recourse was to destroy every last soul within the strike zone.

The order had been given three times against Fionn's armies, and Fionn had outlasted them three times. Angus would be lucky to outlast the first bombardment.

"Never seen poverty before?" the captain asked. He'd stopped his march and plucked at Michael's black uniform, fine by comparison, with his thumb and forefinger.

"I've seen it," Michael responded, giving a pointed look at the two fingers pinching his damp sleeve.

"I can tell you think yourself better. You look down your nose at us." The man's hand fisted in the sleeve of Michael's uniform.

A blast of power rolled over Michael like an explosion. He flinched, stepped backward as though pushed by a high wind. He tightened his aura even as the power, Sinful in nature, raked at him, trying to use his own energy to fuel its course. In a few seconds it was over. He panted, out of breath, as though he'd been in a battle. He looked around, surprised no one else had reacted. He half expected widespread panic.

Avaritia. The sun suddenly seemed brighter, the grass greener, the bricks of some of the buildings a deeper red. A child began to laugh. A wilting garden behind a half-collapsed fence didn't seem as close to its withering demise.

Michael had never felt *Avaritia* unleashed in such magnitude before. Like a hologram, it cast a false perception on the world. The colors seemed brighter, but that would fade in a matter of hours. Whoever was using this much power was either foolish or diabolical. Trying to cast a false view of the world, just to give it the appearance of wealth, only decreased its value two-fold. The power of *Avaritia* was immensely valuable for locating things, like gold. But using it to create gold from nothing was an illusion. Using this particular power to increase one's wealth from nothing backfired, often causing widespread death. There were still rumors that the plagues from thousands of years ago were originally caused by the greed of an *Avaritia* controlled by Roman legionnaires.

"What's wrong with him?" one of the soldiers asked.

Michael spun a slow circle, searching for the source. His gaze landed on the fortress. This much power couldn't have originated from that dirty child. No child was this strong. The child was powerful, but not this powerful. Still, the power had come from the castle. This Angus might prove to be dangerous after all.

"Did you hear me?" the captain said, his hand tightening the fabric of Michael's uniform into a band around his bicep.

Michael tried to stave off the panic building within him. He was a pot on the fire, the water ready to boil over onto the flames and vaporize.

Once, he'd been hung by his arms for days by Jacqueline and endured the whipping at her hand, just because she wanted to see his blood run. The ceaseless crack of the leather against his skin, the burning salt in the wounds, the burn of his shoulders as they strained in their sockets. The whirring of a healing chamber causing him to itch as his skin knitted back together, half as fast as the *Industria* could split it.

Michael clenched his fists. He would not show weakness, ever again. His aura snaked out, sinking its fangs into the man. The captain yelped in surprise as though he'd been burned. Beads of blood welled up from under his fingernails. His angry red face turned as pale as the gray mist that lay heavy over the moors.

"I would appreciate if you refrained from touching me," Michael said.

The man nodded, turned, and led Michael across a wide moat. As they crossed, the moat's murky water began to clear. The castle was a gray citadel, all spikes, weaponry, and a mishmash of new building techniques to reinforce age-old defenses. The place was no Magistrate hall, but while its walls did not gleam with expert craftsmanship, they were grime free. Still, no amount of *Avaritia* power could erase the centuries old stains between the brick work.

"Halt!"

Another troop of armed guards stood at the other end of the lowered drawbridge. "State your business."

"Emissary from the Yukon here to see the King," the captain shouted back.

The soldier considered Michael, taking in the uniform, before he tipped his head in permission. "He's expected. Continue on."

Michael looked past the high walls, the barred gates, the spikes. His pulse roared in his ears with the howl of a storm. Once he crossed the bridge's threshold, he'd be trapped behind those walls.

No, I won't. He thought, as logic overrode his emotions. *Not for long.*

If he failed to report in, Fionn would alert her special ops team. Atticus and Darci were on that team. Neither of them would allow him to be taken prisoner, Darci least of all. She knew exactly what it meant to be trapped by the memories of what he'd endured, and even more what those memories would do to him if he were imprisoned again.

Seven hells, even after that wave of power he could sense he was the most powerful Sin in the castle. He'd killed a man less than an hour ago with only the surface tension of his abilities. If these hardened highland survivors attempted to imprison him, he'd paint their castle red with the depths his desire ran to remain free.

The cracks widening in his mind stilled. He took the last step through the castle gates into the courtyard, and froze.

He took a deep breath, scenting the air, his nostril's flaring. *Harley.*

Her scent wasn't physical, but something he sensed on a mental level. It was a shout in a place of whispers left by the *Avaritia.* The nearness of her was painful, jarring. He hadn't believed it when her picture flashed up on Tobias's screen. He'd thought that maybe, just maybe, the woman with the blonde hair, evenly shaped eyes, and soft cheekbones that drew his gaze to her sweet lips, had been a look-a-like, some woman on the other side of the globe fortunate to share a striking similarity. All these what-ifs were shattered the moment he crossed the threshold into the castle proper.

Harley was here.

The unmistakable sensation of her psychic power permeated the walls, and he responded as a starved man confronted with a feast. He reveled in it. The predatory nature he'd kept as closely wrapped as his aura trailed out. Those parts of him that were whole stirred, and the desire to strike out and tear the castle apart until he discovered her churned as strong as the desire to paint the castle with blood.

The edges of his aura trailed outward and other psychic scents hit him. *Invidia,* like Tobias, but stronger and more mature than the young tech he'd left at home. The other belonged to the *Avaritia.* As expected, the aura was small, a tiny flickering flame.

"Something the matter?" the captain ground out when Michael paused. "The King doesn't like being made to wait."

Michael wanted to snarl, take the weapon from the guard standing too close to his left shoulder and ram it down the captain's useless throat.

Avaritia, Invidia, Luxurian. A trifecta of Sins here all at once formed an undeniable threat to the small town and keep. Too much Sin created an imbalance. Without some kind of Virtuous presence to balance the Sin, it wouldn't be long before they came to blows. Michael could consider the *Avaritia* out of the picture, after using so much power, which meant he and Angus would be circling each other like fighting cocks ready to spring at one another.

"Let's not keep Angus waiting," he replied calmly, surprising himself by his own nonchalance. Inside, he was a storm of severely repressed violence. He was not here to release his abilities upon the small folk.

That didn't mean he wouldn't.

Harley was in this forsaken ruin somewhere, and he would find her.

The castle was dimly lit, and again Michael paused at the entrance. He'd come through three check points, the town, the curtain wall, and now he stood before a dark hole waiting to swallow him. He could smell damp stone. A cold sweat broke out over his body.

The panic struck. Lightning fast, it burned through him with cold fire. He held out a hand, bracing himself with the doorframe, and felt the rough wood under the pads of his fingertips. The wood grain promised the threat of splinters if he were to run his hand along it with any force.

Wood. He relaxed. The Magistrate's dungeons were devoid of anything as organic as wood. The rooms, doors and instruments were all comprised of cold stone or freezing metal or plastic. He stepped through, ignoring the suspicious looks of Angus's soldiers, and moved into a large entrance hall.

"Peculiar," one of the men muttered, only to be silenced by his commanding officer.

Michael adopted a military stance, his shoulders straight, hands clasped behind his back. The castle gleamed in its simplicity. He'd half expected it to be filled with garish decorations, leavings from a long dead era. Instead, the stone wall facing him was hung with a simple banner, a gold dragon's silhouette on a green field. He'd seen it sewn onto many of the uniforms.

The captain left two men to "accompany" him, although babysit was more appropriate. He disappeared down a long hallway. A door opened, shut, and the low murmur of voices followed.

Harley's aura was stronger here, underlying the scent of *Invidia* and *Avaritia* that had leeched into the walls, but still weakened, not as strong as he knew it to be. He frowned. If she lived here, the trail of her should fill his senses, not tease him from the shadows.

"The King will see you now," the captain said stiffly.

Michael blinked, releasing his hands.

He was shown down a close, low-ceilinged hallway and left before a steel door. The captain left without bothering to usher him in.

Michael pushed open the door, his sweaty hand leaving a print on the cold metal. He didn't knock first. Any Sin worth his weight would have sensed him the moment he entered the building.

"Please, come in," came a pleasant voice. It held the echo of command.

"King Angus," Michael said, examining the man before him. Angus was taller than him, and, when they shook hands, his grip was firm and callused, similar to his own. His eyes were sharp, as was his aura. A quick glance, and a quick psychic scenting, had Michael tightening his grip and closing his own aura. "Admiral Fionn sends her regards."

"Thank you for coming at such short notice." Angus sat down behind a metal desk. "I'd expected Admiral Fionn to inform me who to expect, but she never did."

Michael took the hard wooden chair across from the King. "She didn't?" He knew this, of course. "I am Michael Knight."

"You have rank in her command?" Angus inquired.

"Lieutenant," Michael replied.

Angus was silent. By the shrewd squint to his eyes, the conversation wouldn't continue until Michael had given up the information Angus wanted. Which meant this was not a meeting, it was an interrogation. He'd known that from the beginning. But then, he was here to perform his own interrogation, and that leveled the playing field.

"I belong to a certain task force close to the Admiral's

command. She sent me ahead as an advance to ascertain the nature of your request."

Angus's aura flickered, a candle flame disturbed by a breeze. "My people are doing well, but as your scans will have shown you, the Magistrate forces are at my walls. My request for aid will not be fulfilled by one man."

Michael sensed Angus's simmering anger. One did not live in the same location as Fionn without attuning to the depths of rage in another person. It could boil over at any second and he'd learned to sense the nuances of someone's mood. He chose his next words carefully.

"Depends on the man."

Angus was silent. His stare was hard and his nostril's flared with impatience. "I need an army—"

"And I need a reason to call in the cavalry you so desperately need." Michael stood, going to the reinforced window, changing the interrogation into posturing between two equals, keeping the precious balance. "Your town is remarkable. A small rebel population able to thrive above ground in the middle of a nuclear zone."

"We're on the edge of those detonations," Angus said, somewhat defensively.

"Still, you have impressed Admiral Fionn enough to send me as an advance. The Magistrate wouldn't expose such a large part of their force to irradiation of this nature unless there was ample reason." Michael turned. He examined the room and its occupant, turning a full circle.

There was a set of fingerprints marring Angus's perfectly polished desk. They were small, too small for an adult. On the carpet there was a faded blood stain, brown in color.

"How old is he?" he asked, meeting Angus's eyes.

Angus frowned. "What are you asking?"

"There's an *Avaritia* here. He's about eight, maybe ten years old, and powerful." Michael kept his hands clasped behind his back. "You've been using him to keep your starving town afloat. For how long?"

"You are gifted in your ability to sense auras," Angus said.

"Anyone within a mile radius and any ability at all would have felt that," Michael said. Angus was bluffing, so he waited for an explanation.

"How I keep my people living from winter to winter is not your business, nor is it your Admiral's," Angus said.

"I wouldn't say that," Michael replied, moving to stand behind one of the chairs, his hands held loosely at his sides. "Everything you are doing to attract the Magistrate's attention is Fionn's business. The Magistrate is looking for powerful Sins to bring under its control, and if it cannot control them, it will slaughter them. If you'd left well enough alone, I'm sure the Magistrate never would have noticed your small existence. Keeping the boy hidden would have given your people more time, instead of using his power to attract the enemy like flies to carrion."

"You see more than most, Michael," Angus said, pushing back from his desk. "But so do I. Admiral Fionn doesn't send one of her best unless she's seriously considering lending her support. I've been keeping tabs on her campaign. She is actively looking for allies."

Michael didn't like the thirst he heard in the King's voice. This man enjoyed power over the weak. He wanted Fionn's power backing his. "I highly advise you not to assume the admiral's state of mind. You would not want to incur her wrath by a mistaken guess."

Angus's aura flashed out, striking with accuracy at Michael's heart.

Michael took a slow deep breath as the *Invidia*'s aura crawled along his own shield. He would find no cracks in that defense.

"Then why are you here?" Angus withdrew his aura. He'd failed to ascertain the nature of Michael's heart and was frustrated.

Michael had been right. Without an intervening Virtue, it wouldn't be long before he and Angus tried to rip each other's throats out. Michael kept tight defenses, but one wrong move and Angus would have the better of him.

"Using your aura to attack me was unwise. I am here to find the truth behind your request for aid." He pushed his aura out, drawing his power from its depths to wash over the burly man before him. He wanted Angus to feel his strength as a warning, and as a promise that if he ever attacked him again, the consequences would be brutal and unrelenting.

It was ridiculously easy to slip beneath the King's aura and locate his desires. There were many. Strongest was the drive to secure his people, feed them, and care for them. There were others. To have perfect control, to destroy the Magistrate, and something Michael couldn't quite grasp. Still curious, but knowing any further lingering would be a challenge, he withdrew. The whole incident had taken a handful of milliseconds.

Angus paled. "*Luxurian*," he said. "So Fionn did elect to send her best to spy on me."

"You're Majesty," Michael said, disliking the title as it peeled off his tongue. "The Magistrate is amassing on this isle. The Insurgency's rebellion is measured and would fail if we did not consider the odds of our survival very carefully."

"And what do you consider?"

"Everything," Michael answered.

Angus's face turned an alarming shade of purple. "My people are dying, and by the gods—"

"Don't," Michael warned. A whisper of darkness entered the room. Perhaps it was the clouds increasing in front of the sun, but the shadows deepened nonetheless.

"Excuse me?"

"Don't invoke gods you know nothing about."

Angus's breath hissed through his teeth. "Nothing? The gods are cruel, selfish bastards. Abandoning these lands when they should have risen up and fought the Magistrate instead of rolling over."

Michael smiled. "Do you think the Seven Virtues would have been able to enslave the world if they hadn't first enslaved the gods of darkness? Or that Fionn's campaign would have been so successful if she hadn't begun to free them?"

Angus smiled, and Michael realized he'd let slip a key secret to Fionn's success. He cursed himself. He should have bitten his tongue.

"Then it's true," Angus said. "Fionn freed the Goddess of Wrath and murdered the God of Patience. I'll do whatever she requires to have her power at my back."

Michael considered carefully, unwilling to make another mistake. He already knew that Angus didn't deserve Fionn's assistance, but his people did. "I will need full access to your grounds in order to strategize the Insurgency's defense of your city. If the Insurgency can be successful, I will relay the report."

"The hour is late, Michael. My people don't have time for you to waste on an inspection."

Michael braced his hands against the edge of the desk, leaning forward. "Your people have all the time in the world for my inspection. As the leader you should appreciate *my* leader's unwillingness to cut corners when it comes to securing the Insurgency's victory."

Angus returned his stare.

"We're wasting time, Angus."

The King straightened. "Demark." He barely spoke the name before a door recessed into the stonework behind Michael opened with a low hiss, and a medium height, broad-shouldered and stoic man entered. He bowed, giving Michael a shrewd glance.

"Demark, escort Michael about the grounds."

Demark's left brow rose. "A tour?"

It obviously pained Angus to give a curt nod. "Show him the soldiers, the crops, and our defenses. His admiral wants to make sure we are not working with the Magistrate to trap the Insurgency."

Michael stiffened at the implied insult. He refrained from commenting. Time was of the essence, and this way he would achieve what he wanted and complete the mission.

Demark took the explanation without question. "Follow me," he said.

"Angus," Michael said, "What about the boy?"

The King's eyes narrowed. "He's unharmed. His power has given my people strength to make it through our final hours."

"The Insurgency's assistance will also be contingent upon that child. He's an unusually strong *Avaritia*."

Angus let out a laugh. "You think he's strong enough to be one of your pathetic lost gods?"

Michael stared at Angus. "Don't push your luck, Angus."

"Don't count on luck, Lieutenant Knight. Admirals don't send emissaries to places like this unless they are expendable."

It was an old doctrine, frequently employed by the Magistrate: The sacrifice of the few would benefit the many. Michael didn't acknowledge Angus's threat. If it came to a battle between them, no amount of luck or greed would increase Angus's chances of survival.

7

Brax strode into the Magistrate encampment, bold as he'd been during any other infiltration. A corporal saluted him as he passed and he returned the gesture. If only these boys in their tidy-whities knew who he was. Jack-assed bunch of idiots. He had good intelligence that his face was plastered on every training center bulletin as the Magistrate's third most wanted fugitive. Still, dressed in one of their own uniforms, even their brightest wouldn't recognize him on sight. No one in these cookie cutter armies did anymore.

This time though, they'd picked a different cookie. It was a trap. Even the Magistrate didn't need to drag out a parade in order to dismantle Angus's small starving army. They knew Fionn would be here, and they'd brought out the entire band to play for her.

This was the third such outpost he'd found in the two hours since they'd landed on this waterlogged isle. Each post was populated by at least two full squadrons, equipped with the latest weaponry. The Magistrate was gearing up for an assault of grand proportions.

Brax had to hand it to them. They were using Angus's broken wing routine to bait the trap, and all this spanktastic weaponry to spring it. The Magistrate was getting wise. Had to happen sometime.

The *plink* of water dripping from leaves onto metal surfaces was eerie. The Magistrate camps were ordered, every man doing exactly what he was supposed to be doing, no one chatting idly. Fionn's army was a mish mash of sounds and human interaction. This place moved and worked like a machine.

It gave Brax the heebie geebies.

The soldiers were dressed in their traditional white uniforms, not a speck on them. His stolen uniform, on the other hand, had blood on the collar. So far no one had noticed. The Magistrate soldiers could be spotted from satellites, and by the naked eye for miles. They wanted Angus to know they were coming for him, and by proxy Fionn. Besides, there would be no guerilla tactics with tanks *that* size.

Several tents had been erected on the sidelines next to the tank parking zone. The largest structure caused Brax to stop in his stride. His fingers itched to grab the sidearm on his hip. This was the only outpost with this particular tent. It was much too fancy and luxurious for the common foot soldier to sleep in. It set his teeth on edge, with damned good reason. The flap opened. Two corporals saluted as a man with high ranking gold bars on the collar of his uniform strode out.

Brax jolted to attention and saluted, turning about face as though he were a posted guard. It was plausible, and no one gave him a second glance.

"Commander," a voice cut through the din of machine noise and the sounds of marching and shouted commands.

The man who left the tent stopped and turned on his heel, his gaze skimming over his troops, including Brax. This man was a key player. He carried himself not with the strict training of a foot soldier, but with the easy grace of true leadership and high position.

Another man, ancient by the deep frown lines framing his mouth and pinching his forehead, stepped over the threshold of the tent. He wore a white suit whose lines were so perfectly pressed they could probably cut skin. He possessed the unmistakable air of a man who was used to being obeyed without question. Here were the brains of the operation.

Bingo.

Brax kept his gaze straightforward, pretending to be a good little soldier. He burned to slide his eyes to the left and examine this man with more than his peripheral vision.

No way. They would not be stupid enough to… But they did. Brax fought a rising smile. Fionn was going to love this one. They'd assumed the remaining six Virtues would remain in hiding, so which of them had come out to play soldier? Whichever god of Virtue was here, this implied the Magistrate was concerned with something bigger than Angus's small rebellion. Looked as though it was time to report his findings.

Brax took a deep breath, forcing himself to remain immobile. No matter how badly he wanted to march off, moving now would put him in the center of the game board. The tank across from him was equipped with the kind of weaponized laser that could incinerate him with its automated targeting system. If he was caught now, Fionn would have no warning of what awaited her on the ground. He'd be vaporized first.

"The *Luxurian* is here. Make sure you avoid him," the Virtue said.

"A *Luxurian*, Sir?" the commander responded.

Michael? Why were they getting their panties in a twist for a half-insane ex-prisoner?

If possible the Magistrate official's frown deepened. "Do not make the mistake of underestimating him, Commander. He is… unpredictable. Always has been. If you do meet him, don't give him a reason to kill you. He'll do it as easily as I would."

Wait, what? The god was speaking about Michael as if they were old acquaintances; and not just as if they knew each other, but as if he considered Michael his equal. *Impossible!* Michael wasn't that powerful, was he?

"I understand. May your light overcome all darkness," the commander said as he executed a salute, clicking his heels perfectly. The only thing missing was a pirouette and some applause.

Yet, as the commander strode away from the tent, Brax noted the man's shoulders, their stiff set. He was stressed. The pallor of his skin a little gray and green around the gills. He was afraid. Sick with it, in fact. What would happen to him if he failed to carry out his orders? And what were those orders?

Brax glanced again at the tent housing the Virtue, the true enemy here. The Magistrate wouldn't risk losing another of their precious Virtues. Not after what Fionn and Emerick did to General Tysek, the former God of Patience. So what was this?

The commander paced across the muddy camp, his boots kicking through puddles as though he were forcing his authority on them. He disappeared inside another tent.

Brax decided now was the time to leave and become invisible. He marched with precision steps toward the edge of the encampment and into the shadows of the forest. Then he clicked on Tobias's camouflage technology and blended into the forest as if he were part of it. He watched, waiting for the commander to emerge. When he did, he came out of his tent wearing clothes that were dirty and ripped. Veritable rags compared to the gold bars and white jacket he'd been sporting.

So, you're the spy, Brax thought, and watched as the commander traipsed into the forest nearby. As Brax suspected, the man headed north, toward the castle.

Brax drifted far behind the man, trying to keep up with him and remain silent, a difficult thing to do. The commander kept a quick pace, checking his surroundings often. If Brax miss-stepped, or moved too fast, he'd give away his position.

On some hidden cue, the commander stopped and spun around. Brax froze. His body, even with the camouflage technology, would appear blurred around the edges, like the haze created by heat wave. If the man was observant, Brax was about to lose his cover. After a moment the soldier resumed his passage through the forest, then dropped out of sight.

Brax ducked behind a tree, waited a moment for telltale laser fire, then peered around the thin trunk.

Nothing.

The commander must have suspected he was being followed and gone to ground. Brax approached the area. He drew his handgun.

Brax miss-stepped and the ground fell away under him. He dropped his weapon and spread his arms out, catching himself on the edges of the drop-off. He heard the distant slapping of boots down a wet tunnel. It was a manhole, an old-world sewer opening.

"Sly dog," Brax muttered, pulling himself up, cursing his bruised hip and ribs.

Michael had to be warned. If there was a Magistrate soldier with orders to avoid Michael, then the best way to waylay those orders was to pit him against Michael.

His comm beeped loudly.

"What?" Brax said, answering. "You'd better have a damn good reason for almost alerting the Magistrate to my position. You're lucky I lost the sonofabitch."

It was Michael, Tobias, and his commanding officer Emerick. He turned a slow circle as he gave his report, telling them what he'd seen in the encampment.

Something caught his eye.

Was that movement in the forest? He froze, checking his camouflage.

Then he turned slowly to check behind him, and something sharp jabbed into the side of his neck. Brax grabbed for the handgun and fired two shots into the soldier's chest. Red stained the man's white uniform and he dropped.

"Fuck. I'm humped," he said. It was the code phrase, universal for any man in Fionn's army. It translated into "I've been caught. I'm not coming back. Don't wait up." If Tobias was doing his job right, then any second...

Brax yelled as the comm on his wrist burned out, the incendiary device hidden within destroying any and all relevant information in the chip, and burning the skin around his wrist. Now there was nothing for the bastards to use.

The cool sensation of drugs flowed through his system. He stumbled to his knees. He heard people crashing through the underbrush.

Brax couldn't move. He was staring up at the sky, at the gray clouds. A soldier had followed him. How could anyone follow him? He must not have been as careful as he thought. But he was the best. He was always careful.

Had to happen sometime.

Or they'd been tipped off.

Shit.

8

Michael followed Demark through the main part of the castle, silently listening to the man's stiff and curt explanations of their battle readiness. The man obviously didn't like the duty assigned to him. Not on the eve of an impending attack. Neither did Michael. They both knew Demark had better things to do. And the more Demark talked, the angrier Michael grew.

While Angus's battle preparedness impressed him more and more, he hadn't detected any definite trail of Harley's presence. She was everywhere, taunting him in every hall, every walkway.

"And here you can see the back gardens and pastures."

Michael didn't quite step up to the low wall of the back garden. She hadn't been here either. He glanced over dots of sheep and rows of corn before he gave the man his full attention.

Demark met his gaze fearlessly. The King's second-in-command held a posture as though to say, "we are equals", even though it was clear Michael's powers outstripped his. If Michael's abilities were a river of lust and desire, Demark's were a single drop in the bottom of a rain barrel. Still, Demark wasn't fully cast in light; he possessed a touch of darkness. He was a predator in his own right. With so many Sins present in the castle, the need for Virtues was so clear it might have been written in flashing lights. The powers were unbalanced, to the extent that all the Sins, even someone as lightly touched as Demark, was fighting to remain civil. He still wasn't sure if Demark was sizing him up or getting ready to shoot him in the back.

"Tell me," Michael said. "It doesn't bother you that Angus is using the powers of a prepubescent boy to keep his lands fertile?"

A flash of temper, the sharpening of an aura. "The sacrifice of the one sometimes allows the multitude to survive."

"True," Michael replied. "But I wanted your thoughts, not your master's."

Demark clenched his jaw and looked away, out over the fields. "Angus wants an easy life for his people. But if they wanted that, they'd convert and work for the Magistrate. He sees the boy's powers as protection."

"What do you see it as?"

Demark didn't miss a beat. "Another form of control."

Michael let a thin ribbon of his aura touch Demark's. A flood of desire lay behind the man's thick skin. It wasn't licentious, but the kind of desire that wanted a warm hearth, a good meal, and the satisfaction of freedom. Demark felt betrayed by Angus's use of power to ease their life.

"You've told Angus this?"

"Would it make a difference?" Demark retorted. "Does your admiral take advantage of the one to fulfill the needs of the many?"

"No," Michael answered. "Fionn would never make someone do something against their will."

"Too good to be true." He shuffled his feet "I'm to show you the stores if you're done eyeing the sheep."

"Good," Michael said. "I don't think the state of the sheep will factor into my report."

Demark chuckled, caught off guard. "I shouldn't like you, but I do. It's been years since I've seen anyone stand chin to chin with Angus."

"I suppose you were the last to try?"

"Try and fail," Demark answered.

What was the punishment for failing? The more he learned about Angus, the more he disliked the man. He treated the people under his rule like sheep in that pasture, there to do his bidding. They respected him, he could see that; but not out of something positive, as with true leadership, but out of fear. They didn't dare disobey his commands, and they were the commands of a monarch to the small folk.

Michael turned and came up short. All coherent thought dried up, like a river in a heat wave.

"Pardon me," Harley said, looking down and away, not meeting either of their eyes. She hadn't seen him, sensed him yet. Her golden hair lay across her cheek, sticking to it, as though her skin were damp. She'd aged since he last saw her, the lines in her face deepened just enough to reflect the hardship of life. But it was her.

"My Lady," Demark said. "Allow me to introduce you to Lieutenant Knight from the Insurgency."

Harley blinked, her lashes catching on strands of her hair. She didn't look at him. He wasn't sure she'd even heard the name. Still, she dropped a curtsey, a move that looked disjointed as though her body was stiff.

"I'm glad you were able to meet with Angus on such short notice." Her tone said she was anything but thrilled with the prospect. "If you'll excuse me." She spoke with the flustered air of a person getting the obligatory introduction over with so she could return to her duties.

Michael found his voice. Her name passed his lips in a caress, all that he was and ever had been hidden in the sounds of her name.

Her head flew up like a startled animal's. Her ocean blue eyes were wide. A flush deepened her pale skin.

"M-Michael." His name was a prayer, a curse, and a ghost on her lips.

"You know each other?" Demark asked, a discerning curiosity in his tone.

Michael didn't dare look from her eyes. The moment he did he could sense she would flee. "From a previous life," he answered.

"My Lady," called the worried voice of another woman from down another hall.

Harley trembled, an almost imperceptible shiver, and shadows crossed her face. Then Michael saw the signs of a bruise hovering beneath the surface of her skin. What he'd taken for a scratch he now saw was the mark left by a ring. She'd been backhanded. Recently. Not long enough for a bruise to form. But there would be one, of that he had no doubt.

The growl rolled up from his depths. All traces of weakness in his mind vanished, sealed away at the sight of her injury. The deepest parts of him were called to protect that which was his.

He reached for her and she flinched, and it made him angrier to see the woman he once knew to be proud and headstrong shrink away from him. It wasn't because their lives had suddenly been forced together again. No, her gaze was astonished. Her flinch was because he was a man reaching for her. He didn't pull back but continued to do as he intended and brushed his fingertips lightly against her cheek.

"Angus is a possessive man," Demark warned.

Michael turned his cold gaze on the man. Demark had his hand on his sidearm. In the moment of his distraction, Harley slipped away from Michael and down the hall. Something in him ripped.

She ran from me.

In a hundred years he wouldn't have thought Harley would flee, not from him. Lunge into his arms maybe, but bolt away from him like a terrified doe from a wolf?

Michael watched where she had disappeared. "Angus will never match the depth of desire I have for her."

Demark was staring at him with a mixture of wariness and awe.

Michael forced his aura back, coiling its ribbon-like tendrils against his skin. He'd used his powers far too much in the last few moments. Demark's loyalties were too easy to seduce away from Angus, telling him more about the man as a despot then he'd already discovered. Worse, he'd whipped his aura out and laid claim to Harley with raw temptation, and felt nothing in return. She seemed as fragile as he'd been the first hours after Darci pulled his mind back from the raging storm of fear, rage, and pain left behind by the *Industrias*.

Demark eyed him, then said with wary caution, "I've seen Angus execute men over his wife before."

If the years had been tortuous to him, they must have been worse for her. And Darci wasn't here to sooth Harley's thoughts and push back her fear. He'd have to find some way to...

Demark's words sunk in.

"*Wife?*" Michael growled.

"Aye," Demark said carefully. "She arrived on our shores, bedraggled and storm tossed. Still, she's a pretty thing. King Angus took her in. Two months later they were wedded."

Crack.

Michael shuddered. He needed to be alone. The carefully constructed façade was shattering into knife sharp shards. He'd be cut to ribbons if he didn't...

Didn't what? Collapse into a quivering mass of man flesh?

He straightened. He breathed. The shards settled into place. A few were crooked and didn't quite fit, but he wasn't broken. *Nothing* would ever break him again.

"I need to make my report. Is there an office, or a room I might use?" His tone was smooth, no hint of the emotions shooting through him.

Demark nodded. He didn't ask what had happened and Michael wasn't about to elaborate. He was led to a wide guest room with an empty fireplace and the most spartan of linen on the metal framed bed.

The moment the door shut, Michael closed the shutters at the window, casting the room into an imperfect darkness. Lines of light cut across the floor, the bed, the walls. He needed darkness. Sweet, sweet shadows like air to breathe, to live.

He breathed, once, twice. Steadier, Michael keyed his comm

to life. The connection to the Insurgency compound was bad, but he was lucky to get one.

"Lieutenant Michael Knight requesting secure link to Commander Darci Underwood."

A moment later a crackle came over the line.

"Lieutenant, where have you been?" Emerick. "Where are you? And why in the seven hells is Brax half a league from your position? You were to stick together."

Michael frowned. Why was Emerick on the line? Something wasn't going according to plan. "I'm at King Angus's castle. Brax is investigating the Magistrate forces. We were ambushed as soon as we landed. They are crawling all over the surrounding forests."

"That explains the bodies I saw from the satellite images," Tobias chipped in. Michael didn't even have to wonder why Tobias was on the line. It was his line. "What about my ship?"

"Who gave you orders to split up?" Emerick demanded, overriding Tobias's questions.

"We decided the more information we could gather, the better. Since we parted, I have had no contact with him."

His hands were shaking. He pressed his palms flat against the cold stone wall, taking strength from the solidness.

Emerick's growl of disapproval came in a rough staccato over the connection. "Key him in, Tobias."

"If he's in a delicate spot, we could disrupt his cover—"

"Just do it."

"Fine," Tobias grumbled. "Come in, Commander Braxton."

Silence. Then—

"What?" Brax snarled. "You'd better have a damn good reason for almost alerting the Magistrate to my position."

"Where the hell are you?" Emerick demanded.

"I was tailing a Magistrate commander, and you would not believe who they brought with them. You'd better have our special forces over here in a jiffy."

Michael's heart rate pick up. "Who is it?" he asked.

"Nice of you to join the conversation, Lieutenant. How're

things up at the castle?" Brax replied in a hissed voice. "Dry I hope. It's been months since I was this cold and soaked through." A sound similar to crunching leaves echoed over the link. "And this forest is dead. Whatever's out here has sucked it dry."

"Brax," Emerick said exasperated. "Who's there?"

"No idea, but if I had money on a guess, I'd say it's one of the gods, a Virtue."

Silence. Brax never lost when he made a bet.

"No way," Tobias said, accompanied by a furious clicking. "Intel shows the generals are still holed up in Magistrate Central, Mount Olympus, still locked behind the golden gates. None of them have left."

"Check again. He's a powerful bastard, decked out in a suit."

"Which Virtue is he?" Emerick asked.

"Really, Emerick?" Brax admonished. "I'm a fucking neutral. I can't tell."

"Michael," Emerick said testily. "Did you sense anything?"

Michael searched his thoughts. "No, only the *Avaritia*."

"The *Avaritia*'s there?" Tobias shrieked. "Awesome. You know there's absolutely no intel at all about that particular Sin. You hit the jackpot, boys."

"Sir," Michael said. "If Fionn brings the force here, it's a trap."

"I know," Emerick replied, quiet. "I need confirmation that the *Avaritia* is there."

"I'll get it," Michael said.

"I'm transmitting the coordinates of the Magistrate's camps and its numbers," said Brax under his breath. "I was tailing one of their commanders," he added, "but he slipped away. He's playing spy and dressed in Angus's colors. He's got brown eyes, medium height, medium build, carrying a weapon too shiny to be a rebel rifle. The general ordered him back to the castle."

Then the comm crackled as two very loud gun shots went off. Michael flinched, listening, straining to hear if Brax was shot.

Brax swore again. His breathing had become wheezy. "I'm humped."

"Tobias," Emerick said.

"I'm burning his comm."

Michael felt a line of cold run down his spine. Burning a comm. Brax was compromised.

The silence lengthened, punctuated by the raspy breaths of Emerick and Tobias on the other end. Michael was glad for the darkness pressing close. He couldn't see the room he was in, but he wasn't panicked. He felt calm, collected, in his element, and it gave him the clarity to forge ahead.

"Commander," Michael said quietly. "I'll find him and the *Avaritia*."

"If what Brax said is true, then we've got more than just a little Magistrate cleanup starting. You'll have to fight until we get there. You're alone, you got that?"

"I understand, Sir." And he did.

"No one mentions this to Fionn," Emerick ordered. "Not until we know for sure that Brax is compromised. This has happened to him before. We'll find him."

Michael understood Emerick's desire not to tell Fionn that her closest friend was missing.

"What about Angus?" Emerick added.

"Angus's intentions are mostly good. He wants to protect his people. But he's become a despot trying to do it. There's an *Avaritia*, a boy, whose powers are unusually strong. Angus is using the boy to fatten his herds and ripen his harvest." Michael forced himself to relax, "It's clear he's abusive to his wife. His soldiers fear him. He doesn't deserve the aid he's asking for, but his people do."

"That explains why the Magistrate has a sudden interest in the Scottish lowlands," Tobias added.

"The boy isn't the *Avaritia*," Michael clarified, thinking of the powerful child he'd encountered beyond the castle walls. "But he either knows the *Avaritia* or can find him." He couldn't quite keep the desperation from his voice. He needed to protect Harley, get her out of here, and he owed it to Brax to find him, or his body. There was a lot to do and he was completely alone.

Emerick spoke fervently. "We need to take this ground. Secure all possibilities. Find the kid and find out what you can. Get Angus's men ready to defend the castle. If you can, find Brax. The world can't risk the Magistrate gaining control of another Sin, or keeping control if they have it already. Protecting the *Avaritia* is your first responsibility. We will be ready to depart in an hour. Expect us by dawn, Lieutenant. I'll set an alert. If Brax contacts us, you'll be the first to know. If you see an opportunity to get him to safety, do it."

"Understood, Commander," Michael said.

A hesitation. "Did you need to speak to Darci?"

"Yes," he said without hesitation. Things were happening, things he needed her to understand with her knowledge of his mind.

"You met the girl," Tobias said, adding, "bow-chick-a-wow-wow!"

Michael's temper sizzled. "Get Darci, *now*."

"So it's like that is it?" Tobias said; then, "Darci, stop you're puttering with the deck rats, Michael needs your love advice. Make it quick. We're at red alert."

"Love advice?" Darci's clear, youthful voice was concerned. Michael could hear her frown. "Michael, what's wrong?"

Did he even have an answer for that?

"Tobias," he said, "get off the line."

"Fine," the *Invidia* huffed. There was a click and they were alone, he hoped.

"Darci." His voice shook. "Did you ever find thoughts of a woman in my mind?"

A pause. "The one with the blue eyes?" she said it carefully.

He turned and leaned his forehead against the cool stone wall of the room he'd cast in darkness. "Yes. Harley."

"Gods, Michael. I didn't know. I assumed you had an obsession with old-world motorcycles and knew someone with blue eyes."

"No, she's here."

"*What?*" Darci shrieked. He heard the clang of a discarded metal object in the background. "Michael." Her voice was hard, stern, and she was about to give him an order. Something which, if he failed to obey, would wreck some part or all of the work she'd done on his mind. "You have to stay away from her. Your whole emotional process is tied with her memory. Any contact between you could trigger your subconscious into a downward spiral and you'll *shatter*. If that happens again, there'll be no consciousness keeping your powers in check. No one can come back from mental trauma like that a second time."

"I can't," he whispered. He lay his cheek against the cold stone, wishing warm flesh was there instead. Agony streaked through him. He'd given everything for her. Now he was being asked to turn a blind eye to her, to her suffering, to stay away. He could never do that. To do so would be to bring about the very catastrophe Darci was describing.

"Listen," she said urgently. "You don't know the depths of your powers. Even I couldn't find them. Unleashing that much energy, that much *Luxurian* energy, would destroy everyone around you. You'd tear yourself apart unleashing all of it at once. For her safety, until you are ready for this, you have to stay away from her. Promise me, Michael."

He swallowed.

Swallowed again, and lied. "I promise."

9

Michael emerged from the room composed, sane, dangerous. It infuriated him to know Darci was right. She had to be. Who else knew his mind better? Then there was his commanding officer, Lieutenant Commander Braxton. The man's last location was close by, close to the walls, that is. From the readings Tobias gave him of Brax's last coordinates the Magistrate was beginning to move on the castle.

"Lieutenant," Demark acknowledged him.

"Where is Angus?" Michael didn't mince words. "The castle is in greater danger than I previously thought. There is a god, a Virtue, on your doorstep."

Demark swallowed, but otherwise kept his composure. "Which one?"

"We don't know."

Angus was found quickly. Demark carried a direct line to his King and they found him in their war room, accompanied by various leaders of his garrison. By the tension in the King's shoulders, and the downward cast of most of the council's gazes, this meeting was not going well. Angus's anger was almost palpable, and the lick of his power was in the air. Either he didn't notice that the hearts of his men were growing cold toward him, as was obvious to Michael, or he simply didn't care. Another feather in the cap of his incompetence as a leader.

"Unless you're here to tell me your armies are on their way, you shouldn't be here," Angus said, looking up from the complicated hologram displaying a real-time view of his outer walls.

"Admiral Fionn lends her support," Michael answered. "Her forces are on their way."

"At last some good news." Angus pushed off from the edge of the table with a relieved sigh.

Demark stepped forward, standing behind the empty chair at the King's right. "There's more." He glanced at Michael, subtly giving him his allegiance and command of the room. Demark didn't know it, but the simple gesture had given Michael an advantage over Angus, if only for the moment. And he planned to use it to its full benefit.

Small threads of *Luxurian* power would be enough to gain their ears and perhaps their trust. He could not afford a disunited military unit, and he needed to keep them together until Insurgency forces arrived. It wouldn't be easy. They were already held tightly in the grip of despair.

Michael stood at the end of the oval table and glanced at the hologram. "There are three enemy camps. Here, here, and here. This one," he drew a circle in the air and it appeared on the hologram in red over the coordinates Brax had given him, "is attended by a Magistrate general."

The gasp was collective. Michael took a deep breath and wove the threads of his will around them, binding the men to him, making them see him as a capable leader, one tiny thread at a time.

"We can't hope to match one of the generals in ability," sputtered an aging man with a white mustache that drooped as though carrying the weight of his duty.

"We can," Michael reassured them with confidence he didn't feel. Truthfully, they couldn't hope to overcome a general with the paltry half-trained military Angus kept, or the limited range of Sinful powers present. If these men were the best Angus had to offer, they were in for a long night or a very short one. They wouldn't stand a chance. Not until Fionn arrived. They would simply have to find a way to make it till dawn and hope reinforcements made it in time.

"And how do you propose this?" Angus growled. "Which general? And how do you know this?"

"My companion and I were sent here as a team of two. Lieutenant Commander Braxton was to scout the Magistrate forces, confirming our tech's telemetry. Before we lost contact, he was able to confirm the presence of at least half again the force we expected. And he observed the general himself. Admiral Fionn is aware of the situation and will be here before sunrise tomorrow."

"What does she expect us to do if they attack?" Angus said.

Michael turned his attention from Angus's men and was satisfied when the self-proclaimed King flinched.

"Fight," he said. "Until there is no longer anything worth defending. They will attack before nightfall. With Magistrate numbers at over five hundred and the presence of a general, it's unlikely that I'm wrong. My commander will not be here until morning."

"We must mobilize," Demark said.

"I agree," stated the man with the white mustache. "If there's even a smidgeon of a chance that the lusty lad over there is right, our troops should mobilize. No man left in bed with his wife."

Michael glanced at Angus. It took everything not to kill the man right then. Harley was with him, married to him. Angus and he were rivals, and Angus's chances of surviving were just about gone.

The other council members added their agreement to the man with the mustache. Michael didn't smile, but he had their tenuous trust. They wanted to believe they had hope. Their King had failed to give it to them, but he, their savior, had managed to give them a glimpse.

Angus was silent. He knew a shift in power had occurred, but he hadn't yet discerned exactly why.

"Very well. You all know what to do. Dismissed."

The council members filed out. Michael resumed a relaxed stance, hands clasped behind his back.

Angus stared at him, allowing the room to empty.

Demark hesitated, glancing between Angus and Michael, his loyalty torn. He was unsure who was running the operation, his King, or the man who was more likely to save them all.

"Leave us," Angus said to Demark, making up the man's mind.

Michael held his tongue. He wouldn't completely usurp Angus's position. Not yet. Not until it was necessary.

The door clanged shut on old hinges.

"What in the seven hells was that?"

Michael didn't bother with posturing. It didn't advance his plans or the orders he was to fulfill. In the short hours to come, he didn't have time for a drawn out pissing match between them. His power, when it filled the air with filaments sharp enough to cut, made the shadows leap from their corners.

"*Harley,*" Michael said. The vehemence and anger accompanying her name startled even him.

Angus's eyes narrowed. Sweat had already started to bead on his forehead with the rise of power. "What do you want with *my wife?*"

Michael pulled his gaze slowly down Angus's body, with the speed a predator uses to creep upon its prey, and let it rest on the large gold ring Angus wore on his right hand. It was round, like a coin; with an edge sharp enough to cause the small cut that marred Harley's cheek.

When he met Angus's eyes again, the man had set his teeth.

"Do you know what the Magistrate does to Sins they consider to be traitors?" Michael asked.

He didn't wait for Angus to speak.

"They torture them for as much information they can get. When they're finished, the *Industrias* have their way with whatever remains. The Undesirables are doomed to die anyway. Why not have a little fun? They die quickly, if they are lucky. If they are unlucky, they'll be tortured day in and day out for years while their mind shatters and they are used for sport. Skin shredded by day, healed in their chambers by night. There's a reason why their victims are never heard from again."

"We're on the edge of a battle, Lieutenant," Angus growled.

Michael let more of his power enter the room, making Angus sweat. It wasn't lust he flooded the space with; no, it was pure power, the simple energy behind every Sin. Because he was *Luxurian* the energy made Angus feel exposed, vulnerable, prey-like.

"I'm on the brink of sanity," Michael said so softly it cut the air like a bolt of laser fire. "I allowed myself to be captured by the Magistrate to give your wife the chance to escape. I spent six years at the use of an *Industria*. The last four I've spent with the Insurgency, regaining the pieces of my sanity they shattered so thoroughly."

"What does this have to do with my wife?" Angus asked, less confident than before. Perhaps he was beginning to realize what Michael was: a Sin; one who would utterly destroy him, and would enjoy doing it.

"I gave her escape once. This time, I'll give her revenge."

10

The roll of sensuous power scorched through every hall with fire then froze the air with ice. Harley felt the walls tremble as Michael thrust his presence into the stone's memory. She shivered, heat bursting in her abdomen. He laid claim to the castle as he'd once laid claim to her, only now he did it with the promise of violence. She'd dallied with the memory of his hands on her body this morning, and now he was here. All her worst and best dreams colliding together in a single moment of anxiety and elation.

Gods, what would become of her son when Michael found out?

Angus's jealous power rose up through the floorboards in a pitiful response. Fear laced cold fingers in her abdomen. The King would already know. He had to. The resemblance between Cadence and Michael was impossible to conceal. She wrapped her thin arms around herself and sat on the hard bench at the foot of the King's bed. Who would come for her first? Michael? She swallowed. Or Angus? The thrill of anticipation cut off as if a knife had severed it.

"Did you feel *that*, My Lady?" her maid Rosemary said, blushing furiously as she strode through the door. "There's a war brewing and the lads are fighting downstairs. It's enough to steal my heart the way those auras are going on."

"Sins don't steal your heart," Harley said. She stood,

twisting her fingers together. "They seduce it from you, before they rip it to pieces."

If it were Angus who came for her, would he fetch her or her son? He was furious that she had borne another man a powerful son, but was unable to bear him any children. The thought had her rushing into her bathroom, past Rosemary's protests. She shut the door, slid open the false bottom of her vanity drawer and slipped the slim dagger into her pocket. What she would do with the blade she didn't know, but she'd stood by long enough. He would not hurt her son a moment longer. Neither of them would.

"Lady Harley?" asked Rosemary from the other side of the door.

"Don't call me that." Harley left the bathroom and strode to the door. "After tonight, this castle will fall and titles will mean nothing. Can't you feel the Magistrate closing in on us?" She couldn't predict if it would be the battle brewing between Michael and Angus that would spell the castle's destruction or the army gathering in the forest.

"Certainly we won't be overrun." The woman with her mousey hair turned to the window, looking down into the courtyard below. "The Insurgency—"

"It's the Magistrate," Harley snapped. "We can't outrun them. They're everywhere."

"But you did."

Harley thought back to her flight from the capital, the days and nights of fear that she was being followed, the terrible knowledge that she'd left Michael to die, and fear that his sacrifice would be for nothing when her stolen aircraft lost power over the Atlantic Ocean. And shadowing all those things, the soul shattering terror and grief stricken joy when she realized she was pregnant.

"There won't be any running this time," Harley said bitterly. Here, tonight, Angus would fight for their freedom. And Michael... Was he with the Insurgency as he claimed, or had the Magistrate broken him again? Whose dog was he? If Michael was from the Insurgency, his formidable power might, just might, give the fortress a chance at survival.

Another roll of thunder swept across her as though he could sense her thinking of him. *Michael.* There was a vow in his aura as it sought her out. She swallowed, tracking his progress through the castle. He wasn't moving toward her. Instead he turned toward...

She gasped.

"My Lady?"

An alarm began to sound from the castle walls. It was beginning.

Harley ripped open the door and dashed into the hall. She had to get there first. Cadence wouldn't be strong enough to defend himself for days. If Michael saw him and flew into a rage, she would be the only one able to shield her son.

Gods, she should have told him the moment she saw him again. She should have taken Cadence and left, no matter the danger. No danger could be worse than the father of her son destroying him, the only thing left she loved.

The damage Michael could do with all his power... She ran faster. He would be angry. She'd stood right in front of him and run away. It was no coincidence that she had found herself in Michael's arms, all those years ago. She'd been selected for matching by the Enlightened council. As a valuable Virtue, she could produce formidable children. The man they had chosen was not kind, and any Virtue she may have felt was ripped from her with savage cruelty. Michael found her the next morning, dried her tears and showed her kindness in a city where such things as leniency and soft words didn't exist. Was it any coincidence that she'd given him her heart so quickly?

Her well-worn boots slapped against the bare floors. His aura was all around, permeating the stones, the walls, the very air.

The guard at Cadence's door was not at his post.

She panicked. Michael was close, down the hall, coming closer. His aura dominated, possessed and caressed. Cadence's door was locked. She fumbled at the thumbpad. The pad released a soft beep and the door unlocked.

"Harley." *His* voice and barely a whisper of her name froze her body and stilled her heart.

Then her heart resumed its pounding as he stepped from the adjacent hall. She managed to say his name, acknowledging him. At least she could do that much. Her knees weakened, and her body threatened to swoon. It shouldn't be possible for a man she hadn't seen in years to have this effect. Yet he did.

The shadows drew back, revealing him little by little. He was tall, as she remembered. His profile was strong and pronounced, cut as though from stone and smoothed with refined tools, perfecting the detail. The black uniform suited him, making him a dangerous temptation. It was all she could do not to touch him. She knew that if she did, she would feel the same sculpted body that she'd memorized with lips, finger tips and long nights more than ten years ago.

His aura flashed against hers, and she flinched, but she needn't have. The touch of it was the softest silk against her cheek, cooling the painful swelling from Angus's blow. As soft as his fingers had been. But there was anger there. He knew, then, about Angus. She looked down.

"No," he said gently. His rough-skinned hand and gentle fingers replaced the phantom touch of his aura. His skin was cool against her bruises and she leaned into it. "Don't," he said, his tone rough with emotion. "There's nothing to be ashamed of."

Startled, she looked up at him. He knew her. Even after all this time he could read her with barely a glance. Lines of worry appeared around the edges of his mouth. He hadn't aged a day in the last ten years. Suddenly she was angry. Was she ashamed? Of course. She'd abandoned him to die, given birth to his child, betrayed his memory for Angus, a man every bit as cruel as any barbarian in the Magistrate's capital. She didn't deserve his softness. He must know that.

"What do you want?"

His hand fell away as though she'd slapped it to the side. His aura withdrew, leaving her chilled. "I have my orders to protect the *Avaritia*."

Harley felt the blood drain from her face. "And what does the Insurgency want with him?" She spat the word. This could be a ruse. It most likely was a ruse. She knew the Magistrate would do almost anything to get hold of her son. Who else had drawn them here?

"Whatever your suspicions are, Harley, I am not the enemy. The *Avaritia*, please."

Not Cadence, her mind screamed at her. Did they want him for the same purposes as Angus? Would they exhaust his powers until he died from it? Would Michael dare do such a thing to him?

Why not? her mind niggled at her. *You did.*

"His powers are attracting the Magistrate here." He tried to move past her toward the unlocked door. "With the Insurgency he will be well protected."

"No," she said. "You can't have him. No one can." In a panic, she pushed against his chest, knowing she was inviting painful rebuke. "You're supposed to be dead."

He stiffened. "The Magistrate would never kill the most powerful *Luxurian* at their disposal."

She heard it, then, hiding under his words, behind his careful tone. A hitch in the smoothness he presented as a mask. She wasn't so sure the strength and confidence he exuded was more than that: a carefully constructed mask. She let her hands press against his chest, feeling with her aura and the tips of her fingers. Cracks and fissures, dips and rivets comprised his skin and aura. A shudder went through her.

She'd been so willing to believe the worst. Not Michael. Never him. She knew then what he'd been through, what happened before the wind and tide had brought him here.

"How did you survive?"

His hands came up and covered her own, his fingers curling around them, prying them off his uniform. He took her right hand, and turned her palm toward him, brought it to his lips and planted a single kiss, wrapped and sealed with his aura in the center of it. His tone was soft. "The Magistrate would never allow one of the strongest *Luxurian*s to die before his time."

A tremor coursed through her at his touch. "When did you escape?"

"Four years ago."

So long?

"Why Angus?" he asked, and she heard what it cost him. She heard the tremble in his voice, felt the shudder in his aura.

Harley didn't dare meet Michael's eyes as she pulled away, turning her back to him. "He offered me his protection and a home."

"Is that why he beats you? In exchange for all the *comforts* of a castle?" She could feel his gaze tracing the way her clothes hung off her body. They were starving, everyone in the town, all of them too thin and skeletal.

Still, she flinched at his tone, unable to tell if he was angry with her or with the King. "Only if I use my powers. He hates the Virtuous."

"So you married him. The Magistrate would have at least fed you."

How many times had she had those thoughts herself? She couldn't tell him there was nowhere to run that Angus wouldn't find her, no way to get off this wretched isle and crawl away into some other rural waste where a few people scratched a living from rocks out of the Magistrate's way. So she did as she was told and took her stripes. It was better than what others under Angus's shadow received.

"It was the only choice I had at the time," she finally said.

The wail of the sirens seemed to grow louder. Men's shouts outside the castle grew in pitch and tone.

"I have my orders," Michael said. "I will not be able to protect you and keep Angus from destroying his people. Can you defend yourself?"

"Yes," she said. He closed the distance between them. Her aura twined with his, feeding off his frustration and igniting her own. She spun around, her hands on her hips. "And who will protect me from Angus if he senses my powers?" she demanded. "He has trained his men to tear apart any Virtuous power they find."

The shadows leapt forward, cloaking him. He smiled at her, lazy and with violence such as she'd never seen from him. "You were strong once. An asset to the Magistrate. Have you allowed him to weaken you as he has that boy?" A spark of gold appeared in the irises of his eyes.

She wanted to scream at him. She was not a weak thing. In her silence she had fought, resisted the temptation to give in and let Angus rule her. Her fist lashed out before she realized she'd attacked. Michael caught her with ease. His hand ran down her arm, stroking it and raising the hairs all over her body.

"No," she said angrily. "Don't you dare judge me. You have no idea what I've had to do to survive."

His hand suddenly gripped her wrist. Her inner muscles clenched in response and a flood of heat, hotter than any fire Angus had ever stoked, whipped through her. Gods, he wasn't even *trying* to seduce her yet.

"You're right," he whispered. "But I gave up my sanity to give you the chance to have a better life. Was this really the best place you could find? The Insurgency was gaining ground in the Yukon when you left the City. Instead you married him."

"It was the last place the Magistrate could find me. My craft broke down over the ocean and I washed ashore. There was nowhere else to go," she said, trying to pull out of his grip. "You're hurting me."

He let her go so suddenly she stumbled backward. Then his arms were around her, steadying her.

"I'm sorry," he whispered. "Darci was right. I can't control myself around you. You held me together when they broke me, and now you're breaking me apart." He swore under his breath.

His arm as it curled around her waist, pulling her toward him, was gentle. She could pull away if she wanted. She didn't, caught between wanting him and wanting to run. His lips hovered above hers. Energy trailed in spirals across the sensitive parts of her flesh, the places he knew about, the places Angus's clumsy attempts at romance never found.

"I don't care if you're married," he murmured, one hand tracing up her spine, the other moving over her hip. "I don't care if it's against orders. I will not stay away from you." His lips sealed over hers and thrills of desire rippled through her.

She was angry with him, terrified by what he'd said; and still she wanted him like a fish dangling from a hook wants water. She couldn't bring herself to escape him, nor could she consume enough of him. He pressed her against the wall, breathing her in because he was a man gasping for breath. His aura delved into hers, searing her senses. His hands kneaded and caressed, while hers explored, up his arms, over the two-day stubble of his beard, down his chest.

There wasn't time to think, time to breathe, time to—

The door behind them opened. He slipped from her, leaving her gasping for breath as a blazing furnace of desire roared toward the peak for which they'd been sprinting.

"Mom," Cadence's hoarse voice grated over them. "What's happening? Who's he?"

The embers Michael had stroked to life collapsed in a puff of terrified smoke.

Cadence's door stood open and she could see the long sharp dagger of Michael's shadow stretch behind him, cast by the late afternoon sun streaming through her son's windows. She watched as they made eye contact. Michael went unusually still. So did Cadence. Only their eyes, one pair honey gold, the other forest green, showed how stricken each was with the presence of the other.

11

A mirror.

In the boy's face, Michael saw his own, a near perfect reflection in youth. The boy's chest rose and fell. His skin was gray. His *Avaritia*'s aura was weak, like a dying candle, and this close Michael felt it like a tremor through his own chest.

Michael closed his aura about him so fast his skin stung. Something cracked. The shards of his mind shifted, revealing darkness and with it a deeper knowledge of things forgotten.

Like attracts like.

His legs buckled. Knees struck the hard wooden floor. This knowledge, older than Sin or Virtue both, shook him to the core. The boy flinched, but didn't move. He saw the same wary amazement reflected in his eyes.

To find Harley alive and now this boy… his son. No wonder she'd been so protective of the child.

He reached out, his aura first, his hand following after. His son's weak aura sent out a thin string, meeting him half-way, forming the unshakeable bond of something older than time. A jolt snapped through him, elation, worry, guilt. All of it crashed over him in a symphony of disbelief and wild joy. Unlike his own, his son's eyes were green, *Avaritia* green. Michael sensed his son's slow process, the brief flush of power in his aura as he recognized his father.

My son.

He pulled the boy forward, needing to hold him to know for sure what his senses told him was true. The boy's arms wrapped around him, but his response was with the slow grogginess of the sick.

"You're my father," the boy croaked, sounding amazed.

Michael didn't trust himself to speak. He took a shaky breath and looked at Harley. Her lips were bright red from his kiss, and tears were running down her face. Suddenly, so much didn't matter and so much more gained importance. *How could she let Angus use their son?* He was angry, confused. Gods, he was terrified to the very marrow of his bones.

"What's your name?" Michael asked softly.

His son pulled away first and gazed at him sharply, as though his name was something Michael should instinctively know. His considering gaze was dull, his dark brown hair lackluster, his skin gray. The boy's attention slid from Michael to Harley.

"I used too much," he said with slurred words.

Harley's intake of breath was louder than the siren splitting the air.

Michael tore his gaze from his son's face. Harley's skin was no longer pale but sickly, to match his son's—their son's— skin. She seemed about to faint. The joy was replaced by stabbing panic. His son's hand began to tremble and Michael sensed a great weakness in his son's aura.

"Cadence?" Harley cried. She took Cadence, picking him up and holding him to her.

"I wasn't done sleeping," he said. "But the sirens woke me up."

"Shh," Harley murmured, glancing fearfully at Michael. She went into Cadence's room and deposited him on the bed.

Guarded, Michael followed, closing the door behind them. If he had been on edge before, now he was ready to kill someone. The need to protect his son from harm could not be ignored. It was a spike driving into his thoughts. His aura snapped about him, about the entire room. No one would touch his son. No one. If anyone else tried to enter the room where his weak and defenseless son was, he'd kill them.

Was every bond amongst the Sins and Virtues like this? If the bond was as strong as this, it was no wonder parents were often euthanized when the Magistrate used a Sin for breeding. He would destroy cities, thousands, anyone who threatened Cadence while he was weak. Is this what it meant to be a father? Undeniable love and the desire to protect? There wouldn't be a moment after today when he wasn't connected to his son by this bond.

Cadence's aura flickered dangerously. He looked up at Michael.

"Are you going to kill Angus?"

Angus had done this. Michael fought to keep his anger leashed, to keep from the edge of murderous rage that threatened to overwhelm him. "Yes," he answered. He hadn't made a truer promise.

"Michael!" Harley chided him over her shoulder. "Cadence, you need to rest." Something in her voice told him this was not normal. He knew Angus had done this before to Cadence, but something about *this* time was different.

Michael examined Cadence's aura. It sang to him, but there were similarities to a weakness he'd seen once before. Memories crowded his mind. The day he'd found Atticus, spent and unresponsive, in the rain-choked gutter of the Magistrate capital. He'd used his power and given it to Atticus, then a boy of sixteen. Atticus had woken with a gasp, a spark of golden light fading from his eye, almost totally recovered.

Michael placed a hand on Harley's shoulder. "I can help."

"I've read about you," Cadence said when Michael knelt at his bedside.

Michael concentrated on wrapping his aura, its raw power, around Cadence, and fed energy into him.

"Have you?" Michael asked, wondering what about him would ever reach this distant corner of the world.

Cadence pulled a book from under his tattered blankets. The cover had been torn off, but the title page remained. *Beowulf.* He couldn't help smiling. His son liked to read. So did he, once upon a time. *Beowulf* seemed a little advanced for a ten-year-old, but by the intelligent way his son examined him, he knew he shouldn't be too surprised.

"I'm not in that book," Michael said, flipping through the old, wrinkled pages of verse.

Cadence stopped him with a small hand, halting the turning pages. "Not you specifically. Your type, the hero. You're supposed to stop the monster."

Michael glanced at the page. Cadence's fingers marked a familiar line: "Death was my errand and the fate they had earned."

"There are many monsters here," Michael said. "I cannot stop them all."

A flicker of Cadence's aura bespoke his son's anger. "You can stop the worst of them. Cut off the head and the rest will die. I've read about it."

"Cadence," Harley said. "What are you saying? We're at war, there aren't any monsters—"

"War is created by monsters and ended by the very worst of them." Michael was angry. Harley should have done as he would do. She should have destroyed Angus for daring to lay a hand on her, and she should have burned the man alive for daring to look sideways at Cadence.

Harley paled.

Now she sensed it, the building desire in him to destroy, to unleash darkness where the light burned too bright. He banked his aura. There would be time later to talk, when this was finished.

The castle shuddered when an explosion occurred close by. It was starting, and he needed to end it.

Michael turned away from Harley, back to Cadence. He reached out with his aura, sensing the extent of the damage done to the boy. Whole areas of his son's aura were absent, and those that were still present were shrinking. If it disappeared completely, Michael knew exactly what would happen. He'd forced Sins and Virtues to expend their powers when he rebelled against the Magistrate's pawns. They'd all slowly wasted away, and as their auras dimmed and went out, so did their lives. The same had happened to his son. Cadence was dying.

"Cadence," he said.

The boy turned from the window, looked at him, blinked, then seemed to understand. His chest rose and fell unsteadily. "I used too much," he repeated.

Michael extended his own aura out and wrapped it around him again, and fed more energy into Cadence's aura.

"Is that supposed to be doing something?" Cadence asked.

Michael reexamined Cadence's aura. Nothing had changed. No, the shrinking of his son's aura had stopped. He'd slowed it, but not enough to undo or reverse the damage.

Like but not like. His subconscious spoke from the depths. It wasn't working because he was *Luxurian* and Cadence was *Avaritia.*

Michael turned away. His fist cracked against the wall, echoing some sound deep within him.

No! He'd just found him. He would not lose him. His son was *Avaritia*, he was *Luxurian.* Their powers did not mesh, could not exchange energy as easily as he did once with Atticus.

"What's wrong?" Cadence asked, drawing his elbows close to his body and hunching over his bent knees.

Michael took a deep breath and forced his bruised fist to relax. He turned around and met his son's dark green eyes that should have been filled with confidence instead of uncertainty.

"Michael?" Harley asked, the pitch of her voice rising to match his growing panic.

He had to be sure. He examined Cadence's aura more thoroughly and found that although the well of his son's power was deep, it was not deep enough to hold even half the power he had unleashed earlier. It meant his theory was right and the God of *Avaritia* was nearby. No other being had the reserves to give Cadence that much power.

"We have to find the *Avaritia*," he said to Harley. "He has to be nearby."

"What do you mean? Cadence is the only—"

Michael grabbed her roughly by her shoulders. "He's dying, Harley. He's used up his powers. There's nothing left keeping his aura intact. It will shrink until there's nothing left, and when that happens, he will die." The cracks in his sanity widened. Whole pieces were beginning to fall away into the yawning darkness.

Darci was right. Something close to him would tie him to his sanity and its loss would destroy him. She was wrong that it would be Harley. It was Cadence. If the boy died...

Harley's aura shrank from the room, closing about her in defense. He'd frightened her. She'd allowed Cadence to be used by Angus. This was her doing as much as it was the King's. Good, she needed to be frightened, but not of him. He loosened his grip on her shoulders and, like an animal, she jerked away from him and out of immediate reach.

"Harley..."

"What do we do?" she asked, wrapping her arms around herself.

He meant to apologize for his behavior and he would. That is, if they survived the night. "The *Avaritia*." He turned to Cadence whose glazed expression panicked him further. "Cadence, do you know where the *Avaritia* is?"

Cadence frowned. "Who?" His aura was beginning to shrink again. Michael didn't waste any time. He picked up his son. The boy was too slight. Under his clothing he was nothing but skin and bones. Exhausting his abilities must have thinned the rest of his body as his powers had done to the forest, starving it of nutrients. He wrapped his son in his aura again, protecting him that much more.

"Where are you going?" Harley asked.

"We have to find the *Avaritia*. The one who gave Cadence the power he used earlier. It was too much power for his body to create without it being given to him."

"Cadence is strong," Harley said, blocking the door. "He's stronger than most."

"He's not strong enough," Michael said. "If we don't find

the God of Greed soon, he won't recover. I will not let that happen."

Cadence stiffened in his arms and pushed away from him. "I can walk," he said indignantly. "And my friend is not a god. Those are myths. He has lots of books, and I read them. Gods are myths and he's real."

Michael knelt down. Cadence was just a little taller than him at this height. He would be tall when he was fully grown. "Do you know where he is?" he asked.

Cadence looked down. "The underground tunnels."

Michael's mind spun. Brax, before he had been compromised, said something about tunnels below the forest. He'd even glimpsed his son disappearing into one earlier. The forest then. That was the only lead they had. "I know how to find him," he said to Harley. "We need to hurry. Is there a way to get into the forest?"

"The only way is through the front gate. Are you sure this will help him?"

Was he sure of anything? In the space of a day, he'd found Harley and discovered his son. He was all too aware that they could be taken from him just as quickly. "The faster the better."

Harley nodded. "Follow me."

"Cadence," Michael said, and the boy took his hand without hesitation. He cloaked his son in another layer of his aura. They traversed the castle quickly, emerging into a courtyard awash with men, weapons, and war. Golden rays of sunlight broke through the cloud cover to cast their last curse on the doomed fortress. Artillery cannons on the outer wall fired. A nearby explosion shook the ground beneath their feet. People were screaming.

"Lieutenant!" Demark shouted in the silence left behind from the cannon fire. He jogged across the lowered drawbridges toward them. "The King demands your presence at the wall."

Michael went cold. After his encounter with Angus, the man should know better than to demand anything from him.

"Where is the Magistrate now?"

"They've reached the forest's edge. If they keep this up, they'll be inside the walls within the hour." Demark paled. There was fear, deep and dark, consuming him.

"Angus has the firepower to keep the Magistrate at bay for longer than that. He should be evacuating the townspeople into the castle."

"We're evacuating the women and children. All men have been called to the front. All Sins are being used in the attack." Demark paused. "They will begin the Final Order. We all know it."

Michael swore. How did he skirt the Magistrate forces bearing down on them, and keep Angus's quibbling men from giving up, without getting himself or his son killed?

"By the gods," Demark said, glancing between Cadence and Michael. "*You're his father?*"

The resemblance between them was remarkable. Michael felt heat rise in his chest. "Yes, he's my son," Michael confirmed.

"By the gods," Demark whispered.

"Cadence is dying," Harley said. "We have to get beyond the wall."

Demark ceased his staring and frowned. "Impossible. The Magistrate is bearing down on us. If the Insurgency doesn't make it soon, Angus will be forced to lay down arms."

Michael let his power roll over the courtyard. Those with abilities to sense his growing psychic storm stopped and stared. Angus would also have felt the tremor his power caused, even from his place near the outer defenses. He'd given enough to the Magistrate in blood and pain. They would not get his son as well.

"Listen to me, Demark," Michael ordered. "Surrender is not an option. My orders are to find the *Avaritia*. Without him, Cadence will die and if the Magistrate gets its hands on him, the entire rebellion could fail."

Demark nodded, seeming to understand. "We have some time yet before we are overwhelmed. We'll need you before the last if we are to survive past moonrise. The gates are barricaded. No one is getting in or out."

"The tunnels," Cadence spoke up. "He usually finds me there." He swayed on his feet, and Michael let go of his hand to wrap an arm around his shoulder.

Harley turned to Michael. "We have to get there soon."

"Demark," Michael said. "How do we get into the tunnels?"

"There aren't any," Demark said.

"Yes there are," Cadence said. "They are secret old sewers from cities that fell hundreds of years ago. This place is in the middle of the old ruins and the forest grew up on the rubble. The tunnels are still there."

"How do we get there?" Michael asked. There was desperation in his tone.

Cadence considered. "There's an entrance by the moat, and another by the main barracks. The one by the barracks is closer to the forest."

Michael picked up Cadence. They needed to hurry and he wouldn't have the strength or speed they needed walking on his own. He began tugging on the web of ties he'd woven around Demark's desire to be loyal. "Where?"

Demark nodded. "Quickly. I'm needed at Angus's side. I can assist this much. The rest will be up to you." He broke into a run. Michael followed, with Harley close behind.

They jogged most of the way there. Women and children were being herded toward the castle. There were hundreds of them and all frightened, hardly sparing a second glance for Michael and Demark as they pushed through the throngs of people. The city was noisy, filled with fear, panicked sounds, and the thunder of thousands of footsteps.

"There," Demark said.

"Harley," Michael said. He set Cadence on his feet. The boy wasn't any better but he also wasn't any worse. "Do you hear that?"

"No," she answered. The whole time she'd kept a hand on Cadence's arm, never willing to let him out from under her touch.

"I hear it," Cadence said. "They stopped firing."

"Why would they call a cease fire?" Demark asked.

Smoke was rising from the walls in the south, but the tremors from the artillery and explosions had ceased. The Magistrate couldn't have broken through the wall so soon. The bombardment had only begun minutes ago.

"Demark," Angus's voice issued from his second-in-command's comm. "Report."

"Excuse me," Demark said and he turned away.

Michael watched him. He didn't trust the orders Angus had given the man. Here, he was wildly outnumbered and his son was weak. Even he would barely have been able to sense the boy's aura if they weren't connected. He turned to Harley. He didn't want to leave Cadence or Harley at the mercy of such a man.

He touched Harley's arm and she jumped at the contact. "Can you disable Angus if he attacks you?"

Harley looked away.

He gripped her shoulder tighter and she looked up at him. "Can you?"

"I'm not as strong as he is," she said.

He bit back a growl. Demark was still talking into his wrist. "You have to stay here with Cadence. I'll be as fast as I can. I don't think Angus will hurt Cadence more than he already has. He needs his powers too much."

Harley chewed her lip, uncertain. "You don't know Angus."

"He knows me," Michael replied. Angus had nearly shit his pants when Michael opened his aura. He'd given the King a glimpse into the depths of his power, fueled by torture and madness, which could consume the King as fire consumes a matchstick. The man was intelligent enough to know what crossing him would mean.

"Cadence," he said. "You're good at hiding."

His son smiled. "Yes, I am." He said it as a warning. Michael might be his father, but he was still a child and he knew exactly how to drive his parents to their wit's end.

"Good. I need you to find a place to hide. Don't use *any* of your powers. The shield I'm giving you to keep your aura from shrinking further won't last long. Your mother can't keep your aura from dissolving because she's a Virtue."

"I know that," Cadence said tartly.

Michael hugged his son to him, his heart full but cold at the same time. If he didn't find the god in time it wasn't just his son who would be lost. The deep well of his own power, without a mind to control it, would destroy everyone on this isle, finishing what the nuclear attack hadn't.

"I won't let anything happen to you," Michael promised.

Cadence pulled back and tilted his head to the side. "Don't promise anything when you don't know the outcome."

"Cadence," Harley chided. "What are you saying?"

"Go," Michael said. He wrapped a thick layer of his own aura around Cadence. A moment of dizziness prevented him from sharing his power. He was less able to defend himself now that Cadence carried a large part of his shield with him. Still, it was a risk more than worth taking.

"The entrance is there," Cadence said, pointing to a few planks of wood that covered a damp hole. "I have a good hiding place. They'll never find us." Then he released Michael's hand, took Harley's and led her off around the side of a crumbling building.

Michael glanced at Demark and saw the man hurrying in the other direction. This part of the city was deserted. The sun had set and a gloom descended upon the empty buildings and streets. The boards covering the entrance to the tunnels moved easily. In the dirt, Michael discerned a set of man's footprints, and several repeated prints that he recognized as a child's. Someone else, a man with bigger feet even than Michael's, had been using this entrance into the city. He dropped down into a shallow puddle. The scent of ancient muck and grime greeted him with rank sharpness.

Darkness loomed before him, moss and spider webs draping it as though in warning. He took a few steps, ducked under the dangling mosses and found himself shrouded in

utter darkness. Michael jogged forward, stretching his senses to
the walls and followed the winding labyrinthine trail the God
of Greed had left in his wake.

12

Harley stroked Cadence's head as he slept curled around himself, his back to her. When he'd led her to this secret nook he'd been exhausted. He had found some worn pillows, a few tattered books and a lamp, making the place his own little cubby hole. Her heart sank. The signs of his desperation, of his need for security, were everywhere here. She hadn't protected him. She'd failed. If she could trade places with him, her useless powers being sucked away along with her life, she would jump at the chance. His power was waning, and Michael's shield hadn't stopped it from draining slowly, like a dripping tap. The fighting still hadn't started again in the hour they'd been waiting for Michael's return.

She wondered what Angus had done, what deal he'd made with the Magistrate to keep his walls secure and stop their deadly attack. She wondered when Michael would return. The adrenaline of panic, of time slipping away, rose in a flood. This waiting was worse.

"You never talked about him," Cadence said, startling her, proving he wasn't sleeping.

She took a deep breath and blinked back the tears. No, she had never said a word about his father, not when every year he became more and more like the man she left behind to die.

"You know what the Magistrate does to traitors," she whispered. "Michael was one of their prized possessions. I was supposed to..." she hesitated. Cadence was nearly eleven years old. Soon he would need to know all there was that passed between a man and a woman. Still, the Magistrate's laws regarding reproduction were not a subject she was happy to speak about, least of all to her son.

"Supposed to what?"

"I was supposed to have children with a man I didn't want to."

"Like Angus," Cadence spat.

"No. I married Angus. Even if it was to give you a safe place to grow up, it was still my choice. It was the wrong choice. In the Magistrate city, my superiors determined I would become pregnant in order to further the Enlightenment. I didn't know the man, and I was scared. I ran away and found Michael. We fell in love and the Magistrate discovered us. We had committed treason of the highest kind. Michael is a Sin, I'm a Virtue. We are never supposed to... consort with each other. Michael stayed behind when they found us to give me time to escape."

"You could have said something about him," Cadence said.

Harley looked out through a crack in the wall. The town's lights had been lit, casting it in a blue glow. Fires burned in the south quarter, close to where they were now, turning the shadows into dancing demons. Soldiers were patrolling the main streets in groups. She watched the spot where Michael had disappeared into the ground. Nothing moved.

"Michael shouldn't have survived. I thought he was dead."

"Why?" Cadence asked with the insufferable curiosity of the young.

"Because the Magistrate tortures traitors."

"Angus does that," Cadence said.

Harley closed her eyes, the movement making her tender cheek twinge. "He didn't used to."

"Do I call him Michael or what?"

Startled by the question, she laughed. "I think you'll have to ask him."

"I will. I like him. I hate Angus." Cadence sat up and leaned against her. His skin was cool and she wrapped her arms around him. "Why have the cannons stopped?"

"They stopped a long time ago." Then she heard something, like the scuff of a boot against stone.

Her son frowned. "I've been thinking about it. Something's not right. You don't stop firing until the fight is finished. It's not over— "

Harley covered Cadence's mouth, glanced again through the crack in the wall and gasped.

Angus stood just a few feet away. There were two men with him. One she recognized as Demark by his profile in the dark. The other she didn't know, but felt that she should.

"Where are they?" Angus hissed. He grabbed Demark by his uniform. "If you've lost them, I'll skin you myself."

"King Angus," said the other man. He stood stiffly, as though the military posture had been beaten into him. "Such measures will not be necessary. I can sense the *Luxurian* is not nearby. The *Avaritia* child is. I must remind you of our arrangement. You have six more children with abilities to deliver, in addition to the *Avaritia*. My superiors are patient, but they have schedules to keep."

Cadence pulled Harley's hand from his mouth. "Mom, we need to go."

"Hush," she said, the tight knot of fear growing hard and painful in her gut. She didn't know the man, but knew his words, his stance, and deciphered the origin of his training. He was a Magistrate soldier. What was he doing here with Angus?

Demark pushed away from Angus, and glared at the other man. "Your superiors? Who is he, Angus?"

Neither party answered.

"By the gods," Demark said in total shock. He drew his weapon. "He's from the Magistrate."

Angus was faster. His sidearm was already in his hand and firing before Demark could aim for the Magistrate infiltrator. The bright flash from the laser blast at chest level shot true.

Harley held back a scream as Demark's body crumpled to the mud with a wet slap. A gurgling sigh left his body and he was dead.

"The *Avaritia*, Angus," the Magistrate soldier ordered. He turned and nodded toward the crumbling ruin in which she and Cadence hid.

Cadence stood. He wavered on the spot. Michael's shield around him slipped, and she could sense her son's aura again. It was terrifyingly weak.

Harley stood, pushing Cadence behind her and gathering her own strength. It was hard. Years of disuse made it difficult to call upon her energies from the illuminated depths within her. Her powers weren't much, but they had to be enough. She would not let them take everything from her, not when she had just found it all again. "Stay back, Cadence," she whispered.

"Cadence," Angus called. "I know you're in there, son."

"I'm not your son!" Cadence yelled.

"Run," Harley said. She pushed Cadence toward the exit. He bolted.

Something struck the crumbling wall. A few bricks broke loose at the crack. Another strike and the fragile wall collapsed in a shower of dust and debris. Bits of rubble rolled toward her and she stumbled away.

"Well, well," Angus said, spotting Harley. "You traitorous whore. So it's true what my friends in high places tell me. That *Luxurian* bastard from the Insurgency was your plaything."

Harley held her power like a weapon, letting it enhance her own senses. There! Angus's rage and jealousy flickered in his aura in bursts and flares. If she could overload his emotional centers she could reduce him to a weeping, blubbering fool. She let loose, targeting the reds and yellows in his aura.

"Angus!" the Magistrate infiltrator cried.

Another power crashed into Harley. It ripped through her attack like a blazing wildfire over a dry field.

A *Humilitas*. Her power drained away, as ineffectual at harming Angus as a candle flame was at lighting up the night, when she was blocked by such a power.

"You are strong, *Castitas*," the stranger said. He grabbed her and dragged her from the building, throwing her to the muddy ground. "Your powers over chastity would be as useful as I am if you weren't a deserter. Still, you've served the Enlightenment with your son. For that I will not perform the Final Order. I will leave you in the capable hands of your King."

Harley struggled to her feet. Angus turned to her, his hands balling into fists. The Magistrate spy headed after Cadence.

"No!" she shouted, and started back toward the building. Angus swung his right fist. She ducked. Overbalanced, he tilted and she kicked out, tripping him. He landed sprawled in the mud. She scrambled over the bricks and rubble, skinning her palms and splitting her knuckles.

She sent out a flare of her aura, desperate for help, calling for anyone who would answer. They couldn't have him. They couldn't have Cadence.

"Stubborn." The Magistrate soldier faced her, giving up on Cadence. He focused a burst of power, hitting her in the stomach. She fought against the pacifying effects of Humility. She clawed at his faux uniform, with Angus's dragon emblem on it. She ripped the dragon half off the fabric. He sneered, grabbing her by the wrists, and bore down on her with his aura, suppressing hers.

From the darkness, a shout rang out. Cadence. He leapt onto the back of the spy from the Magistrate, pummeling his neck and shoulders with small, weak fists.

"Let go of my mother!" he screamed hoarsely.

"Cadence, run," she shouted again.

Where was Michael?

Rough hands grabbed her from behind. "I'll show you to disobey my commands, *wife*."

13

Michael cried out, falling to his knees in the trickle of sewer water. His voice echoed loudly. The screech of unleashed powers from where he'd left Cadence stabbed at him like a knife, ripping open his fragile mind. Harley's *Castitas* aura washed over him in uncontrolled bursts. Another power, bright like a polished blade and just as deadly, followed, ripping through hers and leaving shreds behind. *Humilitas*.

Something in him whispered, enraged, terrified, and murderous.

And then there was Angus.

Cadence didn't have a chance. Even if he made it to Cadence's side in time, he still needed the God of Greed to restore his son's aura.

"Where are you!" he cried in desperation. He slapped a dirty hand against the side of the tunnel. He forced himself to his feet. Another blast of Harley's power reached him, weaker than before. She was fighting and losing.

"Cadence," he said. His voice echoed loudly, as any sound did in these damned tunnels.

The god's trail was strong here, his comings and goings creating an overlapping psychic scent. The *Avaritia*'s lair was close.

"*Avaritia*," he called. The sludge splashed under his boots as he sprinted in the dark.

"Who are you?" The growl came from everywhere and

nowhere, stopping Michael with its suddenness.

In front of him, Michael sensed a great openness that he couldn't see. He raised his wrist, and the dim glow given off by his comm diffused into the dark ahead of him revealing nothing. Water dripped from a small pipe in the ceiling, creating the trickle of moisture. Ahead, the tunnel was bone dry, the concrete clean of algae and moss as the tunnel here sloped upward. Michael bent and shone his light on the ground. New concrete had been added over the top of the old. Intentional reconstruction to divert the water without blocking the tunnel access. Then the tunnel ended abruptly. He'd nearly sprinted off the edge into a shaft that went straight down.

Avaritia radiated all around him, taunting. Your close, oh so close, and oh so far.

At the edge of the tunnel, he peered down. "I'm Cadence's father. He needs your help."

"What has happened?" A pair of glowing green spots in the dark below looked up at him seconds before a light flicked on. The open space was a hub of tunnel openings. Hand built shelves with glass doors lined the walls. The *Avaritia* had collected old refrigerator doors, the kind that sealed food inside the cooling units in markets, and created an archive of ancient texts. From what Michael knew of books, paper rotted; as moist as this place was, the refrigerators must create a seal, thoroughly protecting the books. A God of Greed, hording books instead of gold. Hundreds of books were stacked on the wooden shelves, preserved in this place for all time. The pipe Michael stood in was about ten feet from the bottom. The whole shaft was perhaps fifty feet tall. At its base, an ornate bed with tattered sheets, a couch and a few chairs made a ragged living area. The *Avaritia* stood in the center, a heavy, leather bound tome clutched in his gloved hands. He appeared only sixteen years old, but the age that rolled from his aura made it more likely that he was several times that age. Here was a true god of Sin.

"How long have you been here?" Michael asked. This was not a god who had been captured by the Magistrate and escaped. This god had yet to be captured.

"A millenium," the god answered. "What happened to Cadence?"

"He's dying," Michael said.

The *Avaritia* snapped his book shut with a loud thump and set it down on a metal table. "Impossible. I gave him my aura, he should be—"

Michael leapt off the ledge, startling the *Avaritia* into silence. He landed with a bone jarring impact. His knees numbed, but that didn't stop him from striding forward until he had the *Avaritia* pinned between himself and the short, stainless steel table at which he'd been working. The fragments of his mind had begun to crumble the moment his aura connected with his son's, opening him to the madness of full darkness.

"You knew Angus was using him in this way?"

The young god's eyes narrowed. "Of course I knew. It is the curse of the *Avaritia*. We make dreams become reality. We have been used for thousands of years to do the bidding of others. It is an inescapable fate for the children of dreams." He spat the last in anger and pushed Michael away from him.

Michael roared. He could sense in the *Avaritia*'s aura the desires, centuries of them repeated over and over. The God of Greed wanted to live without fear. He wanted to live peacefully, without the threat of being used like Cadence. He desired to remain fruitlessly anonymous.

"Do you know my dreams?" Michael asked.

The *Avaritia* looked at Michael, truly looked. His mouth dropped open and his eyes widened.

"No one loves that way," he whispered. "No one."

Michael grabbed the boy-god by his jacket and lifted him, slamming him against the metal table. There was a metallic screech. Michael spun his aura around the young man, catching him by his desires faster than any spider ever caught a fly. The *Avaritia* froze, his eyes going wide.

"I'm a *Luxurian*. My son is dying because of you, because you've helped give Angus his dreams."

"Dying?" The *Avaritia* relaxed. "Impossible. I made sure to—"

"His aura is draining. Only you can restore it. And you will." Michael lifted the god up from the table, set him on his feet, and didn't waste any time dragging him toward the exit.

"If the Magistrate sees me,"—the *Avaritia* twisted out of Michael's grip—"they will imprison me as they have done to the rest of us. As they obviously did to you."

He tightened his grip. "They won't," Michael vowed.

"Can you promise that?" the *Avaritia* asked. "If the seven Virtues know I exist here, they will tear this place apart. Besides, the balance is shifted so far in their favor, we couldn't overcome them if we wanted to. They've won, *Luxurian*, and there's nothing you or I can do to change that."

Michael felt a vibration along the threads of desire. "But you want to change it." He plucked at the thread, tightening it around the *Avaritia*.

"Damn you!" the god said, his eyes blazing with power.

"If Cadence dies, you and everyone else on this isle will be damned."

The *Avaritia*'s eyes narrowed. Michael felt him probing his aura. "There's almost nothing keeping your aura together, *Luxurian*. You're a danger to him, to anyone living."

"No," Michael said with absolute certainty. "I am not a danger to my son."

The god smiled. "Good answer, *Luxurian*. I will help. But I'm old. I've watched civilizations rise and fall. I've sacked cities, been taken prisoner, escaped, and watched hundreds of my *Avaritia*s be taken as children and exhausted before coming into their own. I thought Cadence could survive the greed of others, but... I can't... I..." the *Avaritia* sagged "I'm so tired. I'll help, but promise me I won't be taken alive if we fail."

Michael nodded. "He's out of time." He climbed toward the sewer pipe. The *Avaritia* followed, his power growing. Michael's comm glowed softly.

"Turn that off," the *Avaritia* commanded. "We are Sin and you more than I should never fear the darkness. *Luxurian* is, after all, King of the Sin; or at least you used to be."

Michael did as the *Avaritia* required. Instantly he felt his body relax, some other sense taking over; and suddenly he could tell where the obstacles were. The walls of the tunnel arched around him, and he sensed the individual bricks and their worn mortar as his aura washed around him. He was more alert, more aware, and less blind than the small light had left him.

The *Avaritia* pushed past him. "You let your precious humanity get in the way of what you are harboring, *Luxurian*. Again. The last time I saw you, you were a dragon in human form, seducing everything you could."

"My name is Michael, and we've never met."

The god laughed, but it was fearful and pitched a little too high. "I fear whatever the Virtues did to you when you were captured. You don't even remember what you are. So what chance do the rest of us have?" He broke into a run before Michael could reply. Michael followed, matching his pace.

"My name is Michael Knight," he repeated.

"You are *Luxurian* first. If you were not, I would have slaughtered you for daring to track me down."

Michael's mind opened more, a yawning abyss reaching up to drag him down.

A voice whispered: Return the balance.

"There's a lot of work for you to do, *Luxurian*."

14

Screams. Her own, burning away in a blaze of light and humility. Harley shot upright, filling her lungs with air. Pain, dizziness, exploded in her forehead.

"Let me go," Cadence cried.

"Don't move," Angus breathed in her ear.

She froze, terror clogging her thoughts. "This wasn't part of the agreement I made with you when I decided to marry you."

Angus's hand in her hair tightened. "No, it is not. But tell me, where is your *Luxurian* lover to protect you now?"

Michael. Harley's mind calmed. She could feel him, the tether of his desire curling like a whisper through the air. He would be here soon.

"Gods help you, Angus," she spat. She swung her elbow back as hard as she could, catching him in the solar plexus. He was pure muscle, and a tingle swept up her arm, ending at her fingertips. But he let go. She launched away from him, toward Cadence's cries. She struck out with her aura and felt the crackle of energy as it fell against the *Humilitas*'s aura.

She couldn't run straight and tripped, falling against the side of a small house. Around the corner, yards away, she saw the Humiliats enter a Magistrate craft.

"Mom!" Cadence yelled.

The Magistrate soldier looked over his shoulder and smiled a cruel smile. His grip on Cadence never changed as he lifted his wrist to his mouth. "I have the *Avaritia*. Begin the Final Order." He dragged Cadence behind him. The door hissed shut and the engines engaged.

"Cadence!" Harley hurled every scrap of her power at them. But the craft's upward movement never slowed. She simply wasn't strong enough.

Angus kicked her from behind, in the small of her back, and she pitched forward into the mud, pain jerking up her spine.

"Never defy me," he growled. "You forfeited Cadence's life the moment you chose that *Luxurian* bastard over me. You are mine. This is my kingdom, my isle, my people, and I'll destroy it all before I let anyone take it from me."

Harley gasped for breath, cringing against what was to come. Angus didn't use his power. He favored physical force and she knew what was coming. She heard the grind of small stones in the mud under his boot as his weight shifted. She rolled to the side, avoiding the kick to her ribs.

Angus was off balance and stomped down hard into the puddle she'd vacated. Her body screamed, her head spun, but her heel caught Angus in the groin. The air whooshed out of him in a squeaky wheeze. He groaned, grabbing at his crotch. He staggered forward and fell beside her.

How many times had they lain like this, the roles reversed? Her, bruised and pained, curling around herself. Him, stretched out on his back, satisfied. But she wasn't satisfied, not by a long shot.

"Bitch," he said. "I'll—"

The cold wash of *Luxurian* power targeted to kill flooded the streets and filled up the township. Michael's power cut off Angus's speech more effectively than a hand around his throat. Harley felt rather than heard the screeching tear as Michael destroyed Angus's mental defenses, ripping apart his aura, even at this distance.

Harley rose to her feet. She gathered her power, what little of it was left, and drove it like a spike into Angus's skull, forcing every bit of her emotions into his.

"Do you feel it?" she said. "Every horror, every fear I have ever felt at your hands?"

"Stop," Angus groaned, his hands moving from his crotch to his head. "No!"

Harley bore down on him. "Yes," she countered. "I want you to love my son, and regret every wrong you have done him. I want you to beg for forgiveness before I kill you." Without his powers shielding him from her, she could destroy him, attack as she'd wished for so long.

Angus began to scream. Tears poured down his face, and he rocked back and forth.

"You should have known that if the Magistrate let you live, I wouldn't't."

Beyond the walls an explosion sounded, followed by another. And another. The screech of missiles striking the walls followed. The Final Order.

"Do you hear that, Angus," she said. "Your friends in the Magistrate are destroying your precious kingdom. You gave them my son for nothing!"

Angus writhed on the ground. With his defenses shattered she had him wriggling on a hook like the worm he was. If he had felt no remorse for his deeds in his never-ending search for more power, he felt it now, and burned from the pure energy of it crushing through him. Had she known a decade ago that agreeing to be with him would lead to this, she would have taken the knife that was suddenly in her hand and bled him dry years ago.

The blade gave her strength. No longer trembling from fear and hunger, still bearing down on his mind, she pressed the knife to his throat.

Angus's cries became gurgles.

With a jerk she shifted her weight and dragged the blade across his neck, downward through the trachea. A spray of his warm blood coated her clothes and her arms. She didn't care. He was dead.

Luxurian energy darkened the streets as it flowed ever deeper around her. It urged her desire onward, stroking and tempting her. *Death and blood*, Michael's power whispered to her. *Revenge*. The lights began to go out and she shivered, but she didn't stop. She wanted it, sweet revenge. She skimmed the knife across the King's face, feeling it grate against his cheekbone. He would pay the full debt for his wrongs. She'd once seen him skin a man for disobeying him. She would skin him until there was nothing left to carve from his bones.

Someone was shouting her name. A hand pulled her up. Scarlet dripped from her blade onto Angus's pale face. His glazed, dead eyes stared at her, tears still leaking from his corpse.

She fought. No one would keep her again. She would have her vengeance and it would be bloody, a reflection of everything she had survived, would still survive.

"Harley," Michael said, turning her to him and trying to pry the knife from her hand. "It's over. Stop."

"No," she cried. "He's not dead yet."

"Allow me, Brother." Power similar to her son's touched her aura.

The moment the strong *Avaritia* power grazed her senses, her fingers opened and she dropped the knife. "Cadence?" she asked, looking for him. Instead she found a teenager, his green eyes shone brilliantly from within.

"Where is he?" Michael asked her.

"He gave him to the Magistrate," she screamed, and tore free of Michael's grip.

The night stilled, darkened, and turned to velvet. Michael smiled, his teeth flashing white.

"He did what?" His voice was a caress, the tip of a knife trailed gently across soft flesh. The promise of pain and death and every desire fueled his words.

Harley slapped at the King's lifeless body with her mind. "Angus gave *them* Cadence."

"Them?" the *Avaritia* asked vehemently.

Michael's power slashed through the air, ready to tear a hole in the sky.

"Never again," he whispered. "They should have killed me

when they had me locked in a box." Golden light reflected from Michael's eyes. The light had been missing before, but now it flooded his irises and made them glow.

Harley stared at her fingers, slick with gore. This wasn't over. She was still off balance, floundering in the sudden void created by Angus's death and the knowledge that she had failed. Cadence, her heart screamed with each pulse. She had failed to keep him safe. The one thing Michael had asked and the one thing she had never been able to do. She had to fix this.

"Sweet darkness," Michael whispered. The voice made the hairs on her neck straighten and prickle. "I've missed this."

Fear jolted Harley to the core. Michael grinned, his white teeth catching the light from distant explosions. The rest of him was shadows and terrible things. The man talking was not the Michael she knew. This man had turned his back on the world and revealed a different face, dredged up from some hidden place within him.

Her heart beat an erratic tempo. The *Avaritia* seemed unconcerned, satisfied even. This was the God of Sin her son had befriended. The teen seemed to have stepped from another time, his clothes old, not of this century. He wore a double breasted coat, its collar turned up, the brass buttons tarnished. The way he moved bespoke a different time when people carried themselves in cock-sure postures, no respect, no military stiffness. He looked too young to possess the power he did, but it flowed from him. She'd only met one other person who had power so vast, and right now he was scaring her.

Michael couldn't be the God of Lust. Could he? She trembled. *Oh, that explained so much.*

"Where did they take Cadence?" the *Avaritia* asked her.

Harley focused on the *Avaritia*. She focused on not panicking and giving Michael a reason to turn his abilities on her. "Over the wall, toward their camp."

The god closed his eyes. She sensed his aura expand and contract quickly. "Cadence's strength is waning. We must leave now if there is any hope of saving him."

Michael blinked. The gold light left his eyes. "Cadence?" he asked. He turned to her. "Where is he?"

Harley didn't dare risk glancing at the *Avaritia* for help. Michael was breaking, or something was breaking through him. He was dangerously unstable, but he was also powerful, in a way she could never be. Without him, she would never get Cadence back.

Michael shuddered, and suddenly the great power in him vanished. He crumpled in on himself. He drew his hands close to his heart. "They have him. They have my son. We're too late."

He couldn't break. She needed him to help keep herself together. "No." Harley grabbed Michael's arms and shook him. "They're still on this isle. They aren't getting away with him. They can't have him, Michael. I watched them take you and I can't watch them take him. I can't fail." Her vision blurred and she began to sob. "We have to stop them. They'll kill him before he breaks. He's not like us. He won't come back if we don't get him back."

He closed his eyes, his hands resting on her arms. His fingers tightened, released, tightened again. She waited as he clawed for self-control.

"They won't kill him," he finally whispered, sounding a little more like himself. "They wouldn't dare."

"I've read about this," the *Avaritia* said. "You're suffering from a prolonged case of PTSD. A full account is in one of my books. When we're done I can explain it to you, but right now we need a dragon, not a worm. Pull it together. Both of you."

Michael flinched, and Harley felt another piece of him slide away.

"Stop it," she ordered the god. "Michael, we'll get him back. They haven't taken him far."

"You don't know that," he said.

He had just found out he was a parent. He had quite a bit to learn on the subject. "I do," she countered. Something in her tone caused a small spark of hope to blossom in his expression, a receding of the shadows. It was a subtle change, but it was there. They could do this.

"If we take the tunnels again," the *Avaritia* said, "we'll be too late. They'll take him off this isle before then."

"We're going to fly," Michael said. He keyed something on his wrist and a comm flared to life. "Tobias, can you hack the craft to automatically fly to my current location."

A tinny voice came on the other end. "Yes indeedy, my good man. Already done. Having trouble?"

"I'll call you back." Michael didn't wait for a response before he shut the comm down. It immediately flared back to life.

"Don't think you can hang up on me and get away with it," the man called Tobias said. "I need a report."

"No time. Just send the craft," Michael said, shutting off the comm again. This time it stayed off. The hum of an engine sounded above them. A moment later a craft flickered into view.

"That is astounding cloaking technology," the *Avaritia* said. "How did you manage that?"

"Besides being a pain in the ass, Tobias is unusually gifted when it comes to technology."

The craft was not quite small enough to land in the street between the packed houses. Its wingtip grazed a roof and several clay shingles clattered to the ground, shattering upon impact. Michael ushered them inside the hatch and into the cramped two man craft, then slammed the door and took the pilot's chair.

"Harley," he said. Some of the strength had returned to his voice. "Up front." There was a lurch as the craft jolted toward the sky, and he heard the scrape of metal against stone. Harley stumbled, landing in Michael's lap. The craft jerked to the side before Michael righted it.

"That's not what I meant," he said. A brief flicker of mischief appeared in his eyes, convincing her that the man she'd once fallen so deeply in love with was still there. His gaze promised plenty of time for that later.

Harley blushed and slipped off his lap. It had been a decade since she'd been in his arms like that. She settled into the co-pilot's chair and gripped the familiar controls, trying to suppress a decade of unsatisfied desires.

The *Avaritia* squeezed into the tiny cockpit between their chairs. "You two are oddly familiar with one another. Tell me, how long has it been since you last saw each other?" He waggled his eyebrows up and down at Harley. She looked at Michael, watching for a reaction.

Michael's eyes glazed over, as though he were somewhere else. Another sense rang warning bells. She'd seen a rabid dog once, and the same alarm had sounded. Michael was very sick. She wasn't sure when he'd attack, or if he'd be in control when he did.

"Strap in, *Avaritia*," Harley said. "I can feel Cadence's presence in that direction." She pointed over the forest, toward the south.

"There," the *Avaritia* said. The display panel indicated a large force of the enemy that had yet to be dispatched to the castle. "They have him there."

Harley blinked at the numbers on the display panel. That couldn't be right. Why would the Magistrate send so large a force? Then it dawned on her.

"There's another god here," she said. Anger boiled in her veins. If Angus weren't already dead, she'd kill him a thousand times and it still wouldn't be enough to repay the debt.

"There are gods here as well," the *Avaritia* said. "Even if their god manages to get past us,"—he glanced at Michael—"our powers will pass to the nearest one of our kind. We won't be stopped so easily and he'll know it. If I die, Cadence will be the strongest and closest *Avaritia* after me. He will inherit my power and become ten thousand times stronger than he is now."

"No one is going to die," Harley said, wishing she could believe her own words. Her son was already so close to death. She feared that Michael's ability to shield himself would be shattered along with the rest of him. The *Avaritia* was right.

They needed a dragon. She knew Michael had it in him, as long as he didn't break first.

"Oh yes they will," Michael said. The words were a sweet caress, and a dagger hidden between silk sheets. His hands returned to the controls and the dragon the *Castitas* wanted surfaced as though her thoughts had summoned it.

"I do believe there will be quite a few bodies when we are through here," the *Avaritia* said. "Does this creaking tub have weaponry?"

"Of course," Michael said.

Harley watched as he clicked a few buttons and flicked a switch. Circles targeted individual soldiers on the ground.

"Let it rain," the *Avaritia* said.

Ffft! Ffft! thrummed the guns. Lasers and conventional artillery fire fanned across the camp below. Soldiers dropped one after the other, some sliced into pieces, others riddled with bullets.

An explosion rocked the craft. The engines whined and the instrument panels flickered.

"What's happening?" Harley shouted.

"Don't worry," Michael said. "They'll shoot us down."

"Don't worry?" she shrieked. "They're supposed to die, not us!"

"Crash land right in the middle of the lot of them," the *Avaritia* said. "The fewer of them, the sooner we can get to Cadence."

"The sooner the better," Michael agreed.

"Seven hells," Harley whispered. She was trusting her son's life to two insane Sins, both of them outrageously strong, but neither one carrying a lick of sense between them. Michael was smiling, the cruel twisted smile of a man who desired the bloodshed to come. He worked the controls and the craft's nose began to tilt down. It continued to tilt as the ground and clean lines of green tents appeared below.

Shadows clung to Michael. His stability wavered. His aura slid over her, over the *Avaritia*, and permeated the air with a lust for violence.

Harley closed her eyes. All she wanted was Cadence back in her arms. She only had to endure what was to come. The instruments beeped warnings. Hands gripping the armrests, she braced for impact. She watched Michael from the corner of her eye, the gleeful smile on the face that was and was not his.

15

They crashed. The craft didn't shatter, it broke apart in pieces. First, the wings as it skidded over the trees. Second, panels popped off the hull as they careened through the encampment, leaving destruction in their path. Third, the sound of the instrument panels crackling and sparking as the craft skidded to a stop. The control panel smoked. Mud spattered across the windshield. The craft shuddered, the engines wheezing. Alert lights and alarms echoed everywhere. Michael unstrapped himself. Auras were everywhere, pushing against his, tasting how he changed the game. The Magistrate had brought some of its best. Most were already dead or wounded. Few stood between him and his son.

"This is why I've never flown," the *Avaritia* groaned from the back. "Do you have any idea how old I am?"

Michael could feel Cadence. Sensed the last few pieces of the strength he'd given him. That strength was failing.

"We have to go," Michael said. To Harley he said, "Stay behind us and let us do most of the fighting. Take out anyone that tries to flank us." He handed her one of the last two automatic weapons.

"You're sure about this?" She freed herself from her straps and fell out of the copilot's seat. He caught her and she froze in his embrace. He'd missed her. The perfection of her skin, her silky hair. He kissed her quickly, a brush of lips, sweeping enough desire over her to warm them both. He drew away. "Don't play nice," he said to her.

She nodded, wide-eyed.

Michael gave the second rifle to the *Avaritia*. "Ever used one of these?"

The *Avaritia* turned the gun over in his hands. "Um, no. No I have never used one of these. I prefer to fight the old fashioned way, as Pandora intended." He handed the gun back.

"Me too," Michael said. But he slung the strap of the rifle over his shoulder, just in case.

The *Avaritia* cracked his knuckles. "So, my *Luxurian* brother. Let us enlighten them."

Harley stood next to Michael. He glanced at her once more and saw her sky blue eyes hardened with resolve. He nodded and she nodded back. They were ready.

The hatch squealed open and revealed a field of chaos. Virtues scrambled to form ranks, as though order would save them from him. Bodies were strewn about, screams from the wounded providing a morbid soundtrack. Crash landing the craft into the middle of their encampment had evened the odds. Instead of battalions of soldiers, perhaps twenty stood between him and his son.

Behind the soldiers, a man wearing a white suit, the golden eagle of the Magistrate pinned to his left breast, emerged from the remains of a destroyed command tent: The God of Chastity. His power rang in the air with the confidence of a man who'd never been defeated.

"Arrest them," the god ordered.

The soldiers snapped to, reacting as though a whip had been cracked across their backs.

"Cadence!" Michael yelled. His gut clenched. What if he was already gone? No, he would know.

Silence.

Then a young boy's shout echoed over the camp from inside the ruined tent.

Michael's fuse burned to the end and set off his temper. The gray clouds darkened overhead. The shadows between the scrawny pines deepened, reached out with thin fingers toward the disorganized soldiers. The unending well of *Luxurian* power rose at his command. It was power that matched the God of Chastity stride for stride. He strolled forward. Nothing and no one would keep him from Cadence.

Beside him he felt the *Avaritia's* power join his.

"Get down on the ground!" the closest soldier shouted. His power struck, formidable but no longer a true threat to Michael. Michael shivered. The man possessed the power of *Industria*, the power to cause excruciating pain with a thought. The *Industrias* had his son. Another cry from Cadence cut the air. They could be using that power on Cadence.

The last piece fell away.

Michael stepped toward the man who'd shouted at him. He was dressed in camouflage gear.

"Stop! Hands up, *Luxurian!*" The soldier fired a warning shot past Michael's ear, hitting the side of the craft.

Michael's aura slipped around the first few soldiers. They desired to kill him, kill the Sins, and bring Enlightenment to the rebel forces. Michael represented those rebel forces, fodder for their gods' enjoyment. Their desires were uniform, singly focused on him.

He smiled, made eye contact with the one who'd squeezed off a laser round. These soldiers were trained, but not enough to protect them from him. He wrapped his mind around the other man's desires and pulled.

The soldier gasped, dropped his weapon and stumbled toward Michael.

Michael caught the man by his throat. "You're here to hurt my son. I want you to die."

The enemy soldier's eyes widened.

Michael unleashed the full force of his power. It rolled over the enemy and they began to die under the weight of his desire to see their lives end. Some attacked with their own power, attempting to withstand his crushing aura. The soldier in front of him dropped his weapon, grabbed Michael by his jacket, blood leaking from his nose, his ears, and his eyes like tears.

"Please…" then the man's voice became a gurgle and he collapsed.

A memory tore through the layers of Michael's mind. *Please.* But the words in his mind came from him. He'd once begged for the touch of his tormentors. He shuddered.

"Michael, stop," Harley shouted. She drew him up from the depths. Her hand on his shoulder, her worry and fear spinning with his, bringing him back.

What was he doing? Men screamed and writhed before him. More than one had blood on their lips, dripping from their eyes. Most were dead already. All were begging for the release death would grant them. He'd expected a fight. He didn't know he would slaughter them all like animals. Some part of him was horrified, another was savagely thrilled. His hands shook.

"Cease this violence at once!"

Michael raised his gaze to meet that of the God of *Castitas.* The god's aura stank of fear.

"No, *Luxurian,*" the *Avaritia* said. He bent over a soldier's body and retrieved a pair of blades. "Don't listen to him. Kill them all. Think of what they'll do to you or your son if you don't."

Michael pulled, twisted and jerked on the threads of desire he still held in his mind's grip. He wanted these men to die, and they wanted it more than anything now. They had taken his son from him. He knew what the Magistrate did to their prisoners. He'd die before he let that fate befall Cadence.

Death was too easy an end for the Magistrate horde. They deserved to scream for hours in torment, fearing death, wanting it, and kept in agonizing limbo until their hearts burst from the strain.

"Stop this and you will be allowed to live." The god stepped around the bodies of his dying soldiers, his gaze falling to the *Avaritia*'s. "Brother, if you agree to join us, you will not have to suffer."

There! The god's desires were strong, light colored threads, and easier to read than a flashing sign. He wanted the *Avaritia* captured. They could recapture Michael. They'd done that before; but never before had the power of greed been at the mercy of the Magistrate.

Michael gave one final yank on the desire of the soldiers. Their hearts gave out, screams were cut off, and sighs rose from their lips.

"Behind us," Harley shouted. The sound of two shots from her gun distracted Michael. A body crumpled to the ground. He glanced and saw her standing over the body of a soldier. She nodded at him, her face pale, but her expression determined.

"The Enlightened way is over," Michael said to the *Castitas*. "And the *Avaritia* will never be yours to control."

The god grinned, his hazel eyes glittering as if he'd already obtained his victory. "Can you stop me from achieving my desires, *Luxurian*?" He struck with his power and it flowed around Michael, unable to touch him.

Michael recoiled, drawing upon his own powers, suddenly aware of his limits and how far he'd pushed them. The unending well of power open to him did, in fact, end, and he was at the bottom. A heavy exhaustion threaded through his limbs. His madness was creeping through him, drawing him further into the black. The god was fresh, and from what he knew of Fionn and Emerick's triumph over the God of Patience, what strength he had remaining would be nothing for the God of *Castitas* to overcome.

The God of *Avaritia* came to stand abreast with him. "We can still do this."

"Little Brother." The *Castitas* addressed himself to the other god. "I have searched centuries to find you. You will be welcomed by our kin with open arms."

"We are many things, but we are not brothers, *Castitas*," the *Avaritia* called back. His power grew and was released like an arrow from a bowstring. The bolt of power struck the god square in the chest.

The *Castitas* flinched, his right eye twitching. "What about the boy? Would you sacrifice him to defy your family?"

"Family doesn't chain a brother in a pit to rot," the *Avaritia* shouted back. He glanced at Michael. "Or torture him into insanity. I curse the day I ever called you family."

"Let my son go," Michael said, "and I won't shred you." He kicked the dead soldier's weapon up into his hands and aimed it at the *Castitas*. He struck with his power, a dark spear of angry desire to see the god suffer, and threw it with his mind. It was the same destroying lust he'd used to kill the soldiers waiting for him.

The God of Humility didn't even flinch. He began to laugh. "We are opposites, *Luxurian*. You cannot harm me with your power, we cancel each other out. You'll have to resort to more primitive methods."

Michael marched forward, accepting the invitation to a fight and unslinging the rifle from his shoulder. He flicked off the safety. The battery pack that comprised the stock grew hot in his hands. He passed through the god's aura. He should have remained out of his reach. The god's aura was thick and, this close, it made Michael's skin crawl. He'd felt this before. The things he'd done, the people he'd murdered, the licentious acts he'd agreed to, just so the pain would end. It had shattered his mind, and the pieces that remained were fragile, many missing. Through all that, the presence of *Castitas* had pierced him in his weakness.

"*Luxurian*," the *Avaritia* shouted. "You're strong! He can have no hold over you if you resist him."

Michael was shaking, the barrel of the gun wavering in his hands. "You were there," he said to *Castitas*.

"Oh yes," *Castitas* said as he pulled a thick golden piece of metal from his pocket, slid the fingers of his right hand through the holes cut through the metal and closed his fist. The brass knuckles flashed as he struck. "And you fought hard, but not hard enough."

Michael fired and missed. *Castitas* hit the weapon out of his hands with a clang of metal on metal.

Michael dodged backward, twisting out of the way as *Castitas* drew a knife from his other pocket. A slice of pain cut across his left bicep and Michael lashed out, instinctively, his powers grasping at nothing, flowing around *Castitas*.

"I told you," *Castitas* said, crouching, Michael's blood dripping from his blade, and his fist with the brass knuckles positioned to strike. "You cannot harm me that way."

"But I can." The God of Greed twisted around Michael, one knife in each hand. He slashed at the God of Chastity with his powers and the blades. His knives split the god's white suit down to his skin, then to the red until he struck white bone. *Avaritia* power sucked at the Virtue's aura, weakening him.

The *Castitas* roared, backhanding the *Avaritia*. The god fell against Michael, then pushed off, leaping forward, blades pointed at the Virtue's heart.

Harley ran toward them, her gun pointed toward the gods locked in battle. "We can't let the *Avaritia* die. Without him, Cadence won't make it!"

Michael spun around towards Harley's voice, then turned back to the struggle between the gods. In the brief moment he'd looked away, the God of Humility had wrestled away one of the blades. He raised the knuckles and struck *Avaritia* in the gut. Then he twisted in a perfect uppercut and dragged the edge of the serrated knife across the *Avaritia*'s torso. The young god staggered back, his hand going to the blood darkening his clothes too quickly.

Michael let out a desperate cry. He grabbed Harley's weapon by the barrel and pulled it from her hands. He swung it and the stock connected with *Castitas*'s shoulder, knocking him away. The enemy stumbled backward, dropping the twice bloodied knife. Greed entered the air, more than Michael had felt when Cadence had unleashed the power. The God of Humility cried out, he punched toward Michael's ribs. Michael heard a loud crack and he gasped, stunned at the force of the blow.

The Magistrate Virtue charged the *Avaritia*, the second blade angled up. It disappeared under the *Avaritia*'s ribs, toward his heart. The *Avaritia* sputtered, blood turning the young man's lips red.

Harley screamed.

Michael shouted a wordless noise as though the knife had struck him.

"We've lived a thousand years," the *Avaritia* whispered to *Castitas* as he staggered back. "Neither shall we live a thousand more."

He gripped the handle protruding from his ribs, and jerked the blade out of his flesh with a terrible sucking sound. The *Avaritia* turned to Michael, holding the blade out to him. The green light began to fade from the god's eyes as his aura drained away with his blood. "Vengeance is yours, my brother." Desire for life flared in the young god's aura and faded. Cadence's aura was so weak. Without the *Avaritia*, his son was lost and it was his own heart pumping the life out of him.

The *Avaritia*'s knees buckled and the bloody knife fell from his palm. Michael caught him before he landed. The knife stabbed into the soft ground.

"No!" Harley screamed. Her aura surged outward, pitifully weak in comparison to the great powers that had been unleashed.

Michael dropped to his knees, laying the boy on the muddy ground as gently as he could. His left hand fell to his side, where the blood slicked blade had landed.

The *Avaritia* drew a ragged breath. "He'll do better than I ever did. I'm glad I chose your son." The boy smiled, the last flicker of light leaving his eyes. "Guard him well, Michael, God of Desires. The world will need you both before the end."

"You have to save him," Michael said. He grabbed the front of the god's shirt. "Save him!"

"My time"—he struggled to breathe—"is over."

The god's eyes stilled. His chest fell and didn't rise.

Michael gripped the blade and roared. Darkness rolled through him. It was over. He had failed.

Harley was sobbing.

He surged upward, power crackling at his fingertips, his aura exploding outward.

"Bring him down!" the God of *Castitas* shouted. From beyond the wreckage a flash of light from the barrel of a weapon caught Michael's attention. A bullet struck him in the side. Pain ripped into his body. Pain. He wanted to laugh. The simple pain of a bullet wouldn't stop him.

"Unless you brought the Goddess *Industria* with you, you won't stop me," Michael said. He smiled to see *Castitas* stumble back as he advanced. "I don't see her here."

He flipped the blade in his hand, holding the tip in two fingers, and faster than his protégé, Atticus, had ever accomplished, he threw the blade toward the tree line. A man cried out and a body fell to the ground.

Michael turned. "I hope he wasn't your only sniper. You'll need a better shot."

He closed his hands into fists, slick with the *Avaritia*'s blood.

The *Castitas* struck, his red stained suit coat flailing about him. Michael ducked, ignoring the wound in his side, and slammed his right fist into the god's gut. The god doubled over and he brought his elbow down on his kidney. At the same moment, *Castitas*'s brass knuckles landed on Michael's exposed ribs. There was another crack and Michael gasped, breathless as his ribs broke.

Michael dropped, avoiding the next blow from the punishing brass knuckles. He landed, hands first in the mud, giving his lower body the leverage it needed. Teeth gritting, he wrapped his legs around the *Castitas*'s midsection and, as pain flamed up his torso, Michael twisted. The god slammed headfirst into the blood-muddied ground. Michael sat up and punched *Castitas* once, twice, three times in the head.

"Shoot him!" the *Castitas* ordered.

Another shot echoed through the night. Something struck Michael's left calf. He yelled and his legs unlocked from around his enemy. The *Castitas* struggled to his feet, his pristine suit a mess of mud and blood, made ragged from the knife cuts.

Michael also struggled to his feet. Behind the *Castitas*,

Harley was bent over the body of one of the dead soldiers. He saw a flash of metal in her hand and nodded. She nodded back.

"Bring him down," the *Castitas* said to his invisible sniper.

Michael dropped as another bullet whistled overhead. He winced against the pain in his leg and ribs. It hurt to breath, it hurt to move, but even this close to failing it wasn't the *Industrias*. He owed it to Cadence to take his son's vengeance. A knife skittered through the mud and landed inches from his fingers. He grabbed it and turned.

The God of Chastity bore down on him, his bone breaking knuckles headed toward his skull. The god had added another pair of brass to the first, and these came with spikes long enough to puncture a lung. Michael brought the knife up, slippery and wet from the muddy water. It cut like butter through all four fingers of the god's hand.

The Virtue howled in pain, blood pouring from the stumps of his fingers, his thumb writhing back and forth.

Another burst of gunfire exploded and Harley was firing toward a group of tents. She dropped to the ground, dodging, and continued to fire. Michael could just barely see the outline of the last gunman hidden behind a row of badly damaged tents. He flipped the blade in his hand, caught the tip and sent it to bury in the back of the Magistrate soldier.

"You can't defeat me," the *Castitas* yelled. "I am a god," he screamed. All illusion that he'd ever been a polished leader vanished. His face was contorted in pain and anger. He cradled his hand, blood running over his fingers and staining his sleeves.

Weaponless and wounded, Michael stood, muddy water sluicing down his arms in rivulets. The god didn't step back. He should have.

"Harley," Michael said.

Harley tossed him the last blade in her hand, and he caught it out of the air, the tip pinched between his fingers. He didn't hesitate, and snapped his arm forward.

With a guttural gasp, the god's screams died. The hilt of the tactical blade was buried in his gut.

Michael strode forward. "Not my best shot," he admitted between gasps. "But it means a slow death."

The god gasped. "Stop, please."

Michael circled around the god and bent down. "I begged them to stop," he whispered in the *Castitas*'s ear from behind. "I fulfilled every desire, every demand. Your *Industrias* never stopped. Why should I?" He reached around the *Castitas* and ripped the blade out.

"You don't want to do this."

"Don't I?" Michael adjusted his grip on the blade in his shaking hand. Anger coursed through him fueled by grief. "You killed my son."

"No, he's—"

Michael slammed the blade into left side of the god's chest, cutting off his last words. As he did, the last pieces of his own sanity trembled. "Shattered," Michael whispered. He knew he was toying with him in his last few seconds of life, and enjoying it. "You shattered any chances you had when you made that deal with Angus."

Michael let go of the blade's hilt, and the body fell forward with a sigh.

He straightened, breathing hard.

Somewhere a child was yelling, and he thought the voice might be his. He had destroyed one of the seven Virtues, but for what? Cadence was still lost to them, his aura depleted by now. He took a step backward, away from the bodies of the soldiers, away from the destruction he'd wrought, and all for nothing. As Darci had predicted, the well of darkness, rose up to swallow him. His grip on his power began to slip and with dread he realized he had barely begun to tap his powers. *Luxurian* energy clawed toward the surface of his mind.

Darci had been right, he realized as his consciousness began to slip away. If he couldn't control this, he could destroy hundreds of lives. He'd failed Cadence. Magistrate soldiers swarmed over this place. He couldn't think of a reason not to let go.

Someone was shouting his name. He turned and found

Harley dragging on his arms, begging for his attention.

Cadence. Her lips formed the name and it slammed into him.

Then, impossibly, "He's alive," Harley shouted at him, shaking him.

He gasped, his senses shooting to life. His hold on his sanity came roaring back.

"What?"

"He's in danger, Michael. They still have him. Can't you sense it?" She was terrified, sobbing, and desperate for him to take action.

He shot his aura out around them. A bright spot greeted him. Another Virtue, Harley, and near to her he sensed his son.

"Cadence!" he shouted. Explosions echoed in the distance. Harley was still sobbing, her body wracked with the grief of losing her last hope.

"Dad!" Cadence shouted back.

Michael's aura was full to the brim with power. The last shards of his mind had revealed a yawning well of *Luxurian* energy, inexhaustible. All he had to do was reach for it. He sensed his son's aura. It was stronger than before, gaining strength. But he was still recovering, unable to defend himself. The boy was fighting against a power stronger than his own. Michael pulled Harley up, and together they raced toward their son. His left leg was stiffening, becoming nothing more than deadweight. He ignored it, his heart soaring. Cadence was alive.

Heart pounding, fear trailing in his wake, Michael ripped open the flap and found an officer in one of Angus's uniforms holding a gun to Cadence's head.

"Stop right there." The man held the weapon with a sure and steady hand.

"No, please," Harley said at Michael's side.

"Mom, Dad." Cadence sounded relieved. "They were going to take me where they took the other kids."

Michael stared at the soldier. "Others?" he asked. He turned to Harley.

"He sold them to the Magistrate," Cadence shouted.

Michael smiled at the soldier. This man wore the uniform

of Angus's men. Here was the mole who'd brokered the deal to sell Cadence to the Magistrate. "You were going to take my son to them." The soldier swallowed. He was another *Castitas*, a minor Virtue by the strength of his aura.

"Stop right there or I kill the boy."

"Don't hurt him," Harley cried, there was power in her voice that hadn't been there before.

Michael met Cadence's eyes. Yes, his son's aura was growing, faster and faster. A green light appeared in his eyes, just a spark, but enough to prove whose power he'd inherited. The God of Greed had died, but his power survived and was filling his son's aura to the brim and overflowing. Cadence would live.

Relief cascaded over Michael, and fire burned as one fear left him and murderous desire took its place.

He turned his attention to the soldier. Quickly, he found the thread tying the man's desire to hold a gun to his son's head and peeled it apart. If the man had been stronger, he might have resisted him, but he wasn't a god, his powers were not equal to Michael's. The gun fell from the man's fingers. Harley pushed Michael out of the way. She punched the soldier twice in the throat and once in the groin. The soldier doubled over and she brought her elbow down onto the back of the man's head with a crack. The soldier crumpled.

"You will *never* touch my son again," she said, giving the unconscious man a kick to the gut.

Michael dropped to one knee, his left leg giving out, and pulled Cadence against him. His son's arms went around him, and he closed his eyes against sudden emotion. He'd thought his son was lost. He'd let his mind give in to the madness. He'd given up. How could he have given up hope?

Harley's arms went around both of them.

He closed his eyes and stroked his son's hair. "I'll never leave you again," he whispered.

"Dad," Cadence said. "You're bleeding all over us."

Michael blinked. All the pain came rushing in. He'd been shot twice. He took a deep breath and groaned as his side pulled. The bullet had only clipped him, but still it hurt like a—

"*Sonofabitch*!" he muttered as pain blazed up his side. Harley pressed a length of rough cloth against the wound.

"If you had worn body armor," Harley chided, "you would only have been bruised."

"I left it back at the castle. There wasn't time." He could sense she had a tart reply. "I'm just happy this worked out."

She laughed, and fresh tears slipped from her eyes. "Me too."

An explosion rocked the night. It was far away, but the crack of rock and the shriek of metal were still loud.

"The castle," Cadence said. "They'll kill everyone and it's all my fault. They came here for me. The man in white said they only wanted me."

"Cadence," Michael said. "None of this is your fault."

To his dismay, Cadence's bright green eyes filled with tears. "It is. I'm the reason why everyone is sick, why we can't grow anything. If I use any power, it sucks the life away. I'm not good. Until I'm stopped by the hero—"

"Cadence," Michael interrupted him. "Angus forced you to use your power. He and the Magistrate are the only monsters here."

His son looked away. "I don't want to go back. Angus is there."

Harley began ripping strips of cloth from the bottom of her shirt, baring her midriff. Michael could see fine lines, pearly marks from her pregnancy, that weren't quite hidden by the waistband of her pants. There was another scar, below her ribs. She'd been shot that night ten years ago, right there.

"Angus is dead," she told Cadence. "He'll never hurt you again. Or anyone."

Michael pulled her closer. He brushed his fingertips over her skin.

"What are you doing?" she asked.

He blinked and composed himself. "I'm sorry, I just... Those weren't there before, and the bullet..."

"No," she agreed with him. "A lot of things have changed

and I healed."

There was much to talk about, so many years of old wounds to reopen and begin to heal, for her, for his son, for himself. They might not ever be whole after what had happened to them. Michael wasn't sure what the future held, but she was the mother of Cadence, and for the moment that was more than enough. And his son had inherited the God of Greed's powers. Cadence would never be used again, and Michael would do everything in his power to guarantee that.

"It's not over yet, is it?" Cadence asked.

"No," Michael said. "Not yet."

Harley wrapped strips of canvas around Michael's calf. The bullet was still lodged in the meat of his muscle, but they didn't have time to dig it out. They might have incapacitated the Magistrate's general, but the soldiers already deployed still had their orders. If they didn't do something, every living thing in Angus's stronghold would be slaughtered and left to rot as an example to the rest of the world.

"We have to go," he said.

"Here," Harley said, taking his arm and slipping underneath it. "You won't get far with that leg or that side. At least the first one went clean through. Let me help."

"I don't think it will fly us back," Cadence said, pointing to the wrecked craft. A whole wing had been snapped off and hung between two half-broken trees. How he'd crashed the craft without turning them into human hash, Michael didn't know.

"You're right," Michael said to Cadence. "I don't think it will fly either."

A high pitched whirring squealed overhead and was soon joined by a chorus of similar whistles, like a mechanical flock descending from the heavens. Floodlights snapped on, bathing them in white brilliance. Michael pushed Harley and Cadence behind him, forcing his injured body to strengthen. Despite the pain, despite the fear of what descended, there was so much to fight for. Energy flooded into him, and the madness, the blood lust, came with it.

"Dad?" Cadence asked. There was a hint of fear in his voice, but nothing of actual terror. He was ready to face the next onslaught.

His son's strength bolstered his own.

"Stand your ground," he said. "Don't hesitate to attack." There was no point in running under that bright spotlight.

"I won't," Cadence replied.

A fleet of craft, blazing stars against the black night, hummed in the direction of the castle. This was not a stealth mission. Each craft was easy to see, easy to hear, their lights scanning the forest and the air space ahead.

"Michael, we have to run," Harley said urgently.

Familiarity washed over Michael as auras passed over him, three, no four of them. They were all here.

Michael? What happened? Darci.

Darci, his personal therapist, was in that craft, lowering to the body-littered field. Unlike the white Magistrate vehicles, the rebellion painted their air craft black, as though wearing a cloak of dark energy. The landing pads squelched in the mud with a hiss of hydraulics, and the hatch opened.

"Cadence, Harley," Michael said. "Don't attack. I think our rescue party came early."

"Lieutenant." Emerick's shout came from within. "Stand down."

"We are," Cadence shouted back.

Emerick emerged with Atticus at his side, both armed and padded in armor, looking more like brothers than comrades. For two people who at first had tried to kill each other, they moved as a team. Both scanned the carnage of bodies and debris, Emerick's mouth set in a grim line, surprised by the level of destruction, the state of the dead, but not that it had happened. Atticus, Michael sensed from his aura, was astounded.

"What in the seven hells happened?" Atticus asked Michael, sheathing the knives in his fist. He rushed forward, looking over his wounds. "How many times were you shot? Was it before or after you slaughtered them? Shit."

"Atticus, don't touch him." Darci exited the craft, wearing significantly less body armor than the men. But she was as deadly as either of them, perhaps more so.

Michael knew what she would say about him and his psychological condition and he knew she was wrong. There was a madness that let him forget who he was, turning him into a terrible monster, but he was in control.

"I'm fine," he said.

"That's impossible," Darci said as she pushed past her husband. "The last time I spoke to you, your mind was on the verge of collapsing. You've had a cataclysmic psychological event. You shouldn't be able to control your powers. You shouldn't be you. I told you to stay away from her"—she pointed at Harley—"and now look. You're bleeding to death."

Michael flinched. He wasn't sure Darci was wrong about Harley, about the woman who'd saved and damned him. Without her, Cadence wouldn't exist, but because of her he'd given his mind, his body, and who knew what else to save them both. He'd do it again if he had to make the choice once more.

"Darci," Atticus chided, "this is war. I've been shot before too."

"What is she saying, Michael?" Harley asked the question quietly, but there was something else pulsing from her. Her aura, rife with emotions. The link between them grew stronger every second they were both near Cadence. She was uncertain, fearful, possessive, and a thousand other things he couldn't put a name to.

"So, this is the woman Tobias won't shut up about?" Atticus asked.

"Yes," Darci snapped. "And she's a risk to Michael. His mind is not capable of dealing with her presence. He's collapsing, and, if my theory is right, Michael is actually the God of Lust, and all that power is waiting to be unleashed. If he goes insane again, and trust me he will, we won't be able to stop him."

Atticus gestured to the field of corpses. "Looks like it

already happened. And when were you going to tell me that you are a god?"

"Damn," Emerick said, shaking his head. "Why am I not surprised? Fionn will be thrilled."

"Not when he destroys our allies because his brain is mush and his powers are completely unleashed," Darci said.

"Darci," Michael said, "I already did all that. She's not a risk to me." Michael reached his hand behind him. Harley hesitated a moment, before her fingers weaved between his. "This is Harley, and she is not the enemy, Darci."

Darci wasn't listening. Her eyes had gone wide. She pointed to Cadence. "Who is that?"

As one they turned to look at Cadence. His smaller hand slipped into Michael's, firm and strong. Something essential settled into place, and for the first time in years Michael felt truly whole.

"Seven hells," Emerick whispered.

"This is our son, Cadence," Michael said. He found a smile on his lips. He tightened his hand around Cadence's, and pulled his other out of Harley's so he could wrap his arm around her waist.

"He's the *Avaritia*?" Atticus asked.

Darci whirled on Emerick. "You sent Michael into this war zone after his son, without telling him? Did you want him to go nuclear and destroy everyone we are trying to save? What about the King?"

"Easy there, Darci," Atticus said. Michael sensed Atticus's aura wrapping around his wife, trying to soothe her ire.

"Angus is dead," Michael said.

"See," Darci said. "He's not stable. Weren't we supposed to form an alliance with Angus?"

"I killed him," Harley said.

"Oh," Darci said. She tilted her head to the side and stared at Harley with her mind-reading gaze. "That's a good reason to kill anyone."

A series of explosions went off in the distance. Emerick's comm beeped.

"Emerick, did you find them?" Fionn asked.

"Affirmative," Emerick replied. "Our God of Greed is also Michael's son." He smiled at Harley. "And looks like we have the God of Chastity here as well. Michael killed him and Angus's wife was the closest *Castitas* at the time of death."

"Wonderful," Fionn said sarcastically. A crackle of laser fire, followed by a scream, issued through the comm. "We have our hands full at the fort. Would you mind picking up the pace?"

Michael stared at Harley, and saw a hint of soft light in her eyes that hadn't been there before. Her aura was also stronger.

"I'm what?" she asked.

Michael laughed and kissed her lips. Everything was going to be fine.

16

By the time the pale blush of dawn graced the morning sky, the castle was mostly in ruins, the houses piles of rubble. The bodies of the Magistrate lay scattered. Very few of Fionn's forces had perished. In one of the undamaged areas that still had a roof, they had set up the medical ward. Michael gritted his teeth as a medic poured alcohol over the bullet wound in his side and began to stich it closed.

"Does that hurt?" Cadence asked. He sat on a stool next to the cot on which Michael was perched.

"Nope," he said. He hissed as the needle dipped into his skin again and the nurse gave it a sharp tug. He flashed a strained smile at Cadence. "Feels like a bee sting."

Cadence's eyes narrowed. "Liar."

Michael checked his son's aura again. It was stronger than before. Another piece of tension left him. Every moment his son thrived was a success, something to be cherished.

"What happens now?" Cadence asked.

"That depends on the admiral, and on where your mother wants to go after this, or if she wants to stay."

"We should go. I don't want to stay here."

"Then we won't stay."

Atticus knocked on the door frame, smiling at Cadence. The boy had been quickly adopted as a nephew by Atticus. "In that case, you and your mother will have to come back with us to command," he said to Cadence. "Especially since your father is getting promoted."

"Says who?" Michael said a little testily. He'd just found the woman he'd been in love with for a decade, and his son. He wasn't ready to go back to war yet.

"Says the admiral."

The nurse finished her stitches and had him lie back. Using a knife she cut away his pants leg and the bandage and began to clean the wound in his calf.

"Cadence," Harley called from the other room. "Come in here and let them talk."

Cadence glanced at him.

"Go on," Michael said. "I'll be done in a minute."

His son hesitated, then flung his small arms around Michael, making the wound in his side zing with pain. His heart swelled as his son squeezed, and Michael clutched his boy to him again. Too soon, Cadence wiggled out of his arms and scampered out of the room.

"I'm not leaving them," Michael said to Atticus. "And Fionn can kiss my pale backside if she thinks I will."

Then Admiral Fionn breezed into the room. "I'm not asking you to leave them," she said. "I want you to protect them with everything you have in you."

"Fionn," Michael said. "How long have you been listening?"

She raised her arm, showing her own bandages. "A few minutes. We're searching for Brax."

"You still haven't found him," Michael said. It wasn't a question. If they had found Brax, Fionn's longtime friend, news would spread faster than fire.

She took a deep breath, her barely contained rage brushing against his aura. "I'm assuming the worst. I need someone to fill his place, and since he disappeared on your watch, you're the man for the job."

"I have a family now, Fionn," Michael said.

Her rage flickered into the atmosphere, a reminder that she was on edge. Battle always brought out the best and worst in her, and Brax's disappearance wasn't helping. "Brax was a brother to me. He's leaving behind a widowed sister and three nieces. Your family is nearly immortal. Braxton knows the location of every one of our allies, all our security measures, our status details, supply schedules, everything. If he's fallen into the hands of the Magistrate and isn't lying dead in a ditch, I need your help to find him. The information he has could destroy us." They all knew the chances of Brax lying dead somewhere was close to zero. The man was the best of them. He didn't have any special abilities, but he could out shoot, out fight, and out run every one of them. He'd been compromised. He was as famously wanted by the Magistrate as much as they wanted Fionn. He wouldn't be dead. They would have taken him alive.

Michael was silent. If they had taken him, he'd be on his way to the west coast of North America, to the Magistrate city. They'd give Brax to the *Industrias*.

"I'm going to have to dig the bullet out," the nurse said, glancing between him and Fionn. She pushed the needle of a syringe into his muscle and injected him with a clear anesthetic.

"Fine," Michael replied, but he was looking at Fionn when he said it.

"Wonderful, Commander," she said with false joy. "Once you're finished here, I need you on the first available craft back to base. Tobias has rigged the engines to be faster. Less stealthy, but we were able to double our speed. Atticus, you and Darci will accompany his family."

Fionn hesitated. Her aura dampened, her eternal wrath flickering like a dying fire. "What are the chances that Brax is alive?"

Michael met her eyes, the twin dots of red should have made him shiver, but they didn't. On many levels they were now equals. She used her power over wrath to shield her deep emotions. He had once done the same with lust. But in this moment they were both unshielded.

"They won't kill him," Michael answered. "They wouldn't risk losing access to that information. I would hope that he was

400

dead, instead of in the enemy's hands."

Fionn's jaw tightened. "He's impervious to a Sin or Virtue's powers."

"And why is that?" Michael asked. "And more importantly, why are you worried that the Magistrate knows?"

Fionn took a deep breath. "Braxton's strange inability to be effected by a Sin or Virtue makes him valuable. He's the perfect assassin when it comes to destroying high ranking enemies. He's not just good with a weapon."

"You think he's something else."

She nodded. "He's something we've never seen before or heard of. Maybe a new kind of power we haven't discovered. If they break him, like they broke you, then everything is lost."

"They'll figure out that he can't be a victim of a *Industria*. But even he's not impervious to conventional forms of torture."

"How long will it take them to break him?"

Michael seriously considered this. "It depends on him. Hours or days."

"We'll need at least a week."

"You won't have a week," he answered honestly.

"Michael," Fionn said. "They didn't just take Braxton. Your—Harley said Angus had sold a large number of children to the Magistrate. I need your help to get them to safety, not just Brax." Then she turned and left. She didn't give him time to accept; she simply expected that he would do as she asked.

Michael closed his eyes against his memory. He could have lied to Fionn or told her some other half-truth. But she'd come to him for assurance about Brax, a friend to both of them, and he couldn't give anything but the truth. He prayed Brax was dead.

"Ready?" The nurse asked. She didn't wait, but quickly sliced into the meat of his calf with a scalpel and inserted her forceps. He couldn't feel the pain, because of the anesthetic. Still, the sight of the instrument inside his skin caused something in him to click. The memories of torture had his muscles trembling, his hands gripping the edge of the medical table.

"Michael?" Atticus asked, suddenly at his side, holding him down. "Make it fast," he ordered the nurse.

"Dad?" Cadence cried out.

He hadn't noticed the sudden flash of his aura rising to the edge of madness. He forced himself to relax, his hand releasing the edge of the cot. Cadence's small fingers curled around his. Another hand threaded through his hair and he looked up.

"We're right here with you," Harley whispered.

Michael reached up and caught her hand. He pressed a kiss into her palm. Things weren't perfect. He wasn't fully healed. Maybe he never would be. But he had them. His son would always be near. So would Harley. Someday soon he could trail his fingers over her skin, kiss her with all the passion and desire simmering under the surface of his skin. He let a tongue of it touch her and smiled when a blush rose in her cheeks.

There was still hope for them after all these years. If there was hope for them, there was hope for the rest of humanity.

ACKNOWLEDGMENTS

Everyone who made this possible: The Writers of Imminent Death: Tiffinie Helmer, Kerrigan Byrne, H.M Turner, and Ariadne Kane. My talented and butt kicking editors: Lynne From Wordy Nerdy Editing and Phillip from All Read E. Also, my horse, for putting up with me and being my anti-anxiety chill pill. Also, a huge thank you to the tea makers of the world. Without you, writing period is not possible.

ABOUT THE AUTHOR

Mikki Kells is both a writer and a rider. She grew up on horseback and started her career by writing stories about her adventures. She lives in Utah and divides her time between her horse, her cat, and her upcoming novels.

You can visit her online at www.mikkikells.com

ALSO BY MIKKI KELLS

THE ACE OF HEARTS
BOOK ONE

UP COMING RELEASES

PANDORA RISING
THE CHRONICLES OF SIN BOOK IV

SUMMER 2015

BLACKJACK

THE ACE OF HEARTS BOOK 2

COMING SOON

WWW.MIKKIKELLS.COM